LOVE, FLESH, AND SPIRIT

By
L. ADLAI BOYD

2023

TABLE OF CONTENTS

AUTHOR'S NOTE

This book details the purposes and struggles of a young, married, protestant minister, as he juggles his primary loves and lusts, while trying to honor his marriage and ordination vows. Unfolding in the sexy sixties, it is a studied effort, in novel form, to understand and demonstrate the evolving changes in the sexual ethos of the period. By putting flesh to those influences in the lives of his characters, the author invites the reader into their hearts, heads, and beds, revealing not only the explicit what and how of their departures from prudential ethics, but also the why, in very personal terms.

The book's confounding love affair between the young minister and one of his younger parishioners is juxtaposed against his lust for a mistress, his commitment to his highly demanding church jobs, his love for his wife and family—and his God. What drives him is his persistent effort to improvise the purest of all possible loves—a perfect admixture of *Agape* (God's Love) and *Eros* (Lust).

The Narrator, the protagonist minister in his later years, looks back wistfully, sifting his clear memories and evocative hard data. Thus, the book is not a memoir (though memory is certainly involved); it is not non-fiction (but truth abounds); it is not a religious treatise (though it unfolds within a protestant Christian context); nor is it prurient (though it is purposefully and appropriately explicit and explicatory).

The author is both an honorably retired protestant minister and a university research psychologist, with over forty years of professional practice and academic experience. The

PROLOGUE: THE GREAT REALIZATION

. . . Only I discern—infinite passion, and the pain of finite hearts that yearn.

Robert Browning

Always be a poet, even in prose.

Charles Baudelaire

Have you ever felt that you could sense others' personal and private truths, or experience their hidden joys or sadness, unbeknownst to them? Perhaps nature's offerings or the effects of music or other arts are similar.

In such moments I feel like a helpless god; one who sees, feels, and understands, but little more. A god who does not matter very much, if at all, because the only ultimate thing about him is some mysterious warmth, finally inexplicable even to himself, that draws him into relationships without anyone else knowing it. A lonely god who can only sense and perceive feelings in lives which are not his creation.

Such a petty being can feel—feel with, feel for, feel as if—feel and maybe reach out. So, feeling, he may take his private pen and write, or his secret tongue and sing—or wail—hoping that someone, somewhere, will step forward and without embarrassment or shame, cry out, or even whisper, "I see; I know; I understand!"

What selfish gods we be, to seek someone seeking me—and yet, that is who we are, when sham is gone. Yet there is also the desire—

8

even passion–to live out the *Great Realization: that the best life is one lived for others.* This is the larger mystery because it is so elusive. Now we have it, and then it is flushed away by torrents of self-concern. But it seems to abide in human hearts–maybe little more–abide.

Nathan R. Scott

April 18, 1960

CHAPTER 1
A BIG ISSUE OVER A LITTLE TISSUE

Yes, Jesus worried about the sins of the flesh, but his emphases were quite different from Paul's tautologies, as was his context. Exemplified by the Sermon on the Mount, Jesus preached such idealized and stringent moral and behavioral standards that no one could possibly live up to them. Thus, the necessity, according to some apologists, for his atoning sacrifice and the new covenant of faith, that the law and all things righteous were fulfilled in him. With grace, even gentleness, he told the harlot, "Neither do I condemn you," and "go and sin no more." But he didn't tell her she couldn't fuck.

Nathan Rhea Scott
September 12, 1961

Oh, Nathan fucked Maid Melanie, his redheaded friend, all right, repeatedly, almost by accident, certainly not by design, since his first night in Durham, to begin his first, full-time Christian ministry. They had fantasized interest in each other since their freshman year at the university, when he was courting Lovely Lenore, his wife-to-be. Because she was Lenore's roommate and best friend, it was unthinkable that either act upon their hidden lusts—for at least the next seven years.

Nathan Rhea Scott, twenty-five, an energetic, outgoing redhead, himself, fourth child in a family of ten kids,

10

and beautiful Lenore Elizabeth Stuart, his brilliant, loving wife and mother of their one-year-old Nathan, Jr., are in Durham, NC, to begin Nathan's first, full-time ministry as an associate pastor at the First Protestant Church of that city. Melanie, quietly ardent and beautiful, living alone in Durham, is innocently hosting Nathan, who is house hunting, while Lovely Lenore and little Nathan visit her parents.

From their sophomore year on, Nathan avidly partook of the precious gifts of his darling Lenore's favors, for they were deeply in love. Because of their mutual love for Lenore, the redheaded friends fostered a hands-off, *sub rosa* dance, to the tunes of unspoken fantasies, never voiced nor requited. On many a night Nathan confounded the enticing bodies of these two, comely young women in his head while seeking relief from his driving lusts, solo, in his dormitory bed.

Nathan and Lovely Lenore were married at Tennessee Christian University (TCU) in 1957, right after they graduated, with faithful Melanie serving as maid of honor. After a honeymoon in the North Carolina mountains, they moved into a married students' dorm at Southern Theological Seminary.

Over the Scotts' four seminary years, Maid Melanie visited often, sometimes managing to surprise Nathan not quite dressed. He looked–sometimes longed–but both repressed the swirling tides of tension awash in their loins.

Now, on the eve of his first official charge, Nathan neither planned nor expected to fall victim to his long-suppressed lusts for Melanie. Of course, he was welcome to stay in her one-bedroom apartment, and to sleep on the couch in her living room. Nothing seemed more practical and innocent to all three trusting principals.

Behind closed doors, however, Melanie's beautiful flaming hair, her perfectly proportioned body, and their long-suppressed proclivities for each other unnerved them both. At first, they bantered coy and cautious, with sly allusions to being alone together, and, oh my!

"Finally, Melanie, I'm discovering the Spartan ways of an available, twenty-five-year-old woman, stuck away in this one-bedroom apartment, with nothing to do each night but her nails. Where do you hide your menfolk when they come a-calling?"

"'Available' in what way, Mr. Scott? Do you keep track of my—my—comings—and my goings?"

"Well, we've known each other, without 'knowing' each other, a long time, Melanie, and I've always wondered about your hidden life. When are you going to bring it out in the open?"

"Why has it taken you eight years to ask that? I've always been willing..."

"And during all those eight years, have you never had a man stay overnight?"

"There has always been room for the right visitor—right there on my couch cushions. I'm sure you'll find them quite comfortable."

"You mean you can't find a more disposing place?"

"Disposing or exposing, Nathan. There's a difference."

"*Vive la différence!* Do I have a choice?"

"If you did, just where would that be, Mr. Scott? It can't be the bathtub, for I have a shower, only."

"I see, said the blind man, as he picked up his hammer and saw..."

"You're not contemplating using any tool that hard just for sleeping, are you, Nathan?"

"I suppose I could come up with something more humane..."

And so it went, back and forth, skirting the potentials, building the tension, teasing the likelihood...

Aware of his mental adjurations for perspective and distance, Nathan kicked off his shoes and reclined on the floor, next to demure Melanie, who sat on the couch, both pretending to watch her small, black and white TV.

Having only teased the possibilities so far, Melanie repaired to her bedroom, "to get ready for bed." What she did, however, was to strip naked, don diaphanous, nighttime attire, and let down her luxurious, knee-length, rubicund hair. Then she came out!

Gone was Miss Prim; present were all the fire and longing of a lovely young woman, alone at last, and in serendipitous compromise with the very man whom she had fantasized for eight years. Every nerve and sinew in their eager, young bodies tingled with the possibilities, as she settled on the couch next to him, hairbrush in hand.

Nathan was beside himself with conflict—unable to stifle his surging desire, thirty million and eight years in the making—he bravely tried for perspective.

I have no intention of making any obvious, first move.

Melanie, in rufescent heat, broadcast her openness through subtle exhibition of her natural grace, beauty, and carriage. Her affect continued straight and narrow but her moves and curves, loosely confined in her silky, sea-green peignoir, were naturally supple and pliant in feminine finesse.

Audaciously, Melanie handed her brush to Nathan, who began to brush her resplendent tresses, long, lush, and lovely. Undulating, as he stroked—away as he began another sweep—closer to him with each languorous tour. Inhaling her exquisite, feminine fragrances, fresh, clean, and inviting, he dropped long warps of crimson fullness over her shoulders and down her front—cascading across her ample breasts—maidenhair floating on a rising sea...

Breezing a delicate zephyr into her ear, their lips met in mutual kiss and surrender. Turning to him, she pressed her lissomness onto him, as he leaned back, his hands tracing her figure. Turning prone atop him, loading herself between his legs, her thighs encountered his sequestered erection-in-waiting. Their hips' involuntary motions, like their breathing, increased in depth and force.

**QI, in sudden, alarm, warned, *Capitulation is in process, here. What about Lenore?! Turn back!*

***Note: QI: Nathan's careful, objective thoughts, facetiously dubbed his "Quintessential I (QI)," will always be italicized, to distinguish such thoughts from other text. QI is best understood as his clear and immediate, objective sense of what is happening, both within and around him, as things occur, regardless of his emotions. Even in the throes of events excruciatingly exciting or difficult, or both, QI watches, evaluates, understands, and takes data. Like a chorus in early Greek dramas, QI is his objective, impartial observer, with few moral judgments, rarely guilt producing—just totally aware—and utterly honest.*

"Melanie let's cool it a minute," he whispered, unsure.

Without a word she stood, blushing with her heat, shrugged off her silky garments, and stood before him as God made her. Captivated, he sat back, feasting on her nakedness with awed, cannibal eyes.

"You are lovely," his whisper.

Eyes closed, her trembling hands fanned her long, red locks across her breasts, increasing their allure, as a like-hued blush colored them. Standing, too, Nathan gathered her in, harvesting her beauty. She nipped his lower lip, which opened to his gasp, as he slipped a caressing hand between her thighs. Sighing, she opened her sky-blue eyes and looked straight into his, acknowledging his welcome trusion.

"Oh, Nathan!"

Enthralled by her promising gaze, he mapped the curve and smooth of her, moving from her breasts, across her flat, canescent belly, to her still whiter groin, dipping into her triangle of ruddy hair–so private, so forbidden, so awing to behold–captured now by Nathan's canvassing hand. A deeper red flushed her entire body, as she pressed into him, with ageless, feminine pride.

Nathan swept her open loveliness, feeling that sure calm, amid the delusions of lust, which gentles its madness and affords men the patience to partner, rather than to rape. Sitting on the couch, as she stood before him, his hands chased the contours of her quivering body, moving to the small of her naked back, pulling her pubes into his eager face. As he filled his hands with her hind, exploring its crevice, his lips glissaded down her belly, to begin the ancient adoration.

Melanie piloted his head, drawing his kiss deeper into her. As his tongue probed, she soughed, shuddering at his arousing appetite…

It was inevitable. The two red-headed *appassionati*, in studied abatement of each other for eight years, easily found and opened the remaining doors to the ancient give and take, swirl and swish, clasp and mold, until they be joined at the apex of nature's finest gift: lusty elation in flushes and flashes of spontaneous, sexual delirium, spend, and release.

Neither remembered, later, how intromission occurred, except that as they lay naked and spooning, things slipped into place! Faster and deeper, they tingled with fitting and refitting pleasure. Their meld jolted, as Melanie's ecstatic mewling alerted him to her coming extremity. Millions of years of genetic search and yield validated and justified their mutual possession of the other's utter vulnerability.

In extremis, she cried his name, as ecstasy triumphed! QI, ever the pedant: *Here is the mortar and pestle of creation. I hope she isn't ovulating!*

Later, Nathan's rampant erection was swallowed up, again, not by a repeat performance with the all-too-willing temptress of the shy and decorous, public ways, but by equally as rampant and overwhelming morning guilt and repentance, evoking an urgent, hand-written forswearing of extra-marital sex, for all the best, daylight reasons, "...both now and forever, Amen!" Then did this would-be man of God charge off in his second hand, 1955 Oldsmobile sedan, seeking a haven far from the luscious parts of his wife's best friend.

Was she a virgin? Who stopped to notice—and what difference would it have made? With safe sex concerns more than twenty years in the offing, and the need for a condom not anticipated, the two redheads began a long, sizzling affair, carelessly consummated on light green couch cushions on her living room floor. Both were dumbfounded! Abashed by their secret treatment of their mutually beloved Lenore, they both vowed never to tell her...

The next evening, an unfurnished apartment not yet secured but several places in consideration, this selfsame resolute returned to the scene of the sublime, where Melanie greeted him in inviting dishabille. Therein did a longer, hotter, and more creative recurrence inevitably conspire, with similar fervor applied, *post hoc*, to Nathan's predictable, guilt-laden repentance and concomitant forswearing. QI did not assuage his disappointment and growing sadness, by recalling Aristotle's morose observation: "All creatures are sad after love, except the rooster—and the human female."

This alternating pattern continued for three nights, each opening new doors, for both novices, in the habit-forming delectability of the illicit. On the fourth day, the yet-to-be-ordained minister, deeply ashamed, shocked, and saddened, secured an apartment on the other side of town. His little family returned, rescuing him from the draining dragons of desire, completely unawares.

*

Throughout the next three years, the consistent availability of Mistress Melanie (it would be fatuous to dub her

"Maid" any longer) salved only a portion of the growing spiritual, intellectual, and moral disquietude which accompanied Nathan's unrelenting quest for truth and salient meaning. His family, whom he loved dearly, his mistress, whom he fucked with abandon, and his work, which, though exhausting, was only somewhat satisfying, did not fill him up, as his fervent prayers would have it. QI admitted, *I am floundering* . . .

It was not arguably harmless, extraneous sex that sapped Nathan's spiritual strength; it was the sense that no matter what, how, how much, or how often he made effort to love others unconditionally, to practice his vaunted "Great Realization"—that life is best when lived for others—he perceived himself unsuccessful.

*

"Nathan, you look like I feel: bushed and beaten about the head and shoulders. Why don't you go home at night, for a change, instead of my repeatedly finding you here at church, hard at work in dark of night?" So spake his boss, the good and very Reverend Dr. George Jennings, on finding him pounding away on his typewriter at 11:00 p.m. on a Thursday night.

"Well, you're here, too, aren't you, George, instead of home with your dear wife and sweet children? You set the example by your endless labors; you know."

"Nathan, to my direct knowledge, you have not been home before midnight for at least the last two weeks. What can be so important that you have to stay here that often and that long?"

Whereupon Nathan recited a lengthy list of duties past, present, and yet to be, in which he was up to his eyeballs.

"Yes; you have tripled our youth program in less than two years, Nathan. I've never known a more effective youth pastor. Yet, you're never satisfied. Why is that?"

"I don't know, George, there's always plenty more, no matter how much I do. To be honest, sometimes I doubt myself, get frustrated, so I work harder..."

His boss and pastor listened as Nathan recounted what his inadequacies, "otherwise known as my failures." George tried to assure him otherwise. Responding, Nathan recounted a conversation he once had with his seminary president:

"Perhaps he was correct when he concluded, from my second-year doubts about the parish ministry, 'Nathan, you just don't love God!' 'I do, too!' was my indignant rejoinder. We both continued to doubt it, though he let me stay—where I graduated near the top of my class. Go figure..."

"Thank God! Now go home, before I turn the lights out on you!"

CHAPTER 2
WHAT HATH GOD WROUGHT?

Jesus was all about love. Agape, the Greeks called it—Godly love—love in spite of, not because of—the kind that does not hurt, stint, or deny, but which spends itself in service to others, without recompense. His judgment of his people was that no one could perfectly hit the mark, but that he, by his own works, witness, and sacrifice loved them anyway, as did his father in heaven. Jesus' reference to Judgment Day, in his parting analogy of the prophesized separation of the sheeps and the goats in Matthew 25, seems a fair summation of the essence of his public utterances: serve the "least of these," as you would serve God. No reference here to the sins of the flesh—not even adultery.

Mind, adultery, in Jesus' day and place, was a capital offense, for God's stern commandment to Moses on the mountaintop was considered an absolute prohibition, one evidently shared by Jesus, as well. Yet, he who could have cast the first stone—did not...

Nathan Rhea Scott
September 15, 1964

A single sentence will suffice for modern man. He fornicated and read the papers. After that vigorous definition, the subject will be, if I may, exhausted.

Albert Camus
1956

19

In the summer of 1961, one month after his first infidelity with Mistress Melanie, Nathan was ordained in the large, baroque sanctuary of his church before God and a thousand people, including Mother, Lenore, Melanie, and only incidentally, an admiring, fourteen-year-old Shara Day Starr—a thin, acned face, lost in the crowd. It was a sober moment as Dr. Jennings propounded the several, official questions, Nathan's affirmative answers to which became his ordination vows.

Nathan publicly acknowledged that: 1) the Bible contains the Word of God; 2) He will adhere to the Church's laws and polity; 3) He freely enters into this ministry, being directed by the Holy Spirit; and 4) He will discharge the duties of his office with faith, love, hope, honesty, diligence, and humility. Honest QI added a fervent, inward vow, *I believe; help thou my unbelief, Oh, God!*

To receive the customary laying on of hands by ordained churchmen, he knelt before the throng, his family, his mistress, his shattered conscience, and his God, and sincerely took unto himself the humble work of a minister of the gospel of Jesus Christ.

*

In college, the freeing and formative wonders of Nathan's leaving home and cleaving unto Tennessee Christian University, with its peerless, classical, liberal arts opportunities, are here simply assumed. Decisively, he declared his major three times (English, music theory, and finally, after four semesters, philosophy) and found the required Bible courses boring, largely because they were so insipid, and his professors so unquestioning.

His actual majors, of course, were Lovely Lenore and the University A Capella Choir, in that order. The closest Nathan ever came to in-depth religious experiences in college occurred whilst lost in the profound ecstasies of those two enthralling subjects.

In May 1957, after four, successful years, he married Lenore, a sociology major, and loaded all their worldly goods into their first car, honeymooned in Tabormount, NC, and then moved into Southern Theological Seminary. There, Lenore taught in a local elementary school, and Nathan spent four years with his insistent hand in the air and his face stuck in Greek, Hebrew, theology, and psychology texts, earning two master's degrees (theology and psychology/education).

Once ordained in his first ministry, in Durham, Nathan, of the ambidextrous conscience, not only laid well into Lenore and Melanie as oft as he could, he also laid heavily into his work, developing a fair reputation as an educator, organizer, counselor, youth worker, supervisor, and churchman—even an effective sermonizer. All he had to do was to preach to himself, proving the truth of the adage, "If you want to know the sins of a minister, listen for his favorite pulpit themes."

Thus, during his first three years of ministry, this young, would-be theolog enjoyed plenty of sex with two, quite willing, beautiful women, both of whom loved him very much. In spite of his growing notion that extra-marital sex, apart from the sneaking, was not very sinful or hurtful, God still did not seem to be very interactive with him, no matter how hard he tried to make him central in his life.

Lenore and Melanie haunt me, but for opposite reasons. Lenore is home base for deep, mutual affection, steadiness, and support, my tried-and-true mate, and the beloved mother of my children. Something is missing, though, or there would be no Mistress Melanie, usually late at night, shamefully, when Lenora is already abed. Melanie provides unbridled sex, always available, something I hesitate—even fear—to ask of Lenore. Paradoxically, in a strange sense, they tend to cancel each other out. Both are necessary but neither seems sufficient, or why do I keenly experience another huge, amorphous need? Alas!

Ever seeking to emulate the love of Christ, Nathan and his QI kept tabs on both his extramarital forays and his frustrating failure to practice his vaunted Great Realization. The forays didn't appear to harm anyone, directly, but he was sorely aware of failing in the second—to live for the sake of others! His calendar became impossible, so he added to it feverishly, hoping that more might approach enough. Thus, Nathan felt his foundations quaking and his life adrift...

Though he experienced minimal sexual guilt, he felt inadequate in most other respects. An exception was in the challenging and energetic hordes of young people ever seeking him out, giving him access to himself, and vice versa. *God, I know you're there, for I see you at work in others; I just don't feel you working in me.* Such was this man's tenuous, existential reality, throughout his first, three years of ministry: 1961-1963.

CHAPTER 3
SHARA

What selfish gods we be, to seek someone seeking me—and yet,
that is who we are, when sham is gone.

She is light dancing in a prismed tear; a jewel of sadness is my fear.

Nathan Rhea Scott
May 14, 1964

Having just come from a third, lust lathered night of initial and unexpected sex with his wife's best friend, Melanie, of the body-length, red tresses and enticing figure, Nathan was still in shock—and determination—not to repeat his first extra-marital indiscretions. This very morning, he had, again, left a handwritten note on Melanie's couch apologizing and foreswearing touching her again. *As the new associate pastor of Durham's First Protestant Church, I hope to atone for our mutual debauch by sincerely plunging into my work. This junior high picnic, my first day on the job, is my first opportunity…*

At the picnic Nathan eagerly sought out and met dozens of his endearing and hyperactive teens. Among the many he noted was fourteen-year-old Shara Day Starr of the acned face and scrawny figure, because she tried so hard, yet seemed wistful and apart, almost unseen by other teens. *She appears to shy from peer interactions in favor of helping adults, seeking their approval and affirmation. Though comeliness may grace her one day, she may have a difficult time of it until she outgrows her eighth-grade infirmities and insecurities.*

*

Amidst the hurly-burly requirements of educational and pastoral work, Nathan's relationship with young Shara developed slowly—and almost painfully. For a couple of years, she was something of a pest. Too often, he felt, she took advantage of his open-door policy, staying long and imparting little beyond incessant, adolescent, homely gripes. He slightly resented what felt like imposition, even though he listened, as with the many who sought him out.

"Mr. Scott, I get so frustrated. Daddy treats us all like slaves, even Mom—though he's nice enough in company. Last night, he made Jimmy stay at table until he apologized for simply asking a question, and he sent me to my room, for taking Jimmy's side."

"I see. The level of control your father uses seems unfair, is that it?"

"Yes, Mr. Scott. Just once I wish he'd treat me as something more than a 15-year-old girl who's good for nothing but to obey his every whim. Both Jimmy and I have ideas and opinions, but he puts them down ever time."

This theme of an unfair, demanding father, prone to ignoring or overlooking the value of each child, repeated itself, in one form or another, throughout at least two years of weekly, sometimes daily sessions or phone calls. Due to those repetitive sessions, Nathan heard a great deal about Shara and the Starr family.

Big J. Carl Starr, Sr., a tool and die salesperson, was gone from his family of five children and his stuck-at-home wife much of the time. Having suffered the shocks of being a line officer in both World War II and the Korean conflict, Nathan heard that he tended toward archconservative, intolerant, uncompromising rule, usually to suit himself. He was, however, a good and steady provider.

Over time, however, Shara and her best friend, Kathy Rogers, became the go-to youth for Nathan, when he needed volunteers. They were particularly good working with younger children and for effecting successful senior high church activities.

"Shara, I cannot thank you and Kathy enough for helping me in Bible School, Junior Camp, Sunday School, and Senior High Fellowship, not to mention babysitting my children. You are very real benefits to me and the church. I don't know what we'd do without you."

"Thanks, Mr. Scott. Here, and at your house, are about the only places I feel I have much value at all. Daddy doesn't think much of girls, especially my need to get out of the house. He wants me to mind my little brother and sisters ever weekend, so he and Mom can go out. I cain't ever go out on school nights, either, except to church, sometimes."

"If you help out at home the way you help out here, I'd be amazed if your parents didn't appreciate your skills the way I do."

"Mom, maybe, but I don't get to meet very many people, except here, and sometimes at school. I almost never get to meet or interact with boys. I'm sixteen, and I have never even had a date!"

"Have you been asked?"

"Only once, sorta, at the neighborhood pool. I have too many zits, my teeth need work we can't afford, Daddy won't let me get nicer glasses or wear tighter, uh, more comfortable, clothes, and I'm not, er, attractive enough for boys to notice. Daddy wouldn't let me date, anyway..."

By November 1963, as juniors in high school, Kathy and Shara manifested excellent social growth and maturity, especially Kathy, who was elected president of their church's large senior high fellowship. Shara worked more behind the scenes. Nathan was very pleased with them, for they made youth work constantly challenging and interesting for their peers–and rewarding for him. Both were warm, giving, loving girls, always seeing need, and rushing to fill it, or to see that it was filled.

Jason Hart, a student at another high school, became Nathan's third musketeer. Jason clearly understood, accepted, and enjoyed the growing closeness with Nathan he shared with Kathy and Shara. Thus, over time, Kathy, Shara, and Jason became jewels of great price and junior partners to Nathan, professionally and, increasingly, personally. Together, these three sparked the senior highs and gave Nathan his greatest sense that he might be accomplishing something in their staid, old church.

In the waning days of November, when an assassin's bullet ended the life of the nation's charismatic young president, Nathan tumbled into grief and spiraling disquietude approaching despair, increasing his doubts about himself, his country, his church, and his God. When Big J. Carl Starr and a few others indicated they were pleased Kennedy was dead, Nathan's young triumvirate shared some of his horror. For the first time, they were allowed to see another, more intimate side to their minister, compeer, and mentor.

"Mr. Scott are you still down about the president's death?" asked Kathy.

"Ahh, Katy-did, I appreciate your asking. Lenore and I were deeply involved in his promise. Then to see him ripped from us was almost too much, after all the hope he engendered. I'm adjusting, just as the world is; but it's still hard."

In fact, Nathan's 100-plus hour work weeks began to tell on him, as did his dejection and his growing sense of helplessness in making a meaningful difference.

It haunts me that this church includes powerful businessmen and politicians, but only a few involve themselves in any but themselves, their own success, finances, and prerogatives. Mostly conservative, they seem to be conservative of unfortunate social strictures, wealth, property, privilege, and business; not of the softer, more enlightened, especially Christian values–other humans, their unmet needs, rights, and potentials.

In late December 1963, Nathan developed a bleeding, duodenal ulcer and was hospitalized. After his transfusion, he was moved to put things into personal perspective. Lenore and Melanie were already in his room, when in trooped Kathy and Shara. When he saw tears in all four females' eyes, he knew something had to change–what, who, how or where, he knew not, but he knew why, *and that it must be soon.*

Why don't I turn to Lenore more often? She is beautiful, a loving, giving, sensitive, intelligent companion, helpmate, Mommy, and wife. Perhaps it is my growing sense of not being worthy of her, especially in the face and fact of Mistress Melanie. Then why not simply repent of that extra lady, have done with her, and go home? QI constantly told himself to do that, and partially succeeded, as he began to sublimate those energies through work, often with Kathy, Shara, and Jason.

"Lenore, you do know that I love you, don't you?"

"Of course, I do. What brought that up, honey, have you been doubting it?"

"I was just thinking how seldom we are both together– and awake–and it hurt my feel-bads. Do you notice it as much as I do?"

"Only that I may be growing a new hymen, if that answers your question. I try not to notice, too much, for I'm sure you love me. I sometimes worry, though, that our children may grow up not fully experiencing the marvelous Daddy you are, when you take the time to be around them. I was just commenting to Melanie that I'm with her more than I'm with you. That's sad, Nathan."

"Yes, let's work on that, okay?"

"How about right now? The kids are asleep, and I'll try not to scream too loudly…"

And it was so!

*

The fateful spring of 1964 sharpened the point on the arrow of Nathan's personal truth in most unplanned and unsolicited ways. He was with Kathy, Shara, and Jason more than with any other human beings. Happily, their relationships grew more synergistic. He dallied much less often with Melanie, even when her roommate was away. Instead, Nathan invested in his teenaged stars.

Of the three, Shara appears to be the neediest, and I'm finding that her growth, values, and emotional needs inspire and motivate me. I almost crave mentoring her, as she is so open, innocent, and sincere. Her caring for others does not seem to have any limits. Not incidentally, that seems to include me. What selfish gods we be—to seek someone seeking me, huh, Scott—but a high school junior?

At fourteen, Shara had been simply lost, immature, and clinging—a bit of a pest and a woeful challenge. Almost seventeen, she had grown admirably in all areas, was well on her way to mature, executive function, and was one of Nathan's dearest, young friends, despite their differences in age and station. As her mutually acknowledged mentor, he felt privileged to see her blossom, in manner, mien, and maturity.

What does it mean that she is becoming somewhat essential in my otherwise, too scattered life?

*

On the portentous date of April 18, 1964, Nathan's relationship with Shara jolted into greater depth and personal awareness. During his spring senior high retreat at Camp Promise, while fishing the riverbank, he saw her standing in the camp's roughhewn, riverside Vesper Dell, waved, stopped fishing, and joined her.

"Heighdy, Shara Starr; what's up that you're in Vesper Dell, when everybody else is recreating?"

"Hey back, Mr. Scott. I needed some fresh air and some thinking time and space. Are you catching anything?"

"Smallmouth bass nibbles, but they're too canny for me, so far. What subjects need time and space out here, alone, or are you waiting for someone?"

"I was waiting for you, if you want to know."

Pause.

"And...?"

"Because you always listen to me, even when I'm not sure what to say–like now."

"What's on your mind, Shara?" he said, gesturing for her to sit down next to him on one of the log pews.

"Well, a lot of things, but the most important thing is how grateful I am to you–for your friendship and how helpful you have been–are being–to me, uh, and to all the others."

"Thanks, Shara. I love being available for you guys. Is there something special I can do for you, now?"

"Not really, Mr. Scott. I just wanted to thank you–for everything. You have been wonderful to–and for–me."

"Appreciation gladly accepted, Shara. But you, Kathy, and Jason inspire whatever good I might do for you. Plus, you help me all the time, so let me thank you for that–but mostly I'm grateful for you, the person, so busy becoming."

Shara smiled her happiness, and they talked easily for about ten minutes, as they often did, of church business, soon turning to her personal life, her home situation, her loneliness, what she had to give, and how much she wanted to find a productive path in life. As always with his youth, Nathan listened warmly and tried to reflect expressed feelings. There came a pause, while she looked at him with a puzzled–and puzzling–look.

"Wail, if I'm going to catch anything before suppertime," he said, standing, "I'd better get back to fishing. What about you?"

Shara stood, too, continuing to look up at him in a quizzical way, cocked her head, and said, "Can I ask you something, Mr. Scott?"

"Anything."

"Can I give you a hug?"

"Of course, you can, Shara, and I'll happily return the compliment."

Shara's arms flew around his neck, and Nathan's encircled her trim waist. Her fervent hug was brief, but not so brief as to leave him unmoved by its sudden and unexpected intensity—and warmth. His guard down, his heart open, he basked in her hug, relishing it—soaking it up!

Releasing her, he saw tears in her eyes. She was so open, candid, and obviously admiring—and longing—that he felt fulfilled by what, heretofore, QI always processed as mere, adolescent adulation. As she left, Nathan returned to fishing, but not without re-thrilling at Shara's guileless display. Nathan would fondly remember Shara's momentous Vesper Dell hug the rest of his days, sudden and searing bolt that it was!

After their return to their church, he drove Kathy and Shara to get their polio Type II sugar cubes, while he got his. Such was the familiarity—not quite the intimacy—of their innocent, symbiotic relationships.

During the next several weeks, life went on as before, but Shara's Vesper Dell hug kept popping into his mind, randomly—and quite sweetly. *Something is brewing here I don't understand. Let's keep it in perspective, though, Scott, and attach no more significance to it than to a nice greeting card.*

*

"Please get up and sit at my desk, Shara," he smiled. "If you're going to counsel me, you might as well do it from the proper chair."

Astonished, she hesitated, then did as he requested, while he took her seat. Grinning awkwardly, she asked, "What am I supposed to do, now?"

"Exactly what you were just doing, Shara," he twinkled, "asking about my welfare, but from the counselor's chair. Ask me anything you should know, as my newly appointed counselor."

Twenty seconds of self-conscious grins and silence passed, from her unaccustomed seat, before she whispered, "Mr. Scott, can I ask you anything?"

"Certainly–I have no reason to hide from you, Shara–and please call me, 'Nathan.'"

Another pause as she leaned across the desk towards him, looking intently through tears welling in her eyes, and with such obvious concern that it startled him. *My attempt at a spontaneous lark has morphed into gripping awareness—and openness. Be careful, Scott!*

"Mr. Sco–Na–Nathan, are you happy?" she asked, through trembling lips.

Caught off guard, again, by this increasingly dear girl, his jumbled world of ulcers, doubt, guilt, infidelity, unfinished, sometimes unappreciated, hard work, god-awful debts, not enough time with his family, an ineffable, spiritual vacuum within, intellectual discontent, the sad plight of the world and the American scene: war, woe, death, greed, hatred, prejudice, hunger, strife, bigotry, poverty, violence, and ignorance all flooded his striving mind.

"Of course, you don't have to answer…"

"No, give me a minute–I'm thinking how best to be honest, but not overwhelming. This is your first time in the

31

counselor's chair, and I don't want to blow you clean out of it."

Like any good counselor, and most wise women, she made no response—which became his permission to proceed.

After a few minutes of his describing things awful but external to his daily world, she interrupted, "I mean, are *you* happy—not the world?"

"Sort of," he responded, dropping his voice, exposed. She waited.

"Shara, no one has a right to be too happy, as long as there is such misery and hypocrisy in the world, and one can still do something about it."

A salty pearl of a tear rolled down her cheek and onto her quivering lip.

"Shara, what's wrong? Do you care that much how—how I feel?" he whispered, handing her a tissue.

"Of course, I care, Mr. Scott, er, Nathan—I've always cared. You are very important to me," and then quickly, "and to Kathy and Jason—and all the kids."

"So, you are crying, because you think I may not be happy," he rejoined, lamely, becoming her counselor, again, despite his chair.

"Mr. Scott, I'm crying because I've seen you work so hard for us, and for all the church—and I'm afraid you may leave, to keep from having another ulcer, and maybe you should leave, if it will keep you alive longer; and if you leave, I don't know what we would do without you. Jason and Kathy and me, and lots of others are scared you might leave. We'll do anything to keep you here. What can I do to help you more? I know there must be something more—to make your job easier—and you happier."

Her words rushed between clipped little sobs from a face so concerned and suddenly so dear, Nathan's heart tucked her into itself, wrapped in the still warming cloak of her Vesper Dell hug.

What he did not tell her was that he and Lenore were flat broke, in debt, and had nothing in the way of assets, except a bank-owned car and a few sticks of furniture. Hospital and credit card bills were in arrears, as well as several outstanding personal loans. First Church was paying him $7,200 a year, plus benefits, but Lenore was not working. He was unwilling to go to Dr. Jennings with his financial woes because he knew the church was strapped, too.

Nor could he confess to her how his affair with Melanie kept him up at night, and not always because he was in her bed. Melanie worried him to distraction, especially when he realized how much he short-changed Lenore. Nor did he share that, dealing on the realistic level for a change, he was considering several more lucrative jobs offers.

"Shara, as long as I have people like Jason, Kathy, and a certain Shara Day Starr helping me, things will be okay."

"Really? You promise?" she said, wiping her eyes and perking up.

Swapping chairs made a profound impression on them both. *The caring and the sharing go both ways, and the lines of communication seem so open—almost inviting—urging—us both to give and take—more.*

The unexpected moment of profundity passed quickly, as their conversation turned to tomorrow's senior high picnic, and to her new, two-piece bathing suit, bought and worn before her father could nix it. Confirming that he could pick her up for the picnic about two, she thanked him, as she always did, especially for swapping chairs.

After she left, Nathan returned to his chair, still warmed by Shara's body, and tried to comprehend his—and her—feelings. *What is there about this girl that moves me so? She is certainly bright, but only an average student, so far. She reveals a very caring, serving nature, here and elsewhere. Her curiosity into the nature of things is only beginning to be piqued. Her acned face and slender form show more than the promise of comeliness, but she is surely untried, naïve, and vulnerable—off limits! Yet somehow, she helps me see myself more clearly, by my seeing her seeing me. "What selfish gods we be, to seek someone seeking me," indeed!*

That night, lying next to his satiated wife, Nathan parsed his feelings further. *I am unable to process Shara's tears and fears. I know I don't want to see her unhappy or hurt. I want her and her obvious values fulfilled. Not incidentally, I haven't thought about Melanie for days..!*

CHAPTER 4
FRUSTRATION AND
CONFESSION

Beloved, let us love one another, for love is from God, and whoever loves has been born of God and knows God.

1 John 4:7

S hara was her usual effervescent self when Nathan picked her up the next day. Their conversation was inconsequential and did not plumb the depths of his increasing wonder at this girl. At the picnic, in addition to being constantly besieged by sixty-plus senior high youth about everything under the sun, Nathan caught one bass, trotted a balky Morgan completely around the bridle path, took several rolls of black and white film of the doings (including one shot of Shara in her demure bathing suit, revealing a surprisingly trim and proportioned figure, at 5'4.5" and 111 pounds, and a fetchingly shy demeanor), ate, led the singing of camp songs, joked and frolicked, taught a brief vesper lesson, prayed, and got ready to leave.

Suddenly anxious, he realized: *It cannot happen soon enough. For reasons I don't fully understand, I need to be with Shara, again—alone—to tell her—what?* QI thrashed, trying to parse surging emotions.

In the gloaming, driving the twenty or so miles to her house, Shara sat against the passenger door of Nathan's car, wearing shorts and t-shirt over her bathing suit, with one slender leg cocked up on the seat. Nathan was aware that she was watching him, as they rehashed the events of the day. As they came to the turn toward her home, his mind was aboil with ambivalence. *Take her straight home and forget all this confusion, or tell her the truth? But what is the truth, anyway? How can I manage, much less justify, keeping her in the car a while longer?*

Knowing he knew to turn left, she looked startled when he turned right.

Silence.

"I don't want to take you home just yet, Shara."

"Good!"

They drove along in silence about a mile, while QI festered. *I want to explain, to tell her that she makes me feel things I don't understand. Surely about her assisting me in my job, but is there more to share, really? Careful, Scott; precious cargo.*

"Would you like to get something to drink, Shara?"

"No, Mr. Scott; let's just drive around for a while."

"Shara, please call me 'Nathan.' I really do prefer it."

"Okay, Na–Nathan. It's hard, after three years of saying 'Mr. Scott.'"

"I know."

More inviolable silence, as she looked at him in her concerned, seemingly all-knowing way. *What in the world am I doing? This is just silly—she is seventeen, and I will be twenty-nine in August. What if somebody sees us so far off the beaten track and thinks we're up to no good? Are we—am I—up to no good?*

Finally, he spoke. "Shara, you are truly amazing."

"I am?"

"It's just that I–I find myself enjoying being with you quite a lot, lately, and each time we are together, I find it harder to see you go–I'm not sure why. Maybe it's because you are so appreciative–so eager to help–not just me, but most everybody around you. No matter–the truth is that I feel–an abiding respect and affection for you which I do not completely understand. I do know, though, that I enjoy being with you—longer, and more often!"

She waited, again, showing either wisdom or confusion.

"You are certainly as valuable to me as you indicated I am to you, yesterday, when we swapped chairs, and I want you to know that. You are special, Shara, and not just to me. I want very much for you to be special to yourself. If I hadn't told you that tonight, I think I would have popped."

"What do you mean, 'special to myself'?"

"You're about the most giving person I know, Shara. You are forever showing genuine concern for folks, by your actions, not just your words. You live your caring, and I love that in you."

I can't tell, clearly, but her eyes are glistening behind her glasses with delight —or tears; either way, it means the same thing!

"I do care, Na—Nathan, more than you will ever know," she whispered, looking at him.

Oh, God, I want to explore her surprisingly welcome words, to stroke and caress them, to make them mean what I dare not let myself believe they mean. I'm afraid that she might bolt at the shocking nakedness of these gathering feelings.

"Yes, Shara, I think I do know, and I love you for it."

Though neither came any closer to outright declarations, Nathan confessed to the happy, startled girl that he was drawn to her. By choosing his words carefully, he knew he had not told her—nor did he know how—or how deeply—his feelings ran. Her responses were warm and accepting, as they usually were, and seemed only slightly clothed in uncertainty.

Shara surely heard me, felt my anguish, but did not know if—or how—to act on their seeming meanings. Complimented, perhaps she was pleased with my confession, but could not quite allow herself to comprehend fully. She has never been loved before...

He took her home, told her good night as warmly as he dared, and watched as she strode up the driveway, towards the lights of her unhappy house, keenly feeling the poignancy of her departure. Back in his church office, Nathan wrote, "frustration and confession" on the May 9, 1964, page of his pocket calendar–and saw his fingers tremble.

The next thirteen days were happy for Nathan. He was upbeat and excited about everything. *Something's happening, I know not what, but it's making me alive, again. The question: For what do I dare hope? 'More' is the answer; 'how' comes next! 'Why' doesn't seem to matter very much–only that it's like living waters. Drink slowly, Scott!* Mare incognita.

*

Having just come in from a family night supper, where Nathan gave a talk on God and emotions, he went to their spinet and began to improvise. Putting her hands on his shoulders, Lenore asked, "Nathan, what's going on with you? You've seemed more unsettled, lately, than any time since we got here. I know you're incredibly busy–you're not home much, anyway–and thinking about moving to Wilmington has got to disturb. But something else may be bothering you. Am I right?"

Turning around on the piano bench and pulling her to him, he responded, "Wail, we're broke, for one thing, Lenore, and I have to float another signature loan at the bank or hit Daddy up for another $500 loan, just to get through this month."

"Yes, that bothers me, too," she said, as she pulled his face against her breasts "Won't the increase in salary at Wilmington help?"

"I'm sure of it, if we can hold out until then."

"You said, 'for one thing.' What other things might be at play, darling?"

"Jeez, Lenore, the look on your pretty face makes me think you've got stuff on your mind about what I might have on mine. Wanna go there?"

"Well, now that you mention it, I'm curious why you gave Shara a watch for her birthday, when, to my knowledge, no other teen in your coterie receives such attention?"

As a birthday gift, Nathan impulsively bought Shara a $19.95 silver wristwatch at Sears and had the Greek word Ἀγάπη (Agape) inscribed on the back. He gave it to her Sunday evening, explaining its meaning, after she helped plan the upcoming senior high retreat, at which she and Kathy would be his informal assistants.

Standing in his wife's embrace, he defended, "But you said it would be all right, considering…"

"That was before I knew we were broke and needed a monetary influx to keep us afloat."

"Honey, we can afford to be kind to the person you have always said is the best babysitter we've ever had. 'Like one of the family,' I think were your words."

"Yes, to both of those–I don't know why I even asked. Forget it, honey."

"No, no; please talk about Shara or anything that worries you, Lenore."

"I get concerned, Nathan, when I don't see you enough to share your—your feelings, good, bad, sad, glad, mad, or indifferent, as you always say. I worry that you worry without me, understand?"

"I understand you are the wiser of the two of us! That's why you're resonant with my very strong sense of loss about leaving."

"Not wiser; just sensitive. You're right, though; I feel your feelings."

"And I love feeling you," he grinned, caressing her breasts. I don't really understand my feelings, either, especially about Shara. She's a conundrum, for sure."

Soon after Nathan left, Lenore called Melanie, eager to share her concerns about Nathan's demeanor.

"How much did he pay for the watch?" asked Melanie. "That usually hints at the value men place on the giftee, doesn't it?"

"Oh, Mellie, it was all of $19.95. So, if you're right, I'm concerned about nothing. Still, there's something going on in Nathan's head, if not his heart, which is bothering him, and I have a hard time not knowing what it might be. Any other ideas? He talks to you when he takes you home from here–and from Koinonia class, doesn't he?"

Melanie colored bright red, glad her best friend could not see her reaction, graced the question, and changed the subject to Beth's potty training.

*

Keeping things on a strictly professional plane, Nathan made no further mention to Shara of his confessions but realized that something was slowly coming into focus. Both were looking forward to the upcoming retreat, though neither dared to hope for anything more, especially in the light of day. *Nights, though...?*

On Friday, May 22, 1964, Nathan drove a busload of senior high students, including Shara and Kathy, to Camp Promise, and to a destiny forged by a freedom unavailable elsewhere.

CHAPTER 5
WITHIN MY TROUBLED BREAST

Il n'y a qu'une seule bonne chose dans la vie, et c'est l'amour.
(There is only one good thing in life, and that is love.)

Guy de Maupassant

Love must have a corpus—let it be thine.
Love must have a spirit—let it be mine.
Love must have a purpose—let it be Divine!

With the wonder of Shara here, beside me, Lord, let her
innocence temper my daring, that I do not exploit her. Amen.

Nathan Rhea Scott
May 22, 1964

*M*ay's twenty-second Night, thrusting so carelessly in this gravid Month, loving her on Nature's couch, is careless of what his spending seed might spawn. In his lusting for May's spreading limbs and fecund musks, Night is mindless of the permissive and provocative influence his open and splendid pulsing have on the young minister—and on the even younger girl—suddenly together in it, aroused, but unawares.

The young cleric is naturally affected by the nocturnal nuptials in full moan and cry all around them. Standing at river's edge, the awkward pair is discomfited by the naked invitations and seminal odors emitting from the conjugality of

41

Night and Month. QI recognizes *the familiar creep of conflict between established propriety and longing. Perhaps she feels vulnerable— and wanton—the very stuff of feminine lust. Belay that thought, Scott!*

"It—it's a nice night, Mr. Sco—er, Nathan…"

"Indeed so, Shara. Indeed so—especially with you in it."

Shara Starr and Kathy Rogers, both seventeen, his assistants at this retreat, stayed up in the camp's kitchen, enjoying their moments of privilege and late hour camaraderie with Nathan, their close minister friend. With midnight coming, Kathy left to nurse a coming cold.

At his invitation, now standing on the lip of the floating boathouse, Shara emotes practiced decorum, innocence, and deference, seeming to ignore the obvious potentials of the play, simply waiting for the curtain to rise. Careful not to reveal too much too fast, Nathan's driving need is—*to admit and cultivate a burgeoning need for Shara Starr: a magnet to my most profound feelings, but not because of the delicious danger and inescapable heats of her youthful, striving body—so help me, God.*

Why, then, God, am I here? Because nothing and no one has proved fulfilling and instaurating to me, regardless of my years of praying? But a seventeen-year-old virgin—a member of my church, under my care and keeping…?

Shara walks to the edge of the deck, gazing out over the somnolent river, wondering. Its currents, like those moving within her, are too deep to be obvious. Nathan waits, pondering.

Here am I, God, center stage, on the lip of this amphitheatrical boathouse, under the flattering spotlight of a gibbous moon, alone with this warm, compliant girl who ever seeks me out. Yet it is neither lechery nor the external effects of Night and Month that cast me here! Dear God, could she become the singular patch on the torn and tattered fabric of my life, that will, at last, more fully costume my spirit?

The ambience of unsuspecting hush and slumber on this moon-blest and frog-sung night heightens their sense of risk. Night's winds, stroking the North Carolina hardwoods, provides an overture, and to this expectant pair, it seems that all the previous moments of their lives have prepared them for the crisis of this pivotal, opening scene.

Alone together, on the boathouse stage, and aware, they breathe the fuel of May's forbidden breath, blowing on the coals aglow between them, kindling their energies to will the heavy curtains of censorious society to rise, and to let the play begin. An aureate cyclorama of stars, flickering in the rippled, river waters before them, are their footlights. Sitting together, now, downstage left, the slender girl, dark of hair and cloaked more in the verve and potential of her youth than in her cotton, printed blouse and creamy shorts, leans against a railing, hugging her chilled knees and waits, ashiver, for her first real line.

Beside her, her minister peers past her striking face and form, through the interstice of remaining decorum and propriety, into their mute, primordial audience of earth, air, fire, and water, in and around the dark, living river. The permeating quintessence here is prayerful longing–longing for fulfillment of purest love, of life, and of unmistakable meaning–almost palpable, now.

With the wonder of Shara here, beside me, Lord, let her innocence temper my daring, that I do not exploit her. Amen.

Shara's slight shiver may be due as much to the nakedness, as to the thrill, of this opening Night. I feel an unaccountable calm—a certainty. For the first time in my personal dealings with amenable females, I am not conjuring or anticipating lust. It is far from my mind.

Close beside her, leaning against the same rail, he studies the appealing lines and features of Shara's well-formed, young face, her delicate neck, her slender, strong arms hugging her knees tightly against her breasts, and her starlit thighs, white and smooth, dipping into her shorts.

"Shara?" A whisper–and enough.

Not yet fully fathoming the emotional whirl within, she stirs. Looking up at him, her face is an expression of trust and expectation...

With a sigh, imperceptible, except to God, to whom it is a prayer, Nathan opens both arms to her in clear invitation. Without hesitation, she flows into them, her quaking head snuggling on his shoulder. He enfolds her unto himself, as she presses against him. Her first line is not poetry, but it cues the truth between them, if not yet the beauty.

"Can I ask you something?" she quavers, not quite settled in.

"Yes, Shara," his deep voice breathes into her Night-brushed hair.

"Why did you do that?"

In that moment, while a new heaven and a new earth begin to form, the young Rev. Mr. Nathan Rhea Scott compartmentalizes his loved and lovely wife, his two, precious children, his delectable and demanding mistress, his far-flung family, his senior pastor, his church, but not quite his God, and with bold strokes writes the signature and the first, most honest, notes of his new opus. In his singer's soul, *Allegro, ma non troppo*, the prudent tempo; for his truth is filled with high risk–and still higher gain.

"Because I need you," began his recitative, "and because you are cold and shivering."

Yet, Nathan's soaring spirit cannot quite muffle nor evade QI's Biblical caveat, which, chorus-like, haunts his heart and the magic of the scene, with its forbidding and foreboding drone, long remembered, long believed, ". . . *whoever causes one of these little ones who believe in me to stumble, it would be better for him to have a great millstone fastened round his neck and to be drowned in the depth of the sea."*

Peace, be still—I will not harm her!

Then does she settle into his arms—and tabernacle in his heart—like a bird into her nest. Their hearts keep the tempo, but not the salacious grips of Night, as they quietly snuggle themselves into the appealing warmth and mystery of the other. The moon signals both caution and comfort in Shara's glasses, as Nathan looks down at her upturned face. Jumbled emotions, those he has felt about her for weeks, surge in him, again. *I must decide, anew, now!*

Their first kiss is warmth and electricity, charging them both with love's ancient fires… *Our kisses are starlight and lightning—and alchemy—turning the lead of "no" into the gold of "yes."*

Inevitably, they inspire many more, spurring Nathan's amazed and impudent QI to note that *Shara is inexpert, but learning rapidly…*

*

The foredeck of the boathouse, damp with dew, reflects the waning moonlight, as the daring couple compress time and space between them. After a span of continuous thrilling, manifest wonder at their closeness, and tacit refusal to consider the rude meaning of tomorrow, the players move inside the boathouse. Cuddling together on a large workbench, they hold and tantalize in their floating cocoon in this initiative Night in May. Their stolen time infuses the present with intimations of eternity, a sacred rite of love's initiating passage. Lying side by side, limbs entwined on the crowded bench, their chaste kisses and delicate whispers caress the ambiance of newness with their mutual dare.

In thrall to the man, the Night, her youth, and her overwhelming feelings of comfort and joy in his arms, Shara's body is as busy and as inspired as her mind. For, as she told him later, she is experiencing her first, recognized, welcome surprise of physical desire and enthrallment to expectation, accompanied by the juices which, she guesses, somehow signal her body's readiness to couple.

More ready than Nathan grasps, Shara seems unsure of what, how, when, where, and even if, she should do—positive only of why. Unaware of her building ardor, the young minister is scintillant, overjoyed at the purer aspects of their present joy, on a more exalted, spiritual plain than he believed attainable—at least for him.

Amazing! I am holding her, kissing her, needing her with all my being, so incredibly close, feeling the wonderful curves and softness of her body pressed against me—and I feel no lust—more telling, no erection! Surely God is at work here, no matter the—the strange newness—or the new strangeness—of this telling night. This feels pure, almost righteous, as though Shara is the coal of fire pressed to my lips, allowing me to hear the voice of God. I may not have a choice in the matter. I feel love ascending, not mere want and need, and certainly not lust. I feel pure because she is pure—my wonder and my miracle!

Reveling in the pristine joys of her first love, Shara notes—and welcomes—the surging of the many new and awing thrills cascading over and through her body, despite an unwelcome monition skulking just behind her eyes. Together, they feast on her unqualified acceptance of his unconventional focus, and on the wonder of their evident investment in each other—basking in the always miracle of caring...

Shara's inexperienced, virginal heat exhilarates them, and they stroke it with their awe. His caresses are familiarizing exploration; intimate mapping, piloted by their creative closeness—nothing more. Taking their time too rapidly, making it last forever, they share their very breathing, lest it escape their moral meld...

*

In the coolness of the early morning riverside, feeling the flux of Night around and through them, their combined body heat no longer keeps them warm, despite their embracing. At Nathan's suggestion, they move their awe into an empty cabin, close by. Shara stealthily returns to hers, to dress more warmly. *The sneaking—the damnable sneaking—has begun—but we'll both feel safer if she's more fully clothed!*

As the moon sinks its shaft into a prudery of trees, Nathan waits, pondering the sense and nonsense of this rare Night. *How and why do I continue to feel such great calm, this overwhelming security, in the face of what must be grim, unnerving risk? How is it that our—our caring—though only just begun, already feels ancient and forever? God help me avoid exploitation for carnal or any other reasons—and to hold this dearest one harmless from the trouble we are—I am—stoking so relentlessly.*

I dare not seek forgiveness or strength to repent—a refreshing change from my previous struggles. I feel elation, ebullience, tranquility, and the beginnings of a precious and long sought condition: fulfillment! Through Agape, this time; Eros has yet to raise its nether head. Not yet, not yet! Perish the thought!

CHAPTER 6
PAS DE TROIS?

Where Eros is the arrow, shouldn't Agape draw and loose the bow?

Nathan Rhea Scott

June 5, 1964

Nathan watched from the door of the stark, empty cabin, with its five bunk beds. The door and windows, tightly closed, made the cabin musty but warmer than the cooling passion of Night. Heartbeat singing in his ears, Nathan grinned in relief and excitement, as Shara's shadowy form re-materialized in the darkness.

Evidently, she hasn't thought better of it, doubted me, or herself, for here she comes!

As her welcome silhouette neared, a flashlight moved near her cabin, two hundred yards away. Nathan literally gulped as he thought he recognized his wife, moving toward the well-lit girl's bathroom (where Shara had changed seconds ago). Quickly stepping outside, trying to still the squeaking door, Nathan hissed, *sotto voce,* "Shara, look!"

Stopping in her tracks, she whirled and squatted in one motion. Looking behind her, she was petrified. Sensing her fright and helplessness, as well as his own, he duck-walked to her, put his hand on her shoulder and was about to counsel running, when the light disappeared into the girls' bathroom.

Reprieved but rattled by the prospect of discovery, Nathan's common sense clicked in. He pulled Shara up and quietly walked her to the cabin. After torturing through the complaining door, he felt sudden annoyance at himself for endangering everyone and everything–especially Shara–and his dear, little family, so close, yet so far...

"Who was that?" Shara asked, breaking the silence like a gong.

"You know how kids love to use their flashlights," Nathan whispered. "Probably one of the girls going to the bathroom."

"Yeah. I almost wet my pants, and I just went!"

As he stared blankly out the door, she leaned back against him, folding his arms around her. Nathan felt the pressure of her back and bottom against him as she moved his arms across her breasts, pinning herself to him.

The light reappeared, moving toward the dining hall– close to the director's cabin, where he was supposed to be sleeping.

"Shara, please stay here and hold my place! I've got to beat whoever that is to my cabin!"

Shara's face turned pasty white in the dark, as Nathan squeaked through the door and ran, pall mall, toward his cabin. Holding her breath, she watched the flashlight slowly cross the field and enter the dimly lit kitchen. She could no longer see Nathan. Her heart was beating in her ears, when the light emerged from the kitchen, moving toward Nathan's tiny duplex.

Nathan, lay on his cot in the dark and waited, trying to calm his panting and tachycardia. His clock read 1:30.

I hope Shara hasn't gone back to her cabin. If it is Lenore, she is probably coming here to tell me something about one of the kids. I hope they are all right. Cool it, Scott. You haven't been discovered–yet!

"Nathan?" came Lenore's soft voice, evoking both relief and long-established familiarity. "Are you awake?"

"Hey, 'Nore. Is everything all right? Come in."

49

"I woke you up, didn't I–but why are you sleeping in your clothes? Yes, all is well. Happy anniversary, honey," she said, kissing him. "We didn't get a chance to see each other before lights out. One of the girls' snoring woke me up, and I saw what a nice night it is. So, I thought I'd come tell you how much I love you, and I missed you, all alone over here, on our seventh anniversary.

"Happy anniversary, Lenore. I love you, too!"

Either this fine lady suspects something and is checking her suspicions, or she is being the Lenore I have always known her to be—loving and caring, even to a fault. I believe it is the latter, thank God!

Warm and welcome kisses soon became hot and heavy, as she caressed his rapidly erecting penis through his pants. His hands followed suit, finding her most responsive spots with ease. As both were on the verge of succumbing, Lenore gently pulled away.

"Whew! That'll do, Mister! We don't have time to celebrate properly, but it's very hardening, er, heartening to realize that you still want me!"

"Any time, every time, all the time, Lenore. I know we haven't been together much, lately, but damn! We'll have to prick this up, again, when we get home, honey."

"Promises, promises, but I'll remind you of that one! Let me go back, now, before I'm missed."

Nathan walked his dear wife and best friend back to her cabin, kissed her, again, and started back toward his director's cabin, parsing his emotions.

I know I love Lenore, never want to lose her, hate how my driving lusts with Melanie cheat her, but now, in a certitude of purest, loving feelings with Shara, I feel no sin. I'm not after her body, at all! I absolutely need her purity! If only I could tell Lenore, perhaps she might understand...

*

50

With wide, frightened eyes, Shara grabbed him at the door and drew him into the musty cabin, dying to hear...

"Tell me, Nathan—but, but kiss me, first."

He did, and he did. Shara was mortified and worried that everything would blow up in their faces. Nathan assured her that nothing had changed, that they were still safe and secure in the cabin—and in their emerging feelings for each other.

"Yes, but I don't want to be the cause of hurting anybody Mr. Scott. What should we do?"

"Believe in what we feel—about each other and pray God to bless these feelings. Trust us, Shara, trust your feelings if you can. I believe you want this as much as I do. We have only just begun..."

"Yes; you're right!"

He kissed her again and felt her tremble.

Shara turned in his embrace, looked up at him, and clung even tighter. Nathan's body continued to pour adrenaline, while his mind barely sipped at the dregs of dread. *Lenore is back in her cabin. We're still undiscovered and safely together, aren't we? Shara is still in my arms, isn't she? Easy, wisely, now, lest we perish...*

Their kisses were legion, restoring mutual renewal and reassurance. Feeling an unfamiliar weakness in his knees, his lips opened hers, and their tongues began their first, sweet explorations. *She is breathing faster, her body melting into mine. I've known deep passion, before—but this is utterly, unaccountably different—and wonderful!*

"Mmm, Nathan," she sighed, "you cain't know how good this is. I have dreamed of it so often—and here I am, in your arms!"

Nathan delighted in her artless honesty, as well as in her lovable, Carolina pronunciations. Nearly restored to their remarkable now, in this rarest of Nights, Nathan placed the tip of his nose and his forehead against hers and inhaled her as he would a fragrant flower.

"I do know, Shara. This is exquisite; you are lovely, and I am experiencing such bliss, it stuns me

"Me, too. Ain't it great?!"

As the audacious couple engaged in the sleight of hand and tentative juxtaposition of bodies so typical of new lovers, Shara led him to a bed and sat herself down. Nathan stood before her, stroking her hair and face, now warming against his abdomen. They continued to test the depth of their nascent passion through deep kisses and familiarizing embraces, while avoiding anything overtly sexual. Thrilling, they held; holding, they kissed, kissing, they tingled, tingling, they hungered, hungering, they thrilled.

Reluctantly, Nathan advised that they better not risk much longer. Feathers of pink in the eastern sky would soon tickle the earth awake. It was nearly 4:00 a.m. Night was in his final throes, having ejaculated his spreading dews in licentious May, who, calm and cool, now, dwindled her winds, pining for her next, nocturnal lover.

Nathan, the gentleman, stepped outside the cabin, while Shara, the virgin, stepped out of her jeans and sweatshirt, slipped back into her nightie, and stuffed the rest under her robe. When she came out, Nathan's first view of her in her bedtime habit stirred his heart, but not his loins, for he treasured another kind of intimacy, unpracticed by salacious Night.

Holding tightly, Shara welcomed a man's intrusive pubes against hers for the first time. Their final kiss pulsed and persevered in their bodies, until Nathan pulled away from its searing, lest his reach exceed his gasp...

"I'll try to get away tomorrow afternoon—this afternoon, during free time, Shara. Can you get out to the hogans about three o'clock?"

"I'll try," she sighed, almost panting from the heat roiling her body. "Kiss me again!"

"Yes, my Shara. Good night."

"Until tomorrow–today, my Na–Nathan!"

Nathan watched Shara's strong, young body striding towards the bathrooms. Suddenly weary from need of sleep and the intensity of a well-spent Night, he yawned and stretched, shook his head in disbelief. *I hope I know what I'm doing!*

Nathan waited until Shara reached the girl's bathroom (where she was amazed and puzzled at her well soaked panties). Then, he trekked behind the empty cabins and nearby trees, down by the river, and up the hill, again, to the combo director's and lifeguard's tiny duplex.

He fell into bed in his underwear, resting wonderfully, as the mockingbirds began their sunrise canticle. His last thoughts were of Shara and the exquisite prospects for the afternoon. Several hours later, little Nathan pounced on him, full of jabber, hugs, and kisses, delighting him from a sound sleep and reminding him of his otherwise fully committed life.

It couldn't have been a dream! I still taste her...

CHAPTER 7
TAKE YOUR REST

Regret is pride—the morning after.

Nathan Rhea Scott
May 23, 1964

High school kids, always vivacious and ready for action, needed direction; Nathan directed. Breakfast was followed by a two-hour work project (wash all the windows in thirteen buildings), refreshments, an hour's continuing discussion of last night's movie "Sanctuary," a fair merging of Faulkner's novel of the same name and his play, "Requiem for a Nun," lunch, two more hours of work (staining four cabins and a small dining hall), and recreation (games, sports, swimming, and free time), from 3:00 to 6:00 p.m. Nathan's job was to plan, staff, coordinate, facilitate, oversee, troubleshoot, and enliven everything.

Is it my imagination, or is Shara acting strangely?

Being old hands, Shara and Kathy were to help with projects, as needed. Usually, Shara found a way to assist him. Not this time. He caught only glimpses of her during the meals and the work activities. She sat quietly, almost morosely, during the movie discussion, and busied herself in the kitchen while he supervised work projects. When he finally walked up to her after lunch, she looked down as he spoke.

"How are you doing, Shara?"

"I don't know how—or what—I'm doing; I'm so mixed up," she lamented, looking up and then away.

"I thought maybe so. Is there anything I can do?"

Her voice, already filled with confusion, added tears. "Mr. Scott, I—what are we going to do?"

"Nothing, right this minute, Shara. Meet me at the hogans a little after three. We'll talk—and figure things out. I know it's hard..."

They were interrupted by two freshmen girls, sent to fetch Mr. Scott. Shara turned her misery away, staring down the hill at the river and the boathouse.

"See you later, Shara," Nathan said, returning to his duties.

I should have anticipated something like this; was I too sure of her? Is it her age? Is it daylight doubt? Have I already ruined everything? Is it too late to cut our losses? Why—how could I have let myself get so carried away by her, in the first place?

What do I see in this thin, little, teeny bopper, anyway? She's only a C student, so far; she manifests no great intellectual depth; her family is nuts; her teeth need fixing; her acne is prominent, and who the hell am I trying to kid? Manifestly, I have profound feelings for her—I need her—maybe I love her—perhaps breathtakingly so, despite her age and stage. Her present conflict may be that she wants/needs me, too—I hope so, anyway.

Nathan's heart raced with angst. *No matter what, I need and want her affection and regard, her priceless focus and giving ways. Of course, she's upset; it's daylight, and lusty May is in satiated siesta. I need to hold her, to get her talking and expressing her ambivalence and guilt, if that's what it is. That's natural, isn't it? What is the best—no, the right—thing to do? Protect her, even from me? If that is what it takes, I'll do it!*

As he assured that more green stain went on the cabins than on the teens, Nathan reasoned that Shara could also be ruminating the relevancy of "Sanctuary," last night's provocative movie. He chose it to show the interplay of morals and immorality with faith, repentance, and forgiveness and used Biblical theology in analogizing the slavery, sex, drugs— and the struggle to be free of them; hatred and prejudice—and the outpouring of honesty and human love which transcended both; wealth and power—and attempts to use them righteously; hypocrisy and pretense—and stark, spiritual nudity; even murder and death—followed by faith that almost transfigured the one who faced her own execution, marking her a rare beacon of faith *"Believe, chile; just believe!" the condemned Nancy told the twice-bereaved Temple.* There was also repentance and atonement, bought by the death of innocence. All these horrors—and blessings—were in the movie, so interpreting it was *apropos* for Nathan's retreat's theme: "What Do I Believe?"

Mulling the film, while he brushed green stain on a cabin and worried about Shara, he reprised a rhyme he wrote a year earlier, after seeing "Sanctuary" at the Daisy Hills Drive-In:

> Halting, stilted, roguish man,
> Along the grueling trails of quest
> For inner rest (from outward sham),
> Ain't worth a damn.
> Jealous, looming, nettled God,
> Heeling his beast upon the leash
> Of dimensions, time and space,
> Hides not his face.
> The two converge, almighty surge.
> To still the urge for wreck and purge.
> The coal of fire pressed to my lips.
> Becomes the birth in Mary's hips,
> And Jesus Christ is born—forlorn.
> The life, the Word, the Death absurd!
> Two nights in Hell, without a word
> An empty tomb becomes a womb,

For rebirth of my tarnished soul.
Helpless, sulking, petty beast,
This man who knows his sin, at least.
And falls upon his face, at last,
Can rise anew and fire the past,
May not be worth a damn.
But, to God, I am!

*

Lenore and their children found him and seven teens painting an unused cabin, and his heart leapt up with caring. He dismissed the painting (and painted) teens to supervised recreation and turned to his little family.

"Hi, honey," she chirruped, "Beth saw you painting and wanted to come see her daddy. How are you doing?"

"Well, after your 'in and out' visit, last night."

"Nathan, you and your puns. Think you could get away tonight?"

"It depends on how well tonight's recreation and my sermon prep go, honey. Perhaps we should save it for home, Sunday night. I'd like to be at my best."

"You're always good for me, Nathan," she whispered, making his heart throb and his penis tingle. "But I can wait; I'm used to it. . ."

Ouch! Lenore always says—and means—the most truthful thing!

As his children chased each other around, she volunteered, "I took Kathy and Shara some of the cake they baked for our anniversary. It's delicious. Our children were delighted to see both of their sitters, though Shara looked worried about something; not her usual effervescent self."

"Did you ask her what was wrong?"

"No; I figured she'd talk to you about it, if it's anything serious."

"Okay, I'll look into it. Thanks for the tip."

In addition to his internal, *Ah-ha!* QI did back flips and yo-yos, throughout their entire conversation, trying to discern both his and her feelings.

Don't find issues where there aren't any, Scott. Time will tell.

After hugging his children and kissing his wife goodbye, he recalled the feel of Shara's lips and was almost confused as to his double emotions.

I adore them both, dammit, but how is that even possible?

It was almost 3:00 o'clock. Worrying about Shara, the pain he was courting, and repeating inwardly the final couplet of his rhyme, he repaired to his tiny cabin to clean up.

What if she doesn't show up? Will she tell anyone? She certainly has a penchant for blurting out her deepest feelings, especially when in distress. Dear God, don't let Shara lose her faith in me now. Hang in there, kid; help is on the way!

*

In the rec hall, he was finishing the order and materials for the night's recreation, when he saw Shara on her way to the hogans. Despite QI, he felt his heart levitate into his throat, and his knees weaken.

We are on, hopefully for better—not worse, please God. I want to dash out and grab her and soothe all her angst away. Instead, I'll wait a discreet interval and follow her. Don't rush it, Scott.

Entering the darkest part of an old stagecoach road, Nathan identified at least six bird species by their calls, singing the song of the woods. Around a sharp bend and thirty yards deeper into the woods, he saw Shara sitting on the base of an empty, uncovered hogan. Intent on a cobalt blue shard she held up to a stream of sunlight falling on her like a halo. He stopped in his tracks, to take in this vision.

Shara placed the shard on the hogan floor beside her, pulled her knees up to her chest, wrapped her arms around them and dropped her chin thereon. He appreciated the natural curves of her legs, as they rounded her tightly clothed thighs and bottom. Awakening from his reverie, he coughed lightly, and she turned toward him, with a look of wary expectation. When she saw him through the trees she grinned in relief and stood, as he walked into the hogan's clearing.

"Hi," she said, with warmth but folded arms.

"Hey, Nature Girl," he smiled back. "Hope I didn't frighten you."

"It's a little spooky out here, all by myself. What took you so long?"

"I was doing a little bird watching–listening would be more accurate," he responded, motioning for her to sit down next to him. "Also, I wasn't sure I would be welcome–thinking that you might be having second thoughts..."

"I think I'd better stand, Mr. Sco–Nathan–I don't want to be tempted."

"I take it you've been thinking since last night, and that you have some feelings you'd like to express?"

Turning her face from him, her shoulders heaved, as she tried to stifle a sob.

"Mr. Scott," she wailed, suddenly facing him, streaming pain, tears, and confusion, "I feel dirty!"

Her words, their vehemence, and her obvious distress flayed Nathan's cool demeanor, racking him. Hopes, fears, dreams, panic, love, guilt, and apprehension all crashed and piled up together, in a twisted, tangled wreck of logic. He was speechless!

Acting on his deepest, truest sense, he stood, and simply held out his arms to her, her misery beginning to fill his eyes and face, as well. Through her tears, she looked into his face, saw his misty eyes and his open arms and was unable to resist. In that moment, as his arms enfolded her, his calm returned, settling upon him like a mantle of great honor and responsibility, though she was sobbing, trying to talk.

"Last night, you said we should believe in and trust our feelings, and—oh, Mr. Sco—Nathan, I do feel dirty! And I'm scared to death. I want you so bad, and feel I—I have no right to you, at all. I don't want to hurt you, or Lenore, or your kids, the church, my family, and friends—or God. I keep remembering Temple in *Sanctuary*, how she lost one of her children, and almost lost everything, just because she couldn't resist Candy Man; and how Nancy just kept telling her to "Believe! Just believe!" even though she was going to be executed. I know I'm not them—but I don't know how to keep being the me I was with you last night. What are we going to do?"

Her words shot out of her like vomitus, an expurgation of feelings incompatible with her painfully emerging emotions, a wretched sign and seal of her rejection of a world with—or without—Nathan. Clinging to her, Nathan knew one thing, and one thing only: *I have hurt this girl, and I must make it all right again. Every cell in my body cries out to hold on to this life-giving vessel, this fresh, young, hurting human, so miserable and broken in my arms, to love her back into serenity of self—with me, please God!*

As she blubbered and clung, God herself wrote finis to his doubts and questions, and turned Nathan over to himself and the future with this young one, as he must, whatever the consequences. Renewed with her every sob and syllable, he kissed her tears, rocked her in his arms, and poured his affection: fresh rain on a sere, tear-salted earth, in soft, relentless torrents, filling her up, floating her above the chasm, with its swirling currents of conflict and discord, until he could feel her warmth returning, her simple belief in him, and in their unity, crying out more than the doubts within her, until he knew he—she—they—were safe, again—in each other's arms...

But what about Lenore—and my kids? How...?

Sitting with Shara relaxed in his arms, weary and teary, still, a few lines from one of Nathan's favorite poem/sermons came to mind: quotes from *God's Trombones*, by James Weldon Johnson, a collection of Negro sermons in the old, Black preacher dialect. Nathan's love for them sprang from their simple, enviable, unquestioning faith.

Shara welcomed his loving, sensitive voice whispering lines from, "Go Down Death–A Funeral Sermon," and wept anew, recognizing the depth of his feelings. She knew he was using the dynamics of the poem, not its literal application. He surely was not Jesus, and she surely was not dead. But, as he spoke, he did as the lines described, and she felt the new life of their union burgeoning in her breast, as surely as though she were being raised from the death of hope.

> …And Jesus took his own hand and wiped away her tears,
> And he smoothed the furrows from her face,
> And the angels sang a little song,
> And Jesus rocked her in his arms,
> And kept a-saying: Take your rest,
> Take your rest, take your rest…

Shara calmed down and turned so she could recline in his arms, their chests pressed together, while he sat upright. Their kisses blended with the song of the woods, until Shara's panting and clinging told him it was time to stop. She left the campsite first and was just disappearing into the girls' bathroom, when he exited the woods and returned to the hurly-burly of the retreat.

LOVE, FLESH, AND SPIRIT

CHAPTER 8
RISE UP MY LOVE

*Why does one love? Why does one love? How queer it is to see
only one being in the world, to have only one thought in one's mind, only
one desire in the heart, and only one name on the lips; a name which comes
up continually, which rises like the water in a spring, from the depths of
the soul, which rises to the lips, and which one repeats over and over again
which one whispers ceaselessly, everywhere, like a prayer.*

Guy de Maupassant

Recreation was a lark. Nathan led his teens through their
frenetic paces, calling and leading square and folk dances,
line and balloon games, and other foolishness, ending with a
brief worship service. Nathan was witty; Shara was reassured;
Lenore joined in the fun, holding him tightly during a slow
dance. Little Nathan and fourteen-month-old Beth were both
delightful, holding onto their parents' legs while they danced.

During one of the slower rock tunes Nathan allowed,
Shara asked him to dance. Holding each other demurely,
Nathan did his best to be dignified in time with the music, as
he asked her to wait until all seemed asleep, steal to the girl's
bathroom, dress, and come to his little cabin.

*

It was close to midnight before Nathan put aside his
Bible and his notes, prepared to preach tomorrow's sermon.
Exhausted, he lay down on his blanket and closed his eyes. An
hour later, soft lips caressed his eyes.

Uncertain whose lips, "Who–?" was all he could get out. "Shara?" he whispered, "What time is it? I hope no one saw you!"

Her lips silenced his queries. Dressed in jeans and a sweatshirt, she lay on him, straddled. Sporting an involuntary, nocturnal erection, he was agog as she innocently positioned herself astride it. Persisting with stimulating nips and nibbles about his ear, she waggled her body on his, without realizing what she was doing, except that she felt the fire. Alarmed that things were going (and potentially coming) too fast, he tried to break away.

"Shara, wait a minute!" he laughed, struggling. "I'm a virgin!"

Pleasurably panicked, he pushed her into sitting up, still astride, her crotch directly atop his pulsing penis. Trying to diminish the prospects of *l'orgasme inopportune*, for either horse or rider, he bucked her off. Nathan's dark, bedside light went flying, as Shara tried to catch herself. Both hit the floor at the same time, with a clatter and a thud.

"Shhh!" they hissed in unison, unable to control their giggling.

"Shara, for God's sake, we have to shape up, here," he whispered, sitting her on his lap and clapping his hand across her giggling mouth.

"Okay, Shara, I'm going to take my hand away from your mouth. Think you can handle it?"

She nodded her head, vigorously, exaggerating her motions, eyes wide with pure fun. Warily, he removed his hand.

"I like the way you handle me," she tongued and whispered in his ear, breaking into giggles again.

Picking her up, he walked out the door into another fecund Night in May, and ran with her toward the nearby craft cabin, sixty or so yards away–while yet, she chortled.

"Where are you taking me?" she giggled and bounced, with mock alarm.

"You'll see."

Halfway to his destination, he threw her over his shoulders in a fireman's carry. Her breasts bouncing against his back, and his elbow invading her inner thighs, he ran into the woods surrounding the craft cabin,

"Be careful. Don't drop me! I'll be quiet; I promise," she protested softly. "I cain't see a thing. Where are we going? Please, put me down!"

Unceremoniously, he dumped her at the door of the dark craft cabin, hustled her inside, admonishing, "You little minx, you could've awakened the whole bloomin' camp."

Feeling their way into the dark cabin, he found a long bench and sat her down. His voice so stern, she was unsure...

"Na–Nathan, are you mad? I was just cutting the fool."

Nathan pulled her to her feet and into his arms, saying, "This is how angry I am!"

Sunshine on roses, his kiss. Feeling its gentle power, she stood quietly in his embrace, soaking in it. Drawing her elbows together, against his chest, and taking his face in her palms, she reached up and kissed him back, tiptoeing her feet up and down, like a kitten preparing to lie down.

Her kittenesque display moved him so that he was actually dizzy, so QI kicked in: *How do I explain, even to myself, the depths of this relationship, how it developed so quickly—even to the level of making me feel faint? Should I doubt its origins? Have I manipulated it into being? I honestly do not think so. Can her feelings and actions toward me be genuine; mine, too? How do I answer such questions, especially given Lenore, my kids, my job, and my God? There is no question that I experience her as utterly real and loving! I can actually feel her loving spirit entering, joining mine. Certainly, it's not just physical, though that aspect is enticing. I am driven to say, and mean, "I believe; just believe!"*

The thrilling pair lay down on a large worktable, cuddling and assaying the fringes of ardency. The gusting, Maynight winds, mellow and magnificent, serenaded them, soaring through the night like a mighty orchestra of leaf and limb, branch and bough. Nestling in each other's welcoming grasp, they heard their dreams and aspirations sung by the artful, articulate winds.

The trees became both cathedral and organ, the rude craft hut a sanctuary, and the table whereon they lay an altar on which they felt themselves spiritually joined by Nature, Herself. They spoke no vows during their symphony of souls, but uttered little sighs and cries of delight, in harmonious phase with the priestly winds–blending.

Though there was complete familiarity of bodies, there was nothing sexually purposed between them, even though Shara placed his yielding hands on her covered, braless breasts, erecting their nipples. Nathan replaced them with his head, contentedly resting there. As surely as the winds blew, their second Night of discovery was spent in symphony and ceremony, not in seduction and consummation.

They slept a little, such was the comfort and security of their intimacy, and wakened only when the winds began to sound the last notes of their spring concert. Nathan named the beginning bird calls, as dawn laid out her clothes for the day. Then, holding her closely, he whispered, "Rise up my love, my fair one, and come away. For, lo, the Night is past, the winds are over and gone; the flowers appear in your eyes; the time of the sighing of hearts is come, and the voices of our caring are sung in this land."

CHAPTER 9
"THE IDEA OF THE HOLY"

Discovered

I adore her, and I have said so,
Not yet to her but fully to God;
And all the sweltering agonies of desire
Cannot fairly express my heart's contents.
I love a unique quality—not only youth.
A quality that sings, prays, and sparkles
Of a thousand marvels
In a breast of such tenderness
That only heaven can finally know
And understand why and how
I resonate with her!

Nathan Rhea Scott
May 24, 1964

"My Dearest, call Dan Tennyson about the religious tape to be used for May 31. Thank you! Shara"

Shara had scrawled her audacious message on a pad on Nathan's desk while the returning retreaters departed their church, Sunday evening, May 24, 1964. QI was aghast: *She must have answered my phone, taken a message, and dared to write, "My Dearest," in front of God and everybody!*

About eleven, Nathan turned off the lights in his office and was about to leave when a familiar impulse sparked,

66

turned him around at the door, and walked him back through the huge, unlit building, down three halls–into the dark, cavernous sanctuary. The beautiful, thousand-plus seat sanctuary was evocative of silent awe. The plush, dark, cherry red, velvet pew cushions and rich carpeting, the muted, stained oak and mahogany chancel furniture were shiny-dark, set off in muted luster by the iridescence of available light, filtering through the prisms of the split chancel's two stained glass windows.

Nathan moved quietly up three steps into the chancel and stood a moment before the *prie-dieu*. With a sigh of resignation, he knelt on its velvet cushion and looked up at the familiar Celtic cross between the tall, stained-glass windows at the back of the chancel.

It is time to tell the God who already knows...

The hair on the back of his neck began its familiar, slow crawl in response to his body's spreading tingle. Feeling exposed and vulnerable, his back turned to the huge, dark, and empty church, creaking, and whispering its vacancy, he faced the chancel–and God–alone.

Nathan's prayers, like his life, were handicapped by too much sense and nonsense, and not enough faith. Nathan rarely heard any "still, small voice," except his own, repeating endlessly: *Who am I? What am I for? How do I know the truth? What do I do with it if I find it? What is truth? What is real? Is there a purpose to life? What is good; evil? What is beautiful; ugly? Who, where is God? Where should I go? What should I do? Will I ever be enough? Why? Why not? How? Who the hell are all these people; what are the answers to these questions for them? How should we relate to each other? Why and whom should we love, help, fuck, ignore?*

Nathan shut his eyes in the stillness of the sanctuary, recalling and desperately praying to feel the holy awe Isaiah felt, in an ancient sanctuary (*Isaiah 6:1ff*):

". . . I saw the Lord sitting upon a throne, high and lifted up; and his train filled the temple. Above him stood the seraphim...And one called to another...: 'Holy, holy, holy is the Lord of hosts; the whole earth is full of his glory...' And I said: 'Woe is me! For I am lost; for I am a man of unclean lips, and I dwell in the midst of a people of unclean lips; for my eyes have seen the King, the Lord of hosts!'

"Then flew one of the seraphim to me, having in his hand a burning coal which he had taken with tongs from the altar. And he touched my mouth, and said: 'Behold, this has touched your lips; your guilt is taken away, and your sin forgiven.'

'And I heard the voice of the Lord saying, 'Whom shall I send, and who will go for us?' Then I said, 'Here am I! Send me.'"

Deeply desirous of experiencing the force of Isaiah's awing, spiritual encounter, to fill his own God-shaped vacuum, Nathan fought a swirl of both awe and silliness.

How often I have struggled to surrender myself to Isaiah's confrontation with what Rudolph Otto accurately labeled "The Idea of the Holy:" that universal, human sense of the numinous. Like Isaiah, I yearn to be overwhelmed by the awesome presence of God, praying for the coal of fire to be pressed to my lips, so that I, too, may clearly hear the voice of the Lord, amid the seductive and cacophonic voices within me, some crying, "Woe is me!" others thundering, "Holy, holy, holy," and still others whispering, "Here am I! Send me."

A childhood of Sunday School lessons, eight years of collegiate and graduate level Bible study, three years of Biblical Greek and Hebrew, and a lifetime of sermons and church participation had not allowed Nathan the simple surrender experienced by many committed Christians. Tears of despair at never being able to make such a massive leap of faith fell like drops of molten lead, thudding into the lush red velvet of the *prie-dieu*. His guilt, experienced more as sadness than regret, increased this leaden rain.

Sighing in his continuing despair, he began to pray:

How long, oh Lord? Won't you fill me up? I am so tired of emptiness—of not knowing, not faithing enough. We both know how wrong and ignorant I am—have always been! Will there ever be any answers for me—not just the ones in the Book? They seem so stark, so set up, so full of human error, of hopeless faith, and faithless hope. I'm certain you have heard enough confessions from me—and enough promises...

Did you send Shara to me as a test, God? Well, if she's the test, who the hell are Melanie and Lenore? If you're listening, maybe you could help me cool it with Melanie and try harder with Lenore, who senses a regrettable distance, though she has no idea why.

I'm sorry, Lord. I get carried away in these increasingly one-way conversations. Were you as real to me as you were for Isaiah, I'd be on my face in here, again, as you have seen me so often, praying and waiting—in vain—for the pressure of your coal of fire against my offending lips, that I might believe—just believe!?

God, if I knew how to find it—irrefutably find it—I'd say, `thy will be done,' and mean it, desperately. But the only miracles you have sent my way are my Lenore's constant, undeserved love, my babies—and, and now my Sweet Shara! I look at her; I hold her; I listen to her and feel her need and being. I vibrate to her innocent, untried verve and elan; there is something about her that magnetizes my heart—is that love, Lord? I know it is not lust. Help me discern the truth about my feelings for her...

I do adore our resonance, when together or apart, the way she looks, and feels—even tastes and smells, the way she rushes to help; her loving, forgiving heart, her efforts to understand and forgive even those who wrong her. I love the lilt in her step and the dance of her spirit. I love her openness to life and her eagerness to live it. She is uniquely fresh and innocent at her tender age, yet she seems as solid as the mountains. No will-o'-the wisp, icon, or archetype she, with her realism kicking in, even as mine takes flight. I love her needing me; wanting me, and constantly looking for ways to give herself to me. Oh, God, might she be the One I have been seeking all this time, the One seeking me—or is that your unfortunate role? No typical teen, she draws me out of myself, so I may see myself and others more clearly. I can't fully explain it to myself, though it feels wonderful and natural—not mysterious, at all. I sense you at work in her caring and in her obvious need for me, and certainly in mine for her. We already feel blessed by you...

I cannot promise that lust will not enter our relationship, but please help me keep my need for her unsullied by Eros, alone, God. I have repeatedly confessed that I have an extremely hard time with the notion that fleshly things are evil, despite what eleventy-eleven holy books, prophets, saints, and preachers have to say. Lust, the single, most powerful reason there continues to be the human race—the one you created and instructed to be fruitful and multiply. Did you give us our juices and our drives just to make us slither and slide in the detritus of guilt, God? How can nature itself be bad? Help me keep and foster Agape, your brand of pure love, in all that we do and mean to each other, including any Eros! I do need her so!

I desperately love and adore my Lenore and my babies, too, God! Please help me understand the truths of my need for Shara, without hurting them or anyone. Watch over them all. If you ever do stick your finger in this temporal pie, without destroying our freedom of will, please, guide them, protect them, and continue to show them your face, that your love may abound and rain down upon us, cleansing and directing, at once. Lord, protect me from loving too much— and above all, protect them from me, lest I cause anyone to stumble!

In thy name I pray, Amen!

Feeling the skandalon of faith at the heart of his awareness, desperately trying to believe—just believe—Nathan arose from his knees, turned, and looked around, feeling the throbbing impact of his isolation in the dark sanctuary. Stepping over and up into the pulpit, he embraced the pregnant void in the pews a long moment, sighed and flipped on the pulpit lamp.

Though it was well past midnight, he picked up a hymnbook and turned to, "My Spirit Longs for Thee," his most meaningful hymn... Facing the music, Nathan sang to the Light embedded somewhere in the dark surrounding–and indwelling–him:

> My spirit longs for Thee
> Within my troubled breast.
> Though I unworthy be
> Of so divine a Guest;
> Of so divine a Guest,
> Unworthy though I be,
> Yet has my heart no rest,
> Unless it come from Thee.
>
> Unless it come from Thee,
> In vain I look around;
> In all that I can see
> No rest is to be found
> No rest is to be found
> But in thy blessed love:
> O let my wish be crowned
> And send it from above.

The "Amen" to the hymn utilized a gorgeously harmonized arrival of the hope expressed in its final chord. Nathan sang it forcefully. Waiting for his baritone to stop reverberating through the emptiness, he switched off the light, stood another long minute in the enshrouding darkness, closed the hymnal, and spoke, "Dear God, I do so need them all! Help me perfect that need into pure love," and left.

*

Sunday evenings were often prime fucking times with Melanie, and he knew her roommate was out of town. The habit of reveling in her perfect body was ineffably strong, so he promised himself *he would masturbate while fantasizing Shara (another first), if Lenore were unavailable, instead of making his all too habitual, after-hours sojourn between Melanie's lovely legs.*

Mollified thus, he drove straight home, improvising new words to the tune of the Doxology– which he penned later, more out of respect for their truth, than in thrall to their blasphemy:

> The Seven ride, and turgid in the lead,
> Glistening from that sensate bath
> Of Passion, motionless in time,
> Leads Lust, the father of them all!

When he slipped his freshly spent and washed genitalia alongside his beautiful, sleeping wife, whom he loved, utterly, he felt sadness–not quite guilt–about her and their increased distance. As for Melanie, he discovered that *even fantasized sex with Shara was purer, more meaningful, more beautiful than with her. Surely, this is purity–and not unbridled Lust! How it relates to Lenore and my dear family has yet to be determined. To have and keep them, both? God help us all! Amen.*

CHAPTER 10
GO TELL IT ON THE
MOUNTAIN!

Civilization is a process in the service of Eros, whose purpose is to combine single human individuals, and after that families, then races, peoples, and nations, into one great unity, the unity of mankind. Why this must happen, we do not know; the work of Eros is precisely this.

Sigmund Freud

Florida and home were good for Nathan. A needed respite from his sixteen-plus-hour workdays, he enjoyed his family, rested, and recreated. With Lenore and the kids, he sailed his sloop, caught sea trout, and beachcombed. He took and developed pictures (some of Shara), conversed at length with Mother (who was thin and haggard), and generally enjoyed his two weeks relieved from constant work. Keenly missing Shara, he called her by pre-arrangement twice, and wrote her c/o General Delivery three times (now she had something to hide).

*

June moved into North Carolina before the Scotts and greeted them with day lilies and a lawn very much in need of attention. Kathy and Shara were now proud seniors in the largest high school in Durham. Nathan arranged sexless trysts with Shara as often and as safely as possible–about thrice a week. They both felt their relationship was right, even though Shara constantly appealed to him to make love to her. His explanations satisfied her until the next time. She claimed she needed it and that it was a natural outgrowth of their relationship. He understood and was sorely tempted but always counseled waiting.

"Why?" she repeatedly asked.

"Because I love you enough to keep our relationship as pure as possible, darling!"

Shara's lament: "I feel your pure love in our closeness, confirm it in our kisses, prove it in our cuddling, in our caressing—even in our tears. Yet, how I have burned to hear you say it, expressing the simple truth of us that I have sensed all along! I do love you so!" wiping tears on his shirt. "Do you love me?"

"Yes! Yes! A thousand times yes, Shara! Loving, we hold, holding we kiss, kissing we thrill, thrilling we know, and knowing we love! I know it full well, now: Shara, I love you!"

*

First Church was abuzz that the Scotts were flying to Wilmington, NC, to meet with the board of Christ Church, in response to its heavy recruitment. Every cell in Nathan's being, however, told him such a move was wrong, even though it may restore him more to Lenore's deserving bosom. When he called and told Shara his probable plan, she tried to sound cheery, but wound up in tears of dismay. Typically, she wrote an understanding note, slipped it to him when Jimmy brought her to the Scotts to babysit, forcing Nathan to wait until he found an airport bathroom to read it:

> Dearest Nathan, I am truly sorry I cried Saturday when you called to ask me to babysit—and then told me why. I know you have been in Hell, lately, trying to figure out what to do with me, but the last thing I want to do is to cause you pain. Even though I will miss you terribly if you decide to move,

please know that you have helped me more than any human I have ever known. For that I want to thank you.

I know you love me. I also know that you're a wonderful minister, and that you're uniquely able to help people. When I am in your arms, I hold you as if it is to be the last time. You have a wonderful wife, and two darling children, who need you more than any right to you I might have. If I thought I was the cause of your leaving the church, or having another ulcer, or breaking up your marriage...?

What I want you to know is that no matter what happens, I will be with you always, at least in spirit. I love you, perhaps more than you will ever know.

All my love, Shara

P. S., I don't know if I could stand it if we just stopped, although I know that might be best for all concerned. Even if you decide we should not continue our relationship, could you consider our being together, privately, at least one more time? If not, I will understand. Whatever happens, I LOVE YOU!

The Wilmington church seemed an excellent opportunity, and the salary would be $8,500–considerably more than he could expect in Durham. The ministries were similar, except the Wilmington church was not center city, but nearby in a once-posh neighborhood now slowly being surrounded by slums and projects. Though many members fled to lily-white churches in better parts of town, most decided to stay to minister to the changing area.

Nathan was intrigued by the opportunity to serve both sides of the tracks and immediately liked the Pastor, Dr.

Ralph Morrison. Promising Nathan an almost free hand in developing an integrated ministry with the neighborhood, he was particularly persuasive.

Wilmington was close by Nathan's beloved sea–and was fewer than three hours from Shara. Lenore liked Wilmington, not worrying about leaving Melanie, who was expected to continue to visit regularly, as usual. Thus, for all the right reasons, ignoring the ache of conflict, he told the Christ Church leaders he would seriously consider a call, encouraging them to make one.

As Nathan drove her home, Shara sat demurely against the passenger window, chatting about his children, until he broke the ice.

"Shara, I read your note–forty times, actually–please don't worry. You can't cause me to do harm to anyone. I love Lenore, too, as I think you know. If I err, it is my own fault, not yours; so please, don't worry."

"Well, I do worry, if you want to know…"

"Is it because I won't, can't, er, shouldn't…?"

"…Make love to me, yet, among other things…"

"I think you know why–wait, what other things?"

"I read an article about affairs such as ours. A psychologist explained that the man was often acting out against growing older, or because his wife wouldn't, or couldn't, satisfy him, and that he was just using the girl, until someone better came along."

"You think I'm using you–and dumping you?"

"Well, not using, but because you won't love me the way I want, no matter how I want it–and you *are* leaving!"

"Shara, I understand your feelings, but not your logic. I haven't made love to you, because it's too early. This relationship developed very fast, I don't want to take advantage of you, and I'm leaving because we're broke. I've about shot my wad in this church, and Lenore and I both think we need to try another place."

"See what I mean?" between sobs.

Nathan gently guided her down to his lap and stroked her back and face, while she wept sorrowfully.

"I'm sorry, Nathan. I'm positive that you're not taking advantage of me, and that you're incapable of that. I believe you truly love me, as well as Lenore, but I'm dying inside to think of you leaving, before–before, we, we have expressed our love in a way that neither of us can nor will ever forget. Loving you so much, and not really having you is something I cain't handle. Don't you see?"

"Have faith in me; in yourself; in us, sweetheart. As to your request that we be together, privately, there is the National Youth Conference in Tabormont in July. You and Kathy can attend with me. It's free! Then, there is Bible School for the younger kids and my regional senior high camp at Camp Promise. I hope you'll help me with the first and go to the second. And I still plan to teach you how to drive. So, you see…"

"Nathan, dar–darling, don't *you* see that I want to do all of those things, if Daddy will let me, which he probably won't. He thinks you're too liberal, and that you're a bad influence on me and the kids at church. But I'm not sure we should. Yes, I want at least one more special time with you before you leave, but if I am going to lose you, to see you all those times might just make it that much harder."

Pause.

"How did you like Wilmington, anyway?"

For most of the rest of the drive, Nathan waxed too eloquently about the church that did not cut and run. Two blocks from her house, he pulled into the dark parking lot of a small Episcopal church, turned off the motor, and pulled her up from his lap. She fell into his arms, holding chest to chest.

Their kisses released ravenous need, and Shara grinned sheepishly at his efforts to keep his ready penis from stabbing her in the side. Aware of the unfamiliar pressure, but knowing not what else to do, she kissed him again, *coup de langue.* With his pulse resounding in his ears, he could not stem his cubing desire. QI shouted, *Stop! Take her straight home!*

"Baby, we can't start this. You've got to get home. Your Mama is waiting, and I am dying from wanting more and more of you. Sit up, and let's get out of here!"

Doing as he asked, she straightened her blouse and skirt and reached for her hairbrush. While fixing her hair, she spoke rapidly:

"You just showed me what I needed to know, Nathan. Either you love me, or you are a very good actor–and I know it's the first. I also know you're leaving 'for all the right reasons,' as you say, including your love for your family. This summer, though, is ours. I want to do all the things you listed, if possible. I want us to have this summer of love and leave the future in the hands of God!"

Shara's wide grin, her forthrightness, her dark, sparkling eyes, and her obvious love and faith were so exhilarating that he almost felt foolish. *She's decided to let our caring prevail for as long as it can–improvising! God and tomorrow will take care of the rest.*

Driving home, he thought about Tabormont, a beautiful mountain conference center near Hot Springs, thirty-five miles northwest of Asheville (similar to nearby Montreat), where he had worked his four collegiate summers, spent a two-week honeymoon, and visited many times. *I know Tabormont all too well...*

CHAPTER 11
TABORMONT BOUND!

Dreams are wishes your heart breaks.

Nathan Rhea Scott
September 1, 1964

Through the first hymn everything went fine. No one noticed anything awry, until Nathan began the Invocation. He did not close his eyes or bow his head, but flung both arms out wide, and hurled his words above the high, holy ceiling.

"Now it begins, Lord; now it begins! This little paradigm of piety is cranking up, again, and I'm supposed to use my holy calling to call out the Holy. That's you, God, in case you're listening, and this is your invitation to be present at these presents.

"We are supposed to feel awed; to smell the fire from Moses' burning bush, or from Isaiah's altar, and to hear, in our guilt and shame-filled hearts, the adoring seraphim crying, crying, crying, `Holy, Holy, Holy,' to anyone whose shoes pinch, or has an unholy itch, or wishes to be anywhere else but standing in a Protestant church, and doing anything else but seeking your remarkably invisible face.

"Anyway, Father, Daddy, Abba, Papa, us chilluns is at it, again, and for what it's worth, you're invited. We'll now say the Lord's Prayer. `Our Father . . .'" A rumble of dry voices picked up the ancient chant, complete with the usual confusion between "debts" and "trespasses," reciting it through the amen.

"I believe in God the Father, Almighty, maker of heaven and earth...," Nathan began the Creed, out of long habit, joined by the decent and orderly congregation, which finished without him.

"Instead of taking our text from the Good Ol' Book this fine morning, let's try something from another relevant tome. Hear the word of Dickens..."

It was the best of times, it was the worst of times, it was the age of wisdom, it was the age of foolishness, it was the epoch of belief, it was the epoch of incredulity, it was the season of Light, it was the season of Darkness, it was the spring of hope, it was the winter of despair, we had everything before us, we had nothing before us, we were all going direct to Heaven, we were all going direct the other way— in short, the period was so far like the present period.

Boardmen exchanged raised eyebrows; deacons looked confused, and ushers, one of whom was Big J. Carl Starr, looked bored. A baby cried, and when Nathan ended the reading with "The Word of Dickens," there followed the familiar choral response.

"It's time for the Pastoral Prayer, folks," Nathan grinned, "but this time, why don't we do it a little differently? Instead of my praying for you, why don't you pray silently for me? This preacher is going to need all the prayers he can get. Let you pray!"

Nathan stood, silently, before the bewildered but willing congregation, with his eyes closed, his hands clinging to the lectern, waiting to feel pouring over him the rush of prayers from the congregation, to shore him up. Someone sneezed; another coughed. After several minutes he looked up to see almost every head still bowed.

"Through Jesus Christ, your Lord, you pray..."

Cued by the unflappable organist, the Chancel Choir sang:

"Hear our prayer, O Lord; Hear our prayer, O lord. Incline thine ear to us and grant us thy peace. Amen."

"Immortal, Invisible, God Only Wise" began on the mighty pipe organ. While everyone sang, Nathan scrutinized the congregation, spotting Lenore, Melanie, and Shara in the fourth pew, across the chancel, directly in front of the pulpit. He winked; all three smiled self-consciously and winked back.

Crossing the chancel and climbing into the raised pulpit, he stood poised, looking down at Sunday's season of faces, as the congregation sat down amid the usual bustle of coughing, crossing legs, bulletin flapping, and whispering. He stood as always, the familiar, black- robed anonymity, ready to speak a good word for Yahweh. Now it was mostly silent, attentive, and expectant in the great hall.

A delicious little gasp escaped the congregation as Nathan reached into his robe, pulled out a shiny pistol, and flipped it open, revealing six bullets loaded into its chambers, which he revolved, its metallic clicking almost musical, as it echoed in the hushed sanctuary. He closed it, pulled back the hammer, spun the chamber, again, and placed it in plain view on the left side of the pulpit.

Nathan cocked his head, closed one eye, slowly scanned across the entire, immobilized congregation, and drawled, "Now, don't nobody try to leave!"

With a shock he awoke! Little Nathan was on the floor playing with the only toy gun his parents allowed him, spinning and clicking it. Beth was toddling around the room, exclaiming over a tiny flower she had picked in their yard, and Lenore was in the kitchen fixing their supper.

Slowly, Nathan's wits returned, while he tried to remember the details of his absurd dream. He arose, cuddled his dear ones, joined Lenore in the kitchen, and told her about it.

"That really was a daymare, wasn't it, honey?" Lenore said, chuckling. "Perhaps you've been watching too much 'Gunsmoke,' or God is trying to tell you something–or are you trying to tell Him something?"

"I don't know, babes." he said, still a little shocked at his dream.

"Maybe you're just upset about having told Wilmington you would accept their call."

"Could be. How are you feeling about that?" he asked, already knowing her answer.

"I know we need the money, and that you haven't been getting the support you want from the new Christian Education chairman. Melanie will still visit us, happily, and Wilmington has a preschool and kindergarten right in the church. I can be free to haunt the riverfront stores and nose about the old city, and maybe you'll be home more. I'm quite ready to leave, but how will you ever manage to leave your precious teenagers, Nathan?"

"It will be difficult, 'Nore. I love them very much."

"I know…"

Little Nathan came marching in wearing his Daddy's hat and a mischievous grin. His little arms straight down, he marched and "hup, two, fwee, foured" all over the kitchen. Nathan looked at his namesake, loved him, snatched him up, tossed him on his back, and pretended to be an airplane, flying all over the house. Beth, that thief of hearts, trailed behind them, laughing, and trying to talk.

"Daaddeee, Nattie riiidde!" she chortled, still clutching her tiny flower in her pincer grasp, pointing up to this aerodynamic duo.

Seeing the fun, Lenore grabbed Beth in similar manner and joined the airborne parade. The parents looked at each other the way all loving parents do when they are thoroughly enjoying their children. Nathan gulped, almost audibly, with wistful realization...

How he loved his children! Nattie, with his total trust in people, his "Hi, folks!" when he entered any store, his sturdy little figure, almost four, sandy haired, talkative, with a vocabulary reflecting his intelligence and his obvious problem-solving skills proving it. Calling himself "My Boy," he was their first born, never to be matched–except by his wee and beautiful, little sister, Elizabeth. A precocious sixteen-month-old toddler, she was the apple of her Daddy's eye, cute in her flirtatious ways, sincere in her questions and empathy, even for butterflies and flowers. She sang with Nattie and her father, before bedtime, and said sincere prayers. Just now growing a few blond curls, her cheeks were dimpled, and her eyes shot glee and joy, wherever she looked. She was a feist!

"I shall miss My Boy and my Bethikins when I go to Tabormont tomorrow," he said, in his language of endearment. "Do you want me to bring you a surprise when I come back, Nattie?"

Lenore watched her husband gather a child on each knee, and squelched a sudden sadness, in favor of the joy of the moment.

"Yess, yess, youbetcha!" triumphed the lad. "Bwing My Boy a new cah, or a toy, pwease."

"Oobecha–toyee," echoed his bright little sister.

"And what does Mommy want Daddy to bring her?" Nathan risked, striving for harmony, wanting, genuinely, to please her.

"You can bring me peace and quiet–and then stay home a month!" Lenore pled.

Catching the yearning in her voice, Nathan made obeisance to it by carrying their wee ones to her, wrapping his arms around her, forming a teepee of love, all four Scotts hugging and kissing and laughing together.

"Honey, I'll do my best. I know I've been gone a lot lately, what with the senior high camp, the Bible School, and all the other things I've led," he said, trying to redirect Nattie's wet kisses toward his cheek and away from his eye.

After they shooed their children into the living room, Lenore asked, "Why didn't Shara attend your senior high work camp? I've been meaning to ask."

"Because Big J. Carl didn't want her to have much fun, I guess. Also, camp cost $35.00, and the week in Tabormont costs him nothing. Kathy successfully lobbied Shara's parents to allow her to accompany her there, in spite of me. I don't really know. Why?"

"I was curious. She and Kathy both have crushes on you, you know."

Oops! How do I respond truthfully, without worrying her... I forget, sometimes, how perceptive she is. I can't just tell her the truth—and then leave for Tabormont—with both girls.

"In the unlikely event that you're even a little bit right, honey, there'll be so many boys in Tabormount, I'll have to hold the girls back. It's true that we three plus Jason have a special relationship, but there's a difference between a bit of emotional dependence and crushes, isn't there?"

"Well, be careful not to love them too much, honey, as you're prone to do with almost everyone you meet, certainly counsel, mentor, or lead."

*

At midnight he ventured once again into the darkened sanctuary—to play the organ. Though his ear, fingers, and knowledge of the keys were educated, and he could improvise his own music for hours without too much repetition, he was

84

no keyboardist. Still, improvising always gave him an outlet for probing his continuing dilemmas about himself, his work, his family, his loves, and his God.

Focusing on Shara and Lenore, QI held that *my turning to Shara wrongs Lenore. But how do I turn away when everything about Shara fulfills me? Clearly, I need them, both. Maybe Tabormont will help clarify this dilemma...*

Improvising, his melody was simplicity itself, played mostly on the Choir and Swell manuals, with only a touch of pedaled bass, fully mixed, finally, on the Great Organ. Without thinking, he ended a *fortissimo* coda with a six-part amen, left the sanctuary, and went home, determined to allow events, themselves, to determine his Tabormont behavior...

CHAPTER 12
SHARA'S SONG

Ye shall have a song, as in the night when a holy solemnity is kept; and gladness of heart... ...For ye shall go out with joy and be led forth with peace; the mountains and the hills shall break forth before you into singing, and all the trees of the field shall clap their hands.

Isaiah 30:29; 55:12

Nights are to lovers, as mornings are to children.

Nathan Rhea Scott
July 2, 1964

The three intrepid First Churchers arrived in Tabormont on Wednesday afternoon, July 1, 1964. They deposited their gear in their boarding cottage, and Nathan toured them around, acquainting them with the place. There were teenagers everywhere.

After a quick supper in their cottage, Kathy and Shara trotted off to a hootenanny, while Nathan met with other convention leaders to review teaching plans. Shara is to meet him on the sailboat dock at 7:30 P. M., to climb Mount Tabor, while Kathy meets and plans with other presidents of their local SHFs.

While waiting for Shara on the dock, QI traced their forty-one-day history, taking time to process in some detail, seeking perspective. It had been a delicious and frustrating

86

ride. Nathan and Shara had managed many delightful daylight hours together in relative privacy, since their initial nights of discovery at Camp Promise. They often discussed her need for "full sex" and his need to avoid it, in the near term. After her father acquiesced to her going to Tabormont, Shara corralled Nathan mid-make out.

"Nathan, I'm so hot! Please, please make love to me!"

Gently, he explained why not, to which she responded, "Can you at least promise me we can act like two adults in Tabormont..."

"I won't say, 'no,' this time, darling; I want it, too!" he confessed.

I realized, then, that there might not ever be a better opportunity with needed time to reflect and counsel, afterward, so I capitulated, at least verbally. Shara was ecstatic; I worried about the consequences. Still do!

Now, as he watched a catboat jibe, he realized that *the wait had–has–not been so bad. It has been forty-one days of eager temptation. But does Shara have adequate agency and executive function— informed locus of control–know her own mind, and is she mature enough to take control of her own life and decisions, in this crucial respect? I think so but how will I know, other than by allowing her to act on her needs and desire, and to control them—or not–herself? Even though the legal age of sexual consent is sixteen, I won't push it, but I won't stop it, either, unless I'm convinced otherwise.*

The defense rested...

*

They climbed, chatting easily, stopping periodically to rest, hold, or kiss. She was exhilarated, enjoying the freedom to act and react as his equal partner, away from others' judgments. Clinging to each other, they frisked and puppied their way up the trail, in unabashed search and anticipation.

Reaching the top of Mount Tabor, they gaped at their panoramic view, in full gloam, as the sky crimsoned and purpled the mountains. Finding a familiar, hidden outcropping, Nathan pushed through a thick curtain of brush into their *ad hoc* boudoir of flat boulders, at the edge of the mountain, five thousand feet high. There they sat like children watching a parade, until the last vestiges of sunlight kissed the cooling earth goodnight, and the quarter moon yawned behind darkened, golden-edged clouds.

Shara lay back on the sun-heated rock beneath them, put her hands behind her head, and watched the summer sky begin to sprinkle dusk with its faery fires. She seemed completely at ease. Somewhat nervous about the interplay between desire and caution, he welcomed her guilelessness. Then he kissed her and basked in the very wonder of this loving, lovely young woman in his arms.

"I love you best in the nights, Nathan."

Delirious with her warmth and responsiveness and with his burgeoning feelings for her, which seemed to shore up the very sky, Nathan was unaware when petting became passion, only that both were afire. Shara shivered as she clung to him, moving her body closer and closer, until they lay as one, swaddling themselves into complection. He kissed her neck and ears, sending her into unaffected, yearning sighs and moaned longings. Her initiative was familiar, but he didn't remove his hands from her breasts, this time.

Remembering his promise to her, Nathan allowed his mind to float upward into this first July night; his heart and hardness focused on the writhing femininity compelling him. No questions of right and wrong; no plots or manipulations; no subtle guilt or hidden recriminations inserted themselves into their passion. They were one with nature and with each other, doing what human evolution, their histories, genes, and juices—and their purest love—bade them do.

Shara sat up as Nathan removed her polo and her bra, revealing two starlit mounds of such proportion and beauty that he gasped before he covered them with his hands and mouth. She held him fiercely, drawing him down, her head turning from side to side, as he smoothed her limber, spreading legs, anchoring at her crotch.

Moving gently over her shorts, his fingers traced her swelling labia beneath, until he divined the right spot. Kissing her lips, ears, and neck, while continuing his burnishing, her sighs became an aria of moans.

Lost in the timelessness of giving, he studied the wisdom of lust so beautifully born in her love-washed face. Trembling, Shara's legs stiffened, her bottom left the rock, and she strained to press against his tantalizing fingers, ravening in the pleasure they induced.

"Ahhh, oh, oh, oh God, Nathan!" she cried, grabbing him, as her climax literally shook her body, beatifying her countenance with paroxysms of ecstasy and delight.

She lay quietly in his arms, after her panting and trembling stopped. Her body stiffened, periodically, with aftershocks of pleasure. Nathan was content, though he had not experienced the exultant release that continued to ache within him.

Shara emitted a great sigh, faced his ready grin, and said, shakily, "Nathan—can I—may I ask you something?"

"Anything at all."

"What was that—that incredible feeling? What happened to me?"

So incredulous was he at the portent of her questions, he blurted, "You really don't know?" before he could think.

"No, I don't," said the unabashed. "It was fantastic, whatever it was—I think. I mean, was I supposed to feel that way? Is it all right? I thought I was going to pee—or faint, and you were going to have to carry me to a hospital, or something."

Laving in her precious naiveté, QI cautioned how best to answer her? Then, simply, "Shara, what you experienced was an orgasm. It is the pleasure God provides us to reinforce our love making."

"But what is it? I have never felt anything like that!"

"It's the natural, pulsing release of increased, muscular tension and blood gorged in and around your genitals, resulting in the spasms you felt. It is most easily caused by direct stimulation of and around the clitoris, right at the top of your smaller labia–lips–usually by fingers or penis, stimulating the general area during sexual intercourse. Was that really your first?"

"Yes, it was–I had no idea. Nathan, what is a clitoris–I didn't even know I had one, much less what it's for? Can girls–can I do that to myself?"

Keenly feeling his responsibility, Nathan quietly described her anatomy, its purposes, masturbation, and intercourse, trying not to be too didactic. Fielding many questions, the answers to which he had assumed she already knew, his love for her and his protective sense soared.

"Was it really that good?"

Her answer was a passionate kiss, which stimulated their mutual discovery that she was multi-orgasmic. Still clothed in her tight shorts, she guided his hand a bit to just the right spot. Though Nathan expected to luxuriate in the beauty of her orgasms, he had not considered the bonus–and *aegis*–of teaching her the wonders of her own anatomy!

He turned to the privilege of stimulating even more delight, until her trembling and sighing metamorphosed into a third experiential lesson, but not before she pressed him to make love.

"Sweet, sweetheart, I love giving you pleasure, watching and feeling your excitement flourish and grow, until you come and come and come. Thank you so much for this rare privilege. However, I didn't come prepared, as I didn't think we'd have as much privacy and comfort as we have. Next time…?"

Though disappointed, she contented herself with his kisses and his hands all over her tingling body. They remained clothed, except for Shara's exquisite, bare chest, bathed in the softest of summer nights, revealing a lusciousness of breasts, whose very nipples touted their own erections. If he was smitten by her charms before, now, he was vanquished.

Starting and sitting up, Shara turned to him, wide-eyed with realization, whispering, almost reverently, "Nathan, what about you? Don't you get–don't you want–to have pleasure, too?"

In truth, Nathan had almost forgotten about himself. It was 10:00 o'clock, and he did not think they should stay on the mountain much longer. *Yet, she has a right to know.*

Gently, Nathan moved her hand atop his stiffened penis, just over his fly. As he watched her cup it–over his pants–Nathan's heart melted, seeing her so agog. He placed her willing fingers on his zipper, and she unhesitatingly pulled it down, daring to move inside, feeling the heat of him through his shorts. Shara's awed gasp confirmed her precious wonder.

"Take it out, if you'd like, Shara."

"I'd like," she whispered, eyes wide and mouth open, in the purity of this signal moment of additional passage.

She gazed in awe and wonder, as Nathan folded her hand around his shaft, and moved it up and down, until she tentatively assumed the ancient rhythm. Involuntarily, she leaned down and touched her lips to the head of his penis.

"Nathan, may I ask you something else?" Not waiting for his answer, she expressed her manifest curiosity with the universal, virginal question, "How does it get inside–I mean it's so big? My little brother's is always soft and small; won't it hurt?"

Nathan stifled a chuckle, saying, much too casually, "God made you to stretch in just exactly the right places, at exactly the right times, Shara. To be honest, there might be a little pain, the first time; unless your hymen is small or already broken, it will need to give."

On the rock, on the mountain, under God's benevolent sky, his penis in her adoring, exploring hand, Shara, enrapt with the wonder of continuing initiation, perused the rest of this chapter of the story of the ages.

Afterward, fulfilled and fulsome with his richest love for her, Nathan sat up, helped her clean his effusion from her tendering hands with his handkerchief, put his penis back in his pants, pulled her yielding body down upon his, and kissed her sated lineaments, especially her admiring–and marveling– eyes, still widened by a sudden surfeit of inside information.

He had kept his promise to her–and to himself–not to harm her, use her, or compromise either of them, beyond the chance of discovery. Proud of her, he pulled the clutch of her to her feet and, with growing contentment, hustled back down the mountain.

Later, just past the stroke of midnight, Nathan sat alone in his bedroom musing the face and feel of Shara. Recalling their music on the mountain, he softly sang a few beloved words from Randall Thompson's *The Peaceable Kingdom*, derived from the prophet, Isaiah:

> Ye shall have a song,
> As in the night,
> When a holy solemnity is kept...
> The mountains and the hills
> Shall break forth into singing,
> And all of the trees of the fields
> Shall clap their hands!

CHAPTER 13
TO LOVE AND BE WISE?

Lust's adherents sprout horns and seek pleasure.
Love's devotees sprout halos and seek to please.

Nathan Rhea Scott
Tabormont, July 4, 1964

Rain halted most of the planned recreational events for nearly three days, allowing too much unplanned free time for the conferees. With rain pouring, boredom soon followed. Nathan knew two Sutherland, hometown boys, Terry and Bill Grant, were summering in Tabormont with their parents. Thinking to promote a party for man-hunting Kathy and the other girls in his cottage, he drove to the Grants. Successful beyond his hopes, they immediately invited him to bring as many young people as he could to their place, to be chaperoned by their mother, who volunteered refreshments—and a Bible lesson, should one be required.

Nathan touted a party. The word had a magical effect on the bored, rained out girls, and suddenly eight were available, including Kathy, several of whom had made masculine contacts whom they volunteered, if Nathan could get them there in the rain. It was perfect—except for Shara—who used cramps as her excuse for staying behind. Kathy begged Nathan to attend, to add his wit and experience with teens—and to provide escape, should the party drag. Demurring, he pled needed preparation time. Though Shara flashed happiness in her smile, her eyes told him that something was amiss.

Having deposited his adopted teens (all calling him "Father Nathan") at the Grant's by 1:30 p.m., Nathan looked to Shara. Dolefully, she joined him in the front seat. Wearing maroon shorts and a long-sleeved striped blouse, she volunteered that her period was still flowing, but that she was pleased with the freedom afforded her by the tampons Nathan got her–a first. Then, silence.

"Hey, pretty girl, in case you haven't noticed, we're alone, and we have this entire afternoon to ourselves. What would you like to do with our new freedom–at last?"

Shara looked at him, smiled wanly, but did not speak.

"I'm pretty sure someone else is in this car…"

"I'm sorry, Nathan–what did you have in mind, this awful, wet afternoon? Shall we go somewhere to–talk?" said the girl who had already held his penis in her hands.

"Sure. Have I done something wrong? I wondered when you got in the back seat, while I transported kids to the Grants."

"I don't think you could do anything wrong, if you want to know. I'm the one who's wrong."

He waited.

"Kathy and I were talking this morning, and…"

Shock arced through him, wrenching his bowels. Still, he waited.

"…I asked her about her sex life, such as it isn't, and she asked me about mine. I didn't tell her about us, of course, but then I asked her if she had ever wondered what it might be like to be with you–you know–physically."

"Why did you ask that, and what on earth did she say?"

"We were talking about sex, and you became a natural topic. She admitted that she had thought about you that way and told me she knew I had, too. Even though she was just teasing, she said that it was fine to enjoy you and your giving ways, but that since you are happily married, we–I–should never expect to have you–that I should save myself for someone who is available–because you are not!" she crescendoed, weeping.

Oh, my very own God!

"I can see how that might upset you, Shara. Let's drive up to Glencrest, my old college summer place and talk. What do you say?"

"I say what I always say, Nathan–that I love you and always will–no matter what. But it's the what that scares me," wept the girl.

"I know; me too, but let's talk about it in Glencrest. We're here. Come on, Shara, let's run for it."

Weeping no more, but not smiling, Nathan led Shara up the long, wet path to Glencrest, the cottage of his youth. She sheltered under the small overhang, while he slogged around back, returning with a key. Unlocking the basement, they hurried in out of the rain.

"Let's take off our shoes, so we don't track up the place. I don't want to advertise I've been here, even with standing permission."

They padded barefoot into the simple apartment, with its meager appointments of two sofa beds, assorted sea-green painted furniture, a small electric stove, a refrigerator, a bathroom, a small oil heater, stocked linen shelves, and sundry lamps and knick-knacks. He lit the heater and sat on one of the sofas, drying himself with a towel. Shara took a towel to the bathroom.

Joining him on the couch, she sighed, looked longingly at Nathan, and started. "I'm sorry, Nathan. I just get so mixed up, sometimes. For the past several days all we've been talking about in group is the response of Christians to

Christ, and you reminded us that–who was it? Bon–Bonhoeffer? who wrote, *The Cost of Discipleship* and was hung by the Nazis. You said that he wrote, 'When Christ calls a man, he bids him come and die.'

"Then you explained the many things a Christian might seek to die to–like all those horrible things we do to each other, out of selfishness, pride, envy, greed and so on."

"Do you remember the most difficult price the Christian should *want* to pay?"

"Yes. You told us that the best, and most difficult death a Christian experienced was not physical death, but the unselfish death of self, in helping others–your 'Great Realization.'"

"Shara, my Shara, do you have any idea how pleased I am that you understood and took me seriously–how utterly and completely I love you?"

"Uh-huh, I do," sobbed Shara, pouring it out and into him, "and that's just the trouble. All I can think about is how much I love you, and want you, and want to be with you, always. But that is pure selfishness, Nathan, and nothing at all like the dedication you obviously have for loving and serving God and people–especially young people."

"Young people like you, Shara."

"I know. But look what I'm doing, right now! I'm holding on for dear life to the man I love, but he–you–are married, have two little ones of your own, and if we got caught you might lose them along with your chance to serve, period. I think I would die, just die, if I was the cause of you losing everything. All I've been doing for days, now, is trying to get you to fu–to make love to me–because I know I shouldn't, and probably never will have you the way I want. Sure, I think I would love the sex and all–probably more than either of us could imagine–but what I really want to have is you, and I know I cain't, shouldn't, and probably won't. I feel so miserable, so selfish, so *dangerous* to you, to your family, and to your calling. Oh, Nathan, what are we going to do with me?"

Fair spitting it out in great rushes and spurts of woe, Shara the Sentient became Shara the Shamed, having no other place to lay her strife than on the man most responsible for it. He held her and let her talk, until her voice simply died...

"You will do what is best and right for you, my darling, because you are great of heart, and though not dead, certainly more giving of self than I will ever be in my fondest dreams, and as much as any human I have ever met."

Her nose pressed tightly into Nathan's neck, her head on his shoulder, and his arms tightly around her, imprinting into his chest, Shara calmed and cuddled. Nathan simply loved her back to her essential self, without prescription. Pooling in his love, she lifted her face and tendered her lips. Their kiss signed their misery as it sealed their commitment, despite the conflicts, the dangers, and their mutual fears. Nothing resolved but the clear fact and pure vitality of their caring—no matter what...

CHAPTER 14
REQUIREMENTS

What is it men in women do desire?
The lineaments of gratified desire.
What is it women in men do require?
The lineaments of gratified desire.

William Blake

Needing a break, Nathan suggested a run to Hot Springs for some soft ice cream. Quiet after her outpouring of feelings, Shara pillowed her head in his lap while he drove. Resonant with her mood, he hummed while massaging her face and hair. Soaking in their closeness, she wrapped her arms around his waist and nuzzled. Nathan, he lay low...

Returning to the cottage, they dashed through the rain and splashed through the basement door, again. Both toweled off, and Nathan relit the oil heater. Shara gesticulated before a wall mirror with her hairbrush, then disappeared into the bathroom.

As the cabin cozied, Shara emerged, still a bit damp, but pert and pretty. He watched her moving about the cabin, marking it for her coming accommodation, opening the sofa-bed, stopping before a window, gazing past the swirling mists seeking, perhaps analogizing. Nathan cherished her attractive, svelte form, damp clothing clinging to her curves, legs lithe and inviting. QI forced contextual objectivity about his lady, with evaluation anew.

At seventeen, Shara stands 5' 4 ½" tall, about 111 pounds, slender, rather than thin, nicely developed. With dark, enticing eyebrows and long lashes, she wears her hair in a becoming, short cut, neck length, full bodied set, curved and curling around her ears, a slight part to the right of midline. It shines burnt auburn in sunlight. If her pubic hair has that same quality, our babies could be redheaded...

With high, symmetrical cheek bones; enviable model's nose, mouth, and chin; and the darkest of brown eyes, her lineaments are most attractive, verging on beauty. The body she is made to hide is well curved and proportioned. An exquisitely feminine neck, set over equally alluring shoulders, collar bones, and perfect breasts enhance the affect. Easily a nymph, or a mannequin, with shapely legs and a trim waist advantaging her torso between a neatly rounded bottom and the comely expansion of her thorax. Junior size seven, maybe. Even so, Shara is no mere, adolescent, spring-blossomed flower, ripe for plucking. Standing before the window, contemplating and anticipating this passage, she is awakening to her own awakening.

"Come stand by the heater with me, Shara; it'll help dry us—unless you would rather hang your clothes in front of it..."

In the expectant ambience of the moment, without the invocation of desire stimulated by kiss and caress, Shara seemed tentative, surprising him. *Already*, QI suspected, *she may be thinking that this signal event is not as she anticipated.*

"No, I think I'd better keep them on—for now."

Leaving the rain-washed crystal ball of the window, she joined him before the seething, flickering heater, feeling its weal and warmth on her back and bare legs, as she faced him. Nathan held her waist, breathing easily and confidently.

"May I ask you something, Nathan?" looking up into his adoring face.

"Yes, darling."

"What—what are you thinking, right now?"

"I am thinking about this simple place, unadorned except for the jewel of you–how quiet, intimate, even romantic, with you here, feeling the fire of the heater–and your love. I think about the rain, loving its nurture, despite its inconvenience. Of course, I think about you; how beautiful you are and growing more so. And I'm wondering what you are feeling now, too."

Silent for a moment, forcing focus on her emotions, sorting them out, she spoke quietly, "I'm thinking–I'm wondering–I guess I feel a little bit scared; you know? The time and place of my first, uh, intercourse–have always been so distant–so future, to wait until I got married–and now it's here, if we both want it. It feels different, and I admit–a little strange.

"A bit daunting, I know, Shara. Fact is, we don't have to do anything. I can love you either way. Relax, darling, we can be and do only as we both want–nothing more."

Shara nodded and turned to face the heater, equalizing its warmth. She folded her arms across her breasts, staring into the little windows of fire; the one in the door of the heater–and the one opening to her life and her love for Nathan. Slipping his left arm around her damp waist, he pulled her to his side. She came willingly, but awkwardly, with a hint of the virgin's reserve.

Facing him, again, she loosely clasped her arms around his neck, pressed her body to his, leaned back, and looked intently into his eyes–trying to fathom her previous desire, now cloaked in the ambivalence of trepidation. His arms encircled her trim waist, as she slowly reached his mouth with hers, kissing him lightly, eyes open, seeking that expected spark that sets friendship afire. Emoting his love with all his strength, Nathan returned her kiss. Deliberately, like the slow swirl of deep, dark waters, Shara felt the tide rising, within, as she continued to mark him with her genes and her intuition.

She liked the look, the touch, the smell, the taste, and the fact of the man standing before her, almost like a petitioner, and knew he loved her, wanting only to please her. Her wellspring of feminine power began to roil, somewhere in her loins, causing her to try to discriminate its source and meaning; fight or flight; love or lust; demand or submission; victory or defeat. She decided it was all of them, and more. The swirl grew warm; the warmth grew liquid, and flowed through her body and her mind, immersing the loved and loving vessel she knew herself to be—for him—a fountain head for her maidenhead.

Nathan felt accommodation building within her and her fears dissolving into streams of trust and familiarity. Taking his cue from millions of years of evolution, he pulled her into him and cupped and smoothed her bottom as he kissed her, presenting his credentials of strength, fealty, intent, and invitation.

The oils of her longing reached her strikingly dark eyes, calming their tempests, and gentling their seas—while lubricating her desire. Nathan watched her face transform itself from that of a seventeen-year-old virgin into a deliberate, aware, young woman, filled with mature want and resolve.

She evinced universal femininity, in her countenance, while his love and lust for her mingled with pervasive awe in the presence of such rare and priceless opportunity. Inward, he heard the voice of the angel she was to him crying, *Holy, holy, holy—for whom shall I send, and who will go into me?* His heart exploded with joy, as his mind triggered its elated response, *Here am I; send me!*

Kissing her neck, he swam himself into her rising tide of giving, confirming the righteousness of his own rushing blood and risen seas. A feast of kisses, more intimate than thought, combined the steams of their breaths with the pooling liquids of their desire, inspiring and instructing their love, prepared them to couple. The flows of their yearning ran so pure and deep that, mingled, were created inexorable wind and tide aswirl in their vortexes, with the breaking waves and tugging currents of both sex and selves.

Neither remembered, later, their move to the sofa bed, or how their garments came off. Shara startled to that awareness, feeling a rush of cool air around her breasts, as Nathan removed her bra. Looking up from the bed, she saw his muscled chest and his swollen stiffness distending his white jockey shorts, his sole, remaining garment. Looking down, he saw her lying on her back, legs akimbo, her white, silky panties darkened at the crotch by her mystery patch.

Caressing her limbs, kissing her everywhere, Nathan blew his heat upon her most intimate, still clothed niche, then burnished it with gifting caress. Lost in a cascade of initiatives, each second of newness produced the most provocative stimuli, quickly replaced by more, until Shara's arousal rushed her into ecstasy.

Standing before her now, luxuriating in the contours of her climax, Nathan removed his shorts. Reaching past her spreading legs, he grasped the waistband of her panties. Shara lifted, as he whisked this seventh veil from her body. For the first time, his adoring eyes beheld his beloved's full, well formed, peccant nakedness, naturally drawing him to her thatch of dark hair, and its glistered parting. Shara closed her eyes, adding grace to her lovely lineaments; her arms outspread; her hands lying open in validation.

Kneeling into her welcome, he tendered his penis to her vulva. Eyes widening, Shara felt it gliding along her nether kiss. Her head fell back, chin up, mouth slightly open, as she felt him begin to press...

Shara sat up! Sudden fear shocked her eyes. "No, Nathan, stop! I cain't do it. Please stop–I–I'm too afraid.

Please. I'm sorry, please forgive me–don't hate me. I just cain't do it!"

Nathan drew back, stung by the hornets of her turmoil. Aghast and forlorn, Shara sat naked in the center of the bed, her arms around her knees, drawn up to her breasts, her head down in shame, tears coursing down her trembling body. Overcoming his shock, and comprehending her sudden misery, Nathan stroked her sobbing head.

"Oh, baby," he commiserated, "don't cry. I'm sorry, too. I wouldn't hurt you, knowingly, ever. It's all right, darling. We've stopped, and we won't start again. It is you who need to forgive me."

Lying next to her, Nathan swept her soft, woeful vulnerability into himself, and held her as securely as he knew how, feeling sick with shame, and no little fear, that he had caused this misery. *I believed her too readily, not considering that her young mind might not be up to her ripened body's urging. I denied her repeatedly; I was right.* Filled with the wretched rue of regret, having hurt the one person in the world he most wanted to love and protect, he joined her in that misery–and shuddered at this unexpected plight.

Shara's tears flowed freely, as he sought to comfort her. Facing each other, their bodies puzzled together in sinking despair, unable to stifle their coursing wretchedness.

"Please forgive me, Nathan. It's not your fault! I've led you on, all along. But when you started to–to put it in–I–I panicked!"

"It's all right, darling; it's all right. I love you, and will not hurt you, again. I love you, Shara Day Starr. I love you. I love you," rocked Nathan, soothing her with the balm of his being.

Shara's crying subsided as Nathan rubbed her back, holding her warmth and softness against him. Her reddened eyes moved him to find a washcloth, hold it out the door, filling it with cooling rain and anointing her eyes and forehead. Lying morosely on the bed, her limpid loveliness in a curl, she watched Nathan slip on his rain-damp shorts and pants. He tendered her clothes to her in haloed wonder and sat at the foot of the bed, his back to her, putting on his wet shoes.

Feeling movement on the bed, Nathan assumed she was dressing. He started, as her arms curled around his neck, her breasts pressed against his back, and her lips titillated his neck and ears. Wary and confused, Nathan stood, hoisting the clinging, naked girl to her feet on the foot of the bed. Turning in her arms, her breasts smoothed against his face. Her nipples caressed his eyes and mouth, as she felt for his limp penis over his clothes. Full of love and humility, she stepped back on the bed, legs wide, and held her arms out to him in humble invitation…

"Shara, Shara, what are you doing? Please put your clothes on. I've hurt you too much already. I know you will regret it, if we don't get dressed and get out of this place."

"Nathan," she murmured meekly, pleading with him with the darkling of her eyes, "I'm all right, now. I was just scared. I am not afraid, anymore, and I want you; I want to give to you as you just gave to me—as you always give to me—no matter what you get in return. You are so gentle, so loving; you have wiped away my fears. I was just scared—that's natural the first time, isn't it? Give me another chance. Besides, if we don't do with it now, I'm afraid I'll never find another man as gentle and loving as you. I want you! Please!"

As Shara pleaded and explained, she placed his hands on her breasts, her nipples imprinting his reluctant palms. The lust Nathan had earlier recognized in her reappeared, as she wrapped one leg around his, convincingly humping his thigh.

"Shara, Shara, my Shara, don't torture me! How do I know you won't be sorry afterwards? I'm not convinced you will be all right. Please get dressed, and let's call this off, for now. Maybe we can approach it again, later, okay?

Kneeling at the foot of the bed, Shara kissed him hungrily, where he stood, moving her nakedness against him. As she unzipped his fly, she whispered, "I love you; I want you. I want you to take me. I want you to make love to me. Please, Nathan, that was just the little girl in me. She's gone now, cain't you feel that?"

She took his hand and moved it through her vulva, spreading its lips with his fingers. Nathan's body betrayed his mind, which was still trying to stay convinced that *this could not, should not, be happening.* She unbuckled his belt, opened his pants, and pulled his erecting penis out through the fly of his shorts.

Returning her kisses, despite his misgiving, her musks reached his sensitized, searching nostrils, as she pulled him, still semi-clothed, onto the bed. On his knees now, between her widely spread legs, Nathan protruded through the fly of his undershorts, as Shara pulled him over her. Her arms prayed around his neck, and she pulled him down atop her body's urgently compelling vincibility.

Nathan lay perplexed between her thighs, his mindless penis thrilling in her pubic hair, as she writhed beneath him in convincing heat and requiring desire. His belt undone; his pants slipped past his knees. Shara could not wait.

"I am not afraid, anymore, Nathan! I want you inside me."

Feeling the head of his cock twisting and sliding in her wet vulva, teased by her writhing, he raised his weight on his elbows, looked down, and realized that he was pushing into her yearning with his seeking. Their moment of fulfillment, at last...

"Oh!" she cried, as together they felt her hymen give, and his penis quickly slide halfway into her virginity. The welcome wrap of his penetration sent surges of pristine joy and realization through both of their fused bodies.

"You're in me. You are *in* me, Nathan! At last! Thank you, thank you, God!"

Mutually priming and perfecting this very God-given congruence, made especially for their species, his penis utterly filled her cunning. To Nathan, Shara felt unexpectedly different, warmer, softer–like velvet–and more clinging than he had imagined. Perhaps it was her renewed, unfettered sexuality, astonishingly forward, and dedicated to that giving and taking that uniquely frees and gratifies–and surely typifies and glorifies–her gender. She was neither ashamed nor prudish, as she met each thrust, feeling him filling her again and again. Rather, inflamed with passion and possession, holding him tightly, exhorting him deeper with her legs and upheaving pelvis, she praised and fully met the full-blown requirements of both Agape and Eros.

"Slow down, Shara, please. You'll make me come!"

Fucking with all her allure and nature–and that of her progenitors for millions of years–Shara moved her body more deliberately, drawing him in, pulling away so he could move outward, then pressing towards him again, hissing her desire, "Nathan, Nathan, I want you to come. I want you to pour your love into me, filling me up."

Lost in the pleasure of loving and giving, her head rolled back and forth, and her legs locked around his still clothed back; he could hold back no longer.

"Oh, God, Shara!"

"Oh, God, Nathan!"

Together, they rolled and tumbled down the lush and verdant slopes of their erotic heights, wrapped in the twin mantles of Eros and Agape, Nathan pushing up on all fours, lifting her body off the bed in her clinging engagement with his deepest, rapidly repeating thrusts–as he spent. After his final, claiming thrust, they lay writhing and shivering, enrapt, now fully enrolled and engaged in the daring dialectics of desire.

Their loving requirements met, Nathan still thriving deeply inside her, they wept–quietly, together, in their mutual relief and happiness. *One flesh, at last! Forever is my prayer!*

Reluctantly emerging as individuals, back from their ecstatic synthesis, Shara was amazed and proud. She wanted to talk, to apologize for her prior ambivalence, and to continue to explore the remaining secrets of his mysterious body. Nathan returned the compliment, no less in thrall and adulation to her than she to him.

She became playful and kittenish with him. Like young children, they played with each other, naked and free in the sunshine of their fulfilling innocence, where guilt was impossible, because nature–God–was the master craftsman of their new world–one neither fearful of, nor fettered by, Eden's false claims and caveats.

With characteristic delight, Shara rediscovered Nathan's vulnerability–to her tongue's snaky-lick–slithering under his jaw, tickling, and thrilling him, unmercifully. Nathan caressed and memorized every inch of her proud, yielding body, delighting in her youthful strength and verve.

Noting that his undershorts were splotched with blood, Nathan conjectured that the source of this red badge of courage was her menstrual flow, which they simply forgot. A cursory examination revealed only a slight tear in her small hymen.

About five o'clock, the consummate lovers reluctantly realized they must leave their connubial nest. Nathan relished Shara's easy, unembarrassed ballet around the apartment, as she gathered her clothing and dressed, leaning over, showing him her nubile body from every possible angle, cleanly, proudly, naturally. She did not close the door when she sat on the toilet, washed her vulva, or gingerly inserted a tampon into her doubly issuing vagina.

"Nathan, I feel so, so—complete! I feel alive and wonderful, like I won a victory or something, and, and—I love you! It was even better than I thought. I was amazed when you just slid right up inside me, and it only hurt for a moment—then the pleasure took over. I'm sorry I didn't come with you, but we can work on that tonight, or at least tomorrow, cain't we?" she rhapsodized, as they proofed their trysting place.

"If we play our cards right, Shara. But we must concern ourselves with Kathy. I don't want her to know, as much as I am certain you would love to tell her—and the world."

"You are so right, Reverend Mister Darling. I would love to tell Kathy all about us. God, she has no idea what she's missing. But I'll act sorrowful and left out of the party, instead."

"You will be circumspect with Kathy, won't you, Shara? It is very important that neither of us slip up and somehow apprise her of our love and love making.

"Nathan, I realize how important our secrets are, even though I really would like to share these wonderful things with her. I wouldn't even mind if you did it with her. Of course, I won't slip and tell, nor will I suggest that you—you fu—fuck her. Satisfied?"

They slipped and slid down the dripping, bush-swept path to the road and ran to the car. The rain continued, but lighter and not as drenching. They decided to tell Kathy, if necessary, that they went to the auction in Hot Springs, watching tourists pay too much for items they didn't really need.

"Nathan," she burbled, as they neared their cottage. "I'm already hot again. Next time, let's make it last longer."

QI, finally back in business, after being in lost in cathexis, opined, *as with so many excellent plays, the dress rehearsal was ragged, but opening night was a smash!*

CHAPTER 15
WISDOM'S SIMPLICITY

The past inhabits us and defines us—and often haunts us. We need to go back to it, to sift it, in order to know who we are and how we became what we are.

Lance Morrow

The past is never dead. It's not even past.

William Faulkner

I *have taken her virginity—no, not really. She gave it to me, more than willingly; virtually pleading, after stopping me. What does it mean for her; for me; for my married, family life; even for Mistress Melanie and my extraneous sex life; for my vocation—more importantly, for—no, to my God?*

Such were QI's ruminations as he walked the sunset mists of Tabormont after rain. His reflections needed expression in the footfalls of ambulation, or through contemplative creativity, words, or music—or both. Walking thus, while the earth drip-dried, he needed to make his mark.

But what should be my message to myself or to anyone? Was it worth it? Will it be so in a month, after moving to Wilmington? How will it change us—her—me—Lenore— everything?

So, thinking, Nathan wished he could get past exulting in the fact and get into the meaning of the signal event still roiling him. *Is it all a tawdry re-enactment of Eden's eternal thrall,*

110

unworthy, unoriginal, uninteresting, even banal, condemned to be unleashed again, and again, and, awfully, yet again, by all of humanity? Perhaps. But, to me, it is ontologically important—the pleasure and the probable pain. The only crucial questions still resounding in the mountains and valleys of my being: What might it mean? so I can ask that question's existential twin, what might it matter? Is it a mutual commitment? If so, what about Lenore and my babies—I am mutually committed to them, too!

At the doors of the college chapel, currently absent the surge of hundreds of teens, he entered to find a piano—his favorite thought processor. He needed to play, freely improvising, focusing these questions. As he had done many times during his collegiate summers in Tabormont, Nathan uncovered and opened the Steinway concert grand kept on the stage of the familiar, unlit chapel. He sat himself down and began to probe, play, and pray, improvising whatever came through his mediating mind, into his fingers, not caring that he could barely see the keys. He only needed to feel them—and to hear their—his—expressed and evocative voices.

What might it mean for the church and to God—the mysterious, often silent One who loves, forgives, and challenges me? P.S., What might it mean for me?

Sensing that someone beside God might be listening, he turned his head in time to glimpse a male figure dart past the narrow windows of the chapel's rear doors. *It is of no consequence, someone going thither from hither.* Intent on finding that combination of dynamics and melodies that would provide both catharsis and denouement—and the ultimate, resolving, authentic cadence that would allow him to stop, he played on...

Again, he sensed a movement just through the rear doors. Continuing to play, he looked more discreetly. What he saw unnerved him: a boy, facing the well-lit, outer hall wall, barely in Nathan's view, with both arms uplifted. Pressing against that wall were two hands, both with only a thumb and little finger, crookedly spread, widely apart, in two, failing, flailing vees, writhing in time with Nathan's playing, along with the boy's repeated, bodily humps against the wall.

Aghast at this startling sight, Nathan abruptly stopped playing. The boy was gone, but Nathan heard a sob and a little cry, as the outer chapel door rang closed. Heart pounding with the intensity of his own music and his astonishment at the fleeting apparition, QI searched. *Perhaps the boy heard my banging, wandered in, and, in frustration and disappointment at not being able to play, beat both against the wall.*

Drawn so poignantly back into the world of others, Nathan tried to sort out his thoughts and emotions regarding this woeful specter: *a boy who longed to express himself on the piano, perhaps, without the necessary equipment? I should have thought to call out to him to wait, come in, and talk. Maybe my playing will draw him back; maybe I'll see him again. He will be recognizable by his infirmities.* With that hope—and sad realization, Nathan picked up his probing music where he left off.

Finding his concentration broken by the vision of the handicapped lad, he determined that *more data should help me resolve these questions. Shara and I will simply have to do it again—soon—ghost or no ghost!* Ending his playing with a flourishing coda, Nathan calmly closed and recovered the Steinway and left the darkened sanctuary. Suddenly able to recall every intimate detail of his afternoon's engorging enterprise, he felt his heart quicken—and his nether self stiffen...

CHAPTER 16
INTEGRATION

...To serve Him–in the tangle of our minds...

Thomas More

Sitting quietly with Shara in the little prayer house, on a pier jutting out into the lake, Nathan related his strange experience with the boy with truncated hands.

"I've seen that guy ogling the girls. He gave me the creeps! Who do you think he is?"

"One of God's children to whom nature gave a raw deal, Shara. Why did he give you the creeps?"

"Well, he didn't hide his–his hands; he held them out and fluttered them, so everybody could see, like he was trying to shake something off them. That grossed me out."

"I can understand your reaction to strangeness–but can you feel your way into why he did that?"

"What? You mean you don't think he's gross?"

"I think he hurts awfully, honey, and when I get past the unexpected and the different, his pain hurts me, too."

"Na-than?" she cried, aghast at what felt like criticism.

"Pardon me for coming on like a preacher, honey, but I felt his anguish. I don't think he feigned his sob and cry, running out of the chapel–and even if he did..."

"I hadn't thought about how he might feel. I–I just reacted to his..." The suddenly heavy heart of his young lover cracked with self-accusing recognition, filling her eyes with tears. "Oh, Nathan, I hadn't thought past how strange–weird–he looked, with those creepy hands flapping, and his eyes darting all around the room. I'm sorry–I'm sorry that I let myself think those things. Should we go find him and–and–and I don't know what, but shouldn't we–do, say–something…?"

Shara's own little sob and cry finished and answered her own question, revealing the Great Realization alive in her heart.

Handing her his handkerchief, "If we meet him, we might greet and be open to him."

After the realization and the weeping came the holding and the sweet, familiar caressing, closing the emotional loop, smoothing spiritual wrinkles.

"Come here," he sighed, sweeping her into his arms." Kissing hungrily, their hands began to warm themselves in the other's friendly fire, until Nathan pulled away, as Shara began to unzip his fly.

"Whew! Let's cool it; it's only seven, and we have until midnight."

"I'd like to start right now," she whispered.

"Wait, honey, I want to tell you something."

Curiosity overcoming her heat, Shara got up and moved to a chair away from Nathan.

"I'll sit over here. If I'm too close, I'll want to be closer. What's the big secret?"

"It's certainly no secret that my love for you is peremptory, Shara."

"I like the love part, Nathan, but I have no idea what 'per-' 'peremptory' means. Is that a good thing?"

"It's what I meant by Chalmers' quote, 'the expulsive power of a newfound affection,' as you have heard me spout, and that is what I want to talk about."

He paced to the door, returned, and sat on the porch ledge overlooking the lake.

"We have a few problems to overcome, if we are to give our love any chance of flourishing, without hurting people. We need to continue cautiously, avoiding serious mistakes. The larger issues for me are three: Shara my love; Shara my parishioner; and Shara the girl/woman, soon to be sought by other males. Along with those come the overwhelming issues of Lenore, my children, my church, my calling, God's place in all of this, our families, our further growth and maturity, individually and as a couple—and Wilmington."

Shara—she lay low.

"Good. You aren't crying, and I have mentioned just about everything that might dismay. I need your strength, now, Shara, for beneath all my bluster is a very needy man, hoping that we can be together a long time. It sometimes makes me a little crazy, wondering about how quickly our relationship moved from a Vesper Dell hug to, well, to fucking. Then, there are the size and nature of the potential conflicts we will undoubtedly face if we are to be successful. My mind and ethics warn me about these things, but my heart—which you inhabit and fill—is the dictator."

"I'm listening."

"The good part is that this evening, as I was improvising on the piano, I finally realized that we are going to have to improvise, too. If I can bring my body and heart, so hungry for you, in line, I think we may be able to—to find ways around the conflicts and be together. Let's make love, but let's do so, oh, so carefully. We can be—and should be—free, but our freedom must not imprison others. We have only just begun…"

"I understand—and, of course, I agree. But you won't be the only one who'll have to bring body and heart in line."

"I know. I don't mean to preach. Here you are fresh from one of the most important experiences in your life, and aching to re-taste that joy, and all I can do is blither. You may as well be warned–I'll probably do so the rest of my life."

"Hush, Nathan. I see; I know; I understand. You cain't possibly know how proud I feel right now–in us, both, for your talking to–treating me as an equal–and in me, for loving and understanding you in my own, growing way. Keep talking to me like this, and I'll do my part. My love is per–peremptory, too–at least as much as any scrawny, uneducated, little teenager can love–which is turning out to be about as much as anybody."

"I knew I could count on you, Shara. What I really want to do is to hold you and kiss you–and to be honest, get into those tight jeans you have plastered to your body."

"No more than I want you in them–and in me. But I also think we should be responsible with our love, as well as express it physically."

"There is no way that virtually anybody else could understand and accept our relationship–especially the sex. Were I on the outside looking in, as I sorta was with Kathy and Terry about an hour ago, when they asked me if they could go to a drive-in movie, I wouldn't fully understand it, either. The age of sexual consent here is sixteen. Despite that legality, I would probably conclude that an older, more experienced, married man, in a position of power, found a needy, giving, vulnerable, young girl, and callously took advantage of her, regardless of the potential cost to her, or to anyone else."

Studied concentration on Shara's part.

"As God is my witnesses, I do not–cannot–believe that is what is happening here; or in the boathouse, in the woods, in the church, in my car, on the mountain, or in Glencrest this afternoon, and it will not be what happens tonight, either."

"I may be young, but I'm not stupid. Of course, I have asked myself whether you are taking advantage of me. Never once have I felt or thought that might be true. On the contrary, I sought you out, hounded you, even, until you, somehow, understood. Perhaps I have been taking advantage of you!"

"Not a chance, Shara, but please share with me your understanding of us, now, including our sex?"

"Nathan, I'm no philosopher–not very educated, yet. I don't know what some of the words you use mean, except in a general way. But I'm smart enough to know that you are the best thing that has ever happened to me. I am more complete, more mature, more whole, more purposed, more Christian, now. Your loving me has shown me the value I'm certain I have–not only to God and others, but to myself, and just as wonderfully, to you. I never thought I would know what love is, but I know you love me and are not taking advantage of me–and that is the miracle you are to me. What happened this afternoon was living proof of all that!"

"You do see; know; understand..."

"What worries me is how to continue–to improvise, as you say–if you are in Wilmington and still married. We should talk about that, and the obvious risks involved."

"We'll probably need to talk about it on a daily basis..."

"It's all very scary, Nathan. That's why we have to move cautiously toward any future we may have–but we do have to keep moving, don't we?"

"Yes; one cautious step at a time..."

Nature's improvised music of tree, wind, and lapping wavelets filled the silence following their determined non-plan, outlining only the improbable, and defining nothing so much as their intrepid faith in each other, and their hopes for the future: "*. . . substance of things hoped for, and evidence of things unseen.*"

"Nathan, I know it will be difficult—maybe even impossible—and particularly hard on you. You know—you must know—that I love you, that I trust you, and not just as a dumb teenager. I am entrusting my future to you—to us—for as long as possible. You describe an incredible now and a desirable future for us, if we are careful. Besides the thrill that gives me, you provide me the security I need to be able to risk—everything. The more you see me as mature, the more mature I am. You do that to people, you know; I've seen it bunches of times. So, I'll leave the improvising mostly to you, at least for now, responding as well as I can with my limited experience, and adding to it when I know enough to do so."

Nathan stood, walked to the corner, took Shara's hands, and gently drew her into him. They held, and held on, until Shara suggested they pray. Urgently, they prayed to God, and to each other, with their hearts and with their heads, seeking a path around tortuous pain for others, to the steepling of their growing temple of love, with its golden, pealing twin bells: *Agape and Eros.*

"We believe, Oh God. Help thou our unbelief! Amen," concluded Nathan, taking his lady by her strengthened and courageous hand, and walking with her into a parlous future.

CHAPTER 17
NATHAN'S SONG

Oh God of hearts, hate not our sighs!
Bless, instead, our love's sharing.
With fear and trembling in our eyes,
Fill our scheming with thy caring.

Nathan R. Scott
July 5, 1964

How still the gloam embracing them, upward moving on the trail, recreating their tyro emotions, as they retraced their steps—to a farewell mounting on the mountain. The July sun, meting its waning splurge of heat and light, colored their faces and warmed their bodies with its final passion, as it awakened and cheered other worlds.

At the mountain's peak, behind a cover of greenery, on a great, flat rock, overlooking the Tabormont microcosm and the undulance of the Great Smokies, the dazzled couple faced west, longing for more—of everything. The eloquent sunset enfolding them colored their awe. With Shara leaning back between his outstretched legs, her head on his shoulder, Nathan hummed their mood, needing no words.

Basking in privacy, in collaboration with the dusky thief of light, they were elated, but wistful. Tomorrow an entirely new sun would rise, flooding their shadowy love with lights too bright. She must revert to the diffident daughter, locked in at night by the proprieties. He must re-engage the demanding roles of loving husband, father—and pious man of God. How difficult it will be, they thought, to resume their separate lives, while trying to stretch their Tabormont consummation across the chasm between their stations. Experiencing the inevitable pain too early, they shook it off, preferring to milk the intimate moments left—and to suckle at their shrinking breasts.

"Are you cold, Shara?"

"No, darling; I was just thinking about tomorrow. But I would rather think about tonight, to savor it and take it with us."

They kissed, tasting desire, hungrily gulping the other's breath, inhaling essence, feasting on a symmetry of self and senses.

"Nathan—I—I need to tell you something."

"Sure, sweetheart."

"I—don't—quite—know how—how to begin. It's sorta about sex. I—I, oh, Nathan, I'm so ashamed!"

Dread arced the poles of his emotions, wrenching his bowels and opening his mouth, but paralyzing his tongue. On cue, QI took over: *What can be wrong that she is so ashamed? Is she repenting of our sexuality? Could she have had earlier sexual experiences? No! That doesn't make any sense, at all. Shut up and listen, Scott, and stop racing.*

"What—what is it, Shara? Of what are you ashamed?"

"Well—it's—about my father. He—he—I've never told anyone this, Nathan, and I'm a little scared..."

"Whatever it is, I'll listen and love you."

"Give—give me a minute. It's just that it's been inside me so long, and I couldn't tell anyone," she whispered, crawling back into his sure warmth. Nathan stroked her face, rocking her, until her trembling stopped. Gentled in his embrace, she nestled her head on his chest and began...

"About three or so years ago, after my periods started, and my body was maturing–you know, I had breasts and all–Daddy came home one evening, when I was the only one home. I was in the den, watching TV. He got a drink and lay down on the couch behind me. I was into the TV. Then, he told me to come give him a hug. I went over and sat on the edge of the couch and gave him a little hug. When I tried to get up, he didn't let go!"

She paused, warily scratching at scars of avoided remembrance.

"Anyway, he pulled me down on the couch next to him, so I was lying in front of him, sorta spoon fashion, you know? His arms were around me, and he commented about how I had grown up. Then, he moved his hands up on my chest under my breasts, and his thumbs began to rub them, until he had moved both hands on them and was sorta squeezing and rubbing and pulling me closer to him at the same time."

Another pause amid heavy breathing.

"It's okay, Shara; I've got you, and I love you."

"Well, I felt trapped and had no idea why he was rubbing–sorta squeezing–my breasts, with his thumbs up to my nipples–only that I was confused and scared to death. I didn't dare get up and leave–you don't deny my father, no matter what. He just kept on rubbing, and occasionally, he would say something–sometimes about how I had grown, and sometimes just about nothing. I tried to move away but I couldn't, because he was holding me against him. I didn't say anything–because I–I didn't know what to say.

"We lay like that for maybe five to seven minutes, when I heard a car drive into the carport. I knew it was Mom because I heard the kids. I didn't know what to do, but I didn't want her to see me with Daddy like that. It wasn't up to me, though, for when the car doors opened, he just let go, gave me a shove, and I tumbled to the floor. When I got up and looked at him, he had already turned over, like he was asleep!"

As she talked, Shara's voice softened to a childlike whisper, increased in volume, then just stopped—hating the memory—sucking it up, so she could spit it out.

"Shara, my Shara, are you all right?"

"No—but I will be. Let me get through it."

"Okay," he whispered."

"Well, I was real confused; I went to my room and looked in the mirror—and I felt bad. I felt dirty! I couldn't look Mom or Dad in the eye the rest of the night. He didn't say a word to me, either, acting like I wasn't even there. It was horrible!"

Nathan ached through her next silence, unwilling to interject. As she began again, her troubled voice seemed far away, haunted by the distant shadows of a dismal yesterday.

"That wasn't the end of it, Nathan. Several times—at least three or four—over the next three years, he did it again. I don't remember as many details about those as I do the first. I tried to avoid ever being alone with Daddy, but I couldn't avoid him all the time. I know one time he grabbed me while I was walking by, when everybody else was gone. He sat me on his lap, hugged me, put his hands on my chest and did it again. I got up as soon as I could and got out of there. Another time I was standing, and one time I was lying on the couch, sleeping, and didn't hear him come in."

"Has it occurred recently?"

"He hasn't done it for over a year now, but it may be because I avoid him. Daddy had to know I was avoiding being alone with him, because I would do anything I could to leave. Anyway, that's pretty much what I needed to tell you."

Pause.

"First, Shara, I deeply love you, and I hurt that you have been hurt. You've been harboring this difficult truth for years, and now it's out. I'm moved that you trust me enough to tell me. To be honest, I'm appalled and so sorry you underwent such experiences. You must know and believe that your father was wrong–terribly, irrevocably wrong."

Quietly waiting, Shara hugged him tighter.

"My major, more important reaction is concern for you–what you think of him–but more critically, what you think of yourself."

"Dirty! I feel dirty!" sitting up. "I wanted–I have always wanted love from and for and my father, but how can I when I know what he is capable of–with his own daughter? I could overlook his strictness and his mean streak–always treating everyone like slaves–even Mom. I could attribute that to the fact that he's gone all the time, has a tough job–and was maybe shell-shocked from two wars. But I just get all mixed up, when I think about what he was doing, especially now that I understand and appreciate what sex is all about–what it should be! He was using me, and who knows what he would have done if Mom hadn't come in, or if I hadn't managed to avoid him–or, even worse, if he somehow convinced me it was okay…?"

"Say some more about that and why you feel dirty."

Almost spitting, "Because I didn't stop him! Because I wanted him to appreciate me–but not that way. I've always wanted him to be proud of me–to think I was special for what I knew, or did, or said, or felt. He never seems at all interested in my feelings, or dreams, or hopes, especially not my opinions–only to criticize or correct them. I was–am–just a young, dumb, kid to him, a girl, at that; good for nothing except to do everything I am told; to have no brain, values, or decisions of my own. I want–wanted–to be important, special to him–and he used me instead, like a piece of meat!"

Nathan feasted on her anger, letting it feed his indignation, believing it good for them both.

"So, you feel dirty because you believe you should have stopped him and never let it happen again?"

"Yes! But I was afraid of him, too. I thought if I tried to get him to stop, or told on him, he would just deny it, and then really make me pay. On the other hand, I thought that if Mom believed me, they might get a divorce, and I didn't want to cause that. How would we support ourselves? It's hard enough as it is. Mom doesn't know how to do anything but be a mom—it frightens me for the kids—as well as for Jimmy and me. Who would pay for Jimmy's college—or mine? It was—is—awful, Nathan!"

"I know, my darling; I feel the awfulness."

"I knew you would. I love you for listening, and understanding, and not judging."

Snuggling even closer in his arms, she looked up at him with renewed comfort shaping her visage and pressed her lips into his neck.

"So, you didn't stop him, or tell on him, for fear of the consequences—anything else?"

"Maybe... At first, I tried to convince myself that, if he was doing it, it might be all right, so I sorta leaned in that direction, to protect us both, I guess. But I really knew deep down that wasn't right, so I just felt dirty."

As she spoke, Shara's hands gently explored Nathan's face, touching his eyes, lips, palming his cheeks and temples, running her fingers in his hair, feeling the man behind the loving, listening face, soaking him up...

"I used to wish he'd die, or be killed in an accident, so Mom would get his insurance, but then I'd feel guilty for thinking such things. Was I terrible, Nathan, to have such thoughts?"

"Even though you couldn't see any clear way out of your dilemma, apart from his dying, so it would stop, you felt guilty for even thinking, much less wishing..."

"Yes! I tried to get beyond my feelings, and to forgive him—which I did, until it would happen again. Then, the bad feelings would start all over. It wasn't so much that it was happening all the time, 'cause it wasn't. But I thought it was going to happen ever time he walked in the door, so I was constantly on my guard, and constantly angry, scared—and guilty!"

"Say some more about why you felt guilty, honey."

"That's hard, Nathan, because it still bothers me. When I realized he was touching me in a sexual way, I was ashamed of the tiny little bit of pride or acceptance, or whatever you want to call it, I felt when he paid attention to me—held me! Then I was disgusted with myself for liking it for even one tiny second. That's why I felt dirty. I finally decided, once and for all, that it was simply wrong, and I just had to stay away from him—but I worry about Jennie and Amy. And until you came along, I found myself thinking that maybe all men might be like my father—just take, take, take, whatever, whenever he wants. But you were—are—the exact opposite."

"I hope so!"

"You make it all right for me to like myself, again, and you always encourage me to be my best self. You would rather give to me than take from me, and I know you love me. That is why I love you and have no trouble at all giving you anything and everthing. Your giving to me made—makes—me want to give back—and all I really have to give—is me."

"Much more, Shara; much, much more," he whispered.

"Because you love me," she whispered back.

"Have you decided what to do about it, now, or if he ever tries it again?"

"Yes. I guess I have decided to do nothing but tell you. And I guess he has decided to stop, because he hasn't tried it for over a year. I'm beginning to believe he never will.

He can't believe I liked it, and he's bound to realize how dangerous it could be–is–for him–and me."

"Shara, I think you have about got it sorted out, except, if that–that–if he ever tries it, again, I want you to promise me that you will call or come to me, immediately."

"What would you do, then, Nathan?"

"I honestly don't know–but I would do something to ensure that he never did it again. One thing, Shara: you are not at fault, in any way, for what your father did–no matter what! I certainly understand why you have had–may still have–a small doubt about that, but it is simply not possible. There is no way a thirteen to sixteen-year-old girl can be responsible for such actions by her father, period!"

"I believe that, Nathan."

"I understand and respect your concerns, and I honor your reasons–you did what you had to do–and apart from your legitimate worries about Jennie and Amy, it appears you have effectively handled the situation. Considering how much more lovely and desirable you are now than you were even a year ago–much less three years ago–it's likely that he would still be after you. Evidently, you have been quite successful in squelching that."

"Do you really think so? I want to believe that, but ever now and then, I worry, especially if we are alone in the house–which I still don't let happen, much. And do you know what, Nathan? I have wondered about whether he might be doing it with somebody on the road. As far as I can tell, he and Mom don't have sex very much, and I would be surprised if he is all that faithful."

"It happens all the time, honey." Nathan wryly agreed, immediately flashing to their own situation. That fact was not lost on Shara, either, who smiled grimly at his words.

"Nathan, you don't think that my behavior with you has anything to do with my father, do you?"

"Absolutely not, but which behavior might that be, Miz Ma'am?" trying to lighten things.

"Probably the most important: my loving you–needing you–almost literally haunting you, until you couldn't help but, but…"

"…Fall head over heels in love with you, almost from the very moment of your surprising and wonderful Vesper Dell hug? If you hadn't done that, you'd still be a virgin!"

"What? And turn into a pillow of salt?"

"Pillar."

"Huh?"

"The word is 'pillar,' meaning a post or a column–not pillow, you Bible-believing little minx. Lot's wife disobediently looked back at God's destruction of Sodom and Gomorrah, and he turned her into a pillar of salt."

They clung to each other atop God's mountains, deep in their longest night of striving. All other roles were shunned, as their bodies appeased their minds, and their hearts fed on the increasing friction of their urgency, recreating the ancient, healing fires of righteous and requiring love: Agape and Eros, welded, wedded–and wonderful.

Fastening himself to her, reclaiming her, Nathan forecast their future with the depth of his thrusts, fully met by a reciprocating Shara. Pulling him into her hot center, with its innate unctions, as the full-blown woman she was, she absorbed the depths of his priming, becoming the willing mortar for his eager pestle.

A fortissimo song echoed from ridge to ridge, across the valleys of God's holy mountains, deepening its reverb and vibrato, strengthened by the depth of its utterance, as Nathan's aria crescendoed in climax and lavished its prophet sostenuto on this new, holy night. One word, his libretto, preserved in the very rocks by the depth of its force, sent soaring into the rent heavens, with startled, awakened birds–a word which

Nathan cast and memorialized in the golden, operatic tones of his awesome extremity:

"Shhhaaaaarrrrraaaaa!"

CHAPTER 18
HOME FROM THE HILL

The Well of Faith

Residual, sedimentary, layered Lust,
Building on the bedrock of Self,
Becomes so thickly veiling, that
As we live, we are covered,
Smothered, buried, caught immobile,
Enraptured and entombed—
Pyramids of Pleasures Spent
And Sepulchers of Sense.
Amid the tears,
Astride the vehicle of Love,
    Is there naught but dumb, blind Hope
To bore the well of Faith?
Come, fill the Cup!
I thirst!

Nathan R. Scott,
Tabormont, N. C.
1:00 A. M. July 8, 1964

Into the darkness they go, the wise and the lovely.

Edna St. Vincent Millay

They came down the mountain–and came down.

Maintaing the intensity of their mountain-top relationship proved impossible. Both found their homes unchanged, filled with familiar challenges, banes, and blessings. Nathan's conscience added despair to his slowly returning guilt, not about his actions with Shara, but regarding his otherwise, disheveled life–and his wonderful wife and children.

Meeting him in the driveway of their rented house, Lenore was delighted to see him. At 5'9", lovely, long-limbed and lovable, she was dressed smartly, as she ran to his car with their two little ones, Nathan, II. and little Beth, smiling and jabbering their warmth and welcome: a trinity of love and acceptance crowding around him, covering him with needy wifely arms, and touching him with expectant, reassured, childish hands. There was no denying their joy, nor his, as his heart gladdened to realize how much he had missed them–and had been missed.

"Golly, Nathan, I'm so glad you're home; Beth has been haunting the front window all day, pointing to the traffic, and exclaiming, `Daddee car? Daddee car?' Of course, Nattie and I came running. We got your postcards; couldn't you have written me a letter? No, I take that back; it's just that we–I–missed you. I enjoyed our telephone call, though. Did it ever stop raining?"

"I missed you, too, 'Nore. Yes, it stopped; let's go inside; I'm pooped."

Thus, Nathan re-entered an accustomed normality, and sanctuary, too, from the unleashed energies of Tabormont. Sitting at table to his favorite meal, he regaled Lenore with the antics of the conferees, inhaling the jollity embracing his presence–nagged, also, by his heart's growing vacuum, shaped very much like Shara Starr. Lenore was lovely, and he found himself wanting her...

Afterward, with his arms around her sleeping, naked loveliness, QI purposefully rehearsed his history with her, Melanie, and now, Shara, seeking to understand, as much as possible, the dynamics now at play. To do that, he needed to sift and evaluate...

At twenty-eight, Lenore is a looker, a thinker, a reader, a writer, an artist, an empath, an excellent lover, fine cook, patient Mommy, careful listener, cheerleader—and my better, in most things. My height, she is willowy, long-limbed, green-eyed, and beautiful. Never one to express her sexuality openly, except while participating, Lenore is the near perfect mate for me, one would think—and most do.

In college, Lenore already knew how to study, make better grades, but was excited, if a bit overwhelmed, by my sudden, urgent attentions. Once committed, she stuck with me, despite my willful, gratuitous emphases on total openness, availability—and sex. Somewhat diffident in public, Lenore was—is—a private person, preferring her modest pursuits to almost any public ones.

Lenore delves into us, poetry, art, books, music, nature, family, her closest friends (Melanie!), and, of course, our children. Her chief, legitimate complaint about me is my constant absence from our home. She has not the slightest idea of my dalliance with Melanie and only recently has shown a tad of wariness about my interest in Shara.

I respect Lenore more than anyone I know, love her in my own, deep, complicated way, and always will. Yet, she, like the Church, prefers a world of middle-class decency and order, into which I was born, for which I was trained, into which I committed myself, despite my doubts—and in which I feel ill-suited—even stifled!

Lenore and sex: over time, I felt increasingly insecure regarding Lenore's truest feelings about my prodigious sexuality and my desire—need—for the exploratory, the graphic, and the vicarious. I suspected that it surprised and somewhat disgusted her, but I lacked verifying evidence. Giving hesitant, loving permission, she submitted to my honeymoon efforts at photographic erotica, involving ridiculous, studied angles, film speed, f-stops, focus, tripods, and an air-bulbed, remotely controlled shutter! Due to what I perceived as silent, negative judgment about such, after a few more photographic sessions, with her somewhat wary, but uncomplaining cooperation, I decided that she merely tolerated it, because she loved—loves—me.

One weekend in late 1961, I needed to avoid a tryst with Melanie, while Lenore visited her parents. Determined not to accept Melanie's enticing invitation, I chanced upon a full-page magazine ad, touting the wonders of a certain soft drink. Featuring a trio of beautiful, young females, I was driven to sublimate my libido, by using them to express and relieve my needs and frustrations.

The ad featured fully clothed, long, young legs cocked and positioned to be innocently open, alluring, and sexually inviting. In my fervor, I traced the bodies of the sexy ladies, nude, filled and colored in the necessary anatomical essentials, and added faceless males, gorged penises erect and deeply ensconced within the dripping orifices of the smiling ladies. Working feverishly, I finished all three of the fleshed-in fuckers, before I allowed myself the predictable anti-climax which my crude and lurid drawings stimulated, just before dawn.

Woebegone, I fetched Lenore and little Nate from the airport, put the baby down, and crawled into bed with my beautiful wife. During our preliminaries, I timorously showed her my lurid drawings. She took them from my trembling hands, emitting a little gasp, as she saw the blatant sex depicted. Speechless for a full minute, she turned my crude art this way and that, almost gawking.

"Gracious, Nathan, it's very salacious, isn't it? Can, uh, will you tell me about it, please?"

"Not a lot to tell, honey. I was terribly horny, you were gone, so I found this ad, with the clothed girls made to look sexy, traced them, and filled in the blanks, so to speak. I'm not exactly proud of it, but it is somewhat emblematic of how much I needed you and your luscious body. Are you disgusted?"

"No, you've done a good job of depicting your, er, lust, as well as making believable representations of their anatomies—male and female."

"That's what I was trying to do. It took me most of last night."

"Yes. I'm rather amazed at your efforts, honey. What shall you do with it?"

"After I make love to you, I'll decide. I apologize if you're disgusted. Are you?"

"Not really. No need to apologize, though, for I see no, uh, wrong.

"Are you sure, sure, sure?" I sang, emulating our mutually loved Amahl.

"Wouldn't the real thing be better, honey?'

With that truism hanging in the air, we fucked.

Those drawings, long destroyed, still make me feel foolish in Lenore's eyes. Though she proffered true Agape, as always, I felt—feel—a judgment, somehow, which continues to warn me away from further revelation of my deepest, most challenging, erotic fires. Except for tolerating slight, sexual feints toward my fantasies, my wariness began to conflict with her sex appeal. Almost never suggesting sex, but usually open to it, Lenore typifies Agape and de-emphasizes Eros, while for me, the two are massively and inextricably intermixed, inseparable, ideally—and devoutly to be had! Increasingly, the tensions underlying those two extremes worried me.

For three plus years, then, caught between abundant Agape, but muted Eros, for and from Lenore, and a plethora of adulterous Eros, absent Agape, for and from my luscious, red-haired friend, I began to ache for simple, uncomplicated purity, to release me from what had become, almost ridiculously, an imprisoning dilemma.

Amidst the throes of these complex and worrisome circumstances, young and innocent Shara slowly grew from an irritating impatience, into a hallowed resident in my hall of hearts, simply by being herself. Sexualis tabula rasa, she slowly emerged as a pure and purifying vessel—for warm, professional mentoring, only, uncomplicated by desire, a shelter from my world of sexual conflict. Then, I fell hopelessly in love with her, and the dilemma transferred to our relationship, until resolved by our mutual love come to awesome fruition in Tabormont.

Home from the hill, my triple quandary is almost overwhelming, despite the felt righteousness and purity of our new relationship. Though it seems entirely too neat, I now face three, seemingly viable, demanding relationships (if I ignore everything else): 1) Lenore, who provides and evokes deep friendship, love, wonderful history, co-parenthood, welcome obligations, and moderate (normal?) sex; 2) Melanie, with whom I enjoy a greater expression of mutual sexuality, whom I respect, but do not love, and to whom I owe nothing but truth; and 3) Shara, with whom all things seem possible, desirable, and uninhibited – both Agape and Eros, in equal portions: ergo, pure Love!

What to do? Love the more that grace may abound? Something like that? Sigh! Would that bigamy were legal, for I love Lenore and Shara, both! Ruefully, Melanie remains pleasantly habitual, if peripheral, which is not fair to anyone—including me...

Tabormont seemed a dream, now confounded by competing desires and responsibilities. Duty clashed with desire; desire clashed with religion; religion clashed with nature; and nature clashed with the civilization and the complicated circumstances in which he lived. QI fought for duty, religion, and civilization; Nathan's heart and body fought for desire, nature, and a change of circumstances, to include Shara. God and Wilmington had other plans...

Plunging into postponed work, Nathan received the expected call letter from Christ Church, with a start date of September 9, 1964, two days after Labor Day. He must accept or reject their call by July 20.

*

Soon after Tabormont, Shara visited Nathan's office early one Sunday afternoon—their first tryst since their return. She came carefully bathed, dressed, and effectively preened.

After working together on senior high projects, Nathan covertly met her in a second-floor classroom, where they were unlikely to be heard, disturbed—or discovered.

At first, those surroundings made both a bit timid, standing near a *papier mache* model of a biblical city, in the Primary classroom—until he kissed her. She looked younger than expected but felt as mature as remembered. Their kiss was followed by a mutual outpouring of whispered catch-up, experiences, feelings, and plans for future trysts. Then, Nathan showed her the letter from Wilmington.

"I'm not going to cry—yes, I am!" she moaned, sitting down on an empty, child- sized table. "You're going to go, aren't you?"

"I—think so, but I wanted to talk to you, first. I don't want to go—but I think, maybe, I should—don't you?"

"No, no, no, and no, again! I don't know what you should do, but I know what I want you to do—stay here and be with me! Damn! I was going to be so noble and tell you to look to your family and your calling, and that I would manage, somehow. Now, I've blown all that and am just being selfish. Please forgive me, darling. Do what you have to do," she sighed, picking at the buttons of his shirt.

"I'm not one hundred percent sure, yet, honey, but I'm thinking about it very carefully. Lenore has left it largely to me, but I think she wants to go. Come here!"

"No, you come down here," demanded the hungry, weeping girl, as she grabbed his hands and drew him down to her body, lying back, now, on the low, teacher-painted table. It groaned under their weight, as Nathan loaded himself between her legs. Her arms went around his neck, pulling his head to her breasts. Inhaling the rare perfumes of her youth, he unbuttoned her blouse and bared her loins. Hungrily, he caressed and kissed the muliebrous delights he exposed.

Her pent passion overtook her earlier tears, and Shara eagerly accepted his offerings. As their orgasms catapulted them into the spheres, a loudly closing door downstairs brought them crashing back to an enamel-painted, sea green, child-sized table in an empty primary classroom. Of such was their new kingdom of heaven.

*

That evening, after teaching his Koinonia Class of young adults, in which Melanie was a staunch member, she helped him close up, and he walked her to her car—and right into her apartment, after she put his hands on her breasts. They made love twice, before he knew he had to leave.

"At least kiss me. I have really missed you."

He did, feeling the wash of lust striving to overcome his tired, sad awareness. Knowing that he was right, but wanting to keep him longer, Melanie took things in hand, anew, until he pulled away. Dressing, his mind already fondling Lenore's familiarity, Nathan complimented her and their lovemaking, genuinely appreciative of her open gifts, and finally sneaked out of her townhouse, his semi-hard tail between his legs.

After (perhaps because of) two women and several climaxes, he was aflame for the safe harbor of his familiar, gentle wife; to her he flew, unmindful of speed limits. Turning into his driveway, he was overjoyed to see their bedroom light still on. Warming his soul on the hearth of hope awaiting, his two blessed events, so trusting, so wonderful to hold and behold, and Lenore, the soft, secure, inner core of the past ten years, seven of them married to her, he wanted, needed, and desperately loved his wonderful, innocent wife.

Of course, she welcomed him into her heart and into her svelte, smooth body, surrounding him with stability and her heat. His love was more ardent than usual, in his attempts to wash away his quandary with each healing thrust, and to claim the future for God, for Lenore, and for a mended, productive mission. As they released their lusts for the second time, together in heat and harmony, he promised God that he would sojourn in (escape to?) the distant climes of Wilmington, and seek there the true, promised land.

Weeping softly into his wife's hair, kissing her neck, and needing her peremptorily, he whispered, "God, it's so good to be home! I love you, Lenore!"

Loving and accepting her man, no matter his straits, she snuggled him and whispered, as much to God as to her husband, "I hope so, Nathan; dear God, I do hope so!"

*

July boiled away in a steaming hiss of exhaustion. Nathan preached, tought, organized, presented, or otherwise spoke before audiences every day through September 8, his departure date. The search committee at Trinity University asked him to wait as long as possible, as they were considering him for chaplain to students, but were not yet authorized to hire. Nathan wondered at the capricious hand of God when he received the preferable call to Trinity University one day after he accepted Christ Church's call.

Because he was leaving, he added multiple duties and opportunities, leaving him almost no time for anything but work. While steeped in his triple dilemma, compliments, some accompanied by small checks, began to arrive, adding to his guilt that he knew he never did anything as well as he could. Mainly, he was weary of struggling with the never ending, guilt-producing, heart breaking, and stultifying mess he seemed to be making of things.

God help me! I am not enough; I cannot be!

During July and August, Nathan was in his home about six hours a day, on average, counting sleeping time. Though patient, Lenore was left alone too much, and it showed. Though he clung to her, marital closeness was virtually impossible.

Shara became much more the woman, realistically believing that soon she must give him up to God and his family. Until that time, however, she intended to give herself to him as often as she could, realizing that her love strengthened and completed him.

Hot, pall mall August continued to scorch Nathan's life, significantly abated only by the cooling prospects of trysting with Shara, during his coming retreats. With that soothing balm in the Gilead of his mind, Nathan made the best he could of his thickening, suffocating miasma.

*

Nathan's three August, weekend retreats finally arrived, all attended by Shara, as a junior counselor in the first two, and finally as a participant. They were joys to both, though he was not as able to get away with her as much as he had in May. Managing only two furtive, midnight sessions, during the first two retreats, ending deep in Shara, they were determined to be more successful during his final retreat, Sunday, August 30, through Wednesday, September 3, 1964.

For his retreat theme, Nathan chose, "Relationships: Broken and Healed," and risked using the movie *"The Night of the Iguana"* the first night, to kick off discussion. Brilliantly written by Tennessee Williams, and modified by Hollywood, Nathan considered the screenplay to be clear and moving, providing appropriate stimuli and excellent illustrations of his theme.

That the play's anti-hero was an apostate clergyman, locked out of his church for his susceptibility to seduction by teenaged girls, was not lost on Nathan. Its more important themes, however, focused on despair, inhumanity, estrangement, and the rot that seems to permeate strained, broken relationships in the steaming weathers of living. It also projected a hopeful, redemptive calm in the face of dire, personal circumstances. The kids loved it, responding eagerly to the movie and to Nathan's written questions and penetrating, thematic insights.

CHAPTER 19
SANCTUARY

Brooding on God, I may become a man.
Pain wanders through my bones like a lost fire
What burns me now? Desire, desire, desire...

Lord, hear me out, and hear me out this day,
From me to Thee's a long and terrible way...

Yea, I have slain my will, and still, I live;
I would be near; I shut my eyes to see.
I bleed my bones, their marrow to bestow
Upon that God who knows what I would know.

Theodore Roethke

The night's discussion and recreation were over. The teens had a blast, thoroughly enjoying the hilarity of Nathan and his collegiate, younger brother, Stephen, also the camp lifeguard. They played off each other during the folk dances, the line games, the balloon stomp, and other vigorous absurdities. The brothers, used to fulsome sharing things of a personal nature, were cleaning up the rec hall, after the others left for bed.

"The kids really enjoyed you, tonight, Nathan—and so did I. Do you think I'll ever be able to lead discussions like you?"

"Sure, Stephen, when you grow a chin, and lose some hair," came the affectionate response.

"No, really, my group and I were very excited with your discussion of "The Night of the Iguana." How in the world do you find so much theology in things?"

"Which questions did you like, Stephen?"

"The best ones dealt with how Hannah, the caricaturist, saw love, including extraneous sex, as redemptive, when we open our protecting, excluding gates and actually reach out and touch others where they really live, desperation and all."

"I've always loved that part, too, Stephen. What about the sex, though?"

"That's harder for me. There was an abundance of sin in the play's characters, I think, especially in Shannon, who should have known better. He had the poorest excuse for falling apart, as he did, trying 'to take the long swim to China.' How does a grown man allow himself to be seduced by a seventeen-year-old girl, anyway–a preacher, at that?"

"Don't knock it till you understand it, son. Do you think the Reverend Dr. T. Lawrence Shannon is going to hell, because he allowed himself to be finagled into sex by an adoring, all-too-willing, seventeen-year-old Charlotte–or due to his dalliances with the Widow Maxine, and God knows how many others?"

"That's hard. You see him loved–and maybe even a little bit loving–his gates crumbling, consorting with various women, but what was his excuse for seventeen-year-old Charlotte?"

"There are no excuses for lust, Scott-head, only reasons."

"Well, hell, Nathan, I have my reasons, too. Think back twenty minutes ago, when all those cute girls from your church were swishing their bodies all over the place. Didn't you see some reasons for lust? But does that make it right?"

"It only makes it understandable."

"Nathan, I lust all the time–have to fight it like mad. Even when I was sorta engaged to Carol, I was always looking around, and to tell the truth, I had a few grub sessions with a girl I didn't even date! Don't you think that was wrong?"

"All this from the lad who told me in great angst, once, `Nathan, I'm sixteen years old, and have never even felt a tit!' I take it you have crossed that Rubicon, by now."

Grinning, the twenty-year-old Eagle Scout and boy wonder at everything he tried revealed his progress in learning the mysteries of the female form, first with one hand, and then the other. Nathan loved him, wrote Mother that Stephen was "the pick of the litter," and expected great things from him. They were close.

"Seriously, Nathan, what do you do with your inappropriate lusts?"

"Scott-head, lust is never inappropriate, just inopportune.'"

"Meaning?"

"Simply that lust is as natural as hunger, and as easily satisfied–for the time being."

"Lust is just an appetite, then, to be satisfied at the first fast-fuck place available?"

"If that's the way you want to live, and another fast fucker is willing, so you don't have to break or con your way in. Personally, I like my lust layered with love, Agape, most of the time. But, now and again, everybody craves a hamburger, or even some Kentucky Fried pussy."

"Jesus said that as a man thinks in his heart, so is he. He also said that if we look with lust upon a woman, we have already committed adultery in our hearts. How does your liberal theology handle that, Nathan?"

"With some difficulty, Stephen. Put in context, those words were part of Jesus' Sermon on the Mount, emphasizing the universality of sin and the necessity of God's forgiveness. Nobody obeys God's law–all have sinned and fallen short. Inopportune lust may be one of those emphases. Consider, also, Stephen, we are taught that Jesus, the Messiah, was both fully God and fully man–like unto a man in all things. If so, he woke up with erections, had wet dreams, and his body lusted just as most humans' do. Yet, we're taught he was also fully God, ultimate and absolute in every way."

"Erections and wet dreams…?"

"Frankly, Stephen, I think it was the Apostle Paul and his followers, believing in a ridiculous, three-storied universe, who created today's misplaced negativity towards things fleshly. They dichotomized, claiming that flesh and soul are two separate entities, and the flesh, which is the only thing you can put your finger on, so to speak, gets the short end of the stick. Millions of years of evolution preceded both the Old and New Testaments, and millions of years of fucking is one hell of a head start, genetically, over the proposition that flesh and fucking, in themselves, are evil, or at least not as good as spirit and not fucking."

"You're not saying that it's all right to fuck anybody you want to, are you Nathan?"

"No–it takes two to tango, brother mine."

"Are you saying it's all right if both partners agree?"

"Stephen, I'm just trying to stretch–and yawn a bit, too–at the unholy emphasis the church places on the physical aspects of creation. We get so dad-burned concerned about a little harmless sex, making a big issue over a little tissue, that we can't see the dire, human needs that T. Lawrence Shannon emphasized in the play, when he purposefully drove his bus full of sight-seeing Texas school teachers on a tour of entirely other sights, so they would see that there are humans all around us who are literally and figuratively picking the edible pieces of food out of the shit-piles we rich and fat folks leave lying around, after we have gorged ourselves. Let's be concerned about that and not worry so much about what happens to six inches of turgid flesh, or to those wonderful, God-given havens in which we invest them, now and then."

"Nathan, you have just implied, in less than two minutes, that you don't completely believe the Bible, that bodies and souls are inseparable, that adultery should be okay, if both partners are willing, that Jesus had hard-ons and probably lusted, that monogamous sexuality misses the point, and that maybe Jesus wasn't the Messiah. If you believe all that, why are you in the ministry?"

"Good question—you should address it before you take your vows. I'm in the ministry because I believe that if Jesus is who people—and Jesus himself—say he is, then I have no choice but to serve and teach him. I want to believe that, to faith it, but as time goes on, I find I hope it most of all. There exists no minister, priest, or other cleric who has not had many of my doubts, harboring them just beneath the surface. Christians place far too much stock in the notion that the flesh is weak, even evil, when it is one of the strongest characteristics of humanity. Erroneously, skin and sin have been positively correlated for five thousand years, when skin is actually what keeps the species going. I think we need to question that correlation."

"Go on, Nathan; I'm listening."

"I am in the ministry, Stephen, because it is a good place to serve people—certainly not the only place—but a good one. I care to live out what you've heard me call 'The Great Realization': that the best-lived life is one lived for others. I don't fear hell; I doubt it exists, nor is the promised reward of heaven the inducement it once was.

"What I really fear, and tremble about constantly is that I will see needs I can fill, and not fill them—because I am lazy, or uncaring, or just a plain, selfish son of a bitch. Forget the reward; being on the point of the arrow of the truth of millions of years of evolution is reward enough—I am alive and aware, and I am afraid I won't be worthy of my existence. It's a hell of a sin to be thinking, caring, loving humans, with the excellence of both God and evolution alive in them, and to throw it away mostly on themselves."

"Wait, Nathan, you're confusing me. Answer just one question with a yes or a no. Is sin real?"

"Yes. We miss the mark of being excellent humans all the time, and we ignore the Great Realization."

"What are the wages of sin?"

"Not death. We die whether we sin or not. The wages of sin are ignorance, meaninglessness, and man's inhumanity to himself and to his fellows. Misery: un-remitted misery, caused by the barriers we build to keep others out, that's the real pay-off for sin. The thoroughly sinful man is the useless, uncaring, uninvolved man, lost in selfishness, which is another word for loneliness, so deep, he is his own crowd, his own *raison d'etre*, and his own hell."

"Okay, is sex sinful?"

"As Miss Hannah Jelkes, spinster caricaturist in "Night of the Iguana," said to the calmed down Reverend Doctor T. Lawrence Shannon, after she fed him poppy seed tea, suffering with him his painless atonement—trussed up in a hammock, over the rain forest and the still water beach, `Nothing human disgusts me, unless it's unkind, violent.' Sex surely doesn't disgust me—nor should it disgust the God who figured it out—the God who created lust to make sure we could `be fruitful and multiply, establish the earth and subdue it.'"

"You're on a roll; Nathan, but whether it's leavened with truth remains to be seen."

145

"Steven, if eating the fruit of Eden's Tree of the Knowledge of Good and Evil convinced Adam and Eve that their sexuality was somehow shameful, in and of itself, making them suddenly aware of their nakedness before each other and before the very God who created their precious parts, then that fruit was as bad and as rotten–and just plain wrong–as the reputation that sex and other fleshly sins have gotten from the pulpits and the bully-pulpits of the world, ever since."

"Does Lenore know you think this way, Nathan?"

"Stevie-boy, you just quit preaching, and done gone and went to meddlin,' as they say. But, to answer your question, the distance between the proposition and the deed, between the aspiration to perfection and perfection itself, is vast. That is why we need each other and why we need God– to make it all right to fail–to forgive ourselves and to be forgiven. I'm certain Lenore knows I think this way, but she and God love me, anyway–and just maybe that's the point!"

"As usual, talking to you is like talking to a mirror with cracks in it, Nathan. I see myself in places, in pieces in your words, but not clearly, and certainly not all together."

"I guess I should be glad, Stephen, because you wouldn't be able to see any of yourself in my words, if you didn't see a bit of me, as well."

"Yeah! That's part of what you have been saying–and the movie, too, huh?"

"Bingo!"

The brothers Scott continued their loving conversation apace, until a breathless, pajama-clad sophomore ran in, calling, "Mr. Scott, come quick! There's a snake in the girls' bathroom!"

"Calm down, Ruth. It's probably just a rat snake."

"Stephen, can you finish up, here? I'm gonna go see if this is the serpent about which we've been talking. We'll talk later, okay?"

"Sure, Scott-head, I'll clean up. Be careful!"

Nathan caught a six-foot black racer and brought it out of the girls' bathroom coiled around his arms, while he firmly held its head. That occasioned the curious to turn aside and see this great sight. Shooing them all back to their cabins, Nathan took the harmless black snake back toward the rec hall, showed it to his brother, and returned it to the woods. The brothers finished cleaning the rec hall about midnight, and both retired to their beds in their little duplex. Shara couldn't get away, but he slept in his clothes, anyway.

*

Sunday night the juniors planned a party at eight. Nathan was so tired he could hardly function. He dared not stay away; this was the last night of his last retreat with this beloved crew. He asked Kathy to come and get him at nine, after things got rolling. Stephen, already Nathan's equal in recreational matters, stood in for him and was a marvelous success. Nathan slept like a dead man.

Good as her word, Kathy came to wake him at nine, but sat down on his bed to talk. She was worried.

"Preacher, have you heard the expression, 'parson's privilege?'"

"No, I haven't, and I'm afraid to ask."

"It's what Ruth Grace called Shara and me, and especially Shara, because she–we–get more of your attention than the others."

"Help stop that foolishness, will you, Kathy? It's unfair, for one, even though somewhat true, simply because you two and Jason do most of the work with me."

"It hurts my feelings. Don't they realize that if it hadn't been for the million times we worked on things with you, when nobody else was willing, this youth group wouldn't be half what it is today?"

"Do many feel that way, Kathy?"

"Shara sorta warned me about it, that some girls were envious of that 'privilege,' that's all."

"Frankly, Kathy, it gripes my royal fanny. One would think we were all shacking up–as enticing as that may be," he laughed, as he jumped up and tickled her.

Squealing, she easily eluded him, and began to giggle. Suddenly, she wilted, plopped back on the bed, put her head in her hands and sobbed. Nathan thought she was fooling, at first, and moved to tickle her, again. Then he saw real tears.

"Katy-did, not you, too! What's the matter? Did I hurt you? What's wrong?"

"You're what's wrong, dummy–and what's right, at the same time," she sobbed. "It's just that I have totally repressed the fact that you're leaving, and then, while we were horsing around, I realized how much I love you and will miss you. What are we going to do without you, Nathan? You've been like a father, a brother, a counselor, a friend–by damn, the only thing you haven't been is a lover!"

Sitting down beside her, putting his arm around her, he slyly nuzzled her neck with his nose, whispering, "K-ration, I've been meaning to tell you for a long time, now. The only reason I haven't come on to you is because–because–I'm gay." Then he pecked her cheek and ran out, knowing she would come howling after him.

"Nathan Scott, you poor excuse for a preacher. Don't you dare run away, leaving me all teary eyed, when I'm trying to tell you I love you–and always will. Wait up, you bum!"

Nathan waited, warmed, and saddened by her little display of genuine affection. When she caught up with him, he swept her in his arms in a bear hug.

"Kathy Rogers, God has not made anyone finer than you. You, more than anyone else in the whole church, including Shara and Jason, have helped me the most. It will be terribly hard to leave you–and I love you, too. This parson has

been singularly privileged to have worked with you, watched
you grow, and seen you develop all those fine qualities which
will make you the success I know you will be in anything and
everything you ever do. I am your friend, forever!"

With that he gave her another peck on the cheek and
said, "Let's go have some fun, Senior Scott woman!"

Smiling and wiping her tears, she trotted with him to
the rec hall.

*

The party was over at eleven, and everyone trooped
to the empty, main dining hall for the final, candlelight service.
The dining hall was dark and empty of everything except one
table, on which stood a single, burning candle and an opened
Bible before it. As the retreaters filed into the dining hall, each
was given a small, flat board with a candle stuck on it and asked
to remain silent until after the service.

When all were standing in a large circle around the
walls, Nathan stepped forward, lit his candle from the central
flame, and spoke.

In the beginning was the Word, and the Word was with God,
and the Word was God. He was in the beginning with God; all things
were made through him, and without him was not anything made that
was made. In him was life, and the life was the light of men. The light
shines in the darkness, and the darkness has not overcome it.

"Dear Ones, this candle represents Jesus Christ, the
light of the world, who cannot be extinguished by the forces
of evil, though they battle against him constantly, desperately
trying to keep us in the dark. By lighting my candle from this
symbol of his light, I signify my willingness to see and be
guided by that light. I have accepted him, his light, and his
influence on my life, forever.

"Yet, his light was not given to me for my own use,
only, but to be a light to all peoples, everywhere. Thus, I offer
this light to my brother, Stephen, saying the words of all who

love one another. 'Stephen, Jesus is the light of the world. Use it to light your path and share his light with others.'"

Nathan lit Stephen's candle, and Stephen turned to the person next to him, repeated the simple phrase, as he lit that person's candle, and so on, slowly, around the growing circle of increasing light. As each person's candle flamed, Nathan looked long into that dimly lit face, praying, *"God keep you."*

Looking about the room, he felt tears of the scandal of faith fill his eyes. These were his babies—and his friends, and though he was leaving them, he was certain God was not. Aware that many were watching him, he saw their tears, and realized *I will never again be so loved by any group of people. Lord, I believe; help thou, my unbelief!*

The room was ablaze with more than one hundred candles of faith, their lights reflected in the faces and tears of those whose hearts were open to the symbols and their realities. Moving to the center of the circle, Nathan spoke again.

"We have shared the light of Christ with our friends and behold how we glow with his—and our own—love, light, and warmth. But it is not enough. Jesus said, 'You are the light of the world. Let your light so shine before men, that they may see your good works and give glory to your Father who is in heaven.' There are others, yet, in darkness, beyond these secure and privileged walls—in the darkness of poverty, ignorance, disease, bigotry, hatred, selfishness, greed, and death.

"As Christians, we must strive to use the light God gives us to light the paths of others. Let us take our God-given lights and move into the world beyond, lighting the first unlit candle we come to, and standing by it, lest it go out from neglect. Then, as you see me place my floating candle on the river, come down, also, and place your light upon the waters, symbolizing your willingness to send Christ's light anywhere in the world where there is darkness. We shall sing a hymn and pray together, then go quietly to our cabins, maintaining silence until you hear the camp bell ring. Then, let joy be unconfined. Follow me."

Outside, Nathan came to the first of a long, curving line of candles on the path from the dining hall to the river, knelt, lit it with his candle, and stepped behind it, others following suit. The night was still, with a half-moon overhead, as he watched the procession of twin lights make its way down to the waterfront. Shara and Kathy passed him, their eyes aglow, and he loved them so much he trembled. Shara's focus embraced him with such fervor, he felt weightless, soaring under the empyreal sky, yet eternally grounded in their love.

At the waterfront, Mr. Ware raised a candle, after the last light on the path was lit. Nathan walked down the path of lights and faces with his lit candle. Stephen, and then the others, peeled off behind him, until all had reached the river, bunched together in a little sea of light, reflected in the dark, moving waters. Nathan stood on the boat deck, faced his little congregation of awed hearts, and began to sing a familiar hymn in his strong baritone, others joining in:

> Come, labor on.
> No time for rest,
> till glows the western sky,
> Till the long shadows
> o'er our pathway lie,
> And a glad sound comes with the setting sun,
> 'Well done, well done!'

"Our God, look now upon these, your precious lights–these men and women of the present and the future– and love them into faith, that they may seek your will and your light, even in the darkest moments of their lives. Where they may stumble, lift them up; where they may love pride and selfishness, show them the needs of others; where there is hatred, greed, sloth, anger, envy, jealousy, or despair, cast them out with your light.

"The Lord bless you and keep you: The Lord make His face to shine upon you and be gracious unto you: The Lord lift up His countenance upon you and give you peace; through Jesus Christ our Lord. Amen."

Kneeling, Nathan placed his candled plank on the water, gave it a gentle shove, and watched it begin to float out onto the dark, living river. Stephen followed suit and then walked back up the path of still lit candles. Slowly, each knee was bowed, and God was remembered, at least for that moment, as the floating, lighted candles inched out onto the deep. Each heart took whatever meaning there was in the time, the place, and the people back up the hill, to their cabins—and far beyond.

After helping Mr. Dare's crew retrieve the candles, Nathan began his last, official walk up his beloved hill, following those whom he had led—behind him, now…

Fifteen minutes after the last soul left the path, Nathan slowly rang the camp bell twelve times. After its echoes found places in the hearts of those who heard it, a great silence continued for a full minute, then, slowly, the chatter began, followed by the laughter of hearts too young to hold solemnity too close—or too long.

Much later, Nathan undressed his pining young lover with reverence. Spending time simply holding, he finally lowered himself between her gifting thighs, and as he accepted her invitation, he prayed softly. "Great God, I do not understand many things, and am too proud and ignorant to wait until I can learn before I act. But this I know: this flesh—this Thou—under me and surrounding me is surely your gift to me in my time of greatest need. I offer my thanks to you for the pure love–Agape and Eros–that indwells her–my Shara. I love her; I cherish loving her this way; I love her loving me back, as we were meant to do, evidently from the foundations of your creation.

"We have both been closer to you than usual tonight, God. Feeling you in what we are doing, we offer thanks. We do earnestly beg your help in avoiding the hurts of our past mistakes, especially mine, in seeking to be married too soon, when it had to be your will that we be mates. Now we are faced with the potential agony of causing great pain to others so dear to us that we would rather die than cause them grief. If it be thy will, spare us and those we love, somehow, that we do not fulfill our joy at their expense.

"Accept this wondrous act of love as a thanksgiving offering for bringing us together. Shara is my sanctuary, wherein I can see you–and myself–more clearly, perhaps for the first time. God bless our love, in all its dimensions. Bring us to our time together, soon, and grant it be forever. We pray in your name, Amen."

Weeping as she thrust her open hips into his, Shara whispered, "Nathan, that was beautiful. Do you think He heard us?"

"I know He did, Shara: He had to, for all of our sakes. I love you, baby; I love you; I love you; I love praying in you–now!"

CHAPTER 20
SANCTUARY, II.

Oh beauty, are you not enough? Why am I crying after love?

Sara Teasdale

The world is a friendly place in which to live because a friendly God reigns supreme!

Nathan Rhea Scott
September 2, 1964

Lenore complimented Nathan's "Finale," preached at both Sunday morning services in the First Protestant Church of Durham on September 6, 1964. Perhaps the afflicted who were comforted outnumbered the comfortable who were afflicted. Resisting the temptation to offer gratuitous prescriptions, his sermon featured a loving assessment of the role of the Church, and the role of First Church, in particular. He reminded his influential, well-to-do congregation that their church existed, primarily, for those outside its doors…

Labor Day morning dawned helter-skelter. The kids were in a dither; the telephone rang constantly; Melanie arrived and braved a furtive kiss; Lenore was already tired; and Stephen wouldn't get out of the bathroom. Nathan helped as much as he dared, then high-tailed it to his office.

Jason Hart, the one First Church youth Nathan hoped would become an ordained minister, helped Nathan through one of the most hectic days of his life, packing, while Nathan visited shut-ins who wanted to see him ere he left. He ate lunch with the dependable Dares, prepared tonight's final, senior high party, visited members in two hospitals, and managed to see Shara for an hour in the afternoon.

Parked in a well-shaded, protected wood, they put the back seat down, spread his cushions, and stroked the time and their love with almost desperate passion.

"God, I love you, Shara! You are so guileless in sex that you would be a virgin were you to fuck hundreds of guys next month. You make it that normal, that natural, and that intensely righteous. My only worry is that the truth of it will surpass me, and that you will just as naturally and righteously be the same person with others, in my absence."

"I don't want to be with anybody but you, Nathan."

"That I know. Our relationship is all consuming now, for I am here, both to feel and feed it. Having recently discovered the righteous purposes of your anatomy, you are a seventeen-year-old high school senior who should be free to date and discover the warp and woof of peer relationships. You haven't been with some fumbling, pimpled-faced boy in the back seat of a car, nervously and too quickly getting his rocks off. I have loved you with all the honesty and truth I possess, and you are an incredibly quick and accomplished study."

"Are you saying you don't think I can be faithful to you—that I'll be driven by my—my sexuality to find someone else to fu—fuck?"

"I expect you to want to be faithful to me, and there is no denying that for you to be otherwise would worry me, but not because of the sex itself. I worry because I will not be here—there—to nourish you in such circumstances, sexually or otherwise, or in the many other ways that letters and occasional phone calls won't be enough. Yet, I don't expect you to stop growing, experiencing, seeking, and discovering more about yourself and the world around you."

"Do you think I'll want to do it with others, if you're not available?"

"Probably, in the normal course of things."

"I hear what you are saying, Nathan, but I'm not sure I like what you mean. If we can't get through the next months, maybe years, seeing each other as often as possible, without my having sex with another, won't it mean our love is insufficient?"

"Perhaps, but not necessarily. It could mean nothing more than accommodation. However, Shara, I would be the biggest kind of fool were I to ignore the possibility, and the worst kind of hypocrite, were I to deny you the opportunity to grow–and do–with others what we do."

"Please explain that; it's a little threatening…"

"It's not meant to be. In a deeply loving relationship, which I always assumed was exclusive and permanent, born of love and lust with Lenore, I looked elsewhere *(Not the time to tell her about Melanie, yet!)*. I needed and found a person for whom I feel an equal or greater love, an equal or greater lust, and, with whom I deeply desire and hope to spend a mated life, 'till death do us part.'"

"I'm still a bit confused, Nathan. I just heard you say you want and hope to marry me. Shriek! But I heard this incredibly welcome hope just after you told me it would be natural and acceptable–maybe not desirable, but acceptable–for me to make love–to fuck somebody else. Maybe I almost understand what you mean. I'll promise you this: in the unlikely event that I find someone else I need, want, love, or lust for, as much or more than I do you, I'll tell you and give you a chance to do something about it, beforehand, okay?

*

156

Having no time for supper, Nathan called Lenore about 6:30 and found things going well. Melanie was still there, and most of the items not to be packed by the movers were boxed and ready. After he drove Jason home, so he could shower and change for the party, Nathan used the shower in the bridal room. He flopped on the couch in his office for five minutes–which became an hour and a half of near coma. Jason wakened him twenty minutes before the teens were to arrive for their final Nathan party.

"Jason, I'll never make it."

"Sure, you will. I'll get some more kids to stay as late as they can, to help. It'll take about two hours to get all your stuff packed. I brought some more boxes. Also, before we go down to the party, I brought you a little parting gift."

Jason's appreciative gift was a heartfelt card and a 45-rpm record of the music from the Viking movie, "The Long Ships."

"Thank you, Jason. As usual, you come through for me. What would I do without you, man?"

"Promise that Kathy and Shara and I can come see you in Wilmington sometime this school year? You can pay me back by introducing me to some of the foxes that you're sure to attract to your senior high fellowship."

"You guys are welcome anytime, Jason. You can preach your first sermon to my new guys."

"Let me get through school, first, Nathan."

"Done."

At the party, Nathan rarely sat down; most every girl wanted a last dance with him, and most every boy wanted a moment in which to thank him. His emotions spiking, it was finally Shara's turn. She picked a moderately fast song, so they wouldn't be tempted to hold too tightly. He held her rather closely, anyway, for the last two minutes, grinning, to deflect his misery. *Again, and again, I ask myself, what the hell am I doing leaving this lively, loving creature?*

"Nathan, isn't there any way we can be alone, even for five minutes? I must kiss you goodbye, or I'll die. It's so hard to believe I'll start my senior year tomorrow, and by noon, you'll be gone."

"I'll find a way for us to be alone," he whispered as the music stopped, and it was time for refreshments.

Kathy made a big deal about the kids' going-away gift of a new briefcase and cards signed by everyone. Grinning broadly, he was too shocked to cry...

An hour later, after an abundance of hugs, tears, photographs, and pained fare-thee-wells, most of the teens were gone. As the rest were cleaning up, Nathan put his finger to his lips and led Shara to the main hallway.

"Where are we going?"

"To the sanctuary—for our last prayer together for a long time. I told Kathy and Jason."

"Okay, Nathan, but someone will be coming in to get me, so we can't linger the way I'd like to."

Silently, the couple entered the front of the dark sanctuary, walked up the three chancel stairs, and knelt together on the *prie-dieu*. Nathan's arm stole around her waist, and pulled her close to him, as he prayed in a low, hushed, voice.

"Dear God, you already know how we love each other, and how much we want to be and grow with each other. Help us to be patient, keeping our love alive and strong, while we are apart. Guide my service to you in Wilmington, and guide Shara to be the best student and person she can be. Give us strength to overcome the miles, and gentle Shara's family, so greater love will abound. Through Jesus Christ, our Lord, we pray. Amen."

"Do you want to pray, too, Shara?"

"I prayed your prayer with you," she whispered. "I just want you to kiss me."

Turning to each other, the distraught couple kissed and clung, focused and incautious in the dark of their desperation. Shara placed his hands under her bra, while he kissed her lips, her eyes, her neck, and her ears.

"*Shara?!*" boomed the resonant, southern voice of Big J. Carl Starr, from the door at the front of the sanctuary, twenty-five feet away. Sheer panic electrified the still unseen couple, who turned and saw her father's long shadow lost in the front pews, as he repeated his call.

"Shara, are you in there? You'd better answer me!"

Frightened beyond description, Shara stood and began furiously straightening her hair and buttoning her blouse. Nathan stood, too, immediately feeling protective–and caught. As they doomed to the door which silhouetted the forty-four-year-old, 6' 2", 240-pound frame of her angry father, Nathan led the way, Shara, a step behind, trembling.

Big J. Carl stood immobile, his face hidden in shadow, but his stance was staunch and in obvious disdain at what he had discovered. Hands on hips, feet wide apart, glaring, he gave Nathan the sense of a man looking for a fight.

"We're right here, Carl," he began, speaking boldly and stopping in front of the man, looking up into what he could see of his shadowy face, while Shara stood to his left, looking frightened–and guilty. "Shara asked me to pray with her one last time, so I suggested the privacy of the sanctuary," Nathan said, simply. "We were just finishing our prayer at the *prie-dieu* when you called. I hope that's not a problem, no matter how it may look."

"Well, I was looking all over for you, young lady. Kathy said you might be up here. I don't like your being alone in this dark place with a married man, minister or no minister! Get over here to me, and I mean right now!"

Shara, as terrified as she looked, somewhat disheveled, with wrinkled blouse, and tousled hair, almost jumped past Nathan to her father's side, looking back at Nathan, pleading...

"Get your stuff and get in the car; I don't want to stand around here all night. And as for you, Mr. Scott, you, you ...I'll take care of you later!"

Feeling vulnerable, but confident, Nathan continued looking full into the face of the larger man, "Carl, please understand that we came in here to *pray*. If there is a problem, it is my responsibility, not Shara's, okay?"

Big J. Carl glared at Nathan, then avoided his direct gaze and growled, "There is a problem, and you are it! You're too liberal and a bad influence on Shara and other children. You're being here, alone, sneaking around with my daughter in the dark proves it."

"Carl, I can see how you might misconstrue our being in the sanctuary, but please consider that it is a place for prayer. I hope you can see past the specifics and look at the bigger picture. There was nothing wrong with two minutes of prayer. As you know, we told Kathy where we were going and why. Does that sound like sneaking around?"

"We'll see about that. It's time for her to go, in any case. School starts tomorrow, and it's past 11:00 o'clock! She should be in bed! Not alone with you!"

Feeling the hair on the back of his neck standing on end, Nathan rejoined, as calmly as he could, "Certainly, Carl. I'm sorry if I've upset you. I assure you our intentions and actions were innocent and prayerful. When you think about it more calmly, I'm sure you'll understand. Good night to you both. Shara don't forget what I told you about studying and doing your best in school. I'll drop you and Kathy a line, soon, to let you know how things are going. Take care of yourself;

consider yourself hugged, and tell Jimmy, your sibs, and your Mom I said hello–and goodbye."

Staring at Nathan malevolently, Big J. Carl Starr grabbed Shara by her arm, pulled her ahead of him, and began herding her down the hall. She looked back, and in a voice both piteous and determined, said, "Okay, Nathan. Thanks for praying with me. Goodnight–and goodbye…"

Nothing more from big J. Carl but his heavy footsteps, as he and his daughter disappeared down the hall and around the corner. As he stared blankly after them, Nathan heard her father's angry voice: "Just wait until I get you in the car, Shara Day Starr!"

Alarmed the more, Nathan trotted after Shara and her father, intending to intervene, when he heard the outside door of the church slam, and from behind him, Kathy calling, "Nathan? Did Mr. Starr find Shara? I told him she was in the sanctuary with you."

"Yes. We were kneeling at the *prie-dieu*, praying, when he came to the sanctuary door looking for her. He was pretty upset with us both. I heard him fussing at her when they left the building, so I'm trying to catch them, to make certain he doesn't blame her for our going in there."

"Uh-oh! Go ahead, Nathan. I'll tell you goodbye when you come back."

The Starr sedan was leaving the curb when Nathan got outside. He thought he saw Shara smile and prayed everything was okay. Back inside, he asked Kathy to check on Shara, if she had the chance. "I expect to see your shining face in Wilmington before Christmas."

"I promise. I love you, Nathan Scott, and I'll miss you like mad!"

"That goes double, for me, Kathy. You are absolutely wonderful! And my new briefcase is exactly what I needed. I know you engineered the cards and the whole thing!"

*

All were gone from the huge church by midnight, except for Nathan and Jason, his loyal, yearning, young friend. With the music from The Long Ships blaring, evoking a mixture of sadness, adventure, and longing in both, the two seekers after God threw things in boxes and dumped others. In good spirits, feeling the importance of his task, Jason enjoyed being a needed friend, indeed.

"Hey, Nathan!" he called from the outer office, "what shall I do with all these old Sunday school lessons?"

"Take them if you want them; otherwise stack them in the library and let my replacement decide."

"They'll never replace you, Nathánski; they won't be able to find anyone as ugly!"

"Oh, true, you laudable cockroach! Go ahead and cast asparagus on me."

Their offhand koinonia did not quite mend the fraying mantle of misery settling on Nathan like a shroud. Continuing to echo in his inner ear was the voice of doom, cruelly issuing from the towering man silhouetted in the doorway of the sanctuary, enrolling his next victim: *"Shara?!"*

The more he tried to reassure himself, the more worried about Shara he became. *Big J. Carl is capable of many indignities, so I have no reason to believe he will forgo this opportunity to think the worst about the innocent (well, relatively) couple, kneeling in the sanctuary.*

Nathan's QI further stole him away from his camaraderie with Jason, trying to focus on the possibilities:

Shara is in deep shit with her father, which means we both are. If so, she will be hurt, quite upset—and needy. She either will or won't crack. I don't believe she will, she's made of sturdy stuff. If he believes the worst, Carl either will or won't react further. What did he discover? Two people, alone, in a darkened sanctuary—one his seventeen-year-old daughter; the other an older, married, too liberal minister who couldn't be gone soon enough. Sigh!

Maybe the fact of my departure will be enough, and he will not obsess. Shara looked a bit disheveled, but she had been to a dance/party involving considerable physical activity. If things get too bad, I'll call Carl in the morning, too. For sure, I'll inform Dr. Jennings–Lenore, too– confessing to most of the truth–naive thoughtlessness.

It's likely that Carl has worried about me for a long time, due to the obvious, deep communication level between Shara and me. Perhaps he fears that Shara told me about his sexual caresses. I don't believe he'll do anything to or about me, now that I'm leaving, despite his threat. His treatment of Shara, however, is another matter–and a huge concern! Yes, it was sorta foolish to take Shara into a dark sanctuary. Maybe I deserve some comeuppance, but Shara does not. Thus, no matter the circumstances, I must protect her, which means I must protect myself as well.

"Nathan!"

"What? Oh, Jason. Sorry, man, I was lost in the spheres. What were you saying?"

"I was talking to you for three minutes, until I realized your uh-huhs were just pad- fill. Then, I asked if I should put your Bibles in the toilet, and you said 'uh-huh' again."

"Put them in the box with my commentaries and lexicons, please, and don't think too badly of your desperately tired and unhappy preacher. I'm having a hard time with this sorry business of leaving."

"You're having a hard time? What about those of us who rely on your smiling face? I think Shara, Kathy and I will miss you most of all. You've always been there for us, no matter what."

"And thank you for always being here for me, too, Jason. I really love you, man, and I hope you'll continue to give thought to the ministry; you'll make a superfine one."

"Thanks, Nathan. If I can find a woman who'll put up with me. Think I have a chance with Anna?"

"Sointainly. With women, Jason, everything is chancy, so you always have a chance. It's the nature of the breast—er, beast."

"I notice you did pretty well. Lenore is a rare beauty. How in the world did you ever manage to find—and keep her, Nathan?"

Looking at Jason, who was watching him intently, Nathan raised both pointer fingers up, chest high, holding them about twelve inches apart, and grinned...

"Nathan, sometimes, you are so full of it!"

"So, be a commodian and flush. If I don't get out of here, Lenore will put barbed wire around our bed."

"We're almost through, aren't we?"

"Yes, thank God. The truck can get these boxes in the morning, so I don't have to take anything in the car but my beautiful new briefcase."

"We knew you'd like it. I helped Kathy pick it out."

At 2:00 a.m.., Nathan parked near Jason's home. Walking to the door with him, Nathan thanked his admirable young friend profusely, feeling guilt about what Jason may think of him in the years to come...

"Jason?"

"Nathan?"

Nathan opened his arms; Jason returned his strong embrace, unable to speak, then hurried inside.

Finally, home, Nathan entered the shambles of his house and fell into bed with his exhausted wife. Lenore snuggled and mumbled, "Are you finished, honey?"

Damn! She would put it that way...

CHAPTER 21
OF SHAME AND SHAM

There is no man so good that if he placed all his actions and thoughts under the scrutiny of the laws, he would not deserve hanging ten times in his life.

Michel Eyquem de Montaigne

"Nathan! Wake up! Shara's on the phone, and she's hysterical. Besides, the truck will be here in a half hour, and they'll need to dismantle the bed."

"Lordy, 'Nore, why did you let me sleep so late?"

Nathan struggled into wakefulness, despite the adrenaline charging his system. Taking the call in the kitchen, Shara was crying and trying to talk.

"Ohh, Nathan, it was terrible! Daddy ranted and raved all night, and again this morning. He swears we were in the sanctuary making out and all, and he's threatening to 'haul that son of a bitch before the board, and get his ass thrown out of the church,' or something like that. I'm so scared! What are we going do?"

I suspected he would overreact, but this could be serious. Keep it cool, Scott!

"Where are you, Shara?"

"I'm at school, at a pay phone, and my second period class is about to start. I had to warn you—I've been trying to call you since Mom dropped me off, but your line has been busy."

"Lenore was letting me sleep. Forget your class and start from the beginning. Start with what he said in the car."

"I don't know if I can remember everything. He grilled me until 2:00 a.m."

Calmy, calmy, Scott! She's frightened enough for both of us. We should be able to handle this, please God!

"It's going to be okay, Shara. Do the best you can."

Haltingly, Shara related the horror of her night and morning, starting with her father's initial tirade in the car, at home, late, and through breakfast. The sum of it, after all the noise, was simple. Big J. Carl was appalled that his daughter was alone in the sanctuary with Nathan, then emerged "looking like you had been doing it on the altar." He was so incensed he threatened to take her to a doctor, to see if she was still a virgin.

Other than that, he has no evidence of anything amiss.

"Did he mention anything about my counseling you?"

"Sort of. He said he didn't think you were trustworthy enough to be working with kids like me. But I think he was referring to my being with you so much."

Maybe he's worried that I know about his abuse of Shara.

Shara had steadfastly and indignantly proclaimed their innocence, throughout, and her mother tried to intervene in her behalf, saying that they ought to believe their own daughter. Carl ordered Donna to stay out of it, which started an argument between the parents.

Having begun his rant, Carl refused to back off, despite his lack of data. He belittled the notion of their praying in the sanctuary, which brought a smart aleck response from Donna, "You ought to try it some time." That didn't help any.

At breakfast, Shara's angry, persistent father resumed his indignation, fuming and threatening, until she left for school in tears.

That sorry rascal had no business treating Shara that way, when I am the person he should be talking to. Shara just followed my lead. Ultimately, it's Shara's word against his suspicions. That's far too much of a load for any daughter! I think I know what to do. First, I need to reassure Shara.

"Shara, please believe it's going to be all right. I'm thinking of a plan that will cool everything off. Trust me, for now, okay?"

As her sobbing and dismay abated, Nathan explained his plan. That did the trick, so after a few more empathetic words and assurances, they hung up.

"What in the world . . .?" asked Lenore, mirroring Stephen's facial inquiry.

"It ain't over yet, folks. Let me get dressed, and I'll tell you. Meanwhile no one use the phone, please. I'm expecting a call from Kathy. Don't worry; no one died. There's been a silly misunderstanding, and J. Carl Starr is on a rampage, with yours truly his target."

"Don't you dare stop there, mister. If I'm going to be a widow, I want to know why."

To both his worried wife and Stephen, "I did an innocent but, stupid, thing, last night, at the end of the party. Shara was upset and asked me if we could go somewhere to pray. The most public, private place I could think of was the sanctuary; so, after telling Kathy and Jason where we were going, that's where we went.

"We had been at the *prie-dieu* a couple of minutes when Big J. Carl stood in the door, calling for Shara. Immediately, I realized how thoughtless I'd been. As we came out, he looked and sounded angry, so I told him what we were about. He immediately began to berate Shara and me, so I reiterated. He yelled about it, said he'd take care of me later, ordered Shara to get in the car, and stomped off. I knew he was angry but hoped my explanation would be enough. Not so! I heard him fussing at her as they left the building.

"In the car and into the wee hours, he lit into her with all manner of accusations, venting his spleen about this liberal preacher, threatening to tell the board and get me defrocked—which is all a bunch of bull. We weren't hiding anything. I'm certain I can straighten it all out if I can talk to him face to face. Now, let me shower."

Nathan caught Lenore's surprised and worried expression and knew he'd have considerable explaining to do, later. Though she lay low, her look revealed much more than curiosity. Nathan gently refused Stephen's unhelpful offer to unpack Nathan's .22 rifle in case Carl Starr got physical, then got in the shower. The phone rang, and he answered it dripping wet. It was Kathy.

Shara was better, but Kathy warned him that J. Carl could be mean when riled. Nathan asked her to stay with Shara until she was picked up, got her ready approval of his plan, thanked her for her part, told her once again he loved her, would see her soon, and hung up, returning to his shower, where he shivered being under—and in—hot water.

*

"Hello?" said Donna Starr.

"Donna, this is Nathan Scott. I'm sorry to bother you, but I believe what is happening is important enough for me to intervene a bit. Kathy Rogers just called me to tell me that Shara is extremely upset, crying, and frightened, and embarrassed to go to class. She is reacting to the absurdity of her father's accusations regarding my foolishness last night, for taking her into the sanctuary for three minutes of prayer, and a final conversation. I take full responsibility for that and would like to apologize to you and to your husband for any problems that may have caused. Shara innocently asked me to pray with her privately. Naively and stupidly, I chose the sanctuary, after telling Kathy and Jason where we were going. As innocent as it was, it was stupid and thoughtless. I am sorry my best intentions have been twisted into something as impossible as Carl's suspicions. I need to speak to him, if he's available, to clear this up."

"Well, Nathan, it was a wrong thing to do, but I don't believe it was as bad as Carl seems to think. I don't know what to do, though. Carl is not here, and I would hate to make him madder than he is."

"I understand, Donna, and no one regrets this whole affair more than I. I would like to talk to Carl as soon as possible, though. Our truck will be loaded before noon. If you will ask him to call me, please, or I'll come to where he is, if he will meet me. Meanwhile, Donna, my greatest concern is Shara. She is crying almost uncontrollably, according to Kathy, is deeply hurt that her father thinks so badly of her–and of her minister–and needs her Mama. Do you think it might be best for you to go get her and try to calm her down?"

Vexed and perplexed, Donna hesitated, "Nathan, is she really that upset? She seemed to be all right this morning, though she was not very happy and was weeping. You know how these teenagers exaggerate things. What did Kathy say?"

Nathan shared Kathy's description of Shara's tears, and that she is terribly hurt that her father doesn't believe her. Donna agreed to go get Shara. He apologized, again, and reiterated that he could not leave for Wilmington with Carl's suspicions hanging over him.

"All right, Nathan, let me see if I can find him. Thanks for calling. Goodbye."

"Goodbye, Donna, and thank you very much."

Off the phone, Nathan whispered a few expletives, as Lenore's eyebrows arched. The more he thought about it, the angrier he got. Realizing that he had no right to be angry, he seethed anyway. QI shamed him for his exculpating logic. Such rationalizing did not help his bowels, either, which were a writhing snake pit.

Dr. Jennings listened carefully, chuckled, advised Nathan not to take Carl Starr too seriously, opined that he would cool down when he realized Nathan was not trying to hide anything; was admitting his silly mistake. Wishing him well, Dr. Jennings repeated his opinion that Nathan was surely the finest, most effective youth worker he had ever known or ever hoped to know. Thanking him profusely for his continued support, Nathan hung up, to await the call of J. Carl Starr.

The truck departed for Wilmington, while the Scotts cleaned and waited. Lenore decided to wait until they were on the road to voice her concerns. Nattie and Beth ran about the naked house, enjoying the echoes and harsh, unfamiliar sounds. Stephen was waiting to be dropped off to his ride back to Camp Promise. No one wanted to go get food for fear of missing something.

Nathan called Donna Starr at one, to check on her reaching Carl, and to inquire about Shara. Donna gave Carl Nathan's message, and Shara was sleeping, exhausted, she said. She offered little more than that Carl would certainly get in touch with Nathan before three. Two p.m. came and went; Stephen went for food.

The station wagon was loaded, the house cleaned, the children were playing in the front yard, and Nathan was checking the air in the tires, when Big J. Carl drove up, wearing a three-piece suit and a fedora. Lenore hustled the children inside with Stephen, while Nathan wiped his hands and prepared to greet the father of his beloved...

"Thank you for coming, Carl. Had you called, I would have come to you. I'm sorry you had to drive out here," said Nathan, extending his hand to the man.

"I would've been here earlier, Nathan, but I had to finish some business. I know you are anxious to get on the road to Wilmington," Carl responded, shaking his hand.

"Yes. We're all a little tired, too. How is Shara, and how are you doing, now, Carl?"

"Shara is asleep. I'm sorry I upset her so much. A father can't be too careful, these days."

"As I said to you last night, what you saw was the world's shortest, most innocent, if somewhat inappropriate prayer meeting. But, if there is fault, it's mine, not Shara's; she simply took my suggestion as to where to go, after she asked me to pray with her before she left. As you know, I even told Kathy Rogers and others where and why we would be in case anybody needed either of us. I apologize for my short-sightedness, and for any worry or concern I have caused you and Donna."

"Nathan, I may not be the best father in the world, but I do try to guide and protect my children. My life has been hard; I fought in two wars, and I know how bad things can be. I realize, now, that I over-reacted and scared Shara too much. But, in today's world, I don't think you can scare young girls too much, about what may be out there waiting to—to get them."

"Your own experiences with the evils in the world and what you have seen and heard make you very alert and cautious."

"Exactly! I have tried to be a good father, and husband, but I haven't been perfect. There were a few times, overseas, when I took advantage of some women. I'm not proud of that, but it seemed to be acceptable. I have made my peace with my wife about those women, and with God, too."

"So, your worries and concerns about the dangers to children are also based on your own failures."

"Exactly right."

"I haven't seen as much of the world as you, Carl, but I am very aware of the pitfalls surrounding all of us. That is one of the reasons I am in youth work, and why I spend as much time as I do trying to educate them to be aware of the troubles of the world, and what to do about them."

"You have been important to my children, and to lots of others, Nathan, but when I saw you both come out of that dark sanctuary, I was immediately reminded of another situation and reacted. A minister friend in Georgia recently announced that he was in love with the church organist, and that they intended to divorce their present mates and get married. Donna and I were horrified. So, you see? Ministers are human, and they have the same frailties as others. So, in the future, we'd like you to stay away from Shara. We believe she's much too dependent on you, giving rise to our concerns. Understand?"

"I certainly do. However, I cannot—must not—turn away from her, or anyone's confidential request. Taking your request seriously and under advisement, I ask that you let me be the judge of that, based on circumstances, please."

"What circumstances?"

Did I just hear anger? Careful, Scott. We're treading water, here.

"The nature and seriousness of her, or anyone's, situation, Carl. It is my duty."

"Nathan, do I need to make it more than a request?"

"There will not be opportunity for much additional contact with Shara, except, perhaps, through the mail. I have to be extremely careful not to be caught in compromising situations, such as last night. I can see how it might have looked to you, Carl, and again I apologize for being so foolish."

"Okay, Nathan, but we do want to avoid any other problems related to her friendship with you. Please think about it very seriously..."

Not so much anger, but menace, instead!

"Certainly, Carl, I can do that."

After shaking Nathan's proffered hand, again, Carl said he would apologize to his daughter, wished Nathan and his family good fortune and God's blessing, got in his car, and drove away. Nathan stared blankly after him, until Lenore and Stephen came rushing out.

"Let's everybody pee and get out of here," said the perplexed, young minister."

After depositing Stephen, Lenore asked, "Nathan, what was all that about?"

"Let me drive a little and calm down, please, Lenore."

For now, clearly, what I must do is to move my heart, my faith, and my family to Wilmington, Shara, or no Shara, and pray God take control of my life. It's that simple—and complicated. Say, "Amen," Scott.

"Amen!"

CHAPTER 22
"MILES TO GO BEFORE I SLEEP "

I find the best goodness I have has some tincture of vice.

Michel Eyquem de Montaigne

How rich the dreams that favor love,
How poor the wretch that loses them.
No hopes are gladder; no losses sadder;
Pity the man who confuses them!

Nathan R. Scott
September 15, 1964

D riving the endless miles to Wilmington, his exhausted children asleep in the back seat, Nathan grieved the passing of every crossroads, sighing his way southeast. Sitting next to him, sensing his compounding misery, Lenore shivered impending despair. Wanting to take him into her arms, she felt exiled to the periphery and banished from relevance. Loving, she hurt; hurting, she suffered; suffering, she resolved; resolving, she loved the more.

So, loving, her heart felt: "Nathan, Nathan, my Nathan, where are you? Where have you gone, so far from me, that I did not see you leave?"

Instead, she said, "You have said nothing of substance for the last twenty miles, Nathan, and I know you are despairing. Is there something I can do to help?"

174

"I'm sorry, Lenore. I'm a bit in shock, I guess. It's so very hard to leave."

"What are you leaving, darling?"

"My world of purpose, I guess, 'Nore. I don't know—it's exceedingly difficult to realize that Durham is over, and that I have torn myself away from the place wherein I felt most whole, despite the overwork, the money problems, and the unmitigating exhaustion."

"Whom are you leaving?"

"God?"

"Really?"

"I hope not, but I feel more than a little desolate, right now."

"Is there anything I can do to help, honey?"

"Just put up with me—as you always do—and understand if I mourn a bit. I–I may need to go back a time or two."

"Oh?"

"Yes. I promised I would introduce the new curriculum to the district, next weekend—and I'll probably go to the first football game with the kids. I also want to be certain Shara is all right, after all that ruckus last night and today.

"Is Shara another word for God?"

"I wondered when you might ask something like that."

"If you have something to tell me, I wish you would do it now, so I can deal with it—and help you deal with it, if you'll let me."

"Well, there is a feeling of unrelenting responsibility and protectiveness for Shara, as well as for several other young'uns—Jason, for instance, and even Kathy. They became more a part of me than I realized. But, as usual, your intuition correctly discerns that Shara has become extra special to me, and I don't really know how to handle that."

"I see. So, you've become so enmeshed in–her–their young lives that theirs have become an extension of yours."

"Pretty much, Lenore. You often understand before I do. But the losses feel very much like death. In fact, it's like poor, dead Tom McNair all over again–except, this time, nobody died."

Nathan then further explained, incompletely, that Shara was one of his dearest little ones, in dire need, due to her family's dire straits, and to her father's restrictive unpredictability.

I need to provide a buffer for Shara, as possible. Shouldn't I hide the depths of our relationship–from this wonderful woman beside me– my dear wife? We're on our way to a new job. Time enough to let things cool of. So, maybe I don't tell he, just yet. It would be too cruel. Sigh!

Lenore, she lay low, despite the tumult roiling her heart.

*

Having mentioned Tom McNair's death, Nathan's mind flashed to a time stark with February grief and dread, almost four years earlier, while he was a senior in seminary. Interning in a church with no pastor, he was responsible for the Sunday worship service and the evening youth fellowship. Jean, a mother of one of his teens, a board member of the church, was also the evening supervisor in a large, general hospital near the seminary.

About 11:30 one Saturday night in February 1960, Nathan received a call from Jean, who asked him to sit with a woman whose elderly mother was dying. From out of town, she knew no local ministers. Lonely, frightened, and Christian, she wanted a clergyman to sit with her through the ordeal. Jean immediately thought of Nathan.

With trepidation, having never seen death or dying up close, Nathan grabbed his Bible and walked the two blocks to the hospital. He arrived shortly after midnight, reported to

176

Jean, who immediately ushered him into the dimly lit room of epilogue and prologue—inspiration and expiration.

Nathan listened for the feelings locked in the middle-aged lady, as they both stood watch. He spoke, read from the scriptures when it seemed appropriate, kept silence, and prayed when bidden. The long night of dying awakened him to the prominence of grief, guilt, and the dreadful certitude of mortality.

About 6:00 a.m., a young physician came in. After feeling for his patient's pulse, he checked her pupils, then injected her heart with epinephrin. Detecting no life signs, he turned to the weeping daughter and the awed minister and pronounced the older woman dead, noting the time for the nurse.

The sun streamed its welcome premonitions, early on that frosty morning, as Nathan almost skipped back to his dormitory. He was glad to be alive and happy that he had seen and sat with death—in gentleness. His step was lightened by the blessings of relief and steadied by the realization that he had ministered to the bereaved and come away a wiser, more understanding person.

Waking at noon, Nathan worked three hours on his studies, supped with Lenore, and drove to his little church. Tom McNair and Peggy Severs, a dating couple at fifteen, led the group that evening, with a lesson on missions. Peggy was prepared, Tom wasn't. A good looking, sandy-haired lad, about 5'10", Tom was friendly, a playful wit, and spontaneous in his discourse, kept changing the subject to basketball games and scores. Peggy, more mature, in both mind and body than her boyfriend, was obviously taken with the lad. He, on the other hand seemed less interested. A dozen young people were tolerant of the couple's meager efforts and appreciative of Nathan's assistance, when they faltered. After the lesson,

Nathan led the group in a Bible quiz game, followed by a trip to an ice cream parlor.

Five teens rode to the soda shop with Nathan, Peggy, and Tom next to him. After their blackberry sundaes, he took the other three riders home first. Tom walked Peggy to her door, talked a moment, pecked her on the lips, and returned.

As Nathan parked in front of the young man's home, Tom played with an egg-sized, black ceramic skull he made in shop, complete with gaudy rhinestone facial features. Nathan noticed the glitter in its rhinestone eyes, as Tom tossed it up and caught it. Tom thanked him for the ice cream and the ride, then sat silently a moment or two, fiddling with the skull, glancing at it and then at Nathan.

"Mr. Scott, would you like me to make you one of these?" he asked, cheerfully, tossing the skull up and catching it again.

"If you'd like, Tom, but I think I'd prefer something different."

"Like what?"

"Well, how about a cross?" he smiled.

"I can do that!"

"Great, Tom, thanks. I'm sure we've both got homework, so I'll see you next week."

"That's for sure. Thanks again. Goodbye, Mr. Scott."

Later that night, almost exactly twenty-four hours after receiving his first death-watch call from Jean at the hospital, she called him again—this time she was crying.

"Nathan, this is Jean, again. I'm truly sorry to disturb you," she sobbed, "but could you get over here right away? Tom McNair just shot himself, and an ambulance is bringing him in. It doesn't sound good at all! They'll take him to the ER. I'll meet you there."

Without socks or a jacket, Nathan ran to the hospital, panting and praying for Tom's life. Lungs aching from the frigid February air, he rushed into the ER where Jean was waiting for him. She told him that the McNairs were in the chapel and then hustled him into an OR, where a surgical team was working feverishly on the unconscious, shivering, gray-skinned lad.

Nathan riveted his eyes on the shocked and shocking lad. An ER doctor and team were working desperately to deal with a fist-sized hole in Tom's chest, just under his heart. Blood was everywhere, and the smell of cauterized flesh filled the OR. The cool, professional demeanor Nathan expected was absent, for young Tom's actions, as well as their devastating results, unnerved everyone.

"Preacher, better pray for this boy. The hole in his chest is nothing compared to the one in his back. One lung is gone, his vitals are critical, he's deeply in shock, and has lost an incredible amount of blood. I don't understand how he can still be with us."

The young physician who spoke did not look up from his work. Nathan grabbed Tom's trembling hand and prayed, feeling empowered by adrenaline—*or is it the Spirit of God?*

"Oh, God, our father, we may not know how to fix this tragedy, but we want this boy to live. For the sake of his loved ones, and for those whose lives he could still touch, reach down your mighty hand and guide these men and women, that they may combine their skills with your love and power, and find a way to hold on to this precious, young life. In thy name we pray, Amen."

A chorus of whispered amens surrounded the boy, as everyone fought to stop the flushing away of life—and to ease their own aching hearts.

"Thank you, preacher. Now you'd better go find his parents. It's going to be pretty busy around here," said the sweating young doctor.

"Okay, God bless you all!"

"Thank you. We're all going to need it this night!"

Nathan found the McNairs in the chapel, inebriated and loudly blaming each other for the tragedy. As he entered, they looked at him blankly for a second or two.

"Oh, it's you, Mr. Scott. Thank you for coming. Is there any word about Tom?" whispered Mrs. McNair.

Mrs. McNair, Tom's stepmother, had married his father, the casket salesman, when Tom was ten, a year after his natural mother absconded with another man. Tom and his older sister took the ensuing divorce hard and resented their new stepmother. The problem worsened when she bore her new husband another boy, and Tom was no longer the youngest.

Tom McNair was a bright, friendly boy, somewhat embarrassed by his father's occupation and macabre humor. Instead of a linen closet, the McNairs used a casket, and they drove a hearse, rather than a car. The face of death permeated the McNair home.

In the hospital chapel, during the next half hour, the McNairs interspersed a ritual telling and retelling of what happened, with searching recriminations, mostly toward each other. They were also speaking the words of gruesome truth to themselves, as though telling and retelling would generate an understanding that would make the fact of Tom's suicide attempt fixable. Such is the logic of personal shock and awe.

After Tom came in from Nathan's car, related his grieving parents, he did his homework, took a bath, got on his pajamas, watched a little television, and went into his bedroom. About 11:15 p.m., he took his father's loaded, double barreled, 12-gauge shotgun, inserted an unwrapped tampon down each barrel and tied a cord to the triggers. Stripping off his pajamas, he removed the centerfold from a men's magazine and spread it out on the bed before him.

Standing with the gun butt on the bed, its barrels against his chest, Tom turned his young, tortured, adolescent world inside out and upside down. When his ejaculate fell on the face of the naked blonde, he pulled the cord, blasting the tampons and two, full loads of buckshot through his chest and into the wall behind him, along with blood, tissue, bone fragments, cotton–and his future.

Ashen with his own shock and despair, the young, trembling ER doctor walked into the chapel in the middle of a parental tirade that Nathan was trying to moderate. Mr. McNair stopped mid-sentence, and stood, open-mouthed, as the doctor, looking down at his blood-spattered shoes, mumbled his message of gruesome failure.

"Mr. and Mrs. McNair, preacher, I'm terribly sorry, but your son–Tom–is dead. We couldn't stop the bleeding. God, we tried, but it was just no use. I'm so very sorry! Is there anything I can do for you?"

There came a sound–beginning in the open mouth of Tom's father, joined by the screech of his stepmother, becoming a trumpeted cacophony of grief and terribly eliminated hope–the wail of the living crying in anguish, angry in agony, somehow surprised by the sudden, shattering, despicable rape of life. The lesser gasps and sobs, emitting from the helpless young minister could not be heard, except in his soul, along with the rending of his own, traumatized heart.

Those sounds crashed and echoed together, as the parents rushed to the middle of the room and stood staring at the ghastly fact of their son's death, cruelly written on the other's frightened face. The sounds collapsed into gasps and whimpers, harmonizing fear with grief, as they sang their own, dreaded *dies irae*. Weeping, Nathan put his arms around the fractured, woeful parents, and drew them together, into the sudden, sodden sanctuary of each other's arms...

*

The next day, Nathan sought the counsel of his homiletics professor, a wise and kindly man, with many years as a successful pastor. He walked him through the steps he must take in officiating his first funeral. After the family, his greatest responsibility was to the young people of the church, and especially to Peggy, who had not taken seriously Tom's twice-whispered determination for death. Making the hopeful mistake of disbelief, she informed no one, thinking his pronouncements were more of his increasingly weird teases.

"Mr. Scott," she cried, "he told me Saturday he was going to do it, and I just laughed. Then he told me he was going to come back as a cockroach—and that he was going to make it snow next Wednesday. I thought he was just being silly because he laughed, too. Then, last night, when you brought me home, he told me again and asked me not to tell you or anyone. I worried about it but didn't want to get him—or me—in trouble, sure he was teasing. When my father told me what happened, I just about went crazy. Isn't it my fault Tom is dead?"

Nathan stood before this frightened, broken heart and opened his arms. Peggy fled into Nathan's embrace, opened to her grief, her doubt, and her guilt. Nathan held her, letting her sob her anguish into his chest, while her parents clung to each other, not knowing what to do or say.

"Peggy, look at me," he said, softly but urgently, tears streaming down his face. "Look at me, honey! Now, listen very carefully to what I am going to say, because it is incredibly important. You—did—not, repeat, not—cause Tom to die. I know it hurts awfully, and you feel responsible because you didn't believe him. You are not responsible. You are not a trained, professional counselor, able to recognize and handle that kind of truth, nor are there many such people. Tom shot himself for reasons that no one in this life will ever know—but—

Tom–shot–himself! You had nothing to do with it. You must believe that!"

"Then why did he do it, Mr. Scott?"

"I know you want to know; so, do I; so, do his parents, and everyone else who knew him, because we want to be able to recognize and help people like him. But, Peggy, we will never know, and to be honest, Tom didn't know, either. What he did was sad, tragic, and a great, senseless loss; it was also sick, childish, and perhaps, spiteful. We must not let his sickness wound us beyond our natural grief and sorrow."

*

Tom's funeral went poignantly, as do most funerals, the living restructuring deadly loss, so they may return to normality. The hardest part for Nathan was greeting Tom's church and school mates, all of whom were frightened, non-comprehending, and deeply sorrowful. When Peggy and six others approached Tom's open casket (one of his father's), Nathan waited until they had made their horrified pass before it, before he opened his arms to them. Seven young people clung to him and to each other, crying, confounded–and comforting.

Nathan executed his duties faithfully through the longer service in the church, determined to provide the comfort of scriptures and hymns to the grieving congregation, especially to Tom's young friends. At the graveside, Nathan led the small procession, consisting of the pall-borne casket, the family, and the forty or so mourners, to Tom's grave. Waiting until all were seated under the canopy, and it was quiet, except for ubiquitous sobbing–and the frigid, unrelenting, February wind: "I am the resurrection, and the life, saith the Lord," Nathan began the burial service, reading some of the great verities in the worship book. Then he spoke.

"Fear not, little flock; family and friends of Tom McNair, take heart. This cold and earthy spot is not the end, nor the last of this boy whom we knew and loved. Think how you loved him; think how you wanted for him a full, abundant life. Think, too, in whose arms he now does lie, comforted and cleansed from the personal ills which beset him, and which, in his terrible confusion, caused him to act so painfully and fatally.

"Out of your love, you would restore Tom to life if you could, as would I. Think ye, then, how much more loved he is now in the all-knowing, understanding, and loving, arms of God. Know ye that God will wipe away the tears from Tom's eyes, and in the end, give him back the life that he in his illness took."

With tears overflowing his own eyes, "We sorrow—my God, how we sorrow—but, not as those who have no hope! We must place that hope now in the hands and heart of the God who created Tom, and believe that he is whole, alive, and filled with the grace of that same, loving and forgiving God."

Nathan closed the service with the formal committal of Tom's body to the grave, "ashes to ashes, dust to dust, in the sure and certain hope of the resurrection," followed by prayer.

"O Lord, support us all the day long, until the shadows lengthen, and the evening comes, and the busy world is hushed, and the fever of life is over, and our work is done. Then, in thy mercy, grant us a safe lodging, and a holy rest, and peace at the last, through Jesus Christ our Lord... The peace of God, which passeth all understanding, keep our hearts and minds in the knowledge and love of God, and of His Son Jesus Christ our Lord; and the blessing of God Almighty, the Father, the Son, and the Holy Spirit, be upon us, and remain with us always. Amen."

The graveyard, cold, dank, and bluster-swept with the bitterness of an angry north wind, lay empty, save for Nathan, two grave diggers waiting for him to leave, and poor, dead

Tom McNair–forever an enigmatic tragedy. Nathan stood by as the casket was lowered, the bier removed, the fake grass rolled back, and the vault's lid sealed.

Ah, Tom, Tom–why did I not see you in your sick, lonely need? I should have been able to discern something of your misery–and the depths of your deadly foolishness. You hinted your intent with your ceramic skull– and your ready acceptance of my suggestion of a cross, instead. I so regret that I failed to understand...

Where are you, now, really, Tom? God grant that you are with Him, and not simply juiced up with formaldehyde, facing one of your father's expensive, satin-lined coffin lids, waiting to decompose. Please forgive me, son. I did not see you as you were; I saw you the way you appeared to be. I will do my utmost not to make such a mistake again! I know I did not kill you, Tom; but, somehow, I should have known to stop you!

Unabashedly weeping before the cold, impatient diggers, Nathan knelt on the ground before Tom's open grave:

Almighty God, to whom all hearts are open, you knew Tom's plans–and you did nothing! How dreadful is the free will you allow us, for you permit us to fling it, along with our lives, right back in your face! Take thou my will, Oh Lord: though I did not cause this little one to stumble, neither did I shore him up, and keep him from falling. In the name of Jesus Christ, I hereby dedicate my life to the service of your little ones, especially the least of your little ones, wherever I may find them. I will endeavor to serve children and young people, that no child I will ever know will need to erase himself, instead of his problems, no matter how large and overwhelming. Hear my prayer and my promise, Oh Lord, and forgive my negligence of Tom McNair. In Jesus' name, Amen."

Nathan's promise to his God determined the direction of his life, as surely as the rising of the sun determined each day. Tom McNair, though dreadfully gone, would be with him always, in the faces of the young persons of all ages whom he would love and serve. He got his next opportunity at 6:30 a.m. the following Wednesday morning.

"Mr. Scott," lamented the hysterical Peggy, "it's snowing!"

It was.

*

The truck was virtually unloaded when they arrived at their newly rented home. Nathan changed clothes, grabbed his notes, hustled his family back into the car, and drove to Christ Church in time to be introduced to the Family Night Supper crowd, and to make a short speech.

I am miserable to the marrow of my bones!

As soon as he could manage ten minutes alone, he let himself into his new office and took a chance on calling Shara. The ringing of the phone sounded loud alarm bells in his ear, warning him of danger, daring him not to hang up. Immense relief when he heard her voice.

There followed a tense conversation between the distant lovers, wherein Shara reprised the misery of her father's overblown tirade, followed by her great fear that he might do Nathan harm. Nathan, in turn, shared the gist of his long, poignant conversation–confession, really–with her father. Shara began to weep with frustration when he told her of her father's unsubtle "request." Nathan immediately reassured her, reminding her that his plan worked reasonably well, getting her off the hook. Bowed but unabashed, they plotted his next visit…

"I'll leave here Friday, arriving in plenty of time to meet you after school. Melanie will be coming here, so I'm staying in her apartment. Do you think you can get away Saturday?"

"I'm sure going to try!"

"Lenore is coming up with the kids, looking for me. I told her I was worried about you; I believe she is beginning to figure out that my feelings for you go beyond the didactic and pastoral."

"You're kidding! What did you tell her about me?"

"Only that I can't simply pass you on, like a baton, that I miss you, am still worried about you, and that one reason for my going back is to see you."

"Doesn't she mind? Nathan, be careful–I'm a little scared. As much as I want to be yours, I don't want her to be hurt."

"I know; me either. Gotta go. I love you–I'll be with you at eleven tonight. Have a good one and think of me."

"I'm juicing just talking to you. Do you realize that we've made love twenty-six times since July 4?"

"But who's counting? Maybe we'll make the top thirty this weekend, honey. Squeeze yourself for me. I love you, Shara! Goodbye."

"Goodbye, darling. I'll see you near the school parking spot. I love you."

*

Though Lenore concurred that he should go to Durham, she expressed her ambivalence with an understandably long face and a long list of tasks. Thus, Nathan's nights involved moving furniture, installing shades and curtains, unpacking boxes, and trying to soothe his understandably disquiet lady. Friday morning dawned a bit awkwardly, with Lenore expressing anxiety about Nathan's three-night trip.

"Now, Nathan, please don't spend too much time with Shara. I'm sure she needs you and thinks you're God, but it really isn't fair to her. You need to wean her from her dependence on you, for everyone's benefit."

"I know, Lenore, and I'll try not to be too godlike. Will Melanie still be there by five?"

"She said to tell you that the key will be in the outside lamp fixture in case you miss her. She's hoping to leave right after work."

"I plan to be there by 5:00, at the latest, and would like to get there earlier."

"Why?" blithely asked the wife.

"I can have the car serviced, if I get there by five."

"Well, just as long as you don't spend too much time with Shara."

"After all that ruckus Tuesday? She'll have to sneak, just to go to the ball game."

"You make my point, darling. See what you may be risking?"

"Wasn't it Roethke who wrote, `What's the worst portion of this mortal life? A pensive mistress, and a yelping wife?'" he grinned.

"Nathan Scott! Honestly!"

Twinkling his eyes at her and pulling her to him with genuine affection, Nathan apologized for his miscreance, admitting that she was right.

"Too late!" she giggled, pulling away, "I'm wounded deeply, sir. I shall hie me to my bed to salve the wounds that you should be kissing."

"That's just your way of saying you're going to go back to bed, as soon as you can get the kids fed and comfortably in front of the TV."

Despite the incipient truths in their gentle banter, they chuckled—and hugged. Such was the soft and shifting ground of their relationship.

Nathan hugged his babies, kissed his wife, took a small suitcase, his new briefcase, his 35mm camera, and drove to Christ Church. His heart was bifurcated with joy and relief on one side, and heavy with strain and regret on the other. He dearly loved the lady most recently in his arms, the mother of his children, his dear friend, and constant supporter—but he had five condoms in his camera case...

*

188

Nervously waiting, Nathan avoided looking directly at the many students leaving. Tingling with anticipation and relief, he saw Shara approach, carrying a load of books. Dressed in a blue skirt, printed white blouse, and loafers, she smiled sheepishly as she got in.

"Hi, baby!" he chortled, as she plopped down beside him.

"Hey, Nathan. Let's get out of here. You can kiss me when we get to–where are we going, anyway?"

"Maybe Melanie's? She's driving to Wilmington."

"Fine with me, dar–darling. It's so good to see you! I was so afraid you wouldn't be here; I almost came when I saw you."

"Me, too! Better lie down until we get well away from here."

Only four nights since we've seen each other, and it seems like a month. I feel giddy and addled-pated. Calmly, Scott; calmly. We have three days…

Shara lay tensely in his lap facing the steering wheel; Nathan's right arm on her waist, gravitating upwards.

"You feel so real, so alive, Shara, I missed you. How are things in Glocca Morro?"

"They couldn't be better. My breasts are swelling, and I'm due in the next three days. We won't have to use rubbers, will we?"

"Do we simply assume we'll make love? How telling is that?"

"It tells me how right and good we are for each other, both wanting–needing–to express our love in that wonderful way. Oh, Nathan, of course we both want it–both the Agape and the Eros, as you often say. I've really, really missed you, especially after Daddy…"

"A close call, that, Shara, but handled well enough. As for rubbers, I'm prepared, but thanks be, not so close to your period. You do know I love you!"

"Of course, I do. It's the one thing I am absolutely sure of."

About to park near Melanie's, he saw her car still in its designated spot and sped up.

"Stay down, honey, she's still there! Damn! Let's try the woods near your house."

Driving past fluttering flags and ribbons on trees, Nathan found a relatively hidden spot, parked, and reached for her.

"Oh, Shara," he murmured against her lips, "I worried about you– dreadfully. Are you still you–and truly all right?"

"Now, I am," waggled her tongue against his, "since you fixed things. I was scared to death I'd never see you, again. I worry what Daddy might do if…"

Their lovemaking was unhurried and lingering, remarking the reality of their essential corpus. Slowly immersed in the heats of their desire, transcending time and place, they luxuriated in their mutual, creative, and interpersonal energy. Restored, spent, and secure, they slept.

"Baby, I don't understand it, but it is four-thirty. You have to be home by five."

Straddling him, she teased his lips with her nipples, until he sat up, hugged her, and put her clothes in her hands. She opened the way-back door of the wagon, crawled out, and found a private spot to pee. Nathan followed suit. Such was their ease with their corporeal reality.

Back in the car, Shara sighed, "Next time, we ought to talk more, before falling into each other's arms. We've hardly talked at all."

"Talking is the glue of our relationship; sex is only the scrap book, Shara."

With that, he kissed her and let her out near her street.

*

Nearing Melanie's, Nathan was dismayed to find her car still parked in its assigned place. Light dawning, he realized she was lying in wait. Caught, he took his paraphernalia from the car, locked it, and with mixed emotions, crossed two thresholds—her front door and the one between her thighs. Therein, almost mindlessly, he dosed her with two of the Reverend Dr. Feel Good's benign, intra-muscular injections...

Shara, my Shara, forgive me; it shan't be forever thus!

CHAPTER 23
HOW MUCH IS ENOUGH?

Life is its own journey, presupposes its own change and movement, and one tries to arrest them at one's eternal peril.

Laurens Van der Post

A coming sense of foolishness pinked Nathan's cheeks. So many at the game hailed him that an unfamiliar role of interloper challenged his sense of welcome. Any thought of sitting with "parson's privilege" vanished well before the kickoff. On his second trip to the refreshment stand, Shara joined him.

"I can meet you about ten tomorrow, at the little church parking lot, Nathan."

"All right; I'll see you at ten. I'm sorry we're not sitting together."

"Me, too, but I'm used to it. You'd better get back, before they think the parson is privileging me under the stands."

*

By 9:45 a.m., he had rented a box at the post office nearest Shara's school, purchased sandwich fixings. Watching the rector of their little church drive away, QI noted the irony of their using it to facilitate their trysts. *High or low church, Father What'syourface, at least my libido is ecumenical!*

Waiting for Shara, the philosophy major in him postulated as to whether his being in that parking lot was

192

predestined, conditioned, pure chance, or by his own free will. Lost in the moot circularities of freedom and determinism, Nathan did not notice the wily creature sidling up to his car, until its gnarled, filthy hands, and its emetic, alcoholic breath intruded through the open window.

"Hey, man, are you the preacher of this here church?" formed the noxious vapors, stimulating Nathan's gag reflex.

He was aged, or ageless, weathered by his own stench, and so bleary of eye and tousled of hair and habit as to nauseate. Repulsed, the contemplative young theolog shrank back reflexively, accosted by a phantom. *Good grief! This guy not only wears his sins on his person, but he has also daubed himself with shit—which he is now smearing on my window!*

"I–I beg your pardon?" was all Nathan could get out.

"What's the matter, man, you fuckin' deef? I said, 'Are you the mother-fucking preacher of this here ecclesiastical irrelevancy?'"

Seeking to escape this foul specter, regardless of his will's freedom, Nathan locked his door and rolled up his window, taking the man's hands with it. Disapproving, the specter used those same shitty hands to pound on the windshield, shouting:

"Wait a goddam minute, you breathless brat of bestiality, I only want to talk to you! I ain't gonna try to suck your pristine preacher's pecker!"

"Get away from my car, you old fool!" Nathan blasphemed, abandoning QI in favor of his fight or flight response.

Starting his car, Nathan began to back away from the cursing apparition when a remarkable thing occurred. The old derelict undid several folds of ragged cloth around his groin, pulled out his red and scabby penis, pointed it at the car–and peed.

LOVE, FLESH, AND SPIRIT

"Come back here, you Episcopal, alimentary ailment. I'm a preacher, too, and I'm going to baptize you in the name of the unholy trinity: the Fatuous Fucker, the Somnolent Sodomist, and the Whorish, Ghastly Ghoul!"

Not wishing to harm the clearly deranged man (with a ranging vocabulary!), Nathan looked for a way out, but the pisser persisted and backed him off at the pass. Squeezing his penis to valve off the flow, he dared Nathan to try to escape his urinary ministrations. To Nathan's immense relief, another car pulled into the lot, a man and a woman jumped out and gave chase to the fleeing, loudly farting figure disappearing behind the church.

"Granddaddy, you come back here, now; and stop peeing everywhere!"

As Nathan fled towards Shara's Street, QI posited: *They should have an easy time tracking their quarry; he left a wet, zigzagging trail of piss—likely another kind of tears. Could this be in store for my own parents, and millions like them—or for me? Could he help his behavior? Why was I so cruel? I should have engaged the old geezer—no, that elderly, played out, desperate human—would it have cost me so much to have shown a little kindness and helped? Where was my vaunted Great Realization when somebody really needed it?*

For the second time in less than twenty-four hours, Nathan felt the full flush of foolishness infuse his cheeks, this time accompanied by hot shame. There were no teen admirers complicating things, only a rare opportunity to aid a shockingly needful human gone aborting. The flame of shame for his foolish sin of belittlement, and for the pride of an unearned sense of betterness, seared him far more than could any sly, sexual sortie.

Shame is unlikely until sham is gone, huh, Scott? There is never any sham with Shara, but my attempts at being the Christian good guy sometimes reek with it. Now is such a time. The psalmist wrote, "Cast me not off in the time of my old age; forsake me not when my strength faileth me."

Chastened, Nathan returned to the church and, as is often the case with efforts to atone, he was too late. The parking lot was empty, except for the sad signature of the old man's madness, wretchedly autographed in bodily fluids

*

Nathan confessed his shame to Shara, as she held her nose at the stench left by Nathan's phantom.

"Nathan, what would have been the most loving thing to do? How are we supposed to help people like that?"

"First, to befriend him, I think."

"Aren't we his friends, if we take Christianity seriously?"

"Exactly. 'Greater love has no man than this, that he lay down his life for his friends.'"

"Does it count that I feel friendly toward him, and I don't even know him?"

"It counts a great deal, for my money, honey."

"I know I never feel that I've done as well or as much as I can. Shouldn't I feel guilty about that?"

"Do you?"

"I'm not sure; what should you have done about him?"

"More. I should have engaged, helped somehow. Instead, I cursed and ran like a threatened schoolboy. To put it more plainly, I should have been willing to get my hands dirty—to put them in his shit—to get out of my oh, so private and protected cocoon and become involved, no matter what it might have cost me."

"Even if it meant not seeing me, right?"

"Right."

Thoughtful pause…

"Nathan, how much is enough?"

195

"It depends, Shara. We are not God; we have our own needs. As humans, especially as Christian humans, we have an obligation (or is it opportunity?) to spend ourselves in aid of others: the Great Realization. Unless we prefer living in moated castles or cocoons disconnected from our fellows, or in the jungle, where what is yours is mine, if I can wrest it from you or vice versa, we need to come out where others live, to help where and when we can, allowing God to sustain and forgive us when we fail."

"Nathan, I don't think there is such a thing as enough. There'll always be more need, no matter how much we do. What are we to do about that?"

"I concur. There is no such thing as doing or being enough for any of us—the needs are so vast. So, as for me and my house, we should try to love and serve Yahweh, spending ourselves in aid of others to the extent we are able, but not stinting ourselves, either, when feeding at the trough. We need to sustain, in order to serve."

Basking in his concentrated sincerity, loving him, she said, "Go on, Nathan; I love it when you listen and talk with me—treat me as an equal, even if I'm not."

With that, he kissed her, and they drove to Melanie's apartment, where the needs they filled were clearly their own—and surely not enough! Somehow, the needy world made do without them, while they strove to please—and to be pleased; to sustain—and to be sustained; more importantly, to love—and to be loved—by and for themselves.

*

In a languid moment of postcoital repose, Shara looked around Melanie's apartment, smiled to herself in private assent, and asked, "Nathan, can I ask you something?"

"'May you ask,' and, certainly, you may."

"May I ask, just what is your relationship with Melanie, anyway?"

Coming up behind her, wrapping her in his arms, crowding her jeans-clad buttocks, he graced her question by telling the truth so as to be disbelieved. "She is a college classmate, Lenore's, best friend, college roommate, and I fuck her every chance I get. Why?"

"Be serious, Reverend Horny," she grinned, wiggling her bottom against him, "She's in love with you, you know."

"Funny, that is exactly what Lenore said about you, before we went gallivanting off to Tabormont, where I plucked your merry cherry from betwixt your cunning thighs."

"Na-than!"

"Yes ma'am. No, I don't know she is in love with me; nor does she. She just craves my body. Doesn't everyone? I've been meaning to tell you about old Miss Brumbly, too."

"Take that, you lecher!" she said, hurling a piece of celery at him, bouncing it off his pate.

"Take this, you little minx," he growled, picking her up in his arms, and running with her to the couch, whereon he had most recently fucked Mistress Melanie. "I'll larn you not to skip sailery off'n my haid-bone."

Laughing, legs akimbo, arms flailing, semi-resisting, Shara was on her back, with Nathan's hands rummaging through her drawers, despite the spoon in her hand, and the eggs on the stove. Unable to guard all erogenous zones at once, she realized that he was stripping her, despite her youthful strength.

"Nathan, wait! The eggs will be done in a few minutes. Be careful of my blouse; you'll tear it!"

"Subtly accuse me of banging Maid Melanie, will you? I'll have you know—on second thought, I'll just have you!"

Shara's laughter metamorphosed into moans, as her excited lover foraged with his lips for the delicacies under her bra and explored her now naked legs and thighs. In less than a minute she was nude, except for her panties, with Nathan kissing her passionately, his hands all over her body, gently pinching, probing, petting—freeing her lust.

"Ohh, Nathan, ahh, God, I'm so hot. Let's do it, baby. Get your clothes off and put it in me!"

Lifting her rump, as he laid her bare, she lifted her arms to him, undulating her pelvis and spreading. He fell into her, kissing her body from top to toe, lingering at her flat midsection, and between her thighs. When she reached a fever pitch, he stood, grinned, walked to the stove and removed the eggs, now aboil for about his fail-safe prescription of thirteen minutes.

"Na—Nathan, don't stop now. I am hotter than that stupid stove. Please come back and make love to me."

"Tell you what. You come and peel the eggs, and I'll show you something you've never seen before."

Not mistaking the desire in his eyes and quaking voice—nor in his evident erection—nor in her own tides of excitement tingling and wetting her down, she moved to the sink, where he was filling the egg pot with cold water. Reaching past him, a breast rubbing his arm, she took the pot and stood facing the sink, very much aware of their mutual heat.

Peeling the eggs, she sensed Nathan behind her. Gasping, she felt his lips and hands exploring everywhere. The pot clattered against the sink. Stepping back, leaning over, spreading, one hand holding onto the sink, Shara offered ready access. Suddenly, he was gone. A few seconds of heavy breathing—then he entered her where she stood.

"Look," Nathan mumbled into her ear, guiding her gaze to the right.

Looking, Shara saw herself clearly mirrored in a glassed hutch, with Nathan's welcome incubus behind—and in—her. She watched their reflection, noting the unmitigated loveliness and sensuousness of their union, until the thrilling co-sensations of coition and caress reached their zenith. Her climax was a thing of beauty, accompanied by voluptuous and involuntary contractions of the muscles capturing him.

"Look at us, Nathan!" she murmured, when she could speak.

"I've been looking. God, you are dazzling," he whispered, watching his reflection press forward, only to ease outward, again. She extended her rump upward, concaving her back, and spread her legs more widely, luxuriating in their reflected doppelganger. Viewing themselves from without, Nathan reached for her breasts, while fully enthralled, and moved another hand down to her pubes.

"Watch!"

His rapid thrusts, coupled with his practiced fingers soon brought them both to the heights. Their mirrored images gloried back at them, doubling their pleasure, epitomizing their fantasies, as all four bodies meshed and engaged, exploding in consummation.

Fulfilled and spent, Nathan slowly stepped away; Shara remained spread before him, hands still holding the sink's edge, breathing hard, until her grip gentled with her spasms.

"Damn, Nathan, that was incredible! I thought I was going to faint. The tingling started in my breasts, and shot down to my clit, until I felt like I was flying. It was wonderful! Let's do it again!"

"After lunch, baby. How far did you get with the eggs?"

Nude, eating at Melanie's table, he toasted her as they tasted their new intimacy.

"Thou preparest a table before me, in the presence of mine erection," he smiled, indicating the simple truth of the matter.

Jumping up, Shara's precious nakedness fair danced to turn aside to see this great sight. Laughing, she gallumphed to the sink, returned, and knelt before him in mock obeisance.

"Long live the king," she solemnized, placing half an eggshell atop his upright penis, "Long live the king!"

*

"Shara, what would you like to do with the remaining four hours of our day."

"I don't care, as long as we're together. What do you want to do?"

"Let's go shopping. There's a mall nearby, and I'd like to buy you a pretty."

Grinning her approval and excitement, Shara kissed him, grabbed her purse, took him by the hand, and said, "I'll drive."

The mall proved a happy choice, until Nathan spied two members of First Church walking toward them. Ducking into a woman's lingerie shop, he lost himself amongst the undies, praying the man would not pick this day to buy something kinky for his wife. Serendipitously, Nathan was introduced to bikini panties, still a novelty in the early sixties, while hiding behind a mannequin wearing a black, see-through affair, sporting little red ants.

The church couple gone, Nathan suggested Shara pick out something sexy. She demurred, fearing parental consternation, settling for a silver mailbox charm for her bracelet, instead. Into it he inserted a tiny missive bearing the Greek words "Ἀγάπη ἀ Ἐρως." *That message will characterize our relationship for as long as it is permitted to last.*

Back in Melanie's, Shara whispered. "I want you to take me as forcefully as you can, on a real bed, Nathan," her hands all over him.

Complying, Nathan swept her into his arms like a child and took the stairs two at a time. *Emulating ol' Rhett, eh?*

L. ADLAI BOYD

Congruent with her need, he dumped her on Melanie's bed, pulled off her jeans and panties, and planted his face, while struggling out of his clothes. Drinking her in, adoring her closed eyes, and tilted, open mouth, he invigorated her softer parts as she undulated with his caresses. She was dripping wet.

"I love you, Nathan!"

Homing into her with all the prescient desperation of the drought of coming months, Nathan loved his woman as she begged, accepting her total gift of self without question. Their love rocked the bed; their cries etched burning love and lust in their hearts, giving notice of the terrible losses to come, and ended with mutual tears and soothings, championing the future, even as they were losing it.

An hour later, they kissed goodbye in the parking lot of the derelict urination, after plotting their next afternoon: tomorrow, after he introduced the new curriculum to the assembled multitudes.

*

Nathan slept through Sunday morning, having stayed up until 2:00 a. m. clearing Melanie's apartment of telltale signs of Shara and studying his presentations.

Nathan taught from 1:00 to 3:30 p.m., while over two hundred teachers and preachers furiously took notes, asked questions, and shared plans and problems. He felt reasonably sure he acquitted himself well. Afterwards, the regional executive wrung his hand for the last time, bemoaning his move to Wilmington.

At 4:10 p.m., they arrived at Melanie's. They had until 5:20 to be together, until God knew when...

After gently making love atop the spread on Melanie's double bed, the couple held closely, whispered their desperate blend of hope and sadness, and looked beyond the hour of separation to an unnamed date when, somehow, they would

201

be together again. Nathan felt relief when she called from the bathroom, informing him of the advent of her period.

Naturally mixing their parting with their prayers, they asked God to hold them together, despite their separation. Avoiding the rending finality of their last moments, their conversation turned inconsequential, their wilting elan incapable of additional peaks. A final hug, a muttered prayer, and she was gone.

*

Toiling through homeward miles, Nathan retraced his sojourn in Durham–not only of the past three days, but of the past three years, and his heart filled with grief, anew. *I was a good journeyman to Dr. Jennings, saw my duty and did it. Yet there swirls in my head the notion that my work was good, but not good enough.*

"How much is enough?" Shara asked of the one man she thought might know. Oh, I answered her facilely enough. Doing what you can with your life, spending it in aid of others, but not stinting at the various troughs of life whereat one must feed. But that only appears to offer a balance between self and the rest of humanity...

Waiting at a stoplight in a little town, Nathan's sense of never doing or being enough lay just beneath the surface. Across the intersection a young Negro lad, about nine years old, carrying a bag of groceries as big as he, was walking with his toddler sister toward the crosswalk. The little girl was dragging behind while the lad was cajoling her to "come on." Suddenly, she broke away and chased something into the street, which was busy with cross traffic. Without stopping to look, the little girl danced into the intersection, stooping directly before the oncoming cars.

Horrified, the boy shouted, "Alethea! Come back!"

The grocery bag crashed to the pavement, spilling its contents, topped by a dozen eggs, all over the sidewalk, as the boy ran into the street, grabbed his sister to the panic of squealing tires, and jumped out of the way of the skidding car just in time. Safely back on the sidewalk, two little pairs of eyes, widened by fear, looked at the loudly honking car, which had skidded to a stop just past the crosswalk, its frightened, angry white driver shouting.

"You God-damned little niggers!" he frothed. "Why the hell can't you black bastards stay out of the street? I should have just run you over! Go home; go to hell–NIGGERS!"

With that, the brave denizen of the civilized world Nathan sought to serve careened away, leaving two trails of burning rubber for several feet. Nathan's big heart was now in his throat. His light turned green, and the cars behind him honked. The Black children were on the sidewalk, crying and picking through broken eggs, mayonnaise, ketchup, pickles, and dried beans, all mixed with milk, dripping into the gutter.

"How much is enough? How much is enough?" Nathan cried out, tears crowding his vision of the small tragedy before him, as he pulled his station wagon through the light, stopping by a fire plug, in front of the children. "How much is enough? How much is enough?" he repeated, as he jumped out of his car and ran to the children.

Seeing a white man jump out of his car, muttering to himself, with tears streaming down his face, further frightened the boy, who grabbed his squalling sister's arm, and ran back down the sidewalk. Aghast, Nathan wiped his eyes, knelt before the mess of spoiled groceries, and began to pick up cans, wiping them off with his handkerchief.

"Hey, mister! Those are my cans–my Mama's cans. Please don't take them; she'll skin me alive."

Controlling himself, Nathan smiled and motioned for the children to return. "I'm not going to take them, son, I want to help you pick them up."

Cautiously, the boy approached the kneeling man, telling Alethea to hush, that it was all right; this man was helping them. Nathan continued to stack cans and brush dried beans into a dry portion of the torn sack.

"That was a very brave thing you did, son; you saved your sister's life, and could have lost your own. I'm very proud of you."

"That mean, ol' man in that big car didn't think so," said the boy, smarting under the profane, blaspheming disdain still ringing in his ears.

"Don't pay any attention to him or to his like, son. He just didn't know any better. I'll bet tonight, when he thinks about what you did for your sister, he'll ask God to forgive him for being so mean. And I'll bet he'll thank God for you, for your bravery, and for your love for your sister, too. What's your name?"

"Jackson Avery, and this here is my sister, Alethea," smiled the boy, warming to Nathan's kindness. "Say hello, Alethea."

Coying, as only three-year-olds can, Alethea peered at Nathan from behind her brother with big, dark, beautiful eyes, and smiled. Jackson knelt with Nathan and began to pick at the mess, too.

"I've got a little girl near your age, sweetheart. Her name is Beth. She's almost as pretty as you."

"Ah dot a hair-ribbon," she giggled.

"I see you do; and a mighty pretty one it is, too."

This little scene at the crossroads of Nathan's life continued apace, through a make-do clean-up of the sidewalk, the salvaging of such groceries as were undamaged, and the walking of a block with the children to a grocery store. There, he replenished the boy's broken and ruined stock, bought each child a box of Cracker Jacks, and slipped two candy bars into the sack, to surprise them when they got home.

Nathan offered the children a ride but was politely refused by the wise Jackson, whose mother told him never to get into a car with strangers. He wouldn't mind, however, if Nathan toted the groceries in his car while they walked. Thus, they left the store to return to Nathan's car, now being ticketed by a local policeman, for parking in front of the fire plug.

Nathan briefly explained what had happened, apologized to the gendarme, who, recognizing the story-verifying children, smiled, and stopped writing the ticket. Offering the children a ride home in his cruiser, which they accepted with delight, he loaded them and their groceries in and turned to face Nathan.

"Mr. Scott, I think you've done about enough for these children, today. I'll take it from here—and by the way, thanks. You're a good man," he smiled, offering him his hand.

"Thank you, officer," said the embarrassed adulterer, feeling the foolishness of his inadequacy. "Not really—just a sucker for children."

"Well, you'd better move your car—before there's a fire," officiated the friendly officer.

As they drove away, Nathan thrilled at the smiling waves from Jackson, and to the precious kiss blown from the still forming lips of little Alethea—whose name came from the Greek word for truth.

Back in his car, heading southeast, Nathan's heart ached the more, both with his sadness at the white driver's hatred and with his own, renewed sense of foolishness. His throat then issued a mighty, agonized cry, resounding through his misery, admixed with the golden kernel of his recent kindness, "Nyaiuhh! It is not enough! It is not enough! There can never be enough! Oh God, help me, I am not enough!"

The sad, too wise, too giving, too selfish, too loving, never-loving-enough man sobbed for several miles, before he gritted his teeth, shook his head, and drove his head, his hands, and his huge, inadequate, cracking heart to Wilmington.

205

CHAPTER 24
FALL, 1964

There is a way in which the collective knowledge of mankind expresses itself, for the finite individual, through mere daily living: a way in which life itself is sheer knowledge.

Laurens Van der Post

Nothing is so firmly believed as what is least known.

Michel Eyquem de Montaigne

The Scotts tried hard to settle into their new world. Lenore loved their large, rented house, delighting in enlivening its nooks and crannies, and Nathan immediately saw darkroom utility in the first-floor mother-in-law apartment. Four-year-old Nattie enrolled in Christ Church's weekday preschool and went to work with Nathan, returning with him at noon daily, delighting both. Eighteen-month-old Beth, Nathan's other childish heart, delighting everyone she met, stayed home with Mommy. Nathan's new schedule was just as hectic, but much less rewarding.

Wilmingtonians were a proud, tradition-bound lot, many with lowlander roots going back for generations in and around the old port city. Though there was interest in improving the riverfront and the downtown areas, progress was slow in the mid-Sixties. Despite its city-like accouterments, Wilmington's ambience was one of rural conservatism, looking forward to greater modernization.

*

During their first two months apart, September and October 1964, contact between the lovers was sparse, limited to furtive phone calls and anxious, question-filled letters. When he dared, he rang Shara's house and hung up, just to signal his pining presence.

As a senior, Shara began to flourish, though her influence dwindled at church, hurting her a bit. Yet with Nathan loving her from afar, urging her to capitalize on her assets, she applied the better self he awakened. Feeling renewed and confident, if lonely, she worked with Kathy, Jason, and others to continue Nathan's efforts, anticipating a new educational director. When Shara despaired of schoolwork, Nathan focused on her native intelligence and encouraged her to stretch, academically, as much as she could.

After several painful visits to the dentist, three teeth pulled, and a bit of overnight orthodontia, Shara's preparations for striking beauty were nearly complete. In early October she sent Nathan a roll of black and white film of herself and her younger siblings. Watching her new, flashing smile, slightly longer hair, and svelte figure emerge in his developing tray was delightful.

Though Nathan and Lenore made fulfilling love regularly, his overriding need for Shara remained an unrelenting force, rarely far from his consciousness. *My continuing enigma is how I can be and do what both loves deserve? Perhaps this question will resolve itself eventually, but for now, it mystifies me. Lenore is warm, loving, and giving, including in our lovemaking. I have no real complaints. Shara, however, encourages me to walk through doors I thought would forever remain closed to me. Even apart, she enlivens—and educates—both my spirit and my fantasies. How to balance the unbalanceable?*

Not really in the equation, harmless Melanie visited the Scotts every two to three weeks, allowing him partial expression of some of his fantasies, after Lenore slept. Though physically satisfied by both women at home, he sorely missed the free and unique admixture of deepest Agape and Eros which colored his memories and dreams of Shara.

Missing Shara and the more exciting and responsive ministry he developed in Durham, Nathan was reluctant to go to work, at first. To assuage his mood, he took an hour, daily, to exercise (sublimate!) at the YMCA. Within a month or two his arduous gym regimen trimmed and honed his body. He was a lean, muscular 165 pounds at 5'9", and in the best shape since he played football. He was miserable...

Nathan admired his boss, Dr. Ralph Morrison, Christ Church's new senior minister, transferred from a large, enormously successful church in Missouri. Beginning each weekday morning at 8:15 with a staff prayer meeting, Nathan reluctantly observed that he was long on verve and concepts but short on organizational acumen and effective follow up.

*

Christ Church spun off many of its younger, more energetic members, who began a new church in the middle of an affluent, lily-white section of the city: a perfect example of white flight. The remaining 1,200 parishioners were mostly older, conservative folks. They acquiesced to staying in the older, once beautiful and rich neighborhood, but had difficulty putting flesh to the skeleton of plans for serving the minorities and the poor whites slowly dominating the area. Nathan drew the neighborhood children into activities and services as allowed, but the promised support from the church was extremely sparse, equivocal, and slow in coming. Hope turned to frustration over two significant events.

To provide recreational opportunities for area youth, Nathan requested funds to purchase and install a basketball backboard at one end of the church's large, paved parking lot. Though several boardmen approved and supported his efforts, the official response was "lack of funds at this time." Finding the funds on his own, he ordered the pole and backboard, helped install them, and painted the lines of a half-court himself.

Two weeks later, upon coming to work, he found the unit had been removed. Complaints from the family that donated the funds for paving the parking lot caused the board to relent. The official reason was that the neighborhood children should not be allowed to congregate on church grounds unsupervised, for they might be hurt, and the church sued.

Swallowing defeat with as much grace as indignation allowed, Nathan turned to supervised programs, integrating neighborhood children into Christ Church's child and adolescent programs. Thus, he planned back-to-back parties for juniors, junior high, and senior high kids, and invited the area kids. Only the party for the juniors took place, in Nathan's mind a great success, until observed by the conservative father of one of the church's sixth grade girls.

Much ado and fervent pleading by Nathan and other supporters went for naught. Nathan was told that he could bring the neighborhood youth into the church for supervised activities in a separate program euphemistically called "The Community Club," but that their integration with regular members would have to wait until the church was "more ready."

The message was inescapable to all the young people and to Nathan, who began to look at his future at this viscose, old church with jaundiced eyes: no promised integration allowed!

Nathan had little tolerance for the minds or works of bigots. When encountering them, he ached for the wit of

Knox, a Black seminary classmate. Knox was once confronted at a local lunch counter by a snide waitress who whined, "I'm sorry, you. We don't happen to serve Negras, here!" Quick as a wink, Knox responded, "Hell, lady, I don't want to eat one. I just want a cup of coffee." He got it.

Operating separate youth programs, now, Nathan stayed even busier, while increasing memberships and attendance in both. Additionally, he was called on to perform all the functions and duties of any clergyman. In a word, he was swamped—and very lonely for his young paramour.

In a loving phone call, the lovers conversed about everything, including Shara's existentially threatening news that she and her family planned to move for a new job for her father soon, either to Rhode Island or Atlanta. Frightened, torn, and almost desperate, they plotted meeting at least one more time, come what may. An away football game seemed the best option.

Lenore acquiesced to Nathan's attending the November 6, 1964, away game of Shara's high school—in Fayetteville, as many of his old youth group were going to this public event. Shara's parents finally agreed to her going via chaperoned school bus. The realities would be quite different…

CHAPTER 25
MR. GREENCOCK AND A
PANTHEON OF VIRTUE

All lovers live by longing, and endure:
Summon a vision and declare it pure.

Theodore Roethke

Let us give nature a chance; she knows her business better
than we do.

Michel Eyquem de Montaigne

Molasses-thick need and patience as thin as water characterized Nathan when the time came for their tryst in Fayetteville. From September 13 to November 6, 1964 (54 days!) was too long to wait to requite their love and to unchain the dragons of their desires.

Nathan left Wilmington about noon on the appointed Friday, happily drove the ninety miles to Fayetteville, checked into a motel about three, and tried to rest in the bed that could soon be another connubial couch. Too excited to doze, he readied his camera, wondering how Shara might respond to his cautious hope for some figure shots.

Mindlessly watching television, Nathan reflected on his work in Wilmington. Though he loved working with all of his young people, aided by several dedicated adults who shared his vision, he was unhappy and wanted out. His most satisfying moments involved seeking forgiveness, rather than permission. *Perhaps it was the prospect of this very trip that emboldened me to take Wednesday's drastic and soul satisfying action—surely, the Lord's work...*

The junior high classrooms in the Wilmington church, utilizing one end of an upstairs wing in the large, twenty-five-year-old education building, consisted of six cubicles for five to six students each. Nathan's Sunday evening junior high fellowship doubled from twenty-five to fifty in less than two months and other than the church's large fellowship hall, they had no room large enough to hold more than a crowded six or eight at a time. He needed a large room for mixers, movies, and preliminary discussions, before breaking into smaller circles.

Nathan and Tim Blake, a deacon and junior high teacher, proposed a plan to knock out those confining walls, creating a room large enough for the entire group. The Board approved the plan, but as with most of Nathan's novel proposals, they were unwilling to establish a timeline for it, due to "the absence of funds for the labor."

Taking the Board at their word, Nathan and Tim borrowed saws, sledgehammers, and other tools and met in the junior high department after Wednesday's prayer meeting. With great gusto but little skill, this determined duo gleefully created the larger room themselves. It was exhilarating! By midnight, six small rooms were transformed into one huge room, as the walls came a-tumblin' down! Nathan delighted in this blatant blowing of his ram's horn of progress. He came away exhausted and filthy, but more gratified than any time since his installation.

Came the dawn, he proudly reported his and Tim's gift of hard labor and led a stunned Dr. Morrison on a guided tour of the new meeting room—a wide-eyed staff following in their train. Though Dr. Morrison seemed pleased with

Nathan's initiative, he had to ward off the more conservative deacons, who groused, incorrectly, that load-bearing walls may have been destroyed.

Workers were called in to smooth out the resulting floor gaps, and to clean and paint the enlarged room. When Nathan returned from his Fayetteville trip, he found everything in readiness for his junior high troops, who hailed him as "Joshua," for fighting their battle of Jericho—and delivering them into the promised land.

Though Nathan realized and rued his own brashness, he could not muster much worry about consequences. He had determined to leave, with Lenore's sympathetic concurrence, and was already in the process of applying to two graduate schools. Confiding his intent to a few younger church officers, they commiserated to a person, begging him to reconsider and trying to convince him that he was their brightest hope for greater, faster liberalization of their staid old church. Thus, guilt plagued Nathan, as it always did, when he realized that his prophet sometimes outstripped his priest. *In my zeal to improvise on what might be enough, I sometimes blunder into too much!*

Awakened from his Fayetteville reverie about falling walls and spiritual dissatisfaction, Nathan drove to a nearby mall, ate a light supper, and bought a new battery for his pocket radio. Unfamiliar butterflies beat their exotic wings against the walls of his churning stomach, lest something go awry, while his mind overflowed with amorous anticipation.

Driving to the stadium thirty minutes before Shara's bus was expected at 6:30, Nathan picked a parking spot about thirty yards from the entrance. Turning on his car's radio, he tried to concentrate on the pre-game warm-up, but heard only the static of his own anticipation.

As fans arrived, the festive, expectant ambience of high school football permeated, evoking the ambivalent, adolescent feelings he experienced working his way through the many minefields of high school. At no time since had he felt more powerful and full of potential, yet more unfocused, beyond the next day. His high school days were filled with action and reaction, while he and his many mates tried out their different selves for size. Recalling and re-experiencing such feelings stimulated QI's queries about *Shara's readiness to focus and commit beyond convenience and adventure, considering my own such inabilities, when I was her age...*

It was dusk by the time three groaning school buses, filled with a dyspepsia of excited students, belched up to the main gate, and disgorged their celebrating, adolescent contents. Shara was supposed to go in with the crowd, spy someone with whom she wanted to sit, and disappear. They planned to meet "close to, but not at, the gate."

Nathan was near panic twenty minutes later, with no Shara in sight. Fearing that something was amiss, he walked toward the gate, only to see her standing there looking forlorn. Resisting the urge to run to her, he managed a low whistle, and she spotted him. He signaled her to follow him and ambled as casually as possible back to his car, passing late-comers from he knew not where. The game was underway when he returned her worried grin, drew her down on the seat, her head in his lap, and eased his car away from the tumult and the shouting.

"Nathan, where were you? I walked up and down in front of that gate for fifteen minutes and was about to go back in, when I saw you."

"Egad, gal, I waited in my car, as planned, looking for you to find me, as planned! Why didn't you look for me, as planned?"

"I–I guess I was a little bit afraid. It looked so dark, and there were lots of people coming in. I figured you would realize I didn't want to be traipsing up and down among the cars, under all those trees, alone. God, I was glad to see you— am glad to see you! You're not upset with me, are you?"

"Shara Auchincloss Starr, we don't have time for me to be upset with you; I'll be upset with you, later. The game will probably be over by 9:30 or 10:00, and it's already after seven. What instructions for re-boarding the bus?"

"We're supposed to leave the stadium and sign in on the buses no later than twenty minutes after the final gun. I'm sorry, Nathan. I wasn't sure how safe it would be to be wandering around out there"

"I should have thought of that. I just didn't want to risk being recognized. No matter; you're here!"

"Are we going to a drive-in theater, or did you get–a motel?"

"A motel, of course! I want to be totally free with you, and private. We're here!"

"The Pantheon Motel. It looks expensive. I hope you didn't spend too much money. We could've stayed in the car–it's not very cold out."

Nathan parked directly outside his ground floor room and self-consciously ushered Shara inside. Shy and unaccustomed to her first taste of all-American sleaze, she moved about the room, exclaiming over its pseudo-Roman appointments, skirting the beds. Nathan tuned his radio to the game.

"Do you want a cold drink, Shara?" he brightened, vaguely aware of her unease and of his own sudden thirst.

"Yes!" she exclaimed, too brightly, sitting stiffly in an chair in front of the television. "My mouth is so dry, if I spit, it will break."

Opening a bottle of Cheerwine and pouring two ice-filled glasses, he handed one to her, raised the other, and toasted too casually, "Here's to the lovely Shara Day Starr, whom I've truly loved from miles much too far!"

Her gentle laughter began to warm the sterile room and coaxed her from her chair into his arms. Holding their soft drinks away from their embrace, they kissed for the first time since the middle of September–fifty-four days. Their tentative kiss became a caution to their expectations, a stranger to their desires. Each felt the unexpected effects of time and distance; both struggled to find the person they knew back then, not quite able to recognize the present one.

"What's wrong, Shara? Are you uncomfortable?"

Sitting tenuously on one of the double beds, Shara cast her eyes down, recognizing discomfiting truth in his question.

"Not to worry, baby," he soothed, kneeling before her, and looking up into her face, "we need to be together a while. It's more than natural to be a little dubious about things, after so long."

"I wanted–I always want to kiss you when I first get into the car, but you usually get me out of sight so fast. I–I don't know, Nathan...," she trailed off, ruefully.

For the first time Nathan noticed how straight and beautiful her teeth were and told her so. Shyness turned to self-conscious pleasure, adding color to two grinning visages.

"Do you really like them? The dentist pulled three, reshaped, and put new covers on my top, front teeth. It was no fun!"

"I can imagine but look how gorgeous you are now— and you were absolutely lovely before!"

"It really does improve my smile, doesn't it? I knew you'd be pleased. While I was lying there, and the dentist was leaning all over me, I kept thinking how pleased you would be, and how much that would please me. I think that helped more than the anesthetic."

Through that wee crack in her innate, feminine reserve, Nathan began to pour genuine affection and appreciation, reawakening her responsiveness to his focus, sincerity, and gentleness. Sitting next to her at the foot of the bed, he eased her into conversation about home, church, school, her awful–and likely–move farther away from him, and other topics of salience.

Slowly, Shara began to relax, sensing and absorbing the familiar warmth of the man and appreciating his ardent focus on her life and times. He made no move to touch her again, willing to await the judgment of her emotions.

Leaning back on her elbows, Shara seemed aware of her prone position, as she spoke of missing him much more than she had imagined possible, and of the adjustments she had to make, learning to depend so much more on herself. Recognizing the truth, Nathan expressed his pride in her growth, more obvious with her every sentence. *Though she looks younger, she seems more mature.*

When he, too, leaned back on his elbows next to her, she turned on her side, placed her head in her left palm, and drew her knees towards her body, self-consciously revealing more of her lithe thighs, enticing and indelicately beckoning beneath her skirt. Relishing and appreciating her growth, Nathan shared a few of his Wilmington experiences to a rapt Shara. When he lay back upon the bed, scooted back, and placed his head on the pillows, she rose to her knees, and looked at him, as though for the first time.

"Good Lord, Nathan, you've lost a bunch of weight, haven't you?"

"I guess I've dropped about twenty-five pounds; I weigh 165 pounds, and very little of it is fat. How about you? You look more filled out than you were in September."

"I've gained two to three pounds, but I swear I don't know where they went–maybe a little bit to my boobs and legs. I weigh about 113. But Nathan, you look wonderful!"

Nathan smiled and held both arms out to her. With a whimper of recognition and restoration, she fell into them, pressing her breasts against his sturdy chest, snuggling her face in his neck.

"Shara, my Shara, I've missed you so. Welcome home! I love you, darling. Do you know?"

"Yes, oh, yes, Nathan! I feel it, now! I feel that same kindness and concern, your warmth and love pouring all over me, patiently pulling me home. I love you, too, dar–darling–so much!"

Nathan pulled her fully atop his body, feeling her legs spreading, and her thighs settling their renewed love and lust on his. Kissing her deeply and rolling her over, he pressed tightly the rigid announcement of his ready desire and held her arms above her head on the bed. Looking down at her yielding, trusting love, he saw the fire in her dark, knowing, eyes, flashing its coded heat to him in unmistakable intent and intensity.

"I want you, Nathan!" she whispered.

Nathan took care to assuage and praise the needs of her every part, while removing her clothes, nurturing her softest, most vulnerable spots with the blessings of his tending. The depth and tenacity of his ministrations produced the miracle of readiness for both desire and fulfillment until, totally cleared of the weeds of uncertainty, Shara spread her curving furrows to receive him, deeper and deeper, until need turned to gift, and newly righteous lust evoked the felicity of mutual love. The initial erotic storm passing, it ended with the most vital rain of all: the mingling of tears of joy and reconciliation, cleansing doubt, and expressing love no longer confined to mere hope or distilled memory.

Spent, Nathan lay between her legs, nurtured by continued spasms and delicious flexing, bathing in her fountain, caressing her gratified lineaments, until she milked him into tumescence, and they began their special, precocious, *pas de deux* again. More prepared for their connate roles than either imagined, Nathan used his increased strength and endurance to honor and complement Shara's growth and maturity. Together, they expressed the truth and beauty of their consummate éclat and natural move and sway, in speechless awe of this singular, evolved propriety, until sigh turned to cry, and love's most elite propositions became deed, indeed.

Shara's gentling sighs were interrupted by the roar of the stadium crowd, as another gladiator in another arena also thrust home. Nathan heard the unwelcome huzzahs and pulled himself from Shara's overflowing, bowing to the inexorable intrusion of time into the fleeting practice and perfecting of their love. Looking at his watch, he despised its message of 8:45 p.m.

"My God, Nathan!" she said, trying to refocus his attention back on her, "I cain't tell you how much I needed and enjoyed that! You seem so much stronger than before; yet you certainly haven't lost your gentle touch. It's so much better than exercising, it's ridiculous! I'm glad we didn't have to use rubbers, and it's a good thing my periods are a regular twenty-eight days. Clocca Morra is due about Sunday or Monday."

Lying in his arms, Shara felt the afterglow of delicious reunion begin to ebb, and the onerous reality of impermanence replace it. Seeking comforting familiarity, she kissed his neck, and then sneakily, snakily, she attacked the vulnerable spots under his jaw with her tongue, producing the desired outcry, escape-dance, and denunciation, followed by his prodigious tickling of her ribs. Squealing, the naked couple bounced about the room, chasing each other over beds, around chairs, and finally into the bathroom, where they were stopped short by their reflections, mature, svelte, virile, and beautiful in their respective reflections.

"Shara, would you allow me to take a few pictures of your lovely form, to tide me over the long weeks of separation? Please?"

Though he saw doubt's shadow flicker her features and enlarge her pupils, he was pleased to hear her say, "I–I guess it will be all right. It may even be our last opportunity... I know you are a very visual person–and you have sense enough to hide things. But what do I do? I feel funny–and skinny! Do I look all right? Let me brush my hair."

"'*Vanitas, vanitas, omnes vanitas!* saith the preacher,'" said the preacher. "Here I am, willing to immortalize you, and all you can think about are your hair and how skinny you are. Just get on the bed the way you are, honey. I like the tousled, just fu–just loved look of you. I'll take some good color shots of you tomorrow in your new duds, and you can primp all you want. Believe me, you look scrumptious!"

Thus, in her eighteenth year, Shara Starr posed nude for the first time, disbelieving that she was close to rare beauty. Wearing nothing but a tiny gold cross on a thin gold chain around her neck, and her grandmother's emerald ring, she readied herself to pose. Nathan did his best to still his trembling hands. More coy than shy, but manifestly both, she knelt on the bed before him and struck eleven mild but increasingly daring poses, ending flat on her back, extending her slightly parted legs, revealing her precious charms as naturally as she breathed.

While photographing her, Nathan's lust (and awe) grew visibly, despite the demands of focus, aperture, composition, and flash distances, causing neo-toothy grins and twinkling eyes, when she grasped his rising star, intending another focus.

He hoped to save his last shot for intercourse, but he soon forgot about his camera. Standing at the end of the bed, sliding into her, smoothing the softness of her bottom, he watched his glistening length thrilling in her, repeatedly, until, in a rush of supreme pleasure, they moaned and sang together the great, two part "Amen!" of their hymn to love—and to incomparably good sex.

Afterwards, with three minutes to play, and the ball on the three-yard line of the opposing team, Nathan and Shara posed, standing together before the mirror, au naturel, and he took his last shot as their team scored, winning the game. Dressing quickly, and realizing they had not talked enough, again, they planned to meet tomorrow at the little Episcopal church near her home, noon-thirty.

Nathan maneuvered his wagon against the jam of exiting cars, and stopped within thirty yards of Shara's buses, blowing their white, condensing exhausts into the cool, North Carolina air. Blending with the crowd, Shara joined two acquaintances, who had not missed her, and boarded her bus with five minutes to spare.

Proud of beating the odds and the best efforts of civilized society to prevent exactly what happened, Nathan waited until the buses left, drove back to his motel, and watched television until eleven, certain that Shara could not join him.

Sitting with two friends on the second bus, Shara listened to their excited chatter about the victory, the players, the cheerleaders, who was dating whom, the teachers, and how glad they were to have attended this game. She joined in a bit but all she could think about was the delightful ooze slowly issuing from her body, reminding her of their restoration and plans for the morrow. In lustful recollection, she squeezed her vagina several times and smiled at the pleasure and the effusions—then drifted into contented sleep.

*

Checked out by ten, Saturday morning, by noon, he was in Shara's vicinity. After a cheeseburger, he waited only ten minutes before she rounded the corner. His mind painted the lovely look of her more durably than a mere photograph, in her new blue denim knee-length skirt, a white, thinly cross-striped, long-sleeved blouse, and Bass Weejuns. She carried a light London Fog raincoat and grinned her presence into his car, delivering a quick, fervent kiss.

"There! I did it! Now let's go! I have news!"

"Congratulations on my kiss! I loved it! God, you look good, baby, and smell fresh and sweet as a bouquet," he said, pulling out of the parking lot. "I love your new collegiate outfit, too. What's your news?"

"Thanks, but don't you think it makes me look skinny? What news would make you happy?"

"Gadzooks, Shara, lots of things. To have and hold you forever, for a starter. Do I have to guess?"

"Yes, you do. It has to do with my—my accessibility. Tell me what you think would be good news about that."

"Let's see, you're not moving to Rhode Island?"

"That's right! But there's more."

"You're moving to Atlanta.'"

"Nope! Keep going; you'll get it."

"You're not moving at all?"

"You got it!"

"Yeehhii! Shara, that's fantastickabobble, as Pogo would say. When did all this not come about?"

"Daddy told us this morning. I almost screamed. That means I can finish my senior year in Durham, and we will still be under two hundred miles apart! He has an opportunity for a raise right here, and he's also promoting a business of his own. Aren't you happy?"

"Ecstatic, Shara! It'll be the difference between lots of visits and almost no visits at all. There is a God, and She's on our side! I was afraid a move could have been the end of us."

"Yes, Nathan, it's a Godsend! I prayed and prayed we wouldn't move. Where are we going, anyway?"

"Yes, prayer works! I thought we'd check out the state park. We can find some privacy there. It's close."

"That's fine with me. It's beautiful and warm enough, now, and there are trails and acres of woods for privacy–the place is huge."

On their way to another few hours of purloined pleasure, greatly relieved of the prospects of a distance-forced attrition of their relationship, the couple's delight in the present increased to unconfined joy, expressing itself in their special, intimate cant and banter, all the way to their woodsy haven. Their laughter rang in plangent peals, bubbling up from pools of simple happiness, too long dammed and damnable behind distance, convention, and inconvenient circumstance. Laughing, they learned; learning, they longed; longing, they loved, loving, they laughed.

They ambled across acres of brown, fallen leaves, past leafless trees, interspersed among the evergreens, and patches of azaleas, all sleeping until the first blush of spring. They hadn't seen a soul in thirty minutes...

Stopping in a small glade among sheltering pines, Shara spread her coat on clean, dry leaves and sat herself down. Pulling out a long, green balloon from his coat, Nathan blew it up and tied it off. Four feet long, six inches in diameter, it was topped by a head-like bulb, with two, four inch long, thin rubber antennae. Holding the long, pneumatic phallus to his crotch, and aiming it at hers, he memorialized, "Allow me to present Mr. Greencock, a symbol of my three most memorable traits, Shara. The size and shape, of course, are but meager representations of your favorite member of my personal congregation of physical attributes; the color is to remind you of my capability for jealousy, should you try to rouse it by taking in another vaginal roomer; and the horny antennae are to help you recall my eternal desire for the luscious likes of you. Now, lift your skirt, that I may introduce Mr. Greencock, to the territory which he is to guard, and well, hell, Shara, it's cheaper than a chastity belt and not quite as uncomfortable."

Laughing, she lifted her skirt to accommodate his prank between her bare legs, grimacing with the cold of it. Pinching it betwixt her thighs, straddling its middle, she cavorted about, as though riding a cockhorse, with the balloon and her skirt protruding fore and aft, rolling her eyes, and squealing.

Instead of chasing after this laughing, nimble nymph astride her green stud, he reached for his color camera, seeking to photograph such indelicacy for posterity. She was much too demure–and quick.

"Oh, no you don't, sly guy!"

Having been in the park an hour, and convinced of their privacy, Nathan caught Shara in his arms, drank in her smiling eyes, removed her glasses, and kissed her sweet lips. As was her wont, she closed her elbows together between them, cupped his face between caressing palms, and tiptoed her feet up and down in place–her cat becoming her kitten. To Nathan, so smitten with her spontaneity, it would ever be one of her most appealing and endearing gifts.

His heart beating its thrill, he swept her up and carried her to her coat, spreading her on it like lily pads on an azure pool. Sitting back on his heels, he surveyed this enchanting creature, liquid with love and expectancy, and made ready to drink.

"Shara, my own Shara, do you have any notion of your overpowering beauty?"

"I almost believe it when I'm with you, Nathan, because you make me feel beautiful. I don't really care if I am or not, as long as you believe it."

"'Well roared, Lion!' A fitting response for one so blind to how Nature has favored her. I love you!"

"I know, and it still amazes me!"

"Me, too! Mind if we make love, now?"

Their movements were as unhurried as a winter's passing. At one with the lure of the forest, they mingled and entwined their limbs like vines, seeking the precious warmth and weal of coalescence, finding the heat and moisture which sustained them, in search of the other in the light of brightest day. As have lovers from time immemorial, they wove together their bodies and their spirits, under the trees and under the sky, love and lust irrepressibly soaring to the heights, again and again, until they lay panting and fulfilled, an irrefragable fact amidst Nature in all her decency, order—and righteousness.

"Are you warm enough, darling?" his soft voice sifting in her hair.

"Inside and wherever your body is touching me," nestled the nested, "but I feel the cold under me, and where I am exposed."

Sighing the dedicated sigh of care and protection, her cavalier arose in his nakedness, and wrapped his sport coat around her, this chivalry instructed by its opportunity. As Shara lay in the sun, he found a small, dried wildflower and presented it to her on bare knees, continuing in his need to bestow. At ease in his protecting presence, she pressed it to her lips, planted it in her hair, and laid herself down to sleep.

In awe of his lady, he took stock: *There she lies, lovely of self and mien, calmly naked, pooled in a fortuitous kiss of sunlight, her long-lashes closed, lost in the comfort of my protective presence, blissfully asleep. Such is her trust in me and of this memorable time and meaning. Such is my paragon—Love...*

"Why did you let me sleep, Nathan? You're dressed already. What time is it?" she mumbled, stretching slumbrously, straining her breasts and pinning his legs with hers. "Come down here!"

Kneeling beside her, allowing himself to be pulled into her embrace, "I let you sleep because you drifted off, and wouldn't have if you hadn't needed it. Besides, I love watching you sleep. I dressed because I was a bit chilly, and it's almost 3:00 o'clock. P.S., I love you."

At one with their surroundings, she kissed him, reached for his crotch, and began to caress him. Though he started to speak, her kisses prevailed, while his hands mapped her smooth, white breasts.

"God, Shara, soft, young, desirable, alive—these are the realties I experience when I touch you. You've turned me on in less than thirty seconds. Be careful with the zipper."

"Lie down, Nathan—I want to kiss it."

And it was so.

As they ambled back to the main trail, they saw another couple walking at about their pace, thirty yards ahead. Shara pointed to the pine needles adhering to the back of the lady's coat and asked Nathan to check hers. Sure enough, he removed a few.

"I hope they enjoyed it as much as we did," she whispered, consciously squeezing her vagina as she walked. "I hope I can keep some of your semen inside me until I get home. That way, I can have something of you after you've gone."

"You're just a little weird, Lady. You know that?"

"Well, it's your fault—no, not fault—it's your particular kind of loving that has freed me to be completely myself, sexually—and ever other way. I love it; I cain't tell you how much I want and need it. Sometimes, while I'm sitting in class, it's all I can think of. I look around at all the other girls, and thank God for you, as I wonder how many of them have lovers anywhere near as wonderful as you are."

"And what do you decide?"

"I decide that maybe a fourth of them aren't virgins, and maybe one or two do it regularly. But I am certain I am the only one with a real man for a lover."

"How does that make you feel, Shara?"

"Sometimes I want to tell everone I meet what's happening to me, so they will see me as something more than that dumb brunette with the glasses on the third row. Other times I want to tell them what they are missing–that, if they want to know true happiness, they should find someone they really love, and–well, get fucked!"

*

On the way back to Durham, looking pensive, Shara's face telegraphed another of her unique inquiries.

"Yes, Serious Shara. What can I do for you?"

"What you can do, and what you may do are probably very different, darling, but that's another conversation, for later. What I want to know is how serious you are about one of the symbols of, big, ol,' horny, Mr. Greencock, here? Would you really be jealous if–if I dated?"

"Quite naturally, I would, Shara, but I am of several minds–not hearts–about that likelihood. First, while I'm married to Lenore and not free to offer you an open, permanent relationship, I have no right to ask you to refrain from seeking normal relationships with other males, no matter how much I want you entire to myself.

"Secondly, I am twenty-nine and you are seventeen and, despite our heartwarming speeches, there are many things you should experience, in order to make a final, intelligent decision about the person with whom you want to spend the rest of your life–college, for instance, and all that goes with it.

"Thirdly, I am the first male you have seriously, uh, dated, certainly fucked, and that hardly gives you enough experience on which to base a final decision, no matter how good it feels, or how committed you are, now.

"Finally, as much as it pains me to say it, if you don't date, you might very well go through life wondering who else you might be, how things could have been, who/what you might have missed, and what you could have done differently."

QI congratulated himself on his moral consistency, despite the ambivalent threat lying just beneath the surface, signaling caveat and grave danger.

Shara started, "Are you saying that you *want* me to date?"

"Without a doubt, yes, and absolutely, positively not, sweetheart. I told you I was of two minds about it, but my heart knows only its inexorable need and love for you. It–I– will become as green as that silly balloon when you do. Naturally, you will, sooner or later. Just as certainly, I'll worry and wonder all about it, doubt you and myself some, and ask you a million questions about your true feelings, sexual responsiveness, and what they might mean. So, proceed at your own risk, as well as mine, daring Shara, but do proceed!"

"How am I supposed to respond to two exactly opposite messages? I don't know why I asked; no one has even asked me for a date, yet."

"Ahh, 'yet;' the lady says, 'yet,' thinking that her old fool of a lover hasn't realized, long ago, that there are any number of boys who have already turned her head, wondering how it would be to–date them–dance with them–kiss them– even fuck them. Right?"

"Na-than! What a way to say it! Of course, I look, just as you do when good-looking girls walk by. That doesn't mean I want to have sex with them, does it?"

"It often does when I look, Missy! Now, 'fess up, and tell me his name, or is it their names?"

"Na-than!"

"Shara, it's all right! I'm sorry I'm being a putz, but I've thought about these things, just as you have, and it really is okay. You are a warm-blooded—scratch that—a hot-blooded, highly sexed, experienced girl—woman, really—who is used to getting right down to it, and you live amidst millions of like-minded males, some of whom must strike your fancy, pique your curiosity, challenge your ego, stimulate your hormones, and gush your panties."

"Well, I just don't want you to think I'm sitting up here pining away for anybody but you. If I look, it will be for one or more of the reasons you mentioned a minute ago, mostly curiosity, not wanting to be left out of some of the normal activities of my senior year, and I guess I'll admit to wanting to be liked, even desired, for my own sake, by my peers. That's natural, isn't it?"

"Most certainly, Shara, and thank you for being honest. I love you for it. Now, tell me about him or them, or whomever."

Shyly, Shara described several boys with whom she had bantered a bit, flirted back, or laughed at their suggestive innuendoes. One boy, Sonny, hinted at dating, and told her he bet she would be a good make out. She saw him daily, in two of her classes, though he was supposed to be dating someone else. Nathan felt his heart sinking as the inevitable drew nearer. She sat quietly, looking guilty.

"Shara, it's okay. I don't want you to feel funny about being a perfectly normal girl—woman, I have abundant confidence in our love and don't believe dates with high school boys to be much of a threat. Secondly, dating others will throw any suspicions about us off the trail. Finally, and the hardest for me to say, the only way I could ever stand to lose you is if I were certain that you love someone else more than you love me. Though I have no desire whatsoever to test our love, I have no right to stand in your way of testing yourself as a woman."

A salty tear dripped down, swelling, at the end of her nose. Reaching over, he deftly removed it, letting it hang on the end of his finger, then kissed it.

"Baby, it's all right. It's not as though I've given you up, or anything close to it. It's just that it's a rational solution to a natural, realistic situation—and I love you for crying."

"Nathan, I don't want anybody else but you, now, or ever! You may be my first love, but I want you to be my only love as well. If I date, I'll do so with you on my mind, and I will share all my experiences with you. Not just because you are curious or even jealous, but because I know I can and want to share them with you, openly, because you care so very much who I am—and what happens to me—you could even advise me. I don't think I can or will ever love anyone like I love you. Please believe that darling!"

"I do believe it, Shara. I want you to be as free as you must, and as faithful as you can. Meanwhile, we will continue to love and see each other as often as possible, starting two weekends from today, November 20, if that's all right with you."

CHAPTER 26
MEANWHILE...

My candle burns at both ends;
It will not last the night;
But, oh, my foes, and, oh, my friends—
It gives a lovely light.

Edna St. Vincent Millay

Fulfilled and restored, Nathan returned to his increasingly unrewarding job. Dr. Morrison scheduled a staff retreat which meant long range plans would be evaluated, restructured, and work assignments made to facilitate progress towards derived goals and objectives. Nathan's heart was not in it, though he strove to involve his mind in the process, trying to influence decisions, in light of his unannounced plans to leave.

He was increasingly discontent with his distance from Shara, his role in the church, its unresponsiveness to opportunities to serve its surrounding community, and with the sadness which Lenore evidenced at the sorry quality of their harried lives.

November elided into December, with all its hyperactive preparations. He took the GRE exams; worked to build up his segregated youth groups; supply preached in area churches fairly often; successfully visited Shara four times; sneaked into Melanie's bed on each night of her four visits to

Wilmington; developed pictures of Shara, his family, and the church young people; entertained Kathy and Jason over a long weekend; directed a regional youth rally; served on the new regional camp committee (and helped plan the upcoming summer's tent camping events on an undeveloped campsite); performed several baptisms, weddings and funerals; and conducted many hours of counseling for young and old, in addition to his regular planning, directing, and oversight duties.

Nathan announced an approved introductory sex education course for his seventh and eighth graders, but the conservative father of a seventh-grade girl put the quietus on it until he himself could study the curriculum. One more project put off until someone was "ready." Such disappointments increased his tension and unhappiness with his work. They also cemented his decision to seek more fertile ground, hopefully on a college campus. He didn't blame Dr. Morrison at all, because Nathan realized that he, too, was dancing as fast as he could under similar reactive and conservative circumstances.

As was true in Durham, the one totally non-contingent area of love and affection in his daily Wilmington life was his love for and from Lenore and their children. Nattie was bright as he could be, and little Beth awingly cute and responsive. Cherishing his nightly singing and storytelling, they provided the high-water mark of each day.

"What shall we sing, tonight, Eee-liz-a-beth?" he crooned, a head lying on each shoulder, bed-ready, snugly and delicious.

"Hooww 'bout, hoow 'bout, `Pwaise Him,' Daaddee?" she asked, looking intently into and touching his face, proud that it was her turn to choose.

"That sounds like a good one, Bethamacallit! Do you want to start?"

"My not `Bethamawcawit,' Daaddee, my Beth! Teekle you!"

And she did. Decorum and sleepy-slow activities halted, as hyperkinetic Nattie and rambunctious baby sister crawled all over their sprawling, laughing, loving father, relishing his exaggerated, tickle-induced yelps and pleas, anticipating the gentle, exasperated admonishments from Mommy, advising all that such carryings-on were not conducive to sleep. Calming, *les trois enfants terrible* began their ritual anew, getting through at least one chorus of a children's hymn and a chorus of a made-up sillysong, featuring Daddy's too loud baritone.

Carrying soon-sleepy Beth in his arms to her bed, Nattie rode on his back. Watching while his father tucked his sister in and rubbed her back to the rhythms of his own lullabies, Nathan's namesake advised, "Sing 'Dear One,' to her, Daddy."

Who's a Dear One? Who's a sweet One?
It's Bethee, today!
Who's my favorite girl? Who's the best in the world?
It's Bethee, lullay.
I love you in the mornin' time; I love you all the day!
Who's my Dearest Girl? Who's my precious Pearl?
It's Bethee, lullay.

Nattie's turn, he crawled down and around, into his Daddy's strong arms, so he, too, could be carried like a baby, even though he was a "big boy," to his own bed.

"Say your prayers, Nattie-boy."

"God bless Mommy, Daddy, Beth, Grammy and Granddaddy, Ma Helen and Pa Jack; make Nattie a good boy; keep us all safe; we baig for Chrissake, Amen."

"Do you have anything else you'd like to ask or tell God, son?"

"Well, I could ask Him to bring me stuff for Chrissmas."

"Yes, Nattie, I suppose you could, but do you have anything to ask that will help others?"

"Dear God, help Daddy stay home more often, and make Grammy feel all better and not be sick. Help Beth leave my toys alone, and help me not drive Mommy crazy, we baig for Chrissake, Amen."

"Amen, laddie, and double-amen! Now, close your eyes, and I'll sing to you."

"Sing, `Nattiemydarlin,' Daddy, so I can sleep right."

Nattie, my Darlin', I'll love you forever.
Nattie, my Darlin', forever and a day.
You are my Dear Son—brightest star up in my sky!
Nattie, my Darlin', I'll love you forever.
Nattie, my Darlin', forever and a day!

Rubbing his back and humming, till his darlin' luxuriated enough in his father's comforting attention to sleep, Nathan checked Beth, again, and tiptoed downstairs to be with his dear wife a few minutes, before returning to church.

"Must you go back again tonight, honey?"

"You know I do, 'Nore. I'll try to be back before midnight."

"I hope so, Nathan. I'm beginning to feel like a nun, all alone in our bed. Then, when you do come home, you fall asleep on the couch, watching that darn tv."

"Hast, thou grown horns, dear heart? If so, sharpen them for me, and I'll do my best to point them in the right direction, when I come in."

"Promises! Promises!"

"I'll do my best, Lenore."

"Do you want me, Nathan?"

"You know I do, honey. It's just that life is a bit too complicated to keep both the church and the home fires burning. I'll do better, really.".

"We'll see. I know you're busy but how many times a day do you go downtown to check your post office box, to see if you have heard from Shara?"

"Once in the morning and once at night, baby," he smoothed, trying not to project his shock that he had been found out. "She is doing okay these days and has even had a warm date or two. She took her SATs several days ago, and because she isn't going to be moving out of state, her dad is planning a career for her in interior design after DTI."

"Why was it necessary to get a post office box downtown, Nathan? She could write you here if you didn't want her letters to go to the church."

"For no good reason, but for several lesser ones. Do you want me to enumerate?"

"Why not?"

"Indeed. First, I have the box so I can receive a few mail-order books and magazines that I'm ashamed to let our postman see. Secondly, Shara is sensitive about your feelings, and asked to find a way to keep her letters totally private. Thirdly, I, too, am sensitive about your feelings and did not want you leaping to conclusions about things which still puzzle the hell out of me. Finally, I can get mail as soon as it comes in, instead of having to wait twenty-four hours."

"You did warn me your reasons would be 'lesser.' How often do you two communicate these days, my love?"

"As often as I can cajole her into it, as you might surmise, having suffered through my push for letters yourself, once upon a time."

"And how often would that be?"

"For her, she does well to get one or two mailed a week. For me, I get something to her about every other day–sometimes more often."

"Why, darling?"

"I assume you have found one or more of either my or her missives, so you probably already have a fair idea. Besides, you know me as well as anybody on earth, Lenore. You tell me."

"Yes, you carelessly left one of her letters in your coat, and I needed some money. Age old, corny story comes to our house. I have it here. I have not read it yet–I may never read it, for fear of what it may mean. Why don't you tell me what's in it that I have a right to know?"

With some relief Nathan recognized the date and remembered its mildly loving contents, but no direct allusion to sex. Feeling his wife's worry and genuinely not wanting to hurt her, he depended on her ethics and her upbringing–and on his own certifiable turpitude–in his response.

"Please, do read it, Lenore. You'll find it nondescript, chatty, about the SAT, griping about her father, and looking forward to seeing me sometime during the Christmas holidays. Oh yeah, she asks about Nattie's fistula, Beth's potty training, and your painting. But go ahead and read it. I don't mind."

Nathan never knew whether she read it or not, for she grimaced and handed it to him. "Nathan, what is really going on between you two–or do you know?"

How much do I tell her? I realize that either way, I'm hurting her. What's the most loving thing to say, now? I do love her, so I'll opt for gentleness.

"I'm not entirely sure–except that I think about her a lot; I miss her; I do an awful lot of counseling and encouraging–and even some advising about her dating. For what it is worth, she knows very well how much I love and need my family, and that I do not want to hurt anybody by helping her. Most likely, I have fallen in fascination with her, and she is infatuated with me, to a degree. I'll be glad to go into it as deeply as you wish, honey, but right now, unless you insist otherwise, I have a scheduled counseling session and a report to write before midnight, and I need to go."

"What's that old love song about discriminating 'a line between love and fascination?'"

"It's fascination with her value, both to herself and to others, including me, of course. It's complicated..."

"How often do you plan to go to Durham the rest of this month, Nathan?"

"I saw her, briefly, with a bunch of other kids, on the fifth, so I may go down once or twice after Christmas, unless you forbid me to do so."

"Nathan, you know I won't forbid you to do anything. I would just like to ask you not to sneak, and to tell me your plans. It's what I don't know that hurts me. When are you going to be able to let her grow without you, as you said you planned to do? I realize she is a sensitive, wounded girl, but you need to wean her from her emotional dependence on you— I assume her dependence is only emotional. It is, isn't it, Nathan?"

"I have confessed many times that I have a strange, abiding affection for her, and though it is certainly not fatherly, neither is it lecherous. I simply care very much what happens to her. As is obvious, I need to be with her, at times, I have invested a great deal of my own emotions in her welfare, and I admit to having a difficult time letting go."

I hate not telling her everything, but the truth would be even worse!

"To your point, I have been seriously thinking about an interregnum, during which we would cease communication, at least for a time–say, thirty days or so. But she is not yet ready for that, nor, in all honesty, am I. I know it is hard on you, but

I can only be who I am. You know very well that I love you, and that I love our children to distraction. As to sneaking, yes, I'm tempted, because I'm afraid of hurting you by doing what I must do. I'll always tell you about any visit, however; that's a promise!"

Lenore folded her arms across her chest, and Nathan noticed her foot tapping, unconsciously. Her face was a mask, but her eyes were searching his. She took a deep breath, followed by a long sigh before she spoke again.

"Honey," she said, slowly, "I know you are not happy, but I don't know what will make you happy, and I don't think you do, either. However, neither of us should believe Shara will do the job. Melanie says someone told her that they saw you in Durham the time you went to Greensboro for the district committee on higher education. Did you drive to Durham?"

"Yes, it's on the way."

"Then, why didn't you tell me, instead of making me suspect it, and then have Melanie confirm my suspicions? I'd call that sneaking, wouldn't you?"

"Technically, yes, baby, but why didn't you just ask me? I was not hiding, or no one would have seen me. It's not really Melanie's business to be telling you such things."

"Mellie simply mentioned it, thinking you would surely call her if you were in town. Her comment was innocent. It is your action that is under discussion, Nathan. Please don't sneak, anymore, okay?"

"I'm sorry, Lenore. Henceforth, I'll tell you."

"I hope so, Nathan. I love you and don't want to lose you, but I can't fight for you when I don't know when or where the battles are."

"Accordingly, I'd like to go to Durham December 26, and the 29th."

"Are you telling or asking?"

"Which do you prefer?"

"Telling, for now. I reserve the right to change my mind, however."

Putting his arms around her waist, Nathan smiled and kissed her. She sought to pull away but relented and kissed him back.

"Lenore, bear with me. Things are going on inside me that I don't fully understand, and my foundations are quaking a bit. This ministry squelches me at the same time it challenges me to triple my efforts. Just keep on keeping on with me. If anything gets too hairy, I'll tell you."

Melting into him, the wanting, loving warmth she always was with him, fought the first of many tears and believed him—and in him, despite the threatening bolts striking all about them.

Hugging him back, she let go and opened the door for him.

"Nathan, I love you; please keep loving me," she said, placing her vulnerability at his disposal, once again.

Fighting his own tears, he hugged her fiercely, whispering gently, "'Nore, you know I love you—and always will. Stand by me, baby. It will all work out..."

Then he was gone. Lenore stood a full two minutes on the front porch of their rented home, until she could no longer see or hear his station wagon.

"Come back to me, Nathan!" she whispered into the night...

CHAPTER 27
ADUMBRATION

There is the greatest practical benefit in making a few failures early in life.

Thomas Henry Huxley

A woman waits for me, she contains all, nothing is lacking.

Walt Whitman

Christmas, a paean to little children, was ever sung *bel canto*, in eight parts with descant in Scott homes, *da capo.* That the Scotts were straining to capture jollity was not noted by their two little ones, who, like most Christian little ones, happily feasted on the sauce of the season.

Sharing that very sauce on Christmas Eve, Nathan drove the church bus, filled with rosy-cheeked make-outs, as they caromed and caroled from shut-in to shut-in, harmonizing their episodic merriment with the twinkling decorations of Christendom. His strong baritone graced many a flat note from jovial carolers and mellowed the ambience from shouts to song. Afterward, the revelers streamed into his home for liquor-less wassail and fig-less figgy pudding.

Though it was after ten, and Nathan needed to return to church in time to assist Dr. Morrison with the Watch Night Service at eleven-thirty, he regaled their guests with story and additional song, while Lovely Lenore poured the punch and produced sweetbreads.

Everything came to a sudden halt when keening sounds, faint at first, then *fortissimo*, pitched down the stairs, heralding a child in distress. Taking the stairs two at a time, Nathan found little Beth holding onto the rails of her crib, full of woe and cry for her "Daddee." Pulling her into his arms, he walked, patted, soothed, and kissed her teary face, while she calmed down, and lay limply in his arms.

"What's the matter with my Beth-baby? Did my darling have a bad dream?" he cooed as Lenore entered the room, casting that, "I'll fix it" look practiced by all mommies on those in their care–including daddees. Sandwiched between them, absorbing their soothe and succor, Beth looked up, grinning.

"Daddee and Mommy hold Beth–*bof!*"

"Bof" it was. The look they exchanged, over the sleepy form of their little one, in "bof" of their arms, said far more than "Merry Christmas!"

As accommodation (and compensation) for his trip to Durham, the day after Christmas, Lenore arranged for Nathan to pick Melanie up on his way back, to stay with the Scotts three nights, returning with him on the 29th. The thought of her willing flesh, beautiful, exposed, and disposed to please, in his house, and utterly available, dismayed him, even as it jolted his body with conditioned anticipation.

Melanie complicates things for me in ways I would rather avoid, though I rationalize her, repeatedly. Lenore evidently feels Shara to be something of a rival, but she has no idea about Melanie. A momentous secret, soon to be told–or discovered?

*

A grinning Shara, carrying her wicker purse, quickly kissed him as she entered the car. Then began a happy babble about Christmas, school, grades, her SAT scores (around a thousand), and her recent date, until they parked in a new subdivision abuilding, a mile from her home. There, she fell into his arms, not wanting to wait any longer than the twenty days that had already crawled by. Love's wordless songs echoed in the valleys of their hearts, again, in concert with the dulcet harmonies inherent in reunion.

In the delicious aftermark, dressed, they ambled in the surrounding woods. An exhausted northeast breeze blended muted December sunshine on a cool, clear day. Alone and secure with each other, under the sky, they walked, swirling dried leaves, frisking as they came. Coyly, Shara removed a small, gayly wrapped box from her coat pocket and presented it to him, her happiness barely hidden by the sheer, see-through delight of giving.

"Merry Christmas, darling!" she laughed.

"Dadburn it, Shara; I thought we agreed we wouldn't exchange gifts, other than the gifts of ourselves."

"I know, but I just couldn't resist. Open it; I think you'll like it!"

Nathan examined the silver tie-clip with a heart-inscribed, silver dollar-sized medallion welded to it. As he was about to make obligatory thank you noises for a gift he was not sure he would use, Shara laughed the more.

"Notice anything about the medal?"

"Well, it's a little smaller than a breadbox, it's silver, has a heart engraved on the front that looks more like someone's naked ass, and there's something engraved on the back. It says `Emergency Fund' except they forgot to add the `d' to `Fund.' What does it mean, babes?"

"Notice anything else, dummy?" she downright cackled.

"I resemble that. Let's see—oh, it opens, like a locket; you put your `emergency fund' inside it, and use it when needed, right?"

"Wrong! Open it, you silly man."

"Damn Sam, Shara! Where in the world did you get this? There's a gold-foiled condom coin inside it–and a tiny message–from you, I take it."

"Yes, read it," chortled the Girl with the Laughing Eyes.

> Yank it out, roll this on.
> Stick it in and have some fun!
> When you're through and oh, so soft;
> Wash it when you take it off.
> Then, roll it up and put it here,
> In my little "box" of Christmas Cheer!

"I love it, Shara! Where on earth did you get it?"

"I found a small catalog in Jimmy's wash with stuff like that in it–nothing too dirty, just smutty. I snuck it to school, ordered this, paying with a money order, and had it sent to my PO box. It came with the rubber coin inside. I dare you to wear it. Do you like it?"

"Of course, I do! Did you really make up the rhyme?"

"Yes, I did, and it didn't take me long, either. I'm around you so much, your way with words must be rubbering off on me."

Nathan cracked up, took her back to his car and followed her poem's instructions! Later, dangling the condom, heavy with ejaculate, up to the sunlight for awed, mutual examination, he suggested she keep it as a symbol of coming attractions. After spilling his seed upon the ground, he wrapped the condom in tissue and put it in his glove compartment, reminding himself aloud, "Better not let Melanie find that!"

"You have to pick Melanie up and take her back to Wilmington, don't you? She's got quite a figure on her. Don't you ever get tempted, being in the car with her so long? She has a crush on you, you know."

"Not my type, girl of my dreams. All this from the girl who hasn't told me about her date with Dooley, or Drooly, or whatever the hell his name is."

"It's Dooley, Nathan, and nothing much happened."

"'Much.' The lady said, 'nothing much happened,' when I can still see the faint marks of a hickey right here on her scrawny little neck!"

Squealing, as Nathan grabbed her, sucking on her neck, just as ol' Drooly Dooley did, Shara banged her head on the window, trying to escape. Apologizing profusely, Nathan cradled her in his jealous arms, despising the boy who had kissed and petted his woman.

At that moment Atlas shrugged, the Turtle farted, Prometheus flunked fire-making, God sneezed, and QI intoned, *Beware!* So ominous was their next conversation that those in charge of the moving finger must have switched to a typewriter. Little about and between them was ever to be crystal clear—or quite the same—again...

The anticipated inevitable had occurred, and Nathan felt his own fire to know—which could bank its coals only after it consumed everything there was to burn. Yet he almost wished she would tell him nothing.

Inconsonant with the serpent in the Garden, QI hissed: *Do not eat the fruit of this adumbration!* Nathan ignored his own objectivity.

Slowly, cautiously, at first, Nathan asked questions about the general course of her date, their actions and reactions. Then, he went back to help her fill in as many details as no one could remember, much less carefully analyze. Yet, such quickly became his steadfast focus, and the only way he knew to overcome the competitive ravages of time, age, and distance. Thus, in those moments was born in Nathan the relentless researcher into Shara's dating experiences, including her sex life. He was hooked!

Timidly, Shara reported caroling with eighteen-year-old Dooley, then parking in front of her house, where they made out for fifteen minutes, before her father turned the porch light on and stood in the door until she came in. As a lark, she dared ol' Dooley to give her a hickey. Several of her girlfriends were embellished with those purply badges of heat and suction, and though Shara had been fucked by Nathan in almost every way possible, she had never sported a hickey, until now. 'Twas Dooley who took her hickey-cherry and, forevermore, things would nevermore be quite the same.

Though he approached things lightly, Nathan's heart pumped so hard, he could hear it in his ears. His head spun with the enormity of the reality–and portent. Then he realized the stark truth–*I am scared out of my skull!* Fear started at his toes, consumed and digested him, and shat him out all over his cool confidence, while from the safety of total objectivity, QI advised, *Stop!*

Of what was he so desperately afraid? Losing her, of course–and of this pregnant adumbration of Shara's attractiveness and his jealousy! His mind processed all of this almost instantaneously, but not fast enough to stop his stammers, a red face, the growing vacuum in his bowels, and the clinching of his teeth, as he tried to talk–and absurdly–the tingling in his genitalia.

"I didn't believe he had succeeded," Shara recounted, "until I saw it in the bathroom mirror. Jennie teased me about it, so I wore a high collar and powdered it, for fear that Daddy would see it and have my hymen examined. Was that so bad? I was just experimenting, as you said. You–you said it would be–all right."

"I also said I would be jealous as hell, would want to know everything there was to know about the whole episode, and that you would tire of my anxiety about such things. See, everything is as I told you."

"To quote the Reverend Mr. Nathan Rhea Scott, 'Anybody who says, "I told you so," doesn't deserve to be right!'"

While feeling some of the unregulated power known to most women, Shara did not know what to do. They had never argued; he had never revealed any weakness, apart from his driving need to be with her, which she counted as strength, and now he was wilting like a dying flower.

"Nathan, what's wrong? Surely you are not all upset about fifteen minutes of..."

"...Grubbin' and rubbin' and lookin' fo' yo' nubbin'?"

"That's not what I was going to say, baby. I was going to say that we were just..."

"...Lickin', slickin', and suckin' up to fuckin'?"

"Nathan stop that! My gosh, you'd think I gave him six orgasms, and that we did it on my front lawn, the way you are reacting."

"Let's face it, Shara, you both liked it."

"I guess so."

Though Nathan's fear and an unnerving excitement continued to attend him, fear faded out. Her manner and affect were so dear, so innocent, that he could not help seeing her drooly, drippy Dooley make-out experience through the awed and amazed eyes of Shara, the first time petter that she was, apart from him. Taking her face in his hands, he bent down, placed his forehead and nose against hers, kissed her as lightly as windsong, sighed deeply, and became an adult, again—noting *I have lost my strange—and surprising—semi-erection.*

"Let's talk about any aspect of your date you want, sweetheart."

Grinning, like the self-conscious novice in such matters she was, Lady Shara of Nathansheart, festooned with his adoring gaze and rapt attention didst retell her story, openly, and without fear, pouring intimacies into him as she would into a trusted diary. Significantly, as she spoke and described, she encouraged, and he enjoyed, his playing the part of Dooley of the incubus lips and elevator elbows.

From this signal moment, very early on in Shara's sharing of the pages of her youthful memory book, on which Nathan was not physically present, she learned–and liked–to show and tell. Fortuitously, they learned to re-enact those episodes, both together and apart, he reclaiming his lady, as she contentedly and truthfully shared her age-related, socio-sexual experiences.

Thus, what could have been, and sometimes was, fraught with fear, despair, and jealousy for Nathan, he found he could transmogrify into a singularly rich and explorable mine of vicarious human experiences–social, sexual, relational, ethical, philosophical, emotional, good, bad, sad, mad, glad, and indifferent.

Nathan gave this budding practice–and concept–a name: *elasticity*. She was free to dally elsewhere, experientially, with her time, body, and with both of their hearts, as long as she didn't stretch so far as to break the loving and elastic bonds between them; and that she faithfully, even eagerly, snap back– to him, to report, to share, and to relive her dalliances. A mutual consummation devoutly to be shared and savored.

Mind, this aspect of their assimilating and accommodating realities had barely emerged in early 1965, with only prodding, hambone elbows and a random hickey or two to exploit. Their newfound elasticity is mostly potential here, as they derive the concept from romantic redoubt, but it is surely prescient. To miss these strangely vicarious seeds would be to fail to understand or appreciate their future yield and produce–and a major theme in this story.

*

While driving Melanie back to Wilmington, they both confirmed, once again, the truths of classical conditioning. After the perfunctories, the two old friends, erstwhile and future paramours, were naturally titillated. She wore dark blue slacks, a long-sleeved white blouse, a blue silk scarf tied around her neck, and flats, looking her usual svelte, well-formed self. Nathan cast sidelong glances at her swelling bosom and casually crossed legs, wondering whether she was wearing her black or her flesh-colored, sexy underwear.

"Well, Madam Hepzibah, how go things in the airline business? Flown any good pilots, lately, or are you still dead set on being a passenger for the rest of your days?"

"You know good and well I am not interested in flying pilots, Mr. Scott."

"Well, then, did Santa bring you that twelve-inch dildo you requested?"

"I needed only a nine-incher, Nathan, for I can count on you for the initial three, can't I?"

"Touché! But it's not the size of the ship…"

"…I know; it's the motion in the ocean, and all of that malarkey."

"Well, it's better than getting seasick."

"Ho-ho; and what did your little friend Miss Starr give you, or don't you care to discuss it?"

"I was wondering whether you'd get around to her. Lenore told me you sicced your spies on me, reporting my presence in Durham not too long ago, when I was supposed to be elsewhere. Can you tell me anything else about my nefarious activities?"

"Only that you didn't call me or come by the last time you were in town, as promised."

"I'm sorry, Mel, but I did drive by your place, and your roomie's car was there, so I didn't think I'd better stop."

"You could have called."

"Next time, if there is to be one, Mel. Anyway, what makes you think I saw Shara this trip?"

"Didn't you?"

"Melanie, I can't see where—"

"You're right! I'm sorry. I have no right to pry. It's just that–that–I–I am concerned for you, of course, and for Lenore and your babies."

Nathan's immediate silence perfectly communicated his thoughts.

"I know, if I'm so damned concerned about Lenore and your kids, why do I–I..."

"...Fuck you? Were those the words for which you were searching, Mellie?"

"Nathan don't be cruel to me. Be politely disdainful, or even impatient and exasperated; anything but unkind."

"And violent?"

"I beg your pardon, sir? Who's talking violence, here? I hope you won't be that disdainful or exasperated."

Chuckling deeply in his throat, Nathan explained that he was quoting Hannah Jelkes, of Williams' "Night of the Iguana," "Nothing human disgusts me unless it's unkind, violent."

"You're quite taken with that play, aren't you?"

"It's a wonderfully revealing, almost scriptural play, Melanie, full of the truth and rot which often attend our wet heats. If you haven't read it, you ought to."

"I saw it last month–with Deborah Kerr and Richard Burton. Perhaps you're drawn to it because of–of certain parallels to–our own situation?"

"You mean, do I identify with the Very Reverend Doctor T. Lawrence Shannon, disputed and disreputable child of God, and erstwhile man of the cloth, locked out of his church, apostate, partially because he couldn't keep his hands off willing seventeen years old and other assorted females? Or do you see yourself as Hannah, the spinster lady artist, traversing the globe on shank's mare, drawing flattering caricatures of fat Aussie underwear salesmen?"

"Though there may or may not be parallels to us in the play, Nathan, that's not what I meant. I was referring to the fact that you have a propensity for telling the truth about God, like Shannon, no matter how unorthodox."

"Then where do you fit, Melanie Charles, of the hungry, heaving bosom, in this parallel? You did say, 'our own situation,' did you not?"

"Well, not the widow Faulk, for sure. I guess I saw myself in the role of one of those nameless, faceless ladies, whom Shannon squired around on his various tours in the tropics–especially the ones whom he–he..."

"...Fucked, Melanie. He fucked them! You do it well enough–why can't you say it?"

"You know what I mean. Do you see either of us the same way?"

"Maybe, Melanie. I am in search of the truth about God; good, bad, mad, sad, glad–or indifferent, though I'm far from decrying him as an 'angry, petulant, old man.' Without trying to be unkind, I guess I do sorta see you as along for the ride, taking in the sights, what few pleasures there are along the way, and for me, from time to time, when we both happen to come together–to come together."

Sighing, she leaned over, kissed his cheek, saying, "I thought you'd never ask!"

"Here? Right here, on the road, forty-eleven miles from nowhere? You want me to stop the car along here, somewhere, and–and..."

"...Fuck me! I want you to fuck me. You say it well enough–why can't you do it?"

Admiring her wit, he pulled into a tiny, roadside park, slightly into the trees, well off the road. She was on fire for him; though, as always, demurely wanton, requiring slight hints, coaching, and shaping to stimulate increases in her freedom, with its concomitant delights. In the darkness of the car, with only tree-filtered moonlight for illumination, Melanie's white-on-white flesh looked almost ghostly. Her murmurs and moans continued the metaphor until, thrusting deeply into the hot, wet core of her, he lost the allusion, and happily pumped his juices into her carnate reality.

Epilogue is equally prologue. So, it was with Nathan this night. For, within five hours of repeatedly making love to Shara, and within two hours of succumbing to Melanie's molten ministrations, Lenore's tender mercies claimed him, after which he was fucking Melanie, again, from the rear, in her bed in the guest room. *Another proof that I'm never enough...*

Finally, at 2:13 a. m., he slid his exhausted body next to his innocently slumbering wife and slept like a baby. His last hypnogogic images were of a faceless boy, sporting an enormous erection, exploring the lovely lineaments of his Shara.

CHAPTER 28
GRIEF AND BELIEF

Words dazzle and deceive because they are mimed by the face.
But black words on white page are the soul laid bare.

Guy de Maupassant

The ringing of his private line startled him. It was his former boss, Dr. George Jennings, calling from First Church, Durham. Haltingly, Dr. Jennings told Nathan that Jason Hart, one of Nathan's most beloved teens, and the youngest child of an active family in that church, was dead, at seventeen. The Youngs asked that Nathan officiate with Dr. Jennings at both funeral services—at the church and at the graveside.

Shocked and utterly dismayed, unable to stem his tears, he whispered, "How and when did he die, George?"

"This afternoon about one. It's not absolutely clear, Nathan, but it looks like suicide."

"My God! Why?" The eternal *non sequitur*.

"The Harts were in hopes you might have some idea. You were so close to him."

Tears continuing to clog his voice: "I've not a clue. He was always dedicated and dependable, a bit shy, and super friendly, but never morose or depressed. As you know, he was planning to be a minister. During counseling, he would pine for a girlfriend, not having much experience with girls, other than Kathy and Shara, but they were like sisters. He had an unrequited crush on Anna which depressed him some. The entire youth group will be utterly crushed–as am I, George. Lenore and I love–loved–him very much. How did he die?"

"That's the strange part, Nathan. He tied a rope and a belt to a doorknob, ran the rope over the top of the door and looped the dangling belt around his neck, and that's the way they found him, slumped toward the floor, hanging from the belt, dead."

Nathan was silent, weeping harder with fear and trembling about what he was thinking: "George, was he–was he fully clothed?"

"I'm not sure. Does it matter?"

Sighing amid his sobs, "Maybe. I've heard of boys using that exact setup to practice 'pass-out sex,' or autoerotic asphyxiation, to have more intense orgasms, while almost passing out from self-induced suffocation or strangulation. It's a dangerous–and stupid–way to enhance masturbation. It's probable, unless it really was suicide, which I doubt. If his pants were down or were unbuttoned, and his feet were on the floor, he was in control, until he wasn't. Whoever found him would know, if that was the case. Was there a note?"

"I don't think so. Good Lord, Nathan, that's awful! What a way to go–at any age–for any reason. Nathan, I'm truly sorry. I know how much you loved him…"

Trying to catch his breath among his sobs, "Thanks, George; Did you see him?"

"Yes," he whispered. "It was truly shocking. They had put him on a bed and covered him, waiting for the medical examiner, when I got there. He was cyanotic, and his features were frozen. There were no scratch marks on the belt, the door, or anything to suggest that he fought strangulation. That is why the medical examiner has issued a preliminary ruling of suicide–whether accidental or not has yet to be determined."

"Let's keep speculation to ourselves, George; it won't help to add that probability to the pain the Harts are feeling. How are they doing? Jason was the apple of their eyes."

"I agree; accidental suicide should suffice, either way. Mildred, whom I'm positive doesn't suspect the sex thing you described, is taking it hardest–Jason was her last baby, and she almost lost him during pregnancy."

Due to all the young people who would attend, Dr. Jennings asked Nathan to take half of the church service and all the graveside service. The remainder of their conversation involved funeral logistics: in First Church at 2:00 p.m., Wednesday, the 29th, followed by burial at Greenlawn Cemetery. Commiserating with each other over the circumstances, known and unknown, the two, deeply saddened ministers hung up.

"It is not enough," Nathan whispered, feeling genuine grief and sorrow flow down his face. "I will not be enough, God, please give me something more than myself, that I may be of real help and comfort."

Nathan moped downstairs, being drawn, inexorably, to the sanctuary: a traditional affair, seating over a thousand souls, with a vaulted, beautifully raftered ceiling, a communion table, and an uplifted, central pulpit. Woefully, he climbed into the pulpit and stood there a moment, gazing past the nave's empty pews, aureate with prismed sunlight and feathered colors cast through the stained-glass windows in the narthex.

Jason, laddie, what happened? I can't think that you meant to die; you're much too smart. You now know more than all of humanity– or nothing at all. God, I wish I knew. Why, son? Was sex or death that intriguing? Was life that–that little to you, that you–did this? Were you jerking off and waited too long to stand up? Please, no!

I'm waiting, again, God–amid every trapping we Christians use to stimulate worship–and I feel–I feel–empty–at least emptier than I did this morning when I prayed the pastoral prayer and baptized the

Dellums's baby. My Jason is dead—God—I—I don't know what to say, or how to say it. Another young one has stumbled, and I feel the weight of his death lying heavy on my heart! Am I guilty again, God? Was Jason my responsibility? If I hadn't reached out for Shara, would I have moved from Durham—and would Jason be dead now? Even though we communicated often, and he and Kathy visited us recently, would my continuing to be there for him have made the difference, somehow? He readily admitted that he was horny all the time and didn't know what else to do about it but…

Fatigued by his guilt, inadequacy, and uncertainty, Nathan left the pulpit, walked across the chancel to the pipe organ, to try to play out and through his mood. He and the organ wept through every modulation: a dirge in—and for—A minor.

Jason, were things so bad? I wish you had called me, because I—

"OHH, NOOO!" rang his cry of anguished memory, through the gilded rafters of the sanctuary, clashing with the organ's loud, last chord, suspended forever in strangled silence—like poor Jason!

Nathan remembered that his response to Jason's last, heart-rendering letter, declaring his love for Anna, was still in his typewriter. In the wretched agony of missed opportunities, he felt that overwhelming sense of helplessness and inconsolable sadness which attends those condemned by their own, failed intentions. As with poor, dead Tom McNair, he had been there for Jason, regularly—but clearly, with too little, and, irreconcilably, too late!

Thus, Jason joined Tom in taunt and haunt of Nathan's conscience. In addition to the pain of deep loss of a beloved friend, he sensed that he had not done what he could have done to alter the awful momentum and sequences of circumstances that led to Jason's sad, absurd death—and no matter how hard he cried and tried, he could not find the light to drive the dark of that doubt away.

*

"Are you ready to officiate at Jason's graveside service, honey?" asked an equally shocked and tearful Lenore.

"I think so; Through her tears, on the phone, Kathy suggested I read the rhyme I wrote for Tom's funeral, in 1960. What do you think?"

"It's bleak, but appropriate, but are you ready, emotionally? You loved him, so."

"Yes. It will be hard, especially due to the stupid way he died. I do–did–love him. He fantasized sex a lot. We talked about moderation and time to find the girl who would love him back. I can't help worrying that my leaving somehow catalyzed his stupid experiment."

In their bed, he talked so long and so effusively of his feelings of repeated inadequacy in not being there for so many, that he disdained Nature's plaintive call and Melanie's musky scents in favor of this wonder of a woman who continued to share her bed, her body–her life–and her huge, empathetic heart with him–his dear wife.

Though Melanie wouldn't pout openly about being slighted, came the dawn, she conveyed a muted sense of frustration. On their return drive, her answers were clipped, her comments trivial, and her affect polite.

"Melanie, I assume you know why I didn't make it to your room last night."

"You were under no obligation, Mr. Scott, to come to my room or to my bed, last night, or ever, as you know."

"That is true; nor or you under any obligation to receive me, as you know. We risk the catastrophe of Lenore's discovering us, each time."

"I know we do, and it worries me, too. To my mind, we don't seem to be hurting her by pleasing ourselves, but we must never tell her."

"Agreed."

By one o'clock, Nathan had deposited a frustrated Melanie, and high tailed it to meet a shocked and frightened Shara. He did not share his speculation about Jason's death, other than saying it must have been a foolish, accidental death, probably not a suicide.

"Are you ready for the funeral tomorrow?" she asked still red-eyed from crying.

"As ready as I'll ever be. What I'm ready for is you. I need you! I need to wash myself in you, to feel you pouring all over me, holding, loving me, cleansing me of—of every other reality, at least for a little while. God, I hate it that we can't be together more, and more often!"

"I love you, Nathan Scott," she murmured, sweeping her body into him, and nestling her head in his lap.

For four hours, in the motel, Nathan reacquainted himself with the delicacies and differences in, of, and around Shara. It was a good four hours, the best in a long time. She seemed more mature, and he became more relaxed, more a partner, less a mentor. Sex was different each time, like golden beads on the growing chain of their love. Conversation ranged from Jason to Dooley, and from his work to hers. Their communication was candid and complete, trusting and trusted.

*

After talking Melanie out of visiting his motel, and a night of fitful, Jason-filled sleep, Nathan joined Dr. Jennings in visiting the Harts, at ten. Mildred and Samuel were their usual, gracious selves, introducing them to the inevitable cadre of relatives and friends, so traditionally and poignantly gathered. Mildred motioned Nathan to step out into the hall, and he complied, aware that the weight of loss was about to spread.

"Nathan, as I told you inside, Sam and I and our family are so very grateful that you drove all the way from Wilmington to serve us in this way. Jason loved you so—I'm sure he would have want—wanted—Oh, Nathan, why did he do it? Do you have any idea?"

Grief and loss are as common as the passing years, but never so sad and devastating as experienced by loving parents. Mildred was that and more—a devout woman, disposed to serving others without thought of reward. She could be found in the poorer sections of Durham, driving people to her own physician. Now, Mildred was in need and did not know how to cope.

Perceiving the depth of need in her face, and in her intense search for understanding where there was none, Nathan was moved almost beyond his own petty efforts for courage. Lips trembling, eyes filling, he did what only human animals do when suffering must be shared—he opened his arms to her sagging form and his heart to her unremitting sorrow, both of which came stumbling, pouring in, pulled there by the God-awful gravity of grief.

"Oh, Nathan, it is so hard to bear—to—to understand!" she sobbed, accepting his lame pats and tears as appropriate credentials for their sad intimacy.

"Yes, Mildred—I know—or to accept."

"How—can I—accept what my soul—and my body tot—tot—totally reject as unacceptable? He is my baby! I love him too much to let him go—yet, he is gone, and the world is no longer firm and steady beneath my—my feet. I know I should be grateful to have had him at all, and for having had my others, but—but it is too hard not to want him—BA—BACK!"

Mildred sobbed inconsolably as Nathan rocked her in his arms. As only the living can do for the bereaved, he spent a little of his life on her, gladly giving what he knew could never be enough, but which he also knew that others, in the aggregate, would give similarly to help her and her family to keep on living. In his own pain, so insignificant when confronted by hers, there was the redeeming sense that this, too, must pass—that despised, but essential, sense not yet allowed to Mildred.

And so, as have done members of the human species since they clustered in the trees, wailing over little ones being devoured beneath, Mildred and Nathan clung to human warmth, instead of to the coldness of the grave. They made the sounds and cried the tears of bereavement, then, they took the quintessentially next, courageous, human, steps, denied to lesser creatures—consciously, conscientiously keeping on…

All that was left after that was ceremony, until somehow, courage—not foolhardiness, not dumb, blind, hopeless faith or faithless hope—but courage to take the next steps of living would come—step by lonely step—until, together, they became footfalls on life's continuing path, and whatever else death might mean, it would not, must not, detain the living for long.

Unwilling to shed light as to what might have catalyzed Jason's absurd death, and unable to abuse devastating grief by forensic speculation, Nathan led Mildred back to her own living room, bringing her grief face to face with life, once more. He knew that there would be countless, dark hours, during which this dear lady would catalogue her sins, real and imagined, and search her soul for reasons that would never satisfy, and guilt that would seem impossible to atone.

In the end, he realized, the living simply keep on keeping on, partly because time and the river have a way of muting and even prettifying the ugliness of death, such that even shame loses some of its force—and appeal. *And most any way you cut it; life is better than not life!*

*

Christians organize funerals as times for worship, praise, confession, repentance, remembrance, thanksgiving, and fellowship. Grief is swallowed up in the victorious apostrophe Christians believe is theirs when confronted by the grave: "O death, where is thy sting? O grave, where is thy victory...?" There is sadness, yes, but not the sadness of those who have no hope beyond the grave.

The power inherent in such funeral celebrations is immense, therapeutic for the believer–and very empathetic, for who does not ponder his own death when confronted by another's? John Donne captured something of this essence in his "Meditation 17: Devotions upon Emergent Occasions." "...therefore never send to know for whom the bell tolls; it tolls for thee..."

A suicide, or a near facsimile, however, may be a different matter. Some churches discriminate between a death that is consistent with the sovereignty of God and one at one's own hand. So strong is belief in God's sovereignty, despite our freedom of the will, that even a suicide may be thought to reflect God's will. If that hyper-hope will not wash away such an ultimate rejection of God, then perhaps an illness construct may serve. Most educated ministers see suicide as the result of delusional minds, more condemning of the society which breeds them, than of the victims, themselves.

Dr. Jennings, the one man Nathan was positive meant every word ever uttered from his pulpit, spoke the ancient verities–and did so by heart–a feat Nathan could not match, though he read his passages and prayed his prayer as sincerely and fervently as he could.

He noted that Shara, Kathy, Anna, Willard, and many others of his old youth fellowships, were sitting together, weeping their loss, but expressive of their own *koinonia*, now endeavoring to pull in and renew the bereaved Hart family. A slow thrill spidered down Nathan's extremities, as he saw their faces so intent on him–so in trust and focus on who he was, what he symbolized, what he meant to them, and what they meant to each other–and to their God.

Sanctuaries are too often filled with weak humankind—the crass, the bored, and the calculating, but those qualities were scarce this day—for a Little One had stumbled and was dead, gone, past forever—like unto the future of every man, woman, and child who ever breathed the flower-scented air, and tasted the fear of death in the midst of life.

The organist must have felt it, for he played the hymns as though it be Easter. Perhaps, it was for many, through the music, the Word, and the palpable *koinonia*. Perhaps it was a variety of Easter for all who came to sip this bitter cup in support of those who were forced to drink it to its very dregs.

If the funeral service in the sanctuary is a time for worship, praise, prayer, and music, by the congregation, of the congregation, for the congregation, the graveside service is uniquely for the family and loved ones of the dead. While riding in the lead car with Dr. Jennings and several pall bearers, Nathan remembered this, and smiled despite himself, as he recalled two funerals which would either plague or delight his memory, forever.

His first recollection was more than sad—almost pathetic. A reformed alcoholic died, whose place in the church was peripheral, at best. The family wanted a Christian burial, and Nathan was elected. There was no service in the sanctuary; only a sparsely attended affair in a funeral home chapel, complete with piped in funeral Muzak, and borrowed, plastic flowers. Two carloads of ill-dressed mourners followed the hearse to Greenlawn, and only a few people stood around the grave.

As Nathan moved steadfastly through the final words and prayers, he noticed that one mourner, a large, well-boned, older woman, stood back from the rest, weeping profusely throughout the brief service. As Nathan finished his final prayer, about to pronounce the benediction, a sound, unmistakable to any farm boy or girl, grabbed the attention of all who heard it. Somewhere nearby, it seemed, a cow was urinating, and its bizarre, interminable outpouring overwhelmed the senses of all.

Looking up, Nathan saw everyone else do the same. He realized that it was no bovine effusion anointing the surrounding graves–it was the large, well-boned, older woman, legs spread, body erect, face sublime in grief, oblivious to her efflux. Nathan stole back the attention of the mourners with a cough and increased volume to his benediction, which he dragged out, keeping one eye on the lady in question, finally sloshing to her car. *Such may be the extremity of sorrow.*

The second funeral flooding Nathan's memory was for one of the most beloved elders of the church. Again, Nathan officiated. This time, however, there were more than a hundred people crowding around, waiting for the officious, little martinet of a funeral director to signal Nathan to lead the pallbearers to the parapet, after he seated the family.

In the face of such a crowd, little Mr. Smithers wanted everything to go just right, especially wanting to be seen in tight control of the proceedings. Thus, he fussed here and tidied there, keeping Nathan and the pallbearers waiting at the hearse. Finally, when things were as he thought they should be, he bowed low to the widow and her children, and gestured to Nathan as though he were imploring to be saved from the hangman.

Miffed at such foofaraw, Nathan concentrated on his role of leading the short procession, waiting again until the casket was placed securely on the lowering device, and for Mr. Smithers to give him a second sign–this time to proceed with the service. All went delightfully for the little man until, just as he was about to deign to signal the young preacher to begin, he noticed the grass skirt surrounding the casket was not to his liking.

Making much over his discovery, he held up his hand to Nathan, ordering him to wait a moment, while he moved to remedy the problem. As he hurriedly approached the head of the casket, his foot slipped on wet clay, or on a wet leaf, or on a puddle of God's own firmament, dropped down precisely for this purpose. No matter: Smithers' feet began to skid–toward the casket.

Graveside services are not usually funny, but all who watched this wee Napoleon of Necromania slip/slide into the offending fake grass, arms aflailing, and thence, to disappear into the grave under the casket, surely had God's blessing to laugh–for laugh they did. From early controlled titters, to loud, prolonged guffaws, until the very earth shook with laughter, as the chastened undertaker was helped from the grave and slunk himself to the safety of his expensive hearse.

As the laughter grew, the widow, a bright, loving woman dressed in black, threw back her veil, leaned over, and gently pounded the casket with both gloved hands, and amidst the peals of laughter emitting her throat, cried aloud, for all to hear, "Ed, Ed, if you could have seen that, you would have died laughing!"

It was a long three minutes before Nathan could gain control of the service, and then only after the widow stood, faced the still tittering mourners, and hushed them with one graceful finger to her re-veiled lips.

Knowing full well that any comment he might make would be anticlimactic, Nathan dared only one sentence: "Jesus said, 'Blessed are you that weep now, for you shall laugh.'"

*

Jason's graveside service was no laughing matter. As the cars parked, Nathan helped the family to their seats, and returned to lead the pallbearers in. When all were settled, all that could be noted were the stark vacuum that inhabits graveyards, the soughing of the wind in the live oaks, the muted hymns of a few birds—and incessant weeping.

As he read the ancient verities, choking up only once, Nathan saw Shara's tear-stained face to his left, loving him as he tried to love everybody there into faith and hope. Having finished reading from the book, he turned to his Kathy-suggested rhyme.

"Dear ones, about a year ago I shared a rhyme with our young people that spoke to the sudden death of a young man still in high school. I bring it to you here and now for two reasons: Jason heard it, and because one of his peers suggested that I read it to you:

Grief and Belief

We are here; (Jason) is there.
Where is our relief?
Confusion came. Who is to blame?
Give God the nod?
We are crying at his dying.
All are wondering.
There is fear, but friends are near,
And we are praying.
This family torn, and so forlorn,
Our hearts contort.
We gather here and see God's tear:
Our sad resort.
No justice here, for our compeer;
His life too dear,
He was too young; had just begun,
Death now his career?
Oh, how we mourn, this life so shorn,
That death prevailed.
Our tears are prayers, our hopes are dares,

How have we failed?
It is not odd—We are not God!
Our choice is His rule.
When all is done, our races run,
Death is the fool!
This sting is real; but victory its seal
Of God's great power,
To love the most, when grief's our host,
Allowing faith to flower.
So, rest in peace; this death shall cease;
Love vanquishes all!
God's word is enough, to call Death's bluff,
And end this poignant pall.
Especially here, before this bier,
To cleanse our hearts of rage.
We trust the love of God above,
To charge our grief with—courage!

"God grant us the courage to live with this loss, the love to heal its ravages, the faith to believe that God loves Jason far more than any of us, the hope that we shall meet him again, and that he shall be fine and whole, as once he was."

After Nathan pronounced the benediction, everybody melted into whatever was left of their own lives—as did he.

CHAPTER 29
INTERREGNUM?

I speak the truth, not my fill of it, but as much as I dare speak;
and I dare to do so a little more as I grow old.

Michel Eyquem de Montaigne

Knowing the truth and being able to share it are two different
animals!

Nathan's QI

Nathan grieved anew when he read Mildred Hart's letter:

Jan. 19, 1965

Dear Nathan,

How can we express the feeling in our hearts for you? When we wanted you and needed you, you came to us, from a great distance. We can only say that we hold a special love for you, as did our Jason, who missed you greatly when you had to leave Durham. Your last talk to us and the beautiful poem and prayers for our dear child will live in our hearts always. With God, you have given us courage–courage to face each day without Jason, but with unlimited opportunities to love and help others.

Nathan, we did ask why. I suppose all humans do. But we know that God has Jason in his gentle and loving care, as you said, and we are striving hard so that one day we will join him. We are praying our faith overcomes our grief, as you said!

May God bless you and your dear family and keep you safe until we meet again. Nathan, our hope, and prayers for you are that you will find the things you want to do in God's service. It seems that your calling is with the young ones like Jason and his brother and sisters. They all love you so much and miss you greatly. Not only my youngsters, but others in the church have expressed themselves to feel the same.

Whatever you do, we shall pray for your success, and for God's blessing on you always. Please keep in touch wherever you go or whatever you do.

With much love, always, Mildred and S. G. Hart

Jason's death and Nathan's roles during his funeral put him into a pensive tailspin—about his love, his family, his calling, and the conflicts that were threatening everything. Among his mood-affecting vicissitudes: guilt about not being there for Jason more, Lenore's sad mood and her mild case of pneumonia, Nattie's preschool misbehavior, bold Melanie's continued push and availability, Shara's needs for him (and *vice versa*), the issues of some of his counselees, the gist of his own sermons and lessons, and his many other church responsibilities—all of this and more, combined, compounded, and activated his natural escape and avoidance mechanisms, rendering him very tired—and increasingly morose.

Usually irrepressible, given more energy than most, fatigue was a familiar burden, but something he could handle. Depression was a stranger. Internal conflict and dismay, even guilt, disgust, and anger cropped up, occasionally, but sudden, unfamiliar flashes of lachrymae and despair momentarily overwhelmed him, urging him to contemplate escape—both from and to...

For the first time since arriving in Wilmington, five months earlier, an ego-weakened Nathan allowed QI to evaluate his life more objectively. *My life is too full, but not fulfilling, with entirely too many fragile plates to be kept aloft, balanced, and spinning on the ends of a veritable forest of flexible, enterprising shticks. Sooner or later, one or more will fall from my fatigue, neglect, carelessness, forgetfulness, or (dare I admit it?) lack of skill, and I, and all my loves and purposes, will suffer needlessly.*

*

Hoping to sooth his mood with a furtive visit to Shara in early February, he was met by an agitated seventeen-year-old almost as worried about things as was he. She had just come from an unplanned encounter with Danny, one of her more daring and exciting suiters, to meet Nathan. After their greetings and a hug or two, still parked in the shadows of the little church, Shara needed to talk.

"Nathan, something has to give. Either I have to stop seeing other guys, or just let it all hang out when I do."

"Whoa, Shara! What happened?"

"Well, I just almost got raped, if you want to know, only I cooperated, until it was almost too late. I escaped just in time!"

Alarmed and aghast, Nathan wanted assurance that she was all right, if she needed help of any kind, and to see what he could do for her right then. Weeping in his arms, she cried through a semi-confession of a make out session that became a near-rape.

Last period in school, Danny invited her backstage, to his theatrical props and costume cage. Cautious, but intrigued (and a little turned on), she allowed his kisses and petting. Suddenly, he came on very powerfully, feeling and probing her everywhere over and under her clothes. She admitted to being extremely turned on and didn't complain when he laid her back on a little bench, and proceeded to open her blouse, while lying between her legs, humping. She automatically humped back. His dick was very hard and pressing against her vulva. Almost casually, he threw her skirt over her face and tried to remove her panties. Realizing that he intended to fuck her, whether she wanted to or not, she panicked, pushed him off, stumbled to the door and ran out, while he lay there smirking, semen seeping through his trousers. Shara was mortified, not so much about Danny's behavior, which she admitted to being almost expected, but about her own. "I loved it, until I didn't, and then it was almost too late!"

"What am I going to do, Nathan?" she wailed. "I don't want anyone but you, but I see you so seldom, I get lonely and needful. Being horny doesn't help either, even though I exercise–do myself–regularly. I think maybe I would be less confused and anxious, if I didn't love you so much. It's nice to be liked, and sometimes I let my guard down–and look what happened this time! I'm afraid of what will happen next time, if there is one. I think I should tell Danny I won't date him, don't you?"

"Sweetheart, that has to be left up to you, though that certainly seems a very viable option, unless you really want to fuck someone else..."

"I don't really want anyone but you, but..." she muttered, placing his hand on her pantied crotch which was soaking wet. She began kissing him hungrily, looking at him with knowing realization, pleading with her eyes. Caressing her, she climaxed in minutes.

While holding her, QI recalled a loving conversation with Lenore two days earlier, when *she asked me if I couldn't just stop seeing Shara for a while and see what might happen. Though not pleased with the idea, then, now it almost seems plausible–and certainly fair.*

269

What to do? I love her, though, no matter what. Maybe if we just cooled it a while, and stopped being so driven, it would give her time to decide when, who, and how to date, and me time to recement with my family and my job.

"Shara, what would you think if we took a hiatus, an interregnum, without seeing each other or communicating–for about a month?"

"Oh, no, Nathan. Let's not do that yet."

"Yet?"

"Well, I admit that there are times when opportunities with my age group are, well, not frustrated, but put on hold or skipped by my relationship with you, and I sure don't want to be raped, but I don't think I could go on without you, if that's what you're thinking."

"I admit to similar kinds or anxieties rising up in me when I know how much I cherish Lenore and my family–as well as you. Wanting you both sometimes makes my life so fraught with conflict that I find myself weeping from frustration one minute and desperately pining for you or Lenore the next."

"I–I know it must be hard for you, honey. But even while I was fooling around with Danny, in the back of mind, I knew I have you, no matter what. Does that make any sense?"

"Exactly the kind of sense I just described, Shara."

Weeping again, she put her head on his chest and sighed, "Maybe your suggestion is a good one, then. Maybe we should take a break and see what happens..."

"When you say it, Shara, it scares me to death–and it was my idea! Yet, it makes sense at the same time. Do you think we can do that–cut ourselves off from each other for as long as thirty days?"

The girl nodded her head, while it nestled securely under his chin.

"Nathan, I love you more than anything or anybody on earth. That said, I just experienced one of the problems that make us both a little bit crazy, and which make me doubt myself, when I probably shouldn't. I'll do it, if you think it best, but it will be damned hard for me—and I think for you, too?"

"Yes, but so be it. God help us!"

*

Lenore immediately approved their interregnum, of course, hoping the solution would be permanent. Two agonizing letters crossed in the mail:

Tuesday, 2/9/65,1:25 A. M.

My Own Shara,

I don't want to write this letter. It will seem small and almost simpering alongside the two I received from you today. This letter will be one more in a long list of "I love yous," one of the last for a long time—at least a month.

I ache for you in the misery that we shared, as we discussed our month without communication. Your quote from J. B. remains appropriate, even prophetic, "You wanted justice, didn't you? There isn't any . . . there is only love." I hear and feel your resolve to last in that love, and it lifts me up and away from the dread, which you voiced by your question, "When will we both be flooded by the total loss or total gain of our love?" I know not which.

You know my love, and you cannot doubt it now—at all! But we must remember what and why we are doing—to give us both (all) a chance (perhaps one of many; perhaps our only one) to try another directing dynamic—apart.

Shara, I am with you always. I thoroughly believe you are correct when you surmise that we will

271

love each other always, no matter what else takes place. One month without you–what will you do, be, say, feel, want, and need. We shall just have to wait and see! I love you so much–so agonizingly and awfully much!

10:45 P. M., 2/10/65

My Dearest Nathan,

I love you! Oh, how silent those words after this letter–one month–only the damnable feelings of loss, insecurity, fear, and doubt. Perhaps there will be moments of great hope or joy because of some little word or phrase, a piece of music, a song, anything that might join us together mentally or spiritually, so our souls and hearts will be nourished throughout this drought.

All this week I thought I would be terribly frightened to write this letter, but I'm not. I believe; I really believe that you know how much I love you, and believing your love for me, I am strengthened in the strangest way. I am now able to look at all the emptier tomorrows and know that you are with me, no matter where you are. What is our love if we cannot live without a letter? Perhaps we will see how strong our love is!

My only thought now is how can I convey my deepest love and devotion to you in this letter? Oh, Nathan, just remember our most tender moments, our feeling of oneness, both spiritually and physically–our great concern for each other–and you will know how I feel. I want only to give now–to show you my strength and courage, so you will be strengthened and courageous, too. I want to look at this test as a beginning, and not an end, for if our love persists, think how wonderful this will be for us! I am sure many of our doubts and fears will vanish if our love remains strong–or even grows stronger in this interim. Somehow, I have that crazy feeling that everything is going to work out–if only I could be sure!

Nathan, I must say something, because it is such a part of me. Please make every moment count at home. Cling to Lenore as you have to me and let her help you. Give her every chance to love you and help you find out what you really want. If I could make you forget me–really forget me–for this month, I would, and yet, as I say this, I die! I totally believe your greater obligation is to Lenore and your children, and not to me. So, I urge you to consume their love, and love them in return, completely, trying to force me from your mind and heart, where I'm positive I dwell.

You once wrote, "We love, and loving, we care, and caring, we cling, and clinging, we live, and living, we love!" Words I cannot forget!

Yours forever, Shara

P. S., Listen for the song, "As Long as He Needs Me." I'll mail your letters back right after I receive them. Oh Nathan, know I care–know how much I love you!

*

On 2/12/65, Daddy called: Mother's colon had been examined, and things were not looking good. Apart from referring to a possible "liquid tumor," he told his anxious son that there was little to worry about, and even less that he could do. When Mother got on the line, she wanted to hear about her grandbabies, whom she missed to distraction. Nathan promised to bring them down in June, when he would have the better part of a month off.

On the third day of their self-imposed interregnum, February 13, 1965, Nathan, unaccountably, purchased a pair of size 5 anty-bikini panties exactly like the black, see-through affair that had aroused his admiration in the mall, months earlier. Audaciously, he mailed a heart-shaped boxes of candy to Shara and Kathy, through Kathy, and ignoring the risk, tucked the panties into Shara's, with a little rhyme:

> This blackened silk, covering similar ilk
> Will make you feel so fine.
> Men will declare, dig her underwear!
> As they check out your panty line.
> The ants in your pants will improve your dance,
> As you jiggle your wondrous hind.
> Wear this frilly black, when you crawl into my sack,
> And be my sexy Valentine!

Missing Shara in the extreme, Nathan lurched into undermining his own resolution. Thinking (hoping) that she would give up their trial soon, he checked his P.O. box at least daily, and sometimes twice, when the waiting got dreadful. During the week of 2/14/65, he received effective GRE scores, called home to cheer Mother, and participated in the church officers' two-day retreat at Wrightsville Beach. There was no breakdown in Shara's resolve, nor the return of his letters, as previously agreed. On Wednesday, 2/24/65, fourteen days after their silence began, he broke it again with a brief *billet-doux*–and a reminder to return his letters.

I am suffering!

CHAPTER 30
TURGID TURMOIL

Where my heart lies, let my brain lie also.

Robert Browning

Life is a foreign language; all men mispronounce it.

Christopher Morley

Thursday, 2/25/65, 8:20 p.m.

My Darling,

Don't hate me, just LOVE ME, for I desperately need it now! I have been to hell three times, so far, and don't think I can stand it much longer! Three times I made up my mind to stop everything, but NOT because my love had weakened. I kept on thinking about the children and Lenore, and I didn't see how I could dare endanger their happiness by continuing with you. I thought about how I felt about my father, and I don't want that to happen to Nattie and Beth. Then, I put myself in Lenore's place, and that didn't help matters any! Lastly, I thought of you–and I guess all that means is that I should call everything off. However, Nathan, I don't know if I can!

Oh, Nathan, Nathan, Nathan, I am so torn! I KNOW I can't just walk out. I can't say I don't care anything about you! Nothing has changed. I still love you very much, and I know it. Trying to imagine having no relationship with you makes me feel completely empty, which is why I haven't returned your letters.

How I have wanted your love—so badly—just to have you hold me—just to know that you still love me (even if it isn't as much, now). I think I care more now than I have cared before (but I keep asking myself if this is fair—fair to love you when I am only hurting you and everything you have!).

Nathan, I just don't know what to do, now—you may have to be the stronger and make the decision. I don't want you to feel obligated or to influence you. I don't want you to feel that we must keep going now, just because of me. No matter what happens, I want us to keep some kind of relationship going—either as friends or whatever. I refuse to destroy the closeness we have shared all this time—it means too much to me. To be frank, I need the understanding and concern you have given me, and I am not afraid to tell you so.

There is nothing else to say except that I love you—right or wrong! Take care and try to understand why I didn't send the letters back sooner.

My love always,

Shara

Nathan devoured her words, taking heart and taking their separation extremely hard. Shara was racked with fear, desperation, and an unbearable tension between believing she should give Nathan up, and her need and love for him. Meanwhile, an equally desperate Nathan concluded that their interregnum was foolishness and ached to restore as soon as possible.

Due to a misunderstanding by Shara, regarding their writing, exacerbated by her inability to get to her post office box, he wrote many times during March, fruitlessly, and she did not write at all for three weeks. Unwilling to suffer any longer, he rang her house twice at 9:00 p.m. one 3/24/65 and hung up. Miracle of miracles, Shara heard his signal and placed a sly collect call back to his office.

Commiserating their communications foul up, they wept their mutual love and planned to meet as soon as Nathan could get away. Their goodbyes were paragons of love and longing...

Communication restored, no matter how shakily, Nathan's spirits soared with expectation. During the next ten days, several heartsick letters passed between them, and his planned trip got postponed, due to several huge storms over the Carolinas. Their communication continued to bounce between joy in their mutual love and Shara's fear that her love would ruin him. Lenore was more accepting, without ceding anything, mostly seeking understanding of the realities.

Emory University's graduate school accepted him, and Nathan began the long promised and unfortunately compromised Sunday evening sex-ed sessions with his seventh and eighth graders. The down-pouring storms outside were no worse than the ones aboil in his life. Shara, too, found herself bashed about and inundated by her own turbulent waves of angst and conflict!

*

"Honey, I've missed my period, now, by almost two weeks."

"Oh, my god, Lenore!" he said, running to her and holding her. "Is that right? How do you feel? Shouldn't you go see Dr. Meckle to be sure? That's wonderful! Mother might be so pleased; she'll hang on long enough to hold a new grandbaby. Any other symptoms? We mustn't get ahead of ourselves, but a new baby may be just what we need! Nattie and Beth will be delighted. Me too!"

"Calm down, sweetheart. Let's not get too excited. We don't want another miscarriage."

"No, ma'am, we certainly don't!"

This news, if true, may be the unavoidable clincher between Shara and me, and may remove all the stress and strife arcing back and forth between us. I am truly excited about a new little Scott, though I wouldn't have planned one just now. Still, I ache for Shara, both for her love and for her distress when, if, I tell her. I'll wait until we're more sure, but I must let her know. I hate to think, no I don't, I am amazed to think that this may be an answer to our prayers—if I can stand losing her…

Nathan's next letter to Shara, before his 3/27/65 trip to Durham, began to douse the fire they had been stoking for two years. He wrote that Lenore's doctor opined that she could be about two weeks pregnant. That seeming fact roiled their fears as it dashed their hopes on the rueful rocks of reality.

*

"Lenore, my soul needs a Band-Aid!"

"Any particular ailment, honey, or is your not-so-secret life catching up with you?"

"Ouch! Why do you always know me better than I know myself? It's unnerving. What do you mean, wife-o'-mine?"

"Probably, that the course of your relationship with Shara is running into unforeseen snags, one of which is probably your worry about my probable pregnancy, and maybe about what I know. Think those probabilities are contributing to your present malaise?"

"Would you like to enlighten me, 'Nore?"

"It's not a matter of 'like,' sweetheart, but 'must,' at this point, don't you think?"

"I agree. I love you too much to keep screwing with our lives, especially with a baby on the way."

"That's nice to hear, but I already knew that. I'll cut to the chase and tell you that I know that one of the things—people— you are screwing is Shara. My doubts were confirmed when you forgot to remove the five condoms in our glove compartment. You are fucking her, are you not?"

"Yes, for some time now, as you have suspected all along, darling. I'm glad you know, for you are quite right about my worrying about that, for my not telling you has been eating at my entrails."

"I knew that, too, honey. I also know you well enough to realize that your fucking Shara doesn't necessarily mean you don't love me, too. At least, I hope that's what you're about to confirm."

"Whew! I wish I were as smart as you, for you have always known me better than I know myself. Of course, I confirm that, and I'll never stop loving you. The confound in all of this is that I love you both, want you both, and I spend the largest portion of my life trying to figure out how to do that successfully, without hurting anyone."

"I know. Of course, I am hurt, Nathan, but not crushed, because I love you, understand you, and at least most of your needs. I want to continue with you as my husband and the father of our two, perhaps soon to be three children. I'm pretty sure you're getting pressure from Shara, too, one way or another. Want to tell me about that?"

"I'm glad you asked, for we both have been worrying ourselves sick over how to continue our love without hurting you, ruining my professional life, and then maybe my winding up without either of you. As you know, we have just completed a highly unsuccessful 'interregnum' of over a month of not visiting or communicating, hoping to evolve some sort of solution other than disaster–to give us all a chance at the best outcome."

Seeing tears in his wife's face, Nathan reached out to her, only to have her turn away.

"You can't imagine I'm any too happy to hear you confirm my greatest fears, Nathan. You know me, too, and you should know that, even hurt, I'm going to fight for what's best for us all, whatever that may be, especially with a new baby probably on the way! Meanwhile, please do go ahead with whatever your so-called interregnum produced, if you think that will help. I'll continue to love you, want you, try to more fully understand both you and Shara, for I know she has to be hurting, too, just as am I–and you, too, or your soul wouldn't 'need a Band-Aid.'"

With that, his amazingly brave and mature wife, still in tears, hugged him briefly, accepted his tender, tendered kiss, and went to attend Beth, who was calling her from her crib.

*

In a March 25 letter to his shriveling Mother, Nathan shared his present disquietude with his job, but not about Lenore's probable pregnancy. Confessing the absence of a goodness of fit for him as a pastor, he proposed returning to graduate school, hoping to teach in a college. Commiserating with her that neither she nor Daddy could attend Stephen's graduation from SCU in June, he promised to be there, and hinted that Stephen might be chosen Man of the Year.

*

Mother was dying. He sensed it but knew it not. Daddy's Florida Cracker distrust of doctors kept her away from a competent diagnostician until her cancer was metastatic. Besides, mothers are eternal to their young– especially this Mother. No matter the ten children, all welcome, all wonderful, all hers; no matter the endless hours of sweltering heat, cleaning, cooking, washing (no car or washing machine for the Scott family until Nathan was a junior in college); and no matter her distance from her beloved Tennessee hills—no matter.

No matter the intellect-stifling prejudices and protocols of her conservative, chauvinist, disillusioned husband; no matter the incredible intellectual energy she burned, urging and splurging on growth, reading at least a book a week, teaching scholarly, adult Sunday School classes, serving eternal presidencies of one or more PTAs, and writing a popular, weekly column in the local paper for 34 years—no matter, for this Mother was essential!

No matter her wonderfully open, liberal attitude, infectious and enlivening, which led her to set aside her own wise and thoroughly informed views, in favor of listening to the queries and imponderables of her brood, followed by penetrating questions and illuminating insights. She loved them all, differently, perhaps, but always equally, using her brand of wisdom, to know what and when to offer each, as she saw the need—or was asked. Nathan didn't merely love and honor her; he was in awe of her.

No matter a life almost completely spent in aid of others, usually without complaint; no matter the tribal cloister of a small town, wherein the greatest excitement and intellectual opportunities were to be found in the stacks of the public library (whose board she chaired so long); no matter her one handicapped child, so loved, so well taught, so like her, yet so empty of her keen mind—no matter. Mother would, no, must live forever, as must all givers of life after life. It simply had not fully registered in the mind of her number two son that she would not.

So, to palliate the gnawing agonies in them both, Nathan's letters to Mother were filled with his babies—her precious grandbabies—surging with their lives, providing him the resources for his ultimate gift of life back to its source, turning the wheel, marking the cycle of birth, death, and rebirth a living reality and not a fantasy fit only for shallow greeting cards and fatuous fawning. Repeatedly, he told her of their growth, their curiosity, and their cute, pithy sayings, their naughties and their wondrously puerile goodness, their cuddles, their slights, and their joys—and of their parents' joy in them.

He sought to cheer her with many photos and the promise of their coming in June, after Stephen's graduation, so she could hold them, cupping their bottoms in her hands, and their essential selves in her heart—and know them to be part of her—extensions of herself and of her gone, gone, once and only, beloved Papa—alive, alive, oh! Oh, God! Why don't Mothers live forever?

Indeed, it was partly because of Mother and her internal and internal influence that Nathan returned to his shaky resolve to extract himself, Lenore, and his babies from the calamity which threatened. Though he did not fear Mother's recriminations, neither did he think he could tolerate her pain a full discovery of his love affair almost guaranteed, especially in light of a new baby.

Due to the heft of this news, Nathan whispered to Lenore his woeful but considered intent to seal the very end of his affair with Shara—on his trip to Durham on March 27, 1965.

"Lenore, you have been extraordinarily patient with my relationship with Shara, hearing and understanding me when I confessed that I truly love you both. If I can muster the will—and courage—I intend to tell her, today, that we must try to end it."

This likelihood, recognized now as such between them, Lenore, acting on her love and her assumed pregnancy, let him go, wishing him Godspeed, success, and gentleness toward Shara, the "featured victim in this entire, unfortunate matter," in her essentially empathetic eyes.

Ten minutes after Nathan left that Saturday morning, Lenore called Melanie to partake of her confidante's concern and friendship, and to inform her of Nathan's trip, his resolve, and her own unsteady feelings of hope and anxiety.

"Mellie, I believe–hope–he's actually going to do it this time. He seems truly happy about the prospects of another baby."

"I hope so, too, Lenore; I know that girl has a strong hold on him, the way he's been running back and forth."

"You see Shara from time to time at church, don't you, Mellie? What do you think he sees in her? It simply cannot be just the sex! She's on the slight side, isn't she? It's hard to fathom that a man of his education, intellect, and religious disposition could be so dangerously involved with a yet to be educated seventeen-year-old girl. It makes me wonder if he has blinders on when it comes to her. What's the attraction?"

"Hard to tell, Lenore. Knowing Nathan, maybe he's caught up in the dynamics of teaching her, well, everything, if you get my meaning. Maybe it was her being something like *tabula rasa* that intrigued him, and now he can't let go. It's easy to see why she's attracted to him, though, due to his pied piper personality, smarts, and total giving to everyone all the time. Everyone under fifty at church loved him, learned from him, and were crushed to see him leave–I hear that still."

"Of course, I know what you mean; I was–still am–caught under his spell. I'm guessing Shara fell under his spell, too, while he invested in her personal and family issues. I've often heard him quote something he wrote in seminary about what he called his defining *existenz*: 'What selfish gods we be, to seek someone seeking me.' Maybe he simply responded to her seeking? Obviously, sex reared its nether head somewhere along the line. But Mellie, why Shara, and why only Shara, if seeking and sex is at the bottom–oops, bad allusion–of it? Why Shara and not any of the others constantly seeking him out, some a lot fairer and savvier than she is–Kathy Rogers, for instance?"

"Are you thinking, er, wondering if he might have another–others–on the side, Lenore?"

"Probably not. I know him pretty well, and I think I would realize it, if so. Even Nathan doesn't have that kind of stamina, regardless of any other Nathan-seekers!"

"Uh, I certainly don't know, but evidently Shara had–has–the greater emotional need, the kind I think he has always been more naturally attracted to."

"That would include me wouldn't it – and maybe you, too, at least at some level? Right, Melanie?"

"Well, of course I find him attractive; he's another redhead, just like my brother," she giggled.

"We'll see what happens. I haven't had a pregnancy test, yet, but my breasts are swelling, and I feel nauseous after some meals. According to what I told him over the phone, my doctor thinks I'm about two weeks in, but he hasn't really examined me yet, he reminded me. I have an appointment with him next week."

The two Nathan-lovers stopped trying to figure out why another woman loved him, too, both women having abundant inside information, unknown to the other. Uncomfortable Melanie changed the subject to her upcoming move to Prospect Park, Pennsylvania and to her new job at the Philly airport. Together, they plotted a visit there by the Scott family in early April, to help cement Nathan's avowed intent.

*

Saturday morning, March 27, 1965, Nathan's felt the purging heat of the sun of his moral determination. By noon, at the outskirts of Durham, that dwindling sun was not only in full eclipse but was nearly replaced by the moon of his reflected need for all that Shara had been—and still was—to him. As soon as he saw her turn the corner, he was totally captivated and could scarcely control his need to hold and to love her forever.

"Hi, lover," she grinned as she got in, kissed him quickly, and dropped her head into his lap, "if it's all right to call you that now. God, I cain't believe how much I've missed you. You look—you feel so good!"

Nathan's hands re-familiarized himself with Shara's curvaceous, youth, as she turned her well-formed face up to gaze at him. Moving his hand between her legs, in the time it took to drive two hundred yards, both were aflame.

"Whew," he exhaled, "we had better slow down, before I stop at a red light and ravish you! Do take your sweet mouth away from me—I can't stand the heat of your dragon's fiery breath much longer."

Shara sat up, smoothed her blouse, fanned the front of her skirt, dropped it over her spread legs, smiled, turned toward him, and said, "Well, Reverend Scott, I certainly enjoyed that laying on of hands."

Too early to register in his motel, they parked in someone's future bedroom, in a close, unfinished subdivision and walked about. Then, they fell into each other's arms, enjoying their first full embrace in fifty days. Heads aswim, neither wanted to be the first to break their kiss, nor disconnect their voracious thighs, insistently absorbing the other's heat and pressure. With a giggle, Shara broke away, grabbed the shaft denting her belly and led it back to the car for its accommodation.

First, they discussed their trial hiatus, hating it anew, but avoided the discussion they both knew was to come. Instead, Nathan spoke about Mother, surprising himself when tears splashed on her reaching hands

As was his way with the furies of sadness, illness, grief, failure, and loss, Nathan slowly turned them into more sentient muses, heralding his nibbles on a most inviting neck, and a few well-placed kisses on its neighborly ear. Eventually, his lips covered an erect nipple, while his hands warmed in the hot springs dampening her pubes.

Taut and trembling with the tensions of long-suppressed desire, Shara allowed herself to be gentled backward to the seat, her legs to be parted, and her panties to drift from her body, like a mist rising from the moist, morning earth, revealing its rich, fertile garden.

As Nathan was about to position himself to plow and plant, he noticed a patrol car slowly approaching. By the time the gendarme was abreast of their car, the lovers were sitting calmly, "just talking."

Leaving, as instructed, Nathan dropped Shara at a hamburger hut near the motel, registered, took his gear into his first-floor room, and fetched his lady. They sauntered in, daring the cleaning lady to look at them with more than passing interest. She didn't.

Inside, Shara stood before her man, removed her glasses, and slid her arms around his neck before she kissed him. Her tongue explored his in neat syncopation with the steady gyrations of her pelvis into his. Both relished his swell and increase, so familiar and responsive to her ageless cues.

Fearing this passion would be their last, they leisured through each step of enticing preparation and each level of burgeoning desire, shepherding their excitement by letting it graze. They wove their limbs together in fabulous friction, let them part, and with increasing creativity, re-blended the heats of their desires, dulled their remaining inhibitions, and expressed the righteousness of their mutual, thriving lusts.

Each touch and worship had its own intimate focus, from the gentlest of nibbling kisses and subtle caress, through the artistry of mutual disrobing, to the molding, petting, probing, and incomparable feasting, accompanied by fulfilling senses too devastatingly dear, too long denied–and too imperative to deny any longer.

Inevitably, their tasting and embracing soared into ecstasy, outstripping the impedimenta of space and time, where minds and bodies were momentarily lost to the exquisite thrill of nature's orgasmic rewards. Thirstily, they drank what they tasted and turned to probe the peaks and valleys of desire to come. Her wet, hot eagerness was a perfect, feminine match for his rigid masculine flesh–humanity's universal salutes to Eros.

Lying within and upon the other, one flesh, each of their senses recalling and reclaiming its responsive role, their liquid heats dripping from and around them, flush with the bloods of longing and fulfillment–they wept. Only those who have distilled such tears, sharing their precious salts in recollection and reclamation, unfettered and unashamed, will fully understand the multiform meanings of such effusions. They loved and longed, lusted and laid together, against all odds and gods, and the fact and meaning of these realities and experiences, no matter their form and content, their time and place, or their hopes for the future, simply overwhelmed them with *Now*.

Close to five, Nathan had not said what he must. Hating the moment, as much as the message, he began. She lay quietly in his arms as he talked, until, afraid it would hurt him to see her pain, she turned her back to him, snuggling, spoon fashion.

The details of their discourse were unimportant to her. She felt the hammer blows before she heard them: A) Lenore knew about their affair, was praying Shara would understand that her pregnancy, the real clincher, would convince Shara to let Nathan go; B) Shara is too valuable to him to let her risk depending on him further; C) He felt his back was turned to God; D) He is worried about his family now, especially when it seems inevitable that his own Mother would probably not last another year. E) Thus, they knew what they must do; F) She should date, even have sex, if she believed it would be best for her; and G) For the good of all, and perhaps even for the glory of God, they must try to fall out of love with each other. She cried throughout his alphabet of tears—but agreed.

The remainder of their stay in their parting nest went by in a blur, with nothing but unexpressed, gut-wrenching fear and angst permeating their mood and conversation. Taking her almost home, he kissed her quickly, before she almost leapt from the car. He asked her to call him after eight at the motel, and sped away, as a car was coming.

Dying, Nathan picked over a meal in the motel restaurant, dragged back to his room, and tried to watch television until her call. At 8:45 p.m. the phone startled him into tachycardia. Their conversation was gentle, and with the catharsis of decision over, almost as if nothing had happened. Yet the strain was there, unexpressed. The subject turned to her future, and he reiterated that he wanted her to date, as her loving another continued to be the circumstance that might allow him to adjust to losing her.

She asked, and he told her, about his conversation with Lenore. She wept, not wildly, but keenly, helplessly, while his voice caressed her and tried to love her back to her usual even keel. Hearing her mother telling her to get off the phone for the fourth time, they mumbled their "I love yous" and agreed to write at least one more letter each, to cement their farewells. His last words, to ring in her ears for days, were, "Shara, call me—come to me—or I'll come to you, if you need me!"

Though he was driving, he staggered home...

*

3/28/65 4:15 p.m.

My darling (Is it all right to call you that, now?) Nathan. It is Sunday–the day after our new beginning, a lonely feeling. It all seems like a dream, yet it is too real for that. The force of separation–real separation, this time–has hit me right in the face, and it hurts! The moment I awoke this morning, I knew you were gone, probably home, and my heart sank. I wanted so to see you once more, to be held once more, to bid you a proper farewell, and then let you go your way.

I know I must not cry, yet the tears have begun to fall; the need to have our freedom still within, and nothing seems changed! This makes it terrible because, as I write this letter, I know things must change. It's almost as if I must let a little part of you die–at least die within me. I must learn to love, and yet, not love, to share, yet not share, to give, but to be careful in the way I receive. For, if I don't learn to replace some of the deep feelings I have for you, I'll only want to continue the way we are (were?).

Oh, Nathan, it's so terrible–so terrible right now! I'm still clinging, and I know I must not cling. I remember what you once wrote me: "We love, and loving, we care, and caring, we hope, and hoping, we cling, and clinging, we live, and living we love." It's so hard to imagine myself not loving, not caring, not hoping, not clinging, as I have before. I keep on wondering what will happen to us both–how much we will suffer–maybe a great deal–maybe not at all.

Nathan, please, please tell me how you feel, really feel. Just thinking about Saturday, I get the feeling that you may be hurting inside, yet you seemed to be covering it up, protecting me, at least until we were on the phone. I think you were trying to comfort me by your gentleness, concern, and caring and, therefore, you couldn't show me what you felt. I think I know how you felt, but then, maybe I don't. To be honest, I need some security in knowing that you feel as deeply as do I–in other words, plainly, I want to be wanted very much–by you!

One thing, though–please don't worry about me. I have the strength to go on, more so than I thought. I'm trying to instill within myself the confidence I think you want me to have, plus the confidence I know I need for myself. If I need you, I promise I will let you know. Just pray for me because that is where our greatest strength lies. I believe this, and I'm willing to let God guide my life. Remember my eyes, my gentleness, my concern, my love, and you will know me!

With all my love, Shara

3/28/65 9:10 p.m.

My Darling Shara:

How valuable you are–have become–will always be to me! I can scarcely believe the truth of our love; it is so precious to me. Since our softest of good-byes, I have been holding you, wearing you on and in and through my heart. I wish I had the words to express my overflowing tenderness and warmth toward you...

I am content, yet so sad; I am happy, yet, disturbed; I am fulfilled, yet I fear the void which must become the future for us, and my need for you is virtually insatiable–in every way. Though we both know what we must do, and what we must cease, my eased and essential heart ruptures, even now, as though you and I were always to supply it with its fill of love.

I shall always love you. It is true that it will fade, and the life of it will give way to the withered impression it will make, all brittle and priceless, all tender and eternally wonderful, between the pages of our memories. Yet, the simple truth, the awesome reality, the final joy of it lies in the fact that it can never be taken from us. We are real—we do love—we have given—and we shall always be different, therefore, and happily so. I pray so intensely that it shall ever feel as magnificent and right as it does now, for as long as either of us lives.

I want to record here for you that you have given me life—when I was freely courting death. You have walked with me on the road to Purpose, and my only regret lies in the different paths we must take to serve that Purpose. Your love, your concern, your Self, your body, the very hopes you have held for us—all of these you have offered me, and I have deeply partaken of them all, so thrillingly, so righteously and redemptively that nothing will ever be the same for me, again. You did and gave because you loved me as purely as any love this world has ever seen!

To me, you are a gift. I recognized something of this when we first met, and I have watched you grow, mature and blossom. How desperately do I long to continue to partake of you and your growing gifts of selfless love! But I know this is not to be—as do you. I want to thank, love, and remember you—to watch you grow. So be it. Give love, My Darling, and remember me as you have known me.

Nathan

Two days later, to his shock, Nathan's secretary told him that he had an urgent phone call from Shara Starr.

"What's wrong, Shara?" worried the minister, after he called her back at a Durham pay phone.

"Hi, darling–I, uh, mean, Nathan. All hell has broken out at home, and I need to talk about what to do."

"Are you okay? Have they discovered my letter or something? Tell me!"

"No, Nathan–nothing like that. It's about mother and daddy–they have been fighting like mad. Oh, Nathan, it was horrible!"

"Okay, darling. Tell me what happened."

Shara described terrible verbal abuse of her mother by her dad, in the presence of the entire family, made worse when Shara tried to intervene. When her mother sank to the floor in utter defeat, sobbing, Shara tried to help her, while shouting at her father, "I hate you! I hate you! How could you be so cruel?" Her father looked hard at her and just walked out of the house. Shara helped her mother to the bathroom, telling her she should divorce him on the grounds of mental cruelty.

In the morning, her mother stayed in bed, so Shara made breakfast for everyone. Her dad came in and told her to apologize to him for saying what she said. She said she'd apologize to him if he would apologize to her mother. He colored and told her she couldn't leave the table until she apologized.

"I'm sorry I was disrespectful, but what would you have done if you saw your father treating your mother the way you were treating Mom last night?"

"Go wash your damned face!" was his heated response."

"I did and got out of there as soon as I could and called you. You don't mind, do you, Nathan?"

"Of course, not, darlin;' I'm incredibly happy you trust me enough, still, to share all this with me. Are you upset about anything you have done, so far?"

"Only that I gave in and apologized–but I was afraid he might do something worse."

"It must have been very difficult–especially since we are going through some trauma, too."

Shara wept, wrenching his heart, as she told him how she missed him, how futile everything seemed without having their relationship on which to fall back. Asking him to be patient with her, she said she might not be able to let go as quickly as he could, but that she had every intention of doing what was right.

She had just started her period, which relieved them both. They exchanged vows of continuing, wrenching affection and hung up.

The black clouds of separation dim my hope, but Shara continues my silver lining.

CHAPTER 31
WHAT ARE WE WAITING FOR?"

Purpose without passion risks being merely pedantic.
Passion without purpose risks being merely prurient.

Nathan Rhea Scott
April 11, 1965

Lenore did not feel well, an evident symptom of her pregnancy, complete with a bit of morning sickness and the queasies any time she ate. Knowing Nathan very well, she neither gloated over his recent decision, nor moved in with too much discussion, suggestion, or demand. Ever patient, loving, giving, and beautiful, she generally acted as she thought people should act toward her. Nathan was particularly pleased with her lately, because she did not pressure him about anything and, evidently, was going to present him (and his Mother) with a very welcome third child!

After his sexually wiser seventh and eighth graders left Nathan's church-sponsored sex-ed program, Sunday evening, 4/4/65, he risked a brief, check-up phone call to Shara. She seemed perky and pleased, not at all as devastated as he had feared—and hoped. Saucily, in a rush, she informed him that she was in her period (beginning 3/31/65), and that on Wednesday, 4/7/65, she would, again, be dating Daring Danny! Further, her father almost apologized to her and seemed to be treating her mother better.

Nathan bit his tongue about her dating Danny. A few sniffles snuck through her bravado, when she thanked him for his 3/28/65 letter, which she said she would keep forever. Finally, she waxed wistful about her church's senior high retreat at Camp Promise the coming weekend, knowing it would evoke happy/sad memories.

During a pause, Shara screwed up her courage and asked the important questions: Was Lenore truly pregnant? (Yes, evidently, though yet to be confirmed.) Is it okay to write Lenore? (Yes and no but go ahead. He had already mentioned it to Lenore, who took it as a good sign that they were serious. Lenore might write first, because she didn't want Shara to worry that she thought ill of her.)

Because they were actually ending their relationship, couldn't they please meet just one last time? (Only if you think it necessary.) She did. When? (Not with Lenore's knowledge, any time soon. Though he didn't want to sneak, maybe he could drive up to Camp Promise next Saturday night, 4/10/65, after his teaching in Greensboro, and meet her somewhere there for an hour or so?) Though she hoped for a longer, easier visit, it seemed their only choice. (So, okay.)

I'll see her one more time, to ease this godawful pain we both feel at such a sudden, jarring stop. How to square it with Lenore? Maybe she'll understand…

*

April 5–7, the Scotts, *sans les enfants*, had a very pleasant trip to Prospect Park, helped Melanie move in, set up her one-bedroom apartment, and tuned her car. Melanie gave up her double bed to the married couple, managed a furtive feel or two under the table at a local restaurant, and invited him to plumb her desirous and desirable depths, should the opportunity arise.

Monday night, because they had not made love for about a week, Nathan and Lenore did exactly that. The moment he returned from washing, and Lenore took her turn in the bathroom, Melanie stole to his bed, quickly fellated him, and disappeared as furtively as she had appeared, leaving him delighted, dared, and determined–all before Lenore returned.

Lenore was asleep in no time, so he waited, his penis pulsing against his belly. He entered the bathroom, left it, and tiptoed into the living room where Melanie was supposed to be on her cot. Instead, this long-haired naked lady was sitting, slouching really, on her settee, legs spread in obvious invitation, her fingers having started without him.

Without a word he knelt between those white stemmed invitations and replaced her fingers with his tongue. The moment her back arched, he quickly slid deeply into her, plunging repeatedly, praying that her coming ecstasy would remain unheralded beyond the couch.

There followed a time of raw, ripe, and uninterrupted sexual expression–with minimal sound. Ass in the air, wiggling its grace and curves, Melanie took him as willingly as he took her–a sexual symbiosis–in every way they could think of. Finally, as if to punctuate their temerarious creativity, he stood her against the front door, sheathed, lifted her by her bottom, as she wrapped her legs around him, and pumped for dear life.

As his pleasure increased, he felt their combined sexual power as never before, and almost expected to see the head of his penis emerge from her mouth, so profoundly did they fuck. Digging her nails into his back, she urged him on– and in–deeper and faster, until their heat ignited their sizzling lust, and they detonated!

For a full two minutes, still afuck, they did not move, so engaged in their fusion. Nathan began to lose tumescence, despite Melanie's valiant attempts to muscle him into a more prolonged captivity. Without a word, he eased her feet to the floor, still impaled, kissed her breasts, her lips, and her hair, slithered out of her, lurched into the bathroom, and cleansed himself of her entirely too distinctive musks.

Falling into bed with his sleeping wife, QI failing to conjugate Melanie's conjugality, he tried to sleep, while Melanie performed her own ablutions, and Lenore slumbered in innocence. QI stared at the ceiling...

There was no repetition the next night, as Lenore was not feeling well. Nathan fell asleep immediately, following a long day doing Philadelphia. As was her lonely habit, Melanie made do without him.

Driving back to Wilmington, Lenore complained that she might be getting a yeast or a bacterial infection, and it worried them, both. She had already scheduled an ob/gyn checkup for Monday, 4/12/65, so she decided to wait before doing more than inserting anti-yeast suppositories.

*

Nathan was simply unable to tell Lenore his furtive plans to see Shara one last time at Camp Promise on the tenth. His Saturday Bible School workshop in Greensboro could be an overnight affair so, when his sessions ended, about 5:00 p.m., he was out of there.

Starrlight magic awaited him in the cool of this rustic, stolen night, when restoration was braved and borne, against all risks and tsks. Making their *lit en terre* in a shallow ditch a hundred yards from Shara's recreating retreat group, they marveled anew at their transcendent hunger for the other, crowning it with audacious love on a futon of their peeled clothing, strategically spread on the cool earth. As Shara held tightly to the man worshipping atop and well within her, she beheld meteors, those spangling her mind and those hurled across the firmament above her, as their mutual climax basted their dark night with golden threads of recommitment.

This daring hour, pressing them together between the whirling earth and the effulgent sky, loosed the ineluctable gravity of their relationship. This major nova in the empyrean of their stars, crossed though they be, became the numinous portal to their destiny. Slyly, before she returned to the retreat, she hid a woeful, hand-written note in Nathan's jacket, confessing her desperation without him, praying for more than the reconciling hour she had been anticipating.

*

After Saturday's incredible bliss in a shallow ditch near the blazing light of the rec hall at Camp Promise, Nathan, beset by drastic loss, fatigue, indigestion, and a very savvy, disappointed wife, called in sick Sunday morning, attended neither Sunday School nor church, and slept until almost two. Lenore was poker-faced when he fixed himself a bowl of chicken soup, but she couldn't resist asking.

He wearily told her the truth. Because their finish had been too sudden and painful for her, Shara pleaded that they meet one final time. For a change, Lenore wasn't buying it, and worried herself into tears when he would not, indeed, could not, elucidate. Finally, she was a bit palliated when he told her they had not written any letters for two weeks and were sincerely trying to break it off. *We really are...*

Lenore's palliation lasted until she went to her doctor the next day. He assured her she was *not* pregnant! Thus, she met an anticipating, worried Nathan at the door.

"Oh, Nathan; I'm so disappointed," she moaned, weeping, and falling into his outstretched arms. "He said I probably have a cyst on an ovary, causing my pregnancy symptoms, but I'm definitely NOT pregnant!"

"Oh, baby, I'm so sorry–and disappointed, too. Like you, I very much wanted a third child. Did he treat you for it?" he asked, holding her, and kissing her tears.

"There is no specific treatment, at this point. It could just be a single event and may not recur, but there might be hormone treatments, if it persists. I'm so sorry, Nathan. He assured me it was nothing I did. Apparently, it's all too common."

"How do you feel, then, 'Nore?"

"Physically, I'm all right, but to be honest, I fear what this may mean between you and Shara."

"'Nore, we're trying very hard to break up. As we all now realize, cold turkey simply didn't work! I can't help my feelings for her, any more than mine for you. They both defy a simple solution, unless you both agree to live with me, all living and loving together as an ethically confirmed family. That's not likely, though it would certainly resolve our dilemma, and the kids could have two loving mothers. That aside, things are likely to be different anyway, after she graduates, so try not to be too hard on us—or on yourself."

"I was afraid you'd say something like that, honey. We can try to get pregnant again as soon as the doctor tells me it's all right. Wouldn't that help?"

"Honey, I don't think either of us should be worrying about that, right now. Things are certainly on a distinct path. *But what about the Starry, starry night, Scott, and our meteors!* Can't we let that momentum play out, and then see about another child? As usual, you've done more than your part in trying to hold things together, no matter any pregnancy. I just want you to be as happy and as settled as possible. Somehow, things are going to work out for us all."

"Must that include Shara? Your lurking about in the dark at Camp Promise last Saturday night didn't—doesn't— make me feel any too sanguine about things."

"Lenore, our intention has been to cool it, so everyone could get on with their lives. Your being pregnant was a critical variable factor in that, but we were desperately trying to stop, even before you told me you missed your period. Plus, as you say, we can always try for a third child, soon, if you want. And, yes, that would make it somewhat easier for Shara and me to suffer the necessary agonies of stopping."

"Oh, Nathan!"

"The truth is that I am blessed–and cursed–with loving, needing, and wanting two wonderful women, though the heavens fall, and the earth swallow me! I can't help that; I can only try to live and work with it, without doing further damage."

"Doesn't that mean that I'm cursed, too, honey? I surely don't seem to be getting any blessings from it! Especially not when you keep placing me, your children, your vocation, and your God on an equal plane with your teenage lover. How should I find any comfort in that?"

"Hope springs eternal, Lenore. Mother's dying: we're all pining and suffering, and there isn't a lot to be happy about, right now, except that love should always overcome, in spite of my perfidy."

"Nathan, to me, the last thing you are, or have ever been, is perfidious. Confused, too caring and loving, too accepting, too giving–perhaps too needy–and willing, and your boundaries seem to be fluid, as well, but no one who knows you can believe you want or try to be or do evil. That's not what bothers me about you and Shara; it's more that I don't want, and shouldn't have to, *share* you! How do you handle that?"

"Probably, I don't, but love might be able to do so. Why must loving be so painful, anyway? It hurts so awfully, at times, such as now, yet generates new life. Forgive the stupid analogy, but it could be like birthing a baby. All that pain before a new life is pushed out."

"That may be, Nathan, but aren't I the one likely to be pushed out–or at least aside?"

"Not if I can help it, darling; not if I can help it!"

With that, they went to bed and held, where–and while–their blessings still outnumbered their curses...

*

Monday 4/12/65, 8:30 p.m.

Dear One:

I have debated writing you long enough. I just cannot hold back. I want to say so much, but I shall restrain from writing the letter I would like to write, giving you the opportunity of responding according to your needs and wishes–nothing more, nothing less. Of course, I love you!

I didn't get home Saturday night (Sunday morning), until five, stopping once to sleep a little. I couldn't allow myself to think on the return trip. It was too excruciating. Lenore was almost OK when I told her it was our last time. I didn't go to SS and church, because of indigestion. Of greatest import, she went to the doctor today, and he found her *not* pregnant! He wants to check her, again, next week. She may have a cyst on her ovary–I'll keep you posted. This could change everything, as I'm sure we are all very much aware! She and I had a long discussion about just that.

Of course, Saturday night was extremely sweet and meaningful to me. I find I cannot resist the question which must come: What did it–does it–mean to you? Further, what do I mean to you, now? Baby or no baby, was Saturday night under those stars, with meteors flashing, truly our last time?

Shara, when you are in agony you are capable of clear and beautiful expression. The penciled note you hid in my jacket (which I only found yesterday), while we made love on the ground, was in that rare form. Your concern for both of our feelings was real, and basically unselfish, just as were/are your feelings of regret for "hurting" me, by keeping your peace in answer to my "giving."

What really hurts me is not your silence towards me, now or then, or to come, but the void which seems to surround you now, when you "will not turn to (me), cannot turn to (yourself), and find it increasingly difficult to turn to God." I am most grievously sorry, for I have never wanted our relationship to do anything but strengthen you, and to help us both discover the more laudable truths about ourselves. As your minister, I feel some guilt if I have come between you and your God, or have, somehow, caused Him to become vague and inaccessible to you. Please forgive me, Shara. There must be a way...

I guess my strongest feeling is one of intense, personal loss, regret, and grief that we may be dying to each other. It seems such a ghastly waste to me—and I trust/hope to you. Shara, is there no way we can keep from making this determined rift so final and so complete? After Saturday night, I find it increasingly difficult to imagine trying to do without you, though I realize that this is, perhaps, what you need most of all, in order to get out from under me—literally. I need your utter honesty, here, my darling!

Write me when you can—tell me what you will—love me as much as possible—accept me to the extent you are able. Forgive me for my continuing love—instruct me in its future use and expression, else I hold its brand-like heat to your heart, forever.

Nathan

P.S. I do like your new and attractive haircut. I shall never forget how you looked and felt in our wondrous Starrlight! Will you still tell me things, now—

like what music you hear, when you "exercise," what you think? Or will these become too private? I am enclosing one of two, pathetic, dry twigs I found in my pants cuff. You have a right to one–if that's not too silly.

4/14/65 12:01 p.m.

Dearest Nathan,

After reading your stirring letter of 4/12/65 (Monday), I find myself sad and taunted, with almost unbearable grief and pain. It is not the pain of anxiety, so much as it is the burden of a great responsibility– that I must tell you as exactly and honestly as I can what I feel. I don't want anyone to have pain, so it hurts, because I know there will be pain.

In your letter I got the feeling that you were losing all hope. That can be blamed on me, probably, for my penciled note gave you every indication of hopelessness. But I want you to know it isn't what I want! Oh Nathan, all I want is to be loved by you, just like before. The moment I saw you Saturday in the dark I knew what I felt inside for you. As soon as you put your arms around me, as soon as you kissed me, as soon as we made our nest in that little gully, I needed nothing but you.

Nathan, can't you see how much I really love you!

These past few weeks have been pure hell for me because I was not sure how I should react to the whole situation. I thought I would be big and mature and keep everything from you. However, as I kept my feelings to myself, they only grew stronger, waiting for the chance to be rekindled again by you. Well, Saturday night did it!

How can I make you fully understand how much I love you? Do you have any idea what that night did for me? It made me happy once more; it filled me with security; it refilled and nourished the growing love I have and shall always have.

You cannot imagine how many times I sat by that phone, just wanting to pick it up and call you, asking that we keep and renew our relationship. I thought we were doing the right thing, Nathan; I'm not the kind of person who could just turn it off, as, perhaps, you thought I could. I didn't want to hurt your relationship with Lenore any more than I had. When you told me she might be pregnant I knew I had to stay out. In my heart I knew what I wanted, but I was too frightened to come to you. I refrained out of my great love for you, just as I am calling out to you now, for the same reason. I love you!

Let me whisper in your ear that I love you, as I did Saturday night, under the stars, while we were coming together—twice! Good night my love, my Darling!

*

Suddenly relieved and reprieved, sending his emotions soaring, Nathan preached the Easter sermon, April 18, (a fateful date!). In so doing, he had to fight against the pull of God (AKA, "the hound of heaven") urging faith and hope, rather than doubt and despair. Not quite able to make that desperate leap himself, he found tears in his eyes, perhaps conditioned, perhaps born of that kernel of faith that brought him into the ministry in the first place. He was drawn to his own sermon, needing to honor that precious kernel, so like his need for Shara, to sing its harmonies of belief, rather than to engage in the babble of doubt.

Of such, he later thought, must be the see-sawing plight of every educated minister, facing his own sins, the spiritual needs and doubts they evoked, and confronted by his own God- shaped vacuum. *"What selfish gods we be, to seek someone seeking me," again, huh, Scott? Will you ever let Him find you?*

That same Easter Sunday, Nathan fashioned a serendipitous, new thrust from and for his love. He wrote how much he missed her and was hungry for her every aspect. Feeling his own fire, he dared to launch a more descriptive, slowly unfolding fantasy:

> Can you feel my lips at your breasts, hardening your nipples—my hands cupping your nether lips, my finger slipping gently into...

There followed two typewritten pages of what became their first "hot letter," an intimate genre consisting of the most vivid, tastefully explicit, erotic descriptions they both could evince of their lovemaking fantasies with the other. The purpose of such outpourings, of course, was to stimulate and express Agape's pining Eros, to the point of private (if delayed) orgasmic arrivals, for both writer and reader, while apart.

Shara's handwritten response was no less ardent:

> My Darling, All I can say right this minute is, "You wanna fuck?" I'm having a terrible time trying to calm down. Boy, can you ever set me on fire... I need the sweetness, the gentle, yet exciting caress of your lips on my breasts. But, most of all, I need you deep within me, loving me with every inch, with every thrust which makes us one...

Easter night, exhausted, after his hot letter to Shara, and still as horny, Nathan drove home, knowing that either of two, quite lovely women would accommodate his physical need for as long and as often as he wished. Mind whirling with lust, love, conflict, QI, Easter, God, and a realization that he and Shara had turned some sort of urgent, existential corner, he staggered up the stairs, undressed, and flopped on the bed beside Lenore. Sound sleeper that she was, she automatically made room for him, returned his gentle kiss, and continued in slumber.

Well past Shara's magic hour of eleven, his erection felt permanent. *If I don't do something about it, I'll never sleep.* Thus, he tiptoed down the hall to their guest bedroom, where he knew Melanie would not be sleeping. She wasn't. Without a word, she sat up, knelt on the bed, and kissed him, then took his penis between her lips. He almost came, but instead, he removed her delicate nightie, moved her to the edge of the bed, bent to her crotch and began to lap, while she lay back, caressing his head and her own, perfect breasts. Within minutes, she humped her orgasm into his face, holding his head tightly against her mons with needing, directing hands.

Widely spread before him, all the sexual energy and drive of a beautiful, red-haired woman, Melanie held out her arms, and he crawled into them, probed for her cleft, and shuddering with pleasure, pushed himself in with one, commanding plunge. Gasping with pleasure, she ground her hips into him, clamping him within her, as he kissed her swelling breasts and captained her bottom.

He began his fastest, pistoning motions, stretching her to accommodate his thriving—until he was only seconds away. Then, before any release, the Right Rev. Mr. Nathan Rhea Scott, deeply in fuck with his old school chum, her loveliness split and parted by him, looked down at this epitome of femininity, lust, and beauty, with utter and calm resolve, said "No!" and pulled out. Melanie was ready for anything but what happened. He sat down, pulled her up and around, face to face, put her nightie in her hand, shook his head over and over, and finally whispered his astonishing truth.

"Melanie, I'm truly sorry, but I cannot do this anymore. You know I love it, that I'll still want you, but please try not to make yourself available to me, and please don't give in if I weaken in my resolve not to have sex with you again. I know you won't understand, but please, please try to honor my determination, especially, if you value me. You need to get on with your life, as I think you've already concluded, and you don't need me complicating things, no matter how pleasant it is for either or both of us. It has been most exhilarating, I'll never forget you, but I will not make love to you again!"

With shocked effort, Melanie held back tears long enough to stammer, "Why, Nathan? Why—why are you doing this? Let me kiss you to—to climax—I know you haven't come."

"As always, Melanie, you want to give, and give, and give some more, never really asking anything in return but a little of my time, and for me to make full use of your wonderful body. I can't do it anymore. Please!"

"Then, tell me why, Nathan, so I can believe it is nothing—nothing I have done to make you hate me, so!"

"You know that I don't hate you, Melanie. You also know that I've been deeply involved with Shara Starr. Please don't ask me to go into further detail—I will have to work it out with her, myself, one way or the other. But I love Shara, and I feel unfaithful to her, fucking you. It's as simple, and as complicated, as that."

"Did Shara ask you to stop—stop seeing me?"

"Mellie, Shara doesn't know about you and me, nor does Lenore. I'll tell Shara about you when it is appropriate for me to do so. Until then, we'll need to continue to trust each other not to tell Lenore."

Weeping now, Melanie threw her arms around his neck and tried to kiss him. Returning her last, brief kiss, without touching her elsewhere, he gently removed her arms, stood, and walked out of her room. Melanie's sniffling crowded his conscience, as he entered the bathroom. Several minutes later, Nathan left his motherlode of spunk draining in the sink. His orgasm came in midst of gratifying remembrance of Shara beneath him, under a starry sky, punctuated by meteors, ineffable joy—and pure love.

It was April 18, 1965, exactly one year since Shara's transformative Vesper Dell hug. This very date would prove even more significant in the future, but now he felt better than he had felt in almost four years.

I disavowed Melanie's charms, before I shot my wad! I'll wait out the resulting future, come, Oh God, what may!

CHAPTER 32
THE RIGHT THING

An air of relieved realism must prevail which acknowledges the immediate hopelessness of our situation, while openly trusting the long term, with its manifold chances and opportunities.

Quintessential I

Nathan received the letter from his father more as a slow curtain rising on Mother's last act than as a shock. Daddy typed one letter on April 25, 1965, with a zillion carbons, one for each away child and close relative: Mother was hospitalized 4/17/65, sustained an operation on her distended abdomen, where the surgeon found a "liquid tumor," which he "drained" (Daddy's way of saying they opened her up, released about a gallon of fluid, took one look at her advanced state of metastasis, and closed her up again), transfused her, ordered chemotherapy, radiation treatments, and palliatives, and prepared Daddy for her death. Nathan felt tears of shame mixed with his realizing grief as he read Daddy's letter. Indulging the mortal's eternal–and futile–*non sequitur*, he whispered, "Why?"

Lenore, sensitive to his sadness and fully recognizing her husband's propensity for guilt and self-blame, stayed both near and far enough to allow him comfort without hovering. This restimulated a list of re-comparisons and options: *Shara or Lenore, or both? Shara my quintessential mate–a necessity; Lenore the wonderful helpmeet, the lover, the mother–ever too much and too little for me, never feeling I deserve her, and that, perhaps, I attracted her under false pretenses.*

QI evaluated as he reminisced. *Nothing clearer, during our college days, than Lenore's searching for a nest—a secure haven in the world, but not necessarily of it. In my typical, over-excited exuberance, I promised her love, fidelity, listening, protection, and me, as we snuck delicious nesting episodes all over the campus, played classical records, read Wordsworth and the latter Romantics, and trapped, banded, and released songbirds. It is sadly obvious that now I am no longer fully delivering on my promises, promises, promises, and that, perhaps, awfully, it may be forever thus...*

To me, Lenore became a loving and living poem, seeking a private world that would be secure and sensitive enough to know, understand, and appreciate her, without exploitation. Characteristically, I offered her most of those beneficent conditions, so she trusted me into her private heart, world, and body, despite the risks. I will always pair her with sensitive poetry, and she will forever haunt me with her essence, whenever I read or try to write it.

I rediscovered that haunting gist of Lenore in a poem by Theodore Roethke, "I Knew a Woman." When first I read it, desperately in love with Shara, and just as desperately in Agape, respect, admiration, and loyalty with Lenore, I wept from sheer recognition of my gentle, sensitive wife. Four lines move me most, and, forevermore, they evoke and praise my lost Lenore:

> *I knew a woman, lovely in her bones,*
> *When small birds sighed, she would sigh back at them:*
> *When she moved, she moved more ways than one:*
> *The shapes a bright container can contain!*

This bright container, my wife, my Lenore, has ever accommodated herself to the shapes and shades of my person and personality: my moods and emotions; my demanding, strident love; my whims and attempts at wit; my curiosity, and my skeptical, searching forays; my family; my poverty; my music and my words, words, words; my strengths and weaknesses; my sense and nonsense; my rampant body; my babies. She has done so heroically!

Yet, her essence, her Isness, her Thou, filled with a lovely penetralia which seeps from her bones, does sigh at birds and buds, and poems and petals, and dawns and dusks, and hymns and prayers, all things wee and growing, and gentle, simple, natural things, especially when they sigh at her. As they always do....!

Lenore is at one with equity as fishes are at one with the sea; it is her medium, and like a fish, when her world becomes inequitable, she seems as vulnerable—or at least as needful. Whenever I see her so, most especially if I am the cause, I am driven to restore her to her accustomed health and happiness, where trust is the air she breathes and steadfast love her daily bread.

Nathan knew his wife to be the soul of sensitivity and feminine, protective warmth, yet he also knew her to be no "Wee, sleekit, cow'rin tim'rous beastie." Though realized over the years, it was emblazoned on his forehead by one striking event, two years earlier. Living in a rented, antebellum home several miles out of Durham, Beth-pregnant Lenore thoroughly enjoyed the old house, grounds, lake, fields, and animals about. An inevitable mama kitty deposited inevitable kittens in their shed, and the entire Scott family took inevitable delight in those soft, new lives.

When the kittens were six weeks old, cute, and playful, they inhabited and subdued the wraparound porch of the old house, attacking and vanquishing shoes, pants legs, toys, brooms, and any other moving objects straying into their territory. Coming in from fishing, Nathan thoughtlessly leaned his rod and reel in a corner of the porch, a treble-hooked lure hanging kitten-high and enticingly available for swatting.

The crash of the fishing rod and the yowling of a kitten clamored for Nathan's horrified attention. He rushed to rescue the kitten, somehow snagged in the mouth by two treble hooks. Catching it, almost by reeling it in, it scratched his hands terribly, as he held it, trying to remove the hooks. Completely unsuccessful, Nathan hollered for Lenore to bring wire cutters.

Entering the scene, Lenore was aghast at the suffering of what had been the furry epitome of a delightful, young creature, filled with trust and playfulness. Now it was a crying, spitting, scratching feral thing, seeking to escape by instinct alone. Immediately, almost shoving Nathan aside in her compassion, Lenore grabbed the bleeding, tormented, furry fury, and, sobbing in her own special agony, wrung its neck in one deft motion!

Now, because of his love for Shara, it was increasingly difficult for Nathan to nourish Lenore enough, this lovely, genteel lady, and he suffered when she did. *At least she still has Melanie; but look how close I came to destroying even that source of love and understanding.*

Since his last traipse into Melanie's bedroom, he remained true to his determination, and had not returned. She looked longingly at him, often, and he still salivated when she rang his Pavlovian chimes. Though undeniably difficult, Nathan's fidelity to Shara seemed easier than his to Lenore.

Though he missed sex with Melanie, he happily focused those freed energies on Lenore and Shara–especially in his fantasies about Shara, nurtured by his periodic, unavoidably limited, excruciatingly desirable contacts with her. She and her guileless, giving ways almost filled him up, even at a distance. Lovely Lenore, almost by default, was slowly relegated to lesser wife, which status did not become her, nor satisfy Nathan's ethics–or his deep regard for her.

Lenore gets the short end of the emotional stick, I fear. Even when I'm with her, I'm often thinking of Shara, how to see her more often, whether her dates are heating up, how she's doing in school, writing her and impatiently waiting for her letters, basking in her focus on and love of me, and on and on.

On the other hand, I trust and co-parent with Lenore, help her run the house, make love with her far more often than with Shara, share ideas about the news and the world situation, invest in her projects, share my church work issues and answers, and get feedback on my sermons and talks. Lenore, essential to my daily life and the best part of my history, is also directly connected to my family, the producer of Mother's beloved grandchildren, and makes up a huge portion of my very identity!

What, then, gives Shara this vaunted place in my heart, my being, my essence, my life? Ultimately, I do not know, other than that I utterly need her to need me. She is so important to me that I daily risk losing Lenore and all the rest, by my existential need for and investment in Shara. Where Lenore is my wife, and a very successful one, at that, I firmly believe that Shara was meant to be my mate from the foundations of God's creation! Talk about faith! Have I created a religion of her? I sincerely think—and hope—not!

Thus, the most ethical, practical, and enduring solution, were it possible, is, somehow, to have them, love them, both, together, in the same home, preferably: two wives. How do I create that at the moment of delivery, Scott? Fat, scandalous chance?

*

Nathan received word that Shara's period commenced May 4, two days after his sermon on scandalized faith, that divine foolishness, and ceased two days following his Family Night Supper address, regarding the methods and benefits of active listening in human relationships. Driving home, Lenore opined it was one of his better talks, surely resulting in increased efforts to hear and understand in Christian homes.

"Is that a wifely hint, ma'am?" he made light.

"Do I have to hint these days, Nathan?"

"Mebbe. How *are* we doing in the communication department, sweetheart?"

"We neither flourish nor wither, but you'll talk to me when you have something to tell me. I have noted an interesting change in you, lately—even Melanie has commented on it."

"How sayest Maid Melanie?"

"She said you seem both more serious and more distant, as if your mind is far away, even when you are looking right at people."

"And my beautiful wife? What saith she?"

"She doubts the beauty, notes the distance, but perceives the seriousness as direction-finding—perhaps even course setting—or correcting?"

"Thou sayest correctly—I am struggling with many things, as you know, and trying to find my way around this combination minefield/cow-pasture earth, without stepping in or on something."

"Nathan, I love you. Do you love me?"

"Did the sun rise, today?"

"You're so romantic!"

"How's this, 'I love you as a brook loves its source!'"

"You used that one in college."

"I love you as flowers love the sun?"

"Seminary."

"How about, 'I love you as gravity loves a falling object in a vacuum?' That's pretty accelerating, don't you think?"

"You do love a pun. I would settle for leisurely intercourse when we get home, instead of your regular fornication with the television."

"You mean you'd rather I fucked you than fuck around with the late show, right, wife-a- mine?"

"Thou hast said!"

"So be it," he grinned, running his hand under her dress, and caressing her inner thighs. The fulfillment he enjoyed that Thursday night lasted him until his next letter to Shara, the following Thursday, a little more than seven days: a record for total, sexual abstinence, since the introductory, orgasmic age of eleven.

Meanwhile, things were heating up in Shara's life. Tight control over her life by her father stifled her. With no prompting, overt or covert, from Nathan, Shara longed for, talked about, and plotted leaving home, so as to be independent, regardless of the outcome of their relationship.

Additionally, Shara accepted a modicum of dates with males about her age, meaning she accepted a modicum of physical intimacies, as well, though she excommunicated Daring Danny, permanently, to Nathan's relief. According to mutual understanding with Nathan, she should pursue her own socio-sexual growth, while they were apart. It also gave helpful cover to her dangerous activities with him: *elasticity!*

The weekend of 5/15-16/65 provided a sample of her dating life. Peter Gordon, a senior from nearby Raleigh, whom she met at a party, called and asked her out Saturday night. Danny called, apologized for his behavior, and begged her to go out with him Sunday. Her body was tempted, but she demurred. Preparing for her date with Peter, she took a leisurely bath and got ready. Wondering if Peter would ever see her nude, she powdered her muff and was immediately embarrassed, fearing such might hurt Nathan. No matter how often he told her it would be all right to date and whatever, she was dubious—and almost afraid, especially of guys like Danny who knew how to push her well educated buttons.

If Shara were expecting the earth to move with Peter (or with Peter's peter), her expectations soon faulted to another reality. Peter, a tall, thin boy with glasses, was very polite. He seemed totally inexperienced—but was cute and male, thus a valid prospect for her elastic wings. A good Christian boy, by his own declaration, Peter avowed respect for her–that he would never do anything to hurt, embarrass, or anger her.

Following the movie and a leisurely drive home, they parked in her driveway, and he kissed her three times, gently and demurely, after asking her to go to a movie with him the next Tuesday. She went in fifteen minutes early, at 11:45 p.m.

Monday, walking from school to her bus stop, two boys drove up and offered her a ride. Recognizing them as fellow seniors, she accepted. Joel jumped out of the front seat, and ushered her in beside driver Mark, so they could squeeze her in between them, hips to happy hips and thighs to tempting thighs.

Full of restless energy, sexual and otherwise, the boys turned their Colgate smiles on Shara, trying to discern how willing–or cajolable–a female she might be. For ten minutes, all three laughing uproariously, she fought off their teasing, daring, darting hands, legs, arms, elbows, wrists, and lips. Despite their hilarity, Shara noted two erections, one enormous, and felt her congestion returning.

Arriving at her home, both boys playfully tickled, smooched, and otherwise teased her, while she laughed and tried to fend off their efforts. Opening both doors, the boys engaged in tug-a-war, with Shara as the rope, with Mark, the driver, winning, pulling her out of his door. Mark walked her to her front door, where he asked her for a date, not trying to hide his woody. Up drove Big J. Carl and parked behind their car.

There ensued an awful scene: accusations that both boys were trying to assault Shara; Shara's attempt to explain harmless, jocose behavior; Shara summarily ordered to her room, where Carl "will take care of you, later;" threats, curses, and demands that Mark get his "piece of shit car" out of Carl's driveway; Joel arriving to back up Mark; louder threats of harm to both boys; Joel pulling Mark away, retreating to their car, ending in their scratching off, with twin, ornithological salutes held out of their windows, as Big J. Carl shook his fist and cursed...

Mortified, Shara made an important decision—at least, she decided she was going to decide to leave—and soon.

Three days later, 5/19/65, Shara reported her progress.

My Darling Nathan:

I have been listening to classical music since 8:00, and my heart is lightened, leaving me feeling as free as a bird. It's hot as blue blazes up here, and I'm only wearing a bra and panties (black, too!).

Nathan, I must admit this whole situation has really got me down. God knows I don't want to hurt anyone, but I want so much. I just need to be me. I don't feel free at home, anymore, always wanting to be alone (Mother thinks I'm just weird), or to get out with people my own age. I don't understand what they want from me—from anyone!

Now, to Peter. He wants to take me to dinner Friday, and to his PROM Saturday! Shriek! I didn't get to go to my own prom, but he and his friend want to take Kathy and me to theirs. I'm going to borrow a yellow, full-length gown, if Daddy will let me go—and if I don't have to babysit the kids. I'll find out tomorrow, so cross your fingers! Kiss! You do understand my wanting to go, don't you? Yes, of course you do. I love you!

I've thought about why I dated Danny, and why I made out with him. I've come up with an answer: I let Danny use me, so I could escape the mess at home. He seemed like so much freedom then that I couldn't see past him. Anyway, I'm sorry I made out with him. I told him that I didn't want to date him anymore, period. I'm satisfied with Peter, if I can't have a certain young minister around to help me enjoy the end of my last year in high school. Try to come Saturday, 5/29/65. My parents will be gone. Yours with a kiss and a penile squeeze!

Shara

CHAPTER 33
POSTING THE GUARD

We do not what we ought;
What we ought not, we do;
And lean upon the thought
That chance will bring us through.

Matthew Arnold

Shara enclosed her class standing in a letter to Nathan on 5/25/65, pleasing him that she fared as well. With an overall grade average of 90, she was 164th out of a class of 649, putting her at the 75th percentile, with a verbal IQ of 121. Not expecting to do as well, she was pleased with herself, but far more pleased with Nathan's encouraging pride in her and her accomplishments. She also enclosed invitations to her graduation, Saturday, 6/5/65, and another plea for him to try to come Saturday, 5/29/65. How to swing that with Lenore?

That evening after supper, Lenore, Nathan, and their two children frolicked in their front yard. Nathan chased the squealing pair, swooping them up and swinging them around, while Lenore tended her rose bushes. Relishing this respite, Nathan admired the setting sun shining golden in Beth's meager curls, and its firing of the red in her little Royal Stewart sun dress, as she curtseyed to a butterfly. Nathan II skulked around the corner, waiting to pounce on the first living thing to come his way. It was his father who, pretending to be caught unawares, allowed himself to be held in a five-year-old's bondage, which soon became a five-year-old's hugs and kisses. *God, I love these little ones!*

With Nattie on his back, and Beth in his arms, he galloped to Lenore: "Where do you want me to put these two monkeys we ordered from Sears and Rareback, Mommy?"

"Oh, in the basement, I think, until we're sure they aren't too wild for the house."

"Ooo-uh-ooo-uh-ooo-ooo!" quoth Beth, in her best monkey-ese.

"I think they should be put in the swing on the porch, 'cause it's like a tree!" opined the other monkey.

"That's a banana of an idea, Cheetah! Here we go! Come on, Mommy!"

Enjoying closeness and the pendulum pleasures of swinging, all four Scotts snuggled together and inhaled the last full gasps of the gloaming. Their simple, living words floated up and away from them, forever lost to memory, but not to meaning. Their Now simply was, and, no matter what, would always be. All four felt that truth, as only humans can, and it further hushed their busy world, waiting for nature's promised amen. It came from wee Beth.

"Mommy an' Nattie an' my in the swing-swing, wif you, Daddee?"

"You are, indeed, my Bethee!" choked the awed, suddenly stricken man. "You are, indeed."

Later, as Nathan prepared to drive back to the church, to continue his never-ending tasks, Lenore confronted him.

"Honey, what is it you aren't quite telling me? Are you plotting, er–planning a trip to Durham anytime soon?"

"Am I that transparent?"

"Certainly–at least to me–and maybe to the children, too. Tonight, on the swing was very special to them."

"And to me, darlin'."

"So, I gathered. It would all be so much easier for you if you didn't have a conscience, wouldn't it, Nathan?"

"It's no big deal, this time, 'Nore. It's just that this Saturday is the only one available, before August, for me to talk to Bruce Kennedy about campus chaplaincy jobs. I called him this afternoon, and he can see me from ten till noon. He's prepared to recommend me to the Trinity University people again; their interim guy has already left."

"And from noon to whenever?"

"I'll doubtless try to see Shara, honey."

"Have you totally given up trying not to see her?"

"You know I'm in quandary. If it helps any, she has a boyfriend—and he's asked her to wear his ring."

"So, you're going up to make sure she doesn't?"

"Not at all, Lenore. I'm going to see the Rev. Dr. Bruce Kennedy, chaplain to students at several area colleges, as he invited me to do, to discuss the likelihood of my getting a similar post. Then, I'll see or otherwise talk to Shara, and rejoice with her, if she's happy about it. Otherwise, I'll do as I always do."

"I sincerely hope not!"

Two wry grins, despite themselves, allowed Nathan to continue.

"As I was about to say, afore I was rudely truthed…"

"How about Shara sexed?"

"Hon-ey! Give me a break…"

"Like the one in my heart?"

"Damn, woman, you are sharp, today. Much more conversation and I'll bleed all the way to Durham—and don't you dare say…"

"…Then don't…"

There was silence in the land, as both finished her sentence in their heads.

Sighing, Nathan said, "Honey, I'm sorry, as usual. You always project such a completely open, accepting, loving persona, that I get too used to it. I don't ever mean to hurt you—yet I'm certain I do, often. Please forgive me."

"I have a confession to make, too, Nathan."

"Huh? You?"

"Yes. I wrote Shara this morning and mailed it in time for her to get it at her box at the mall post office, tomorrow, along with any missive you may have mailed her."

He stifled the *Oh, shit!* forming in his throat, but she heard it in his face anyway.

"Yes, I know that worries you—especially now if she really does have a boyfriend. Frankly, I don't see how she has time for one, the way you keep her hopping. Anyway, it's done, for good or for ill."

"And?"

"And I told her what was in my heart—no more; no less. I didn't try to attack her, accuse her, or even beg her—I simply described...'

"...What a bastard I really am?"

"Nathan, when will you learn that those who love you have an extremely difficult time seeing that aspect of you? No, of course I did not try to put you down—in any way. I told her I love you and want to keep you as my husband, and the father of our children."

QI, calculating and analyzing, checking out the many possibilities, tried to see how much damage there was on both ends of the Durham/Wilmington axis, and was uncharacteristically frenetic with posits, propositions, scenarios, and prospects.

What does it mean that Lenore finally decided to contact Shara, directly, whom she has ever seen as too young, too immature to be confronted or otherwise treated as an adversary? How will Shara, with her great, loving heart, her belief in fair play, and her determination not to hurt anybody, respond to the pain and the inherent plea of an artful, otherwise plea-less letter, written to her as the other woman, woman to woman, by the wounded wife? Did Lenore pull out all the stops in her reference to Nattie and Beth? Would Shara die a thousand guilty deaths to read such? What should be my response to both of these blameless women, who are guilty only of the cardinal foolishness of loving my sorry ass...?

"You ought to see your face, Nathan," she gentled, stroking it as she said his name. "Your brain is going a thousand miles a second, trying to fathom the damage, measuring the depth of the pit into which you are afraid I have cast you. Yet–I also see an effort to understand, and that, dearest heart of mine, is typical of you. Whatever else may happen, you'll struggle to keep love alive–in all its forms–even flames–even if they are destroying you–and everyone else you love."

"I'm sure you did what you had to do, darling, and I know I will understand more when you explain it to me. You are right, of course, about some of your characterization. You know me all too well, as usual."

"I knew you would understand before you understood–it's your way, and one of the ways about you I love. You do see that I have acted out of my love for you?"

"Of course."

"But you are surely worried that I may have hurt Shara in the process, right?"

"Of course."

"I knew you would be, and you are right to be so worried. However, please believe that I was gentle. You see, I knew I would be writing to you, as well as to Shara–even though I suggested, in my fear, that we keep the letter between ourselves, only; woman to woman."

"That's the first time you've granted her womanly status–she's usually 'that poor girl.'"

323

"Perhaps that has been my mistake. Either she is fully a woman, or you have looked past her puerile qualities at the woman emerging, thus making her a woman in your eyes. In either case, I finally realized that you are dealing with a woman, not a girl, so I had better do so, as well."

"I always knew you were brighter than I, Lenore. Your problem is that you are equally as romantic, and more of an egalitarian, so you don't protect yourself very well, always affording others their needs, even when they threaten your own."

"Perhaps."

"Don't make me ask, Nathan-knower. Tell me!"

"I wrote her this morning right after we made love. I described our lovemaking—its gentleness, its passion, its heat, and fulfillment. I described the kittenish quality in you, afterwards, when you want to play, and I described the look on my husband's face, lying on my breasts, his eyes closed in contentment, as I felt his penis slowly slipping out of me.

"The analogy was too much for me to ignore, Nathan. I compared that experience to the growing feeling I have about us now, considering Shara. I confessed that I feel you slowly slipping out of me—my body, my life, my children's lives. I asked only that she appreciate those feelings, because I am positive she has felt them, too—the physical and the threat of loss."

"You are an amazingly insightful woman, Lenore!"

"Then I told her I wanted her to think about her own life, now that she is graduating from high school and bound to be planning future moves—away from home—to college, whatever, wherever. I'm afraid I became a bit prescriptive and asked her to consider all of her many options, reminding her that opening certain doors closes others, and that she probably ought to keep as many of them open, as possible, at her age, until she is sure of what, when, where, who, why, and how she wants to be."

Breathing a bit easier, QI advised: *perhaps my dread is ill founded, for Lenore is incapable of baring her fangs in such a circumstance. Shara might be so taken with the earnestness of the letter, the implied compliment of being treated as an equal, along with its expressions of concern for her welfare, that she might see her own needs as somehow equal. My need, in addition to understanding and accepting Lenore's brilliant ploy, is to get to Shara before she reads the letter, and to coach her a bit as to its meaning for us.*

Thinking thus, guilt flushed over him like the sudden, odiferous flux it was. *Here I am, already thinking how to undo damage to Shara, and not hearing and fully understanding Lenore's feelings!* Shamefully, he realized he could not help it, and felt the bolt of his heart's lock plunge closed on that.

Lenore continued, "Finally, I asked Shara to look at you closely and ask herself, as honestly as she can, two questions: Is this really the person, the man, and the brand, you want, out of all the hundreds of men you will meet? Are you really the brand of woman he wants and needs—or are you possibly a temporary replacement for her, whether I am she or not? I concluded, how can you know the answer to either of these questions, now, with so little time and experience spent in gathering the information, experience, and data needed to answer them with anything like certainty?"

"Impeccable logic, 'Nore, but a bit heavy for an existentialist like you."

Of course, she's unaware of our elasticity, planned to provide just such experiences.

"Sticks and stones. Anyway, I ended it with the thought that we all have an obligation to be true to ourselves, to become our best selves, as you always preach, in all matters. Lastly, I wrote that she need not answer my letter, unless she has an urgent need or desire to do so."

"Love, Lenore Scott?"

"Yes."

"I'll bet you at least thought about signing it 'Mrs. Nathan Rhea Scott.'"

"For about ten seconds. Don't be bitter, Nathan."

"I apologize, honey. You had—have—every right, of course. As you said, I'm trying to accommodate myself to it. It being a new experience for both of us, I don't quite know what to say or ask. To you or to her."

"I'm sure you'll have it all figured out by Saturday, when you see her, if not beforehand."

"Maybe. Is there anything more you want to say before I have to go be a minister?"

"Yes—give her my best when you call her, tonight."

"I shall—if I can get her. She's been going out with Peter Gordon rather regularly, when her Pappy isn't home."

"Nathan," she grimaced, "must you call her tonight? Couldn't you just wait and see how Shara the person handles this, without Nathan the Mentor?"

"It's definitely an intriguing thought, honey, but please note that she was given this signal opportunity to handle it courtesy of erstwhile Mentor Lenore."

"I thought we agreed I have the right…"

"So do I, darlin'," he whispered, hugging her good-bye at the front door. "Kiss our babies, again, for me, and tune in tomorrow for the next exciting episode of this, our version of 'The Preacher-Man Cometh.' Until tomorrow, then, good night, from our sponsors, Agape and Eros."

"Be careful, Nathan, that you don't outfox yourself. You've always had the necessary talent."

*

Three days later, May 29, 1965, on his drive to Durham, QI rehearsed his strategy for dealing with an incredibly distraught and determined Shara. *I must shepherd her*

326

past the notion that she alone bears responsibility for the future of the Scott family, and I must do so through honest active listening, accompanied by my overriding love for her, which colors everything, disproportionately. Though he had called her twice, and written a brief, reassuring letter, still she wept and dismayed in response to Lenore's timely, honest, skillfully crafted, and genuinely beautiful letter.

If it had been Lenore's intent to foment ferment among all our lives, she succeeded measurably. She wisely chose the best possible time: Shara is wearing another male's senior class ring around her neck; she is graduating from high school; other males are noticing and seeking her out, and when she masturbates, she sometimes finds herself fantasizing others, in addition to me; she realizes she need not forever remain an average student; she is gaining both the confidence and conviction needed to leave home; she is an extremely moral, caring, loving, fair-minded young woman, who shudders at the thought of hurting others; she has certainly learned that I am not perfect, and naturally wonders who else might be right for her; she has long been bothered by her failure to take a sister's welfare fully into consideration, after she fell in love with and repeatedly fucked that sister's husband; and, now, that sister has written her an effectively sad yet hopeful letter, the only righteous response to which must be her capitulation to that sister, and, of course, the sacrifice of her relationship with that sister's husband. QED! Quod erat demonstrandum.

Though he tried, valiantly, Nathan could not shake Shara from her conviction that she must magnanimously, with great pain and sacrifice, return him to his children and to Lenore's pillowed bosom. He had not yet learned the truth of the cynicism that magnanimity and sacrifice are more often cloaked in contemplation than in actualization—more so in their propositions than in their deeds...

*

Whom the gods would destroy, they call to Florida. Such was the content of the phone call Nathan received Friday, 5/28/65. Into the current, existential miasma came the Rev. Jack Eastman, associate pastor of the large Bayview

Protestant Church of Miami, Florida. He asked Nathan to consider moving to Bayview as its third minister, with total responsibility for its extensive Christian Education program. In an affluent area, Bayview Church was a wonderful opportunity. With an active membership of over 3,000, a private school, preschool through the ninth grade, and more real estate than the Seminole Indians, it could and did pay its professional staff well, and afforded them a great deal of freedom in developing programs.

Nathan was sorely tempted; only the prospect of even greater, almost impossible distance from Shara, gave him pause. Wondering at the intent of the hand of God, he told Jack that he would think on it and get back to him. Meanwhile, the Rev. Dr. Wesley Flowers, the senior minister, would arrange to meet him on his way back from Ohio, in a week or so, to discuss the job, if Nathan was truly interested. Immediately, Nathan began to calculate the pros and cons, and to worry the possible outcomes.

Later, in Durham, ending their two-hour discussion, the Rev. Dr. Bruce Kennedy thanked him for the brainy stimulation that Nathan always provoked, assured him of an excellent recommendation to campus chaplaincy groups, and then asked about Lenore and his children. Intimating that Lenore was none too happy as a minister's wife, and maybe not very happy as this particular minister's wife, he did not go any deeper into the subject. Shaking Bruce's hand, he departed, pleased with their meeting.

*

"Are we going to the motel?"

"Indeed, we are, babe. Why? You wants to register yo'self?"

"No, but I guess I could if I had to, wearing this."

"This" was a silver wedding band on the appropriate finger. Triumphantly, she reached over and kissed the catsup off his lip.

"Now, I'll look like we're married. I borrowed it from Mother's jewelry box after they left for the coast. Jimmy isn't even home. If it weren't for the neighbors, we could do it on the dining room table. I love you, Nathan, and I want you inside me," she hissed, finally, looking at him with unmitigated lust, and thrusting her newly wedded left hand into his lap.

For someone about to quit me, she seems engaged otherwise. Hope springs eternal...

Little more was said until Shara opened the door to their motel room, pulled him inside, closed the door, kissed him, caressed his neck and ears, and straddled his thigh.

"Ohh, baby," she moaned, as she trundled her body all around his, kissing him everywhere, "let's make love first, and then we can talk, okay? I've been wanting you for days. I even played with it a little bit right before I left, so it would be hot and wet for you. Do you want me? Do you love me? Ohh, Nathan, for God's sake, fuck me!"

He did.

"Kiss it, Nathan," she urged, arching her middle to his admiring gaze. "Make me come that way, too."

He did.

"Nathan! Nathan! I'm going to come!"

She did.

Later, looking up from her mouth's ministrations to his penis, she loved him with her eyes, as she caressed her own breasts and massaged her own genitals. When he was only two throbs away from releasing, she rose to her knees, threw one finely formed leg over him, and scooted up until she could feel his wet glans probing her vulva. There she paused, took both of his hands, held them over his head on the pillow, and slowly sank down, filling herself with him, as she had fantasized for days.

"Now, my darling, I'm going to fuck you until you explode inside of me!"

And it was so!

It was almost 3:00 p.m. before the deprived couple was satiated enough to pause. Looking up from his cradle between her breasts, he saw her gazing intently at him, with tears in her eyes, and knew she was weighing him, per Lenore's suggestion. It unnerved him but he returned her tender gaze, then kissed her.

"Do I detect the unmistakable aura of Lenore in this room?"

"Ohh, Nathan, this is us, our love, all of it is so wonderful to me—and I think, to you—how can it be so harmful to her—and to your children—to anybody?"

"I know, baby. Yet I know Lenore's letter—as well as other things in your life, these days—have made you say and think, once again, that all that we have and are and mean should probably cease."

As planned, his words opened the flood gates to torrents of guilt, fear, not quite shame, and awful resolve, all seeded by Lenore's perfect letter. Shara's body racked with sobbing as she shed her grief and confusion, raining it down on Nathan, washing his spirit's wounds with the stinging salts of her awful onus. He simply held her, wept with her at times, rocked her in his arms, and kissed her a thousand times.

"I love you, Shara. I know, baby; I understand; I hear and feel your ambivalence; I am here; I will not leave you; I love you, darling, and I can no more help it than you can help breathing; let it out—all of it; leave nothing inside; pour it into me; let me love us enough for both of us."

From time to time, she hushed long enough to articulate a question or special feeling. In such pursuit, she retrieved her purse, dug out Peter's class ring and chain, and tossed it on the bed.

"What am I supposed to do with that?" she wailed.

"Return it? Wear it?" he whispered.

"See? I can't even have a normal relationship with a boy, because of loving you. I prefer you a thousand times over, but is it fair to Peter, is it fair to me, for me to date, at all, if it cain't go anywhere? And, no, I didn't say I want it to go anywhere–it's just that I know it cain't! I probably will return it if you want to know."

"I love you, Shara; I know; it seems unfair; I understand; I love you, darling!"

Slowly, inexorably, their love began to refill the shell of his beloved, as she poured herself out, emptied herself, and turned her righteously weakened, vulnerable self back to him. Neither tried to offer facile solutions. They simply were who and how and what they were to themselves and to each other. In the end, Shara uncurled, sat up, managed a grin or two, and began to return to her normal, loving self. Nathan invested in her regeneration, by taking her to dinner.

While waiting for their meals, Shara removed a paper bag from her purse, and shyly placed it before him. Opening it, he found two envelopes, a small box, and a wee diploma tied with a red ribbon.

"Which do I open first, Shara? They all look very special."

"The envelopes. Then decide how special they are."

The first envelope contained her senior class picture, inscribed with abundant love and kisses. The second contained a pink-tinted pencil drawing of a bare-breasted girl with Shara's face, hair, and figure, with pubic hair showing through her bikini anty-panties. The inscription read, "Hey, Preacher, I'm available when Shara isn't."

"I love it, Shara," he said. "I've always wanted a self-drawn nudie of you. Thank you!"

"You're welcome," she sighed self-consciously. "But don't let the waitress see it! I drew it so you'd have something of me, if, if. . . damn! Just open your diploma!"

Removing the ribbon and unscrolling his diploma, it entitled him to eighteen years of unbridled love, sex, trust, respect, and marriage, if he wanted it, with the right to renew the contract at any time, on demand. The small seal on the diploma revealed a silhouetted, naked couple, embracing.

"Don't these wonderful, creative gifts sorta cancel each other out, honey? One is so I'll have something of–like–you, if we stop, and the other assumes at least another eighteen years of continuing. Which one is real?" spake the Man With the Shara-shaped Heart.

"They both represent me–my truth–for they recognize both possibilities."

"Well, as far as I'm concerned, the eighteen years will certainly outlast your lovely drawing. Besides, what's a drawing in comparison with eighteen more years of having and loving the real thing?"

Smiling a baleful smile, "Dear God, please let that be true!"

"Amen!"

Finally, Nathan opened the small box and was pleased to find a small, silver Celtic cross lapel pin, and a short note vowing eternal love and praying God to bless their relationship. Braving their openness, Nathan kissed her and put the pin in his lapel.

"Shara, may I ask you something?"

"Certainly, honey, but that's usually my line."

"Did you prepare all of this before or after you got Lenore's letter?"

"What do you think?"

"I think you probably prepared most of it before you got her letter, right?"

"Wrong. I sat there crying while I was drawing the nudie and the diploma. I planned to give them to you when I graduated, but I was afraid that after today, I might not see you again, so, I finished everything for today. Do you really like them?"

"Of course, I do, darling, if they mean, now, what they were to mean before you got Lenore's letter."

"They do. I know we haven't solved a damned thing. We never do, but still, we keep on loving each other to death, don't we?"

Back in their motel, he hugged her nakedness to him, delighting, again, in the effect it had upon all his senses and his memory, and busied his hands all over her yielding body, anchoring them in her heat.

They lay exhausted and sated an hour later. Slowly they dressed, forcing their unwilling limbs into the habits of another world, where their naked flesh was forbidden, and their intimate touch abominated–a world made neither by God nor Nature, but somehow blamed on both.

It was almost 10:15 p.m., when Nathan stopped his wagon close to Shara's dark house. Not daring to creep closer, he looked down at the loveliness pillowing his lap and decided to tell her the potentially bad news. *There can never again be secrets!*

"Shara, how strong is our love?"

"Uh-oh, here comes something bad. You get that tone when you are about to kill me to death. What?"

"Well, there is something else–and it could augur for good or ill, depending on how we handle it. I have a serendipitous opportunity to work in Miami in the fall."

Quickly, he laid out his rationale for accepting the position. She remained silent but the shining in her eyes was not due to pride. After a car passed them, he kissed her and let her out. She walked quickly up the street, turned into her driveway, heard her telephone, and ran to catch it, disappearing without a wave. It was a long drive home…

CHAPTER 34
AS MOTHER LAY DYING

But often, in the world's most crowded streets,
But often, in the din of strife,
There rises an unspeakable desire
After the knowledge of our buried life;
A thirst to spend our fire and restless force
In tracking out our true, original course

Matthew Arnold

Warmth. Warmth and familiarity. Warmth, familiarity, and myriad memories of creative growth and increasing self-awareness, as he grew to love Lenore. These feelings swept over Nathan as he re-entered the gates of Southern Christian U.

He had seen the lady, talked with her, had classes, and casually interacted with her throughout their freshman year. During Rush Week their sophomore year, Nathan saw considerably more of Lovely Lenore. In what must have been the most uncomfortable and awkward moments of her entire eighteen years, she posed on the campus midway specially constructed for touting the Greek Life, as one of two nineteenth century Riverboat Dancing and Party Girls, wearing garish rouge, lipstick, eye shadow, and revealing black, one-piece bathing suits adorned with red sashes across their voluptuous torsos. For an entire evening, while upper class Greeks vied with each other for the attention and interest of the best of the freshmen class, Lenore endured the catcalls, whistles, and leers of hordes of admiring males, the most taken of whom was Nathan Rhea Scott.

That tall, diffident girl with the classically beautiful face, who was slightly aloof, clearly shy but exceedingly bright, well bred, and sensitive, was also surprisingly well formed, long and lovely legged, and willing to portray herself sexy and available, as well–at least in fun. As was his typical wont, he retrieved his Argus C-3, photographed her–and was smitten!

Now, as Nathan circumnavigated the large campus anew, thinking back on those formative years, he recognized both the omen and irony in his collegiate history with Lenore. The young, pre- ministerial student had turned aside to see that great sight, affording him both more and considerably different views of Lenore, who was only incidentally dressed as a whore.

Enjoying reverie, Nathan entered his old dorm, found Stephen, fetched sister Allison, and took them both out to a late dinner. Allison was debating her return to Christian U, due to Mother's illness, and Stephen was anticipating matriculation at another of Nathan's alma maters, Southern Theological Seminary, in the fall. After returning Allison to her dorm, the two brothers talked until 2:00 a.m.

Stephen's morning graduation ceremony was a carbon copy of Nathan's, eight years earlier, complete with formal academic procession led by his beloved A Capella Choir. Brother Mitch having arrived, the three Scott siblings were proud of the family's newest Bachelor of Arts in Philosophy. Stephen received several awards, none topping his singular recognition as CU's Man of the Year.

By 4:00 p.m., the two students were packed and loaded into their brothers' station wagons, and all were on the road to overnight with Lenore and her parents, two hours away. Calling ahead, Nathan heard his sad and embarrassed wife tell him that her inebriated father had reneged on his invitation to host that many Scotts. Not wanting the hassle of trying to grace their unwelcome, Nathan asked her to be ready to leave. They found a motel instead.

Arriving in Sutherland, Florida on 6/9/65, Nathan found the environs much the same, with a very different ambience–Mother so ill and stifled. He took small pleasure in transporting her to the hospital for radiation treatments and the periodic draining of her fluid-filled abdomen. Having trained as a hospital chaplain, he was familiar with the feelings and thoughts he believed she was experiencing.

But this hopeless patient is Mother, and I cannot bring myself to utter religious platitudes or to play the counselor. I will listen to her every thought and feeling, but she is Mother, and no matter the pall of death surrounding her, she continues that role and august status. I must help her feel her family's love and caring.

Mother asked only once, in her pain, how he and Lenore were weathering the inevitable vicissitudes of marriage. Nathan graced her question, quickly returning to her frame of reference–to her expressed hopes and expectations of living. He needed to believe her optimistic words, as he had all his life, to his betterment. *How can I not? She is so seldom wrong!*

During their three weeks stay, Nathan and his family rested, swam, sailed, and fished with Daddy, visited old friends, wrote, and played with his siblings and his children. They talked, talked, talked; everyone attempting to decoy the obvious and onerous purulence of imminent death, so frightfully infecting their home.

Never far from Nathan's consciousness was the dark-eyed beauty, so busy becoming, some four hundred fifty miles north. Walking the moon-washed shoreline, alone, waiting for the eleventh hour and their telefocus, he compared his feelings with those of, *what? a mere year–and eons ago!*

337

Walking these same shores, we had barely begun our relationship. In a Night rutting in May, at a senior high retreat, we were bound together as inexorably and as inextricably as the passing of time. After two tense and delicious nights of holding and beholding our audacious love and innocent passion, somehow denied me earlier, I brought my unsuspecting family home, here, pining for that fresh, utterly desirable young girl in ways much less physical than those I feel for her now, not only in my heart, but coursing through my body, as well. How fatuous fate, if I believed in it.

How well I remember my early and urgent desire to taste of her essence, but without consuming her, and to partake of her guileless, devastating affection, fulfilling us both, without destroying anyone. Then, I did not want sex! Now, I miss that consonant aspect, equal to my vital need for her essence and her loving focus on me. I was reaching out to someone reaching out to me, both expressing pure, simple, but vast, human need. Now, one flesh, we are struggling to remain so, and to grow into permanence, reaching out together to a world which, likely, will receive us not.

The Scott siblings welcomed the arrival of Patricia, their oldest sister, from Japan, where she had been a State Department coordinator for the last two years. Four years older than Nathan, Patty was well bred, read, and traveled, possessing a wonderfully broadened, highly educated mind. Having lived almost literally all over the world for twelve years, she was liberal, pan-religious and well on her way to reluctant spinsterhood.

Patty came home to say goodbye to Mother whom, she realized, she would never see again. Her necessarily firm plans were to leave in June, to take an executive State Department post in Egypt. Daddy pleaded with her to stay home and help him care for Mother until the end. Patty adamantly demurred; she could not and would not watch Mother die, though she blamed her refusal on her contract.

Daddy refused to believe that she could not break it, and they sparred for days.

It would fall to Patty to load herself with the guilt of desertion and the despairs of denial, and to fly away, so burdened, to her own, far away, uncharted regions. She was miserable to her bones.

In midst of these dynamics, Nathan came to resent a resurgence of the old, familial, seniority system. Patty soon filled the authority vacuum left by Mother's incapacity, and despite her liberal ways, began to issue orders, kindly but firmly, to all her younger siblings, including the esteemed Right Reverend Mr. Nathan Rhea Scott. The clincher—being ordered by his sister, summarily, to mow their large lawn, "Stop putting it off; and get it done before I leave, tomorrow!" Reluctantly, resentfully, but meekly, he complied, lest he show forth the immaturity roiling his wobbly pride, threatening to surface and embarrass him.

Perhaps it was the resentfulness he felt towards Patty for her shabby treatment of his newly earned adult and ministerial persona; perhaps it was the pain and disquietude of his lengthy separation from his lover; perhaps it was the overwhelming sense of denied, looming grief at Mother's last days; perhaps it was both neurotic and ontological guilt, relentlessly suffusing his soul, regarding the quality and direction of his life; perhaps he was simply careless or uncaring. No matter—while mowing near the clothesline, he failed to notice that the exhaust of the mower spattered and covered Patty's freshly washed clothes with dirt and grit.

Completely unaware of the damage he perpetrated, Nathan noted his sister's dour approach, her motion for him to stop pushing the noisy, spraying mower, and to turn it off. He did.

"Nathan, you stupid, thoughtless moron, look what you've done to my freshly washed clothes!"

Fighting the gorge in his throat, Nathan stared at his sister, aghast, seething, and uncomprehending, until he saw for himself the obvious results of his mindlessness. Not knowing what to say, but furious at her uncharacteristic attack, he colored, turned his back, and made to restart the mower. Gone was any vestige of a non-directive, reflective openness to the obvious pain and anger in Patty; present was unfamiliar, disorienting humiliation.

As Nathan reached for the mower's starter cord, Patty grabbed his shoulder, spinning him around, and with angry tears in her eyes, drew back her open hand to slap him. As their eyes met, Nathan instantly recalled another stark drama involving this sensitive, brilliant soul, a million years earlier, when they were but fourteen and eighteen.

That drama began about 6:00 P. M. on a weekday, when Daddy told him to go straight home after he finished work. Doing so, Nathan walked two sides of a right triangle, instead of a straight-home hypotenuse, and was on the corner of their property talking to one of his friends, when tired, frustrated, overworked Daddy got home—and came looking for him.

The penetrating whistle which signaled an angry, threatening father unnerved Nathan, who recalled with dread how recently he had heard the words, "You're asking for it, walking on eggshells! I will not tolerate your disobedience, and one of these days I'm going to wear you out!" As a man to the gallows condemned, he dirged into his house, thirty feet away.

Impatient Daddy accosted him in the kitchen, where several of his children were soberly munching sandwiches and averting their eyes. Wordlessly, he grabbed Nathan by the back of his neck and hurled the lad through two open doors, onto the floor of the laundry room, closed the door, and removed his belt.

Standing over the lad, "I told you to go straight home. You couldn't even do that right. Now I'm going to teach you to obey me, once and for all. This is it; this is what you've been asking for. Stand up, turn around and keep your hands out of the way!"

Perhaps it was the result of Daddy's eternal working, trying to feed and clothe ten children, or his living hand-to-mouth all of his life; perhaps it was too many weeks of eighteen-hour days, seven days a week, or too many years of working through his vacations at double pay; perhaps it was his failure to get beyond high school, despite several unsuccessful forays into correspondence schools; perhaps it was having to squelch himself and be responsible and obedient, utterly, to the needs of his families—to those of his aging parents and younger siblings, and now to those of his large brood; perhaps it was because, as a child, he had been beaten himself, almost daily, by an angry, bitter, frustrated, twice-bereaved, straightlaced, God-fearing Methodist mother; perhaps it was because he was a mean and nasty son of a bitch. No matter: Daddy proceeded to belt his second son, mercilessly, for what, to Nathan, seemed hours, literally beating the shit out of him...

Crying and crying out, alarmed, and fearing for his life, Nathan dropped to his knees, groveling before his father like a whipped, submissive cur, begging, "Please stop, Daddy; don't hit me anymore! I won't do it, again, I promise!"

"Don't you tell me what to do, you jackleg! I'll beat you half to death if I want!"

The belt fell relentlessly, again and again, cutting the slacks over Nathan's legs, creating huge welts, drawing blood, and smushing the excrement in his shorts all over him. Losing all sense of reality, going into shock, he looked up from where he lay to see an angel pushing Daddy away, daring to oppose him, telling him it was "enough, Enough, ENOUGH!" Daddy, never one to brook interference with his almighty will, continued to lash out at his son, over, around, and through his adamant wife. Seeing her gave Nathan strength to try, once more, in the only way he knew how.

"Please, Daddy, stop. I've learned my lesson!"

"Then, you–you g-get out of h-here–NOW!" stammered the furious, sweating, anguished, unsatisfied man.

Crawling through two doors, Nathan stood and limped stiff-legged through the empty kitchen, smelling and feeling the blood and excrement oozing down his legs, leaving rank and filthy spots in his wake. Crawling up the stairs, he staggered into the upstairs bathroom and closed the door.

Looking in the mirror, Nathan faced a horror that would haunt him all of his life: a ghoulish soul, face reddened and awash in tears, belt welts across it; clothing torn and reeking; pants filled with shit–babyish, forlorn, helpless shit; beaten shit; embarrassed, hated shit; shit extracted from him as punishment for being alive, and for being the son of the son of a bitch who sired him; shit; shit for value; shit for brains; shit for his future; shit for a father. He saw and smelled himself as pure, unadulterated shit; he hated the man who shit him into existence, surely from his asshole, and not from his balls. He saw a pile of wrecked, worthless, vile, smelly, defenseless shit– and his only consolation was that, somehow, unaccountably, miraculously, he was born of Mother.

Woefully turning to the task of cleaning himself, Nathan stripped off his ruined trousers and shorts and sat on the toilet, daubing at the bloody, smelly awfulness all over his legs and genitals. To his eternal chagrin and embarrassment, the door banged open, and Patty, crying furiously, stumbled to him, took one horrified look, and threw her arms around him, removing the last shreds of his modesty and manliness in her need to succor. Trying to cover his adolescent nakedness, heretofore unobserved by any female other than Mother, much less by a pretty eighteen-year-old girl, even if she were his sister, he was suddenly giddy with the realization that *there may be some justice in the world.*

This very girl, hugging him and trying to love and reassure him through her choking sobs and tears, was the same girl at whom he had occasionally peeked, through this very bathroom's window, having crawled there from his room onto the roof, to learn all about feminine nakedness—and vanity. This very girl, who had inspired clandestine, adolescent erections, a willingness to risk being caught, and a rooftop crowned with semen, was now clasping his shitty, mortified body, her face buried in his neck, her arms about his torso, her hands nowhere, for she knew not where to touch.

Relentlessly crying, the siblings carved their most intimate scene into their psyches until neither could take it any longer, and Patty burst from the bathroom to go get Mother, even now arguing with shocked, simmering Daddy. Nathan's relief was palpable when Patty left, and he immediately crawled into the tub, turned on the shower, and tried to rinse his body and his clothes of his bloody, shitty humiliation.

Mother knocked and entered, in her own anguish, which she soon transformed into quiet, experienced, sensitive ablutions, tending Nathan's scourged body and spirit with the knowledge and skill that always seemed to seep from her pores, covering him, challenging him, even punishing him, but ever, always, and forever, loving and respecting him, which love and respect she would epitomize for him, then, and forevermore, world without end, Amen!

Mother tended his wounds and his wounded sense of self, walking the tightrope between apology for Daddy's horrific abuse and her repeated affirmations that Nathan was her son, loveable and beloved, and did not deserve what happened. Sleep, she said, and honest tears, would heal—and she hugged him and put him to bed.

"Thank you, Mother!" he prayed.

Came the dawn, Nathan was rudely awakened by a loud pounding on the wall above his sleeping head. Disoriented, he puzzled himself into wakefulness, then into clarion alarm and dread, realizing that the pounding was Daddy's, and that he was shouting at him through the bathroom wall.

"Sir?" he shouted back.

"You get yourself in here to me; I mean right now, and don't make me call you again!'"

"Yessir!"

Beside himself with trepidation, Nathan dragged his sore and weeping body out of bed, noted the blood all over it and his pajamas, and cringed to the bathroom. Mother, robed and standing in their bedroom doorway, gestured for him to go on in, smiling grimly and nodding, perhaps trying to assure him. Patty Pajamas was in her doorway, too, arms folded, sheer, vicarious agony disfiguring her pretty face. Not daring to look at her eyes, Nathan knocked.

"Get in here, Nathan!" came the gruff answer.

"Yessir!"

Daddy was in his white boxer shorts and sleeveless undershirt, shaving at the mirror in which, hours earlier, Nathan had calculated his own excremental conception. Standing, not knowing what to say or do, the boy noted the smell in the bathroom and could not discriminate whether it came from him or from his father.

"Sit down!"

Was it only his imagination that the tone had gentled? Obediently, he sat down on the toilet; he would have stood on his head on the toilet, if so commanded.

"Harrumph!"

Aware that his father was watching him in the mirror, and that he seemed to be trying to say something, the adolescent simply sat there, dumb, broken, and waiting…

"I'll tell you one thing…," returned the threatening tone, but once poised, trailed off.

Silence.

"Harrumph!"

More silence.

"Well, I suppose you've learned your lesson–except for two things remaining."

"Sir?"

"Don't ever tell me to stop while I'm disciplining you; and you had better never mess your pants like that again!"

"Yessir!"

Silence.

"Harrumph!"

Deadly silence.

"Now get out of here and get ready for school!"

"Yessir"

"Is that all you have to say to me?"

"I–I–I'm sorry I messed my pants."

"All right; now get out of here."

"Yes, Daddy."

So, fast-forward sixteen years to Patty's dirt-spotted, clothesline-hanging wardrobe, besmirched by Nathan's mower, and to her frustrated, aggressive anger, shamefully ignored by his turning toward the lawn mower, away from her sudden disdain. As she grabbed his shoulder and spun him around, her open hand poised for retribution, he suddenly recognized old and familiar tears of despair and frustration in the eyes of the same sister who, sixteen years earlier, braved his shitty, bloody nakedness, who tried to speak the difficult words, between her sobs and gags, letting him know she loved him, and that she knew he was hurting, terribly.

345

Seeing her now, again, so alive with pain and fruitless anger, seeking an outlet for the grief and guilt which covered her like God-awful, bloody shit, Nathan's great heart cracked along the fault lines of yesteryear, and he loved her anew. Ignoring her still cocked, slapping hand, he looked into her deeply tortured eyes, opened wide his arms, and spoke her name, reverently, awesomely, in gratitude, and with such empathy as she once afforded him.

"Patty?"

Staring into his face, she, too, recognized the memory unspoken and unspeakable, still alive between them, forever fulsome and aflow, despite the dare and dregs of time. Pausing mid-slap, she sobbed and melted into his offered, sweaty arms, under the clothesline, in the back yard of their childhood home, where, upstairs, even now—as Mother lay dying—the woman who bore them both, and who loved and respected them, even when they were shitty and unlovely.

Aghast that she was leaving the next day, that she would never see her mother alive, again, Patty balled her fists into tight rejections of that truth, and knowing, at last, where to place her hands, pounded her younger brother's strong back, wailing and flailing her guilt and despair, not speaking a word. Then, together, they removed her shitty clothing from the line, and, together, entered the same laundry room, where, together, they enacted a ritual cleansing.

The next day, at the old, unimposing Tampa Airport, Nathan filmed Patty's departure for New York, from whence she would fly to Egypt. Like a movie star, she came back to the loading stairs still pushed against the airplane, stood on the top landing, her red hair glistening above her sunglasses, and waved farewell to her family. Then, Patty was gone.

*

Nathan, Lenore, and two rascally little ones were soon to be gone, as well, for it was almost July, and he knew he could not wait to see Shara until the 8th, when his vacation ended. Her 6/24/65 letter convinced and alarmed him of that, well enough:

10:50 P. M. 6/24/65 (Thurs.)

My Only Love:

It is softly raining outside as I write, and my need for you is like a blazing fire. Peter arrived at four this afternoon, and didn't leave until 9:30 p.m. He ate dinner with us, and to be quite honest, I sort of substituted and symbolized him for you. Perhaps that might displease you some, but in a sense, it helped me.

Nathan, we did make out some, seeing that we were left alone for 45 minutes, but I'm not too happy about it. Every time he kissed me my thoughts would wander to you, to what you were doing.

Time out—it's 11:00 o'clock and I just want you to know how much I love you! I just need for you to hold me tightly now, to love me as a husband, so I can get the kind of affection from you I both need and want. To say the least, I am starved for love and feel frightened because you are not near or with me. The security you offer has meant so much to me that to think of you this far from me is worse than hellish.

I need you to comfort me, to let your hands roam gently over my hair, down my neck, onto my breasts, and venturing further, to my groin, helping to ease the pains of premenstrual cramps, which have me agonizing. I can feel your fingers easing through my black forest, where they gently rub my mound of Venus, until they unveil my clitoris, making it throb with excitement, lubricating me with flowing love. I feel your stimulating kiss upon my lips, our tongues tasting our love and singing our invitations to partake

347

of the pleasure, love, and warmth so soon to come. My nipples are taut as you fondle and play with them.

The time has come when my body can no longer stand the teasing–the flirting with the pleasure which is to be ours–and I want to feel your full thrusts deeply within me. How well I remember, now, the slow, steady entering, with its growing peaks of pleasure for us both. I've always wanted an orgasm with that first thrust, so I could cling to and milk the power of your penis. The first few thrusts always bring such magnificent sensations for me that I simply want to lose myself in them. I want you in me, powerfully, in that way, now!

It is now midnight and I'll have to finish this tomorrow–later this morning. I am tired and very excited from wanting you so much. Does that please you in any way? I shall exercise soon, and dream of you. Good night and good morning, my Love!

7:35 a.m. 6/25/65 (Friday)

Good morning lover! I'm sure you want to know what Peter and I did during our little make out session. Watching T.V., he pulled me up close to him, and during a commercial he began to kiss me. One kiss wasn't enough for him, so we must have kissed (French) for a few minutes. I didn't respond very much, just let him kiss me. His hand dropped to my breasts once or twice, but he didn't try to feel me off anywhere downstairs. All through our making out, which probably took 30 to 40 minutes, I was not the least bit aroused.

Nathan, that experience made me feel like a person who doesn't believe in God, but who still goes to church. I was almost repulsed by the whole thing– it just wasn't anything, not even the sex. I didn't want

348

anything from him—not even for my own pleasure. What are you thinking, now?

About the church in Miami—I don't know what to tell you. I don't want you to go, but you all will be the ones living down there, and if that is where you want to live, work, I want and think you should go. However, I am somewhat unsure about our relationship with you in Florida—or with you not in Florida, for that matter!

Nathan, how long do you think any of us can endure a relationship like ours? It's hard for me to see real light for us, even though that thought tears me in two. Another question I've asked myself is can I have a normal relationship with any of my peers without feeling some sense of guilt about you and about them? Are we ever going to be able to live together under one roof, or are we endlessly hoping, clinging to each other, knowing full well that it will never work out?

Nathan, I also wonder what kind of Christian I am—you are—we are? Don't we owe Lenore something; don't we owe ourselves the memory of love instead of pain? And what about the children? Don't they deserve the kind of father who works for a family united, instead of thinking about a girl in Durham? Don't we owe them trust in you and the security of a sound home, father, and mother together?

Now I look at myself. What do I want? Of course, I want to live with, care for, and be with you always. But, Nathan, I can't be a mistress all my life. I want a family to love, a husband to care for, and a home to build—all the things I have never had—mainly love. Oh God, Nathan, do you understand me, at all?

Throw in a prayer for me when you can. With all my constant love, I leave you until 11:00 o'clock tonight. Me.

Nathan burned to call Shara. Her rational letter, the distance between them and the proximity of Peter made him more than anxious. He informed Lenore that they would be driving back to Wilmington Thursday, 7/1/65. He explained that things were heating up in the Starr home, and that he planned to see her the weekend of 7/3-5/65, unless she strenuously objected. Being Lenore the trusting—and realistic, her objections were heartfelt but mild. For days he could think of little else but leaving.

CHAPTER 35
REFLECTIONS OF
QUINTESSENTIAL I

Being entirely honest with oneself is a good exercise.

Sigmund Freud

Sex and beauty are inseparable, like life and consciousness.
And the intelligence which goes with sex and beauty, and arises out of sex
and beauty, is intuition.

David Herbert Lawrence

We cannot kindle when we will
The fire that in the heart resides,
The spirit bloweth and is still,
In mystery our soul abides.

Matthew Arnold

On their drive north, Nathan shared with Lenore greater detail about past and current stresses in the Starr household, finally including her father's earlier sexual abuse and more about Shara's solid plans to leave in early September. Lenore was shocked at the history of abuse, no matter how mild, or how long ago, and typical of her characteristic empathy, offered to help. She suggested that Shara write Melanie, to probe her willingness to let Shara live with her until she found something of her own. Dubious, Nathan thanked his wife and promised he would follow up.

QI posited: *Though Melanie sincerely wants to help, it's likely that she still harbors breath enough to blow on her banked coals still hot for my sorry ass.*

Home, Thursday night, 7/1/65, Nathan was anxious to get the children and Lenore reasonably settled, so he could zip to the post office. Too tired to offer much resistance, Lenore was convinced that such was not the way to regain the fulsome focus of her conflicted husband. Her wise and simple strategy was to keep on keeping on, lovingly engaging Nathan whenever he would respond.

Mailed 6/30/65, Nathan found a short note announcing that Shara's father would be out of town, and her mother was taking the three youngest to the beach, leaving Jimmy and Shara on their own for four long days, starting Friday, 7/2/65, after her 8:30 a.m. class. Could Nathan possibly take advantage of the situation during the remaining days of his vacation?

That night, lying appreciatively atop his sated wife, he waited for her breathing to return to normal before he said, "If at all possible, 'Nore, I would like to leave tomorrow morning, early, for three nights, planning to return Monday night, 7/5/65."

He could not tell whether the soft sounds emitting from her were laughter, sobs, or both. He waited.

"Will—will you be fucking Shara, this time, honey?" " "

"Why do you want to know?"

"Don't I have the right?"

"Of course; that's not the question. *Why* do you want to know?"

"Why shouldn't I?"

"You tell me why, first, and I'll tell you why you probably shouldn't, second. Fair?"

"Since when do you concern yourself with 'fair' when it comes to Shara?"

"Stab! Ugh! Bleed–bleed! Guilt! Sorrow! Now what?"

"Well, it's true, Nathan. You aren't fair with me about Shara, and you damned well know it!"

"Guilty, your Honor. Shall you pass sentence now, or shall you wait to learn if rehabilitation is likely?"

"You make me want to pass gas!" she grimaced, trying not to chuckle.

"Is that my sentence–to be sworn in as a *bona fide* fart blossom?"

"Tell me what you think you deserve, Nathan–and why! You are not stupid, and you know the difference between right and wrong."

"May I be utterly, completely, unabashedly truthful with you, honey?"

"For a change?"

"I'm serious, 'Nore."

"So am I."

More silence.

"I'm sorry. Go ahead, Nathan."

"Yes, I do know the difference between right and wrong, and part of the truth of the matter is that I know how very right it was for us to make love a few minutes ago, and for us both to enjoy it to the hilt–so to speak. It was glorious! The puzzling part of the unvarnished truth is that it would be equally right with Shara this weekend."

"Nathan! Don't try to soften me up, lathering me with compliments, just to shave me with your outrageous, painful, and self-serving truths!"

"Hear me out, honey. I have no reason to lie anymore, and I have every reason to tell you the truth, as I see it, self-serving or not. You are not stupid, either, and sooner or later, you find me out. You always do. So why not discuss it beforehand, this time?"

"Well, okay, Nathan, but no funny stuff."

"When I said I knew it was completely right for us to make love tonight, you had no trouble with that. But how close to understanding me did you come when I said it would be just as right for Shara and me to do the same thing this weekend?"

"Not very close, I'm afraid, Nathan, but no matter; I'm sure you'll try to justify it."

"There is nothing more to explain, Lenore. It's that simple. I do not know, think, feel, believe that it would be wrong, period, end of story, stop, turn the page! Au contraire, I am utterly certain it would be wonderful, and it would not hurt you a bit–in fact, I guarantee you wouldn't feel a thing. Why, you wouldn't even know if or when it occurs, it would be so remote to you!"

Be gentle, Scott; I love this woman!

"Of course, it hurts me, Nathan. Are you crazy? I love you. You are my husband, and the father of two of the dearest little children in the world. Why would you think it wouldn't hurt me? Don't you know me any better than that?"

"You know how much I love you, too. Of course, I know that you feel pain at the idea of my making love to Shara. My contention is that it does not have to hurt you, and that your pain may be conditioned, not real, nor essential. What have I really done–will I do–that is so terrible? I have taken nothing away from you except time and my doubtful presence, but that would be true, anyway, for I'm a workaholic and would be at the church otherwise.

"Usually, you don't like to make love more than once, each time, and about twice a week–and that's fine! So, if I press the flesh with another enjoyable, warm human being, what is the harm? I can't use it up, yours, mine, or hers, and I still love you."

"Very neat, Nathan; very neat! How would you feel, however, if you discovered Shara was fucking someone else this weekend? You know it would hurt you–and you know you would want to know about it, too!"

"I see your point, honey, but my response would be the same to the hurt part of your question, darling: I would be curious, even interested and concerned about the effect on her, but it would not hurt me, *per se*."

"But, honey, what about love? Mine for you? Yours for me? Yours for Shara? Hers for you?"

"I know this is difficult to hear, 'Nore, but I can no more help loving Shara than I can help loving you. Of course, I shall be loving her, this time, last time, next time, all times, until she loves someone else more than me, or tells me to get lost. You, too! Our dilemma, both mine and yours, is that I love two wonderful women and act on both loves. That existential fact drives me, you, Shara, God, I'm sure Melanie, and most of the fucking Christians in the world up the proverbial wall, if they knew."

Pause

"You know, Nathan, you're sorta right about one thing, anyway. I guess I wouldn't mind much if you–did it– with some other woman–even a prostitute–in a casual way. In fact, I almost wish you would, if it meant you wouldn't need Shara anymore. It is the love you have for Shara that I fear– and don't understand–if you love me, that is."

"I know. Isn't it interesting that when we love the most that we generate fear and needless misunderstanding in others whom we also love?"

"Do you understand what I just said?"

"Yes ma'am. You said it would probably be okay with you were I to get it on with other women, as long as I do not love them–or they, me, I assume?"

"Basically. If you must have more sex, why don't you give that a try, and let poor Shara learn to love someone with whom she can grow up?"

"It's good to know that you consider me all growed up, at least."

I'm serious, Nathan. I don't think it would bother me nearly so much if you did it with someone else, as long as you didn't love her—but you would have to be careful about diseases."

"You confirm my oft-repeated claim that much of sex seems to be a big issue over a little tissue and doesn't disturb the Richter scale of existential import. I'll take your illicit prescription under advisement, baby, but don't hold your breath. I know this situation is hell for you, sweetheart, but it's also hell loving and being faithful to two women already. I've thought about it, of course, have had, and will continue to have, opportunities—more than you imagine. But I can't make myself do it. I love you, and I love Shara—at least for now. Though I look at other women, and fantasize them in bed sometimes, I want to fuck only those whom I love, these days. I'm afraid both of you are stuck with this godawful puzzle, me, at least for now."

"God help us, Nathan. What am I supposed to do? Especially, when you leave me here with your children and go courting down to Durham to love a pretty, budding eighteen-year-old girl, who thinks she loves you back."

"Both the prosecution and the defense rest. You just made both of our cases."

"But Nathan, what is the answer?"

"I honestly do not have 'the' answer, darlin.' But I have a hopeful answer for you if you're interested."

"Yes, of course I am, honey."

"It's simplicity itself—keep on loving me as long as you can, despite Shara Starr, for my sake, for the kids' sakes, for

God's sake, and even for your sake, if you love me. That's what I want. Perhaps we can weather it all, and in thirty years or so look back on all of this and laugh. Until then, I guess you had better trust your instincts and your excellent mind and do what you think you should do. What do you think?"

"I think I'm going to be sick—and lonely—for the next three nights. At least call me, midway, okay?"

"Okay, darlin'."

"I love you, Nathan."

"I love you, too, 'Nore."

"Yes, 'too;' that's the trouble. Why can't it be, 'only,'" as it once was?"

"It can; it just isn't, right now."

"Is that what you tell her, too?"

"Almost word for word."

"Thank you for being honest, even though I hate it, sometimes—such as now. Couldn't you…?"

Eyes glistening, Lenore turned her head from him, into her pillow. Nathan stroked her naked back and shoulders, playing with the wisp of hair on the nape of her lovely neck. Sadly, in their familiar, loving intimacy both felt like castaways on a dark tundra, where those who are frozen out wander in desperate search of the human warmth once thought secure and eternal.

*

Lenore did not stir when he put the rose on her pillow, followed quickly by a little fife on Nate's, and a tiny drum on Beth's, in honor of Independence Day—independent of the man of the house. Well on his way to Durham by 6:30 a.m., 7/2/65, Nathan clinched his teeth and resisted the urge to turn back to Wilmington. Suspecting his honesty to have been a mite too facile, he also knew it had hurt Lenore—a regrettably frequent happenstance lately. Calling on QI to take a vantage point above *sturm und drang*, where reality arced its threats and promises like the rainbow of Cimmerian hues it was, he asked, aloud:

"Just how honest was I with my Lenore, Scott?"

QI's answer was coldly candid. *I know I spoke the truth about loving two women equally, but I also know I favor one or the other, slightly, depending on circumstances, 60/40, here, 40/60 there. For everyone's sake, I need to answer my own question with more exacting ratios. God help me!*

My eternal courtship with ambivalence and open skepticism of too facile, too pretty, too pat conclusions almost dares me to stop the wondrous process of experiencing long enough to see and say, finally, "This is what is!" or "This is what I feel!" As in a living travelogue, in which I play viewer and traveler, narrator and listener, questioner and answerer, in monologue and in polylogue, cameraman and editor, I simply experience and create at the moment of life's delivery, without ultimate conclusions, good, bad, sad, glad, mad, or indifferent.

I purposefully sail many different seas—all at the same time—not exactly sure of where I am going, until I get there, only to cast off, again and again, seeking the why and truth of things in other ports of call. Yet I cannot say it's random, because it's not; it's usually driven by past data (trend), future need (exigencies), the availability of possible fulfillment variables (my Shara and my Lenore—and certainly my babies, and not by mere desire)!

Perhaps it is my eagerness to embrace the dynamics of life, focusing on the process, the impermanence, the change, the ambiguous growth, the ongoing, rather than on pat, summary categories and arrivals: those too neat, too static, too unsubstantial, and too confining little boxes into which it is so tempting to sort truths, experiences, and feelings. Perhaps such thoughts are most productive of suspense—that stimulating essence of 'to be continued,' which most accurately describes many of our more thoughtful and valuable experiences, from music to prose to poetry to science to human interactions.

In improvising much of my life, I don't often arrive at perfect, authentic cadences, in the musical sense of harmonically returning to the tonic. *I suspend them instead, constantly asking, no, requiring, more: more data; more music; more experience; more miles to go before I leap—and promises to evaluate. I am my own* nunc stans, *in which there is only eternity (or impermanence), perhaps even no time or place to be, in favor of just being, as though that being—my journey, either untimed or timeless— shall never end.*

These are the Sixties, and I welcome the liberating aspects of the current evolution of more open minds: about religion, about politics and economics, about education—and certainly about sex. However, mindless euphemisms: "Go with the flow," "Do your own thing!", "Whatever floats your boat," and "If it feels good, do it!" are for mental, emotional, and spiritual masturbation which may not grow green hair on one's soul, or impregnate drug-warped minds with new truths, but are likely to place opaque scales over one's eyes, resulting in passive, undifferentiated victims of life, rather than fulsome, vigorous, challenged and challenging participants, on the move! However, the hedonist/ humanist, philosophical calls to action such as "Make love, not war!" intrigue me. Go to, now, Nathan, and build yourself an operating philosophy that integrates the improvised life with solid realities, such that you might someday light somewhere, cease all this flitting about! After all, whether walking or running, you are always in the process of standing still—at least long enough to take the next step!

Do others experience life this way, or am I somehow unique? Surely not! It is as though any pure rush of feeling, no matter what kind, automatically engenders an objective examination for meaning, for value, for maturity, and amount. Until now, the most notable exceptions to my idiosyncrasy of honest, nearly automatic analysis of my emotions and experiences are my greatest loves, and their most intimate corollaries: Lenore and Shara (Agape and Eros, both shaded by different personalities), Little Nathan and Beth (parental and genetic love?), and music (evolved auditory patterning or numinous Imago Dei?*). These feelings and experiences I do not, cannot long subject to the merciless scrutiny, skepticism, and objectivity, a* lá QI. *I let them be, as I let trees, oceans, mountains, and sunsets be, unfettered by my insatiate, sometimes* *contaminating, intellectual probing. Simply put, they are givens in my subjective, transcendental, eternal Quad, but not very subject to probing scrutiny—or for long.*

Applying meta-mind to what is happening in my marriage, exemplified, perhaps, by last night's exchange of bodily fluids and existential truths in our bed, I seem to be hearing something akin to a death knell for that marriage—sounding and resounding, of late. Sadly, it no longer seems impervious and sacrosanct to my QI and presents more and more data for my processing—and less and less the transcendence, in my mind. This realization does not please me—it makes me feel sick and guilty, which, in turn, kicks in my examination of those feelings in the cold light of reflecting intelligence, and begins the ruminating, blithering cycle all over again.

"Crap!" he hissed to his steering wheel, "efforts at objective rationality are such a pain in the ass!"

How honest and likely is this marital dies irae *I'm beginning to hear, anyway? Shara, I breathe; Lenore is more like a warm cloak in a cold world, a safe harbor in a storm—my dear friend and steady respite in a world of tears. I need and want them both, but without Shara, I believe my life would cease; at least, it would offer far less orienting, purposeful value and good will—and might as well not be. Without Lenore, I would be utterly miserable—but I would still BE. How's that for sophistry, Scott?*

"I hate that!" cried aloud his upbringing, his religion, and his sense of fair play, accusing and abusing his smug reverie of realizations. "Scott, you are a bastard—no doubt about it!"

But I must do what I must do, whispered super-mind.

"Shit!"

And that ended that, excrementally...

*

Fair Friday donned her sunsuit and bade Nathan heed the welcome of the little greensward adjacent to the DTI campus, as he watched for Shara's familiar silhouette to appear against the trees, seventy-five yards away. Working overtime, QI made valiant effort to see this banal campus scene objectively: *almost 30-year-old, married, horny-toad preacher waits for bright, bold and beautimous eighteen-year-old with lovely legs, exquisitely toned and talented pubococcygeal muscles, a determined, almost masculine gait, and the most compellingly attractive eyes ever blown on the face of woman by the kiss of God.*

He could not do it. He had little trouble seeing himself accurately, and thank you QI. Shara, however, he idealized, turning her youth and blossoming maturity into freshness and spontaneity, and her willingness to love and trust into beatific adoration by his Magi. So, thinking, he gave up and gave in to the thrill creeping up the back of his neck and into his prayer, as she suddenly appeared, below, carrying an armload of books, her London Fog, and a pocketbook, already grinning ingenuously, taking the gentle hill in steady, three-foot strides.

"Behold, she cometh!" began the prayer. "For what we are about to receive, make us truly thankful, Oh God, our Strength, and our Redeemer."

Came, also, the familiar, guilt-producing realization that *God has not escaped the scrutiny of my scrutable QI, either, and even now, is pretty much relegated to long, oblong Blur status, a conceptualized entity of abstract, philosophical import only. Perhaps my God is dead—or at least on the critical list.*

"Do not be deceived; God is not mocked…," came his baritone, aloud, as his heart vibrated sympathetically with his mind's acceleration; "…for whatever a man sows, that he will reap," he cadenced, in tempo with Shara's strides. "For he who sows to his own flesh will from the flesh reap corruption; but he who sows to the Spirit will from the Spirit reap eternal life. And let us not grow weary of well-doing, for in due season we shall reap if we do not lose heart. So then, as we have opportunity, let us do good to all men, and especially to those who are of the household of faith."

Paul, Paul, why persecuteth thou me? Why couldn't you simply have advised, as did Jesus, "Be ye kind, one to another!" and let it go at that? Oops! You did! He didn't. Ephesians, about Chapter 4; same chapter in which you berate us poor Gentiles for "... living in the futility of [your] minds; they are darkened in their understanding, alienated from the life of God because of the ignorance that is in them, due to their hardness of heart; they (we) have become callous and have given themselves (ourselves) up to licentiousness, greedy to practice every kind of uncleanness. You did not so learn Christ!"

By the time Shara opened the passenger door and entered his station wagon, Nathan had relegated his theology and his minimal exegesis to QI and turned to greet his beloved, whose breasts were like pomegranates, whose neck was like alabaster, and whose thighs were like unto those of a young hart's.

"Will you lie with me, Oh, woman of the Earth, on this dusty road to Xanadu?"

"Huh?"

"Hi, baby, wanna fuck?"

CHAPTER 36
L'APRÈS-MIDI D'UN FAUNE

*Eros drives the human search for God. Eros is experienced as
the presence of God. Eros is the divine energy that fills the universe and
our own being. It is the work of Agape to set Eros in order.*

Paul Avis

*What shelter to grow ripe is ours?
What leisure to grow wise?*

Matthew Arnold

"All wet, green, and summery, our wood, and brown-eyed Susan-spread, where time is marked by seasons, and steamy dreams of life are bred. A haven and a shelter from all except our love, a fecund soil for Nature's seed, sown within, and from above."

"Take that, Objectivity!" he sang, forgiving the banality of his own improvisation, as he stroked his partner's sweet thighs. "It's Shara time!"

They babbled with reunion like the merging waters of two rippling rills, moving joyously over and around the rocky obstacles before them, gurgling as they came. Rushing and swirling, ingathering the clear passions of heaven-sent rains and run-off, the brook's intercourse, like that of Nathan and Shara, sparkled and flashed in the rare and brilliant freedoms of this, their place upon the earth–if only for the swelling time, before their waters wane, and they must branch, again, into separate channels—or simply dry up. But, for a precious while, moving and flowing together in a single, wider bed of coursing love and laving lusts, their combined, liquid energies sapped the very July sun and bade heaven visit them anew, anointing and appointing them with awing mists and righteous rain.

A hot, dreamy drone of tree frog and insect legions serenaded them as they lay cocooned in his car, dripping sweat and orificial effusions from love's labor's found, like the rain, recently spent. Only steaming droplets remained to mark the passing of the summer storm, spattering the car's roof with gentle, soporific timpani. Outside, the newly washed world wizened in July's searing light. Inside, a newer, saltier rain fell.

Shara wept against his neck, with her lush, flushed nakedness wrapped tightly in his fawning arms, her smooth, damp legs still straddling him, and her vagina vainly trying to retain him, as he slipped from that clinging, delectable pocket.

"Shara?"

"I'm all right, Nathan. Just let me cry a minute."

"Did I do or say something wrong?"

"Yes, yes, no, no, and maybe," she wept, employing his clarifying formulation amid her tears. "*Yes*, you just came in me, again, and you cried out my name over and over. When I heard that, and felt your love anointing me, I came again, too, but it just increased my frustration that we cain't be together, forever, right now! *Yes*, you looked far away and impatient earlier, when I mentioned that we needed to talk about our relationship and where it is going. *No*, because you immediately stopped feeling me off, willing to postpone making love, and to talk right then. *No*, you just gave me three orgasms, and you obviously love me to death. I'm just—it's just that I'm not used to so much happiness all at once, and after a month of not seeing you, it's—it's as if you were dead, and are alive, again—and alive again in me!"

"Gracious, Shara, that needed saying, didn't it? And the 'maybe'?"

"*Maybe* you did something wrong by not being able to last forever when we make love. Just now, after we came, I squeezed you so hard you finally came out of me. That triggered my tears."

"Then, you are crying because…"

"I'm crying because I–I love you so–so totally, and I need you, and when you're deep in me I know I have you, and, just now, when you slipped out, it was like you're leaving me, again. But you're here, under me, and not down in Florida, and you–you are mine at least for right this minute. Do you understand?"

"Of course," nuzzled the puzzled, "you are sad because you are happy. Right?"

"Right!" laughed the most beautiful, tear-stained visage he ever beheld, smiling down at him with such a look of love as to invigorate Lazarus. Grabbing her tightly to him, Nathan rolled her over on the six motley cushions sent to him by sister Patty from Japan, pinioned her, and lavished on her shimmering body a laughter of appreciative hugs, licks, kisses, and love bites.

Neither riant lover realized when their puppy play transfigured into requiring lust, directing his sculping tongue between her thighs. Her lean legs locked his head in place and heaved her bottom, tuning and directing his *Te Dea Laudamus* on Mount Venus, till her tense silence was broken, as she sang another auricular aria of arrival.

Content, the sentient lovers lay, caressing and parsing their love, marking its challenging wisdom. Despite its apparent, mutually irresistible qualities, Shara continued to worry specifics that Nathan could hardly bring himself to contemplate, much less turn over to his calculating uber-mind. She thought logically, realistically, functionally, this time, parsing the concerns in her apt letter of 6/24-25/65. *Though willing to hear most of her questions, I am simply not prepared to answer them.*

"How long do think you can wait for such specifics, Shara?"

"Oh, Lordy, Nathan, I don't know! I don't even know why I get so concerned–it doesn't change my feelings for you, whether I'm with you or not. I know I love you, and that I will do almost anything to be with you one more time, and one more time, and one more time, until they add up to forever."

"I have a suggestion, baby," murmured his deepest bass against her achingly lovely throat. "Why don't we declare a moratorium on these questions, at least until Monday, when I must leave? That way, we can be thinking about things while we enjoy the rest of what I believe may well be the turning point in our relationship–this four-day weekend."

"What do you mean, 'the turning point'?"

"I think we need these four days to restore, renew, and re-cement. Until we have this opportunity, I think we might be either too naive, too realistic, too pessimistic, or too hasty."

With her hesitant concurrence, Nathan then suggested they explore the nearby creek. They dressed; he in jeans and a tee, she in her knee-length, teal green dress with a thin, white leather belt cinching her trim waist. Skittish about trespassing more openly, they followed the rushing creek downstream about two hundred yards, through light underbrush, towering conifers, and hardwoods, until it took a hard turn eastward, and headed for a river about a half mile away.

"We better return to the car before someone runs us off. It's four o'clock."

Walking the final hundred yards up the brook, hand in hand, feeling their freedom and love in their bones, Shara suddenly chortled and broke away. Beneath a huge weeping willow, she slipped off her loafers, hiked up her dress, and waded into the clear, shallow water up to her calves. Giggling, she kicked the singing water at Nathan, sending a large spray fanning aloft. Immediately taken with the challenge, and thinking to respond, the aureate beauty of the scene arrested his mind and his motion altogether.

Nathan well knew when he beheld great beauty. He beheld it now. It was not symbol or caricature which evoked his wonder, in that eternal moment of grinning, perfect teeth, laughing eyes, naked, kicking legs, green dress and leaves, fused in an arcing, prismatic mist. He saw something simple, split-second, and timeless; something to grace his memory and play his heartstrings forever. Gulping, as a freshet of beauty-washed tears added its own prismatic colors to his vision, Nathan painted the scene on his inward eye and impressed its hues of love and scintillations of joy upon him, quite despite the stalwart interrogatories of QI.

Backlit by suffused sunlight, filtered through North Carolina's summer greens, light and dark, broken by a symmetry of ebony silhouettes of snaking limbs and trunks, and by a blanket of ground ferns, young pines, and poplars, amid wildflower hosts, the brook presented itself in four, lovely foci. Gently entering the upper right, from thirty yards upstream, it curved slowly down and to the left, before inverting, slashing back, and broadening to a dozen shallow feet across, filling the center of the scene, then exiting downstream, to the left. The foreground was filled with swaying strands of willow's hair, caressing, and streaming in the risen waters of the brook. As a whole, the view was a study in light, shadow, natural shapes and color, greens and browns, dotted with pinks, yellows and reds, split by the challenge of a moving, flashing, three-dimensional, reflective brook: a curving perspective *sans* clear horizon.

Absent the frolicking girl midstream, the scene suggested a Monet or a Renoir. Present the girl, it scored his personal *L'Apres-midi d'un Faune*. Body perfectly poised in a slow motion *grand battement devant*, Shara's lithe, scissoring legs parted, propelling a rainbow of water skyward, while her beatific face, animate with smiles and larking, glistering eyes, tuned to him in playfulness, seeking and seeing love returned.

As the nymph's perfectly formed and pointed nubile leg emerged from the stream, arcing her love, spraying it heavenward, splashing the willow and the man, her skirts took wing, flying up with the geyser, revealing the exquisite form of her naked limbs, all the way to her bare pubes, affording him a momentary glimpse of her black, triangular treasure of feminine weal and allure, so much more enticing and fascinating for having been hidden, now highlighted by a coruscation of the forbidden white of her inner thighs.

Forevermore, this shimmering, sylvan scene of this beautiful, young creature would flood his memory, at times both odd and seemly, reminding him of her frolicsome, animal nature, freed by the wood, the brook, her youth, the time, the place, and her man. The promise in her rain-bowed aura, and in the complement it expressed between them, would live as long as he could discern green and wet, the fabulous female form, sunsets, babies' smiles, and ospreys on the wing. And when he would die, he fully expected the scene would somehow express itself, *postmortem*, as a promise of heaven, at the least. For one brief, eternal moment, Nathan pictured joy incarnate, kicking up her heels in a sunlight-dappled wood, surrounded by a halo of mystic, watery lights, freed of all constraints save love's, blending with motley hues on Nature's private canvas, to be hung forever in the Louvre of his mind: precious, priceless, and eternally imprinted upon his heart!

*

Back at the car, both thoroughly delighted—and doused—by their spontaneous cavort, they stripped and laid their wet clothes on the hot hood to dry. Meanwhile, he grabbed and pointed his camera, stimulating Shara's playful shriek and rapid run down the ruts in the tractor road, naked Nathan, penis aflop, in hot pursuit. As she ducked around trees and bushes, laughing, and begging him not to photograph her nude, a distant, calling voice interrupted their frolic, froze their merriment, and stilled their voices.

"Haalllooooo!" came the voice from the west, answered by its echo from the east.

Instinctively, Shara squatted where she was, risking chiggers or poison ivy on her fanny from the leaves covering her. Nathan stood still, harking.

"Haalllooo, Molliiee, is that youuuuu? Are you allll riiiighht?"

"It's hard to tell," whispered the naked cameraman to the sylph in the bushes, "but he sounds like he's about a half mile away, way on the other side of the corn field."

"Yeah," hissed the bushes, "but where's Mollie? He must have heard me shriek and thought it was whoever Mollie is."

"Doubtless. Come on; let's get out of here. I don't want to lose this parking spot."

Had Mollie Maid-in-Wood been watching (they never knew), she might have laughed to see two very white, moon-like butts scurrying up the old tractor road, retrieving a passel of damp clothes, only to go into eclipse as they piled, willy-nilly, inside the inner reaches of a dark blue 1963 Chevy II Nova Wagon. Further, as the car made its way out of the tractor road, she might have seen a hilariously laughing girl, in dishabille, trying in vain to remove her white nylon panties from the balding pate of the resisting male driver, where he had placed them.

369

CHAPTER 37
WHAT BLISS IS THIS?

It's good to be happy; it's a little better to know that you're happy; but to understand that you're happy and to know why and how . . . and still be happy, happy in the being and the knowing, well that is beyond happiness, that is bliss.

Henry Miller

Happiness makes up in height for what it lacks in length.

Robert Frost

"H'lo, Dad-dee?" spake Elizabeth, picking up the phone just ahead of her Mommy.

"Hey, Bethee! How did you know it was your Daddy?"

"Dah tellyfoam ring," she sang-song, "an' I tawk to my dad-dee, sil-lee. Hee heee! I luv you, Dad-dee. Come home, see my an' Nattie?"

"I'll be home Monday night, sweetheart—that's after two more sleeps. Today is Saturday, tomorrow is Sunday, the Fourth of July, and the next day is Monday. I'll be home that night, before you go to bed."

"Dad-dee, dat's too faarrr!"

"I know, baby; Daddy misses you, too."

"I give you kiss–(smack!). I go play my drum you gived me. Nattie is outsiiide; I luv you!

370

Here's Mom-mee! Bye-bye!'"'"

"Bye, darlin'."

"Hi!"

"Hey, Lenore. She's so dear! Did you tell her to answer the phone?"

"No, but she surely ran to answer it, saying, 'Dat's my dad-dee.' Are you in the YMCA?"

"No, darlin,' I'm in the Morningside Motel. Is that a problem?"

"You tell me, mister."

"Honey, I called to say 'Hi' to you and to the kids, as promised, to let you know where I am, and to say I am thinking about you, and us, and them, and Shara, and…"

"…And?"

"No conclusions, honey; but enough love and conflict to choke a horse!"

"The way you're treating us, wouldn't you know more about the other end of said animal?"

"Ummphh! Yes, I admit to a certain resemblance to a jackass; a horse is too noble for me, probably. I'm sorry for disappointing you, again, Lenore. I honestly don't mean to do it!"

"I'm sorry, honey, but you leave yourself so open, sometimes, and right now, I need a cushion for the pins and needles I've been on since you left early yesterday morning. And what was the big idea of picking one of *my* rosebuds and leaving it on my pillow, without even waking me up to say, 'Good-bye'?"

"You tell me, 'Nore."

Silence.

"What do you want me to tell people when they ask when you will be available? Two couples want you to marry them, and old Mr. Partee is expected to die anytime now."

"And I'm not even supposed to be back from vacation yet, darn it."

"You didn't tell me that."

"Baby, is there anything I can do for you–from this distance?""

"Come home?"

"Monday, as planned, unless you tell me to come now."

"Come home now, then!"

Silence.

More silence.

"I'll be home in three hours."

"You know damned well I won't make you do that! And you also know why!"

"Yes, and yes, and I love you for being you."

"Oh, Nathan…"

"Well, it's true, darling, no matter what else is happening."

"I–I try to understand–that you are struggling–with your emotions, your convictions, your morals, and with yourself in general, Nathan, but, sometimes, my struggles rise up in me and won't let me see yours very clearly–especially when you are–where you are."

"I know."

"And do you know that I love you, too?"

"Yes, thank God!"

"Let's–let's hang up, now, Nathan, before I blubber."

"Are you sure, Lenore?"

"Umm-hmm."

"Are you sure, sure, sure?" sang their mutually beloved Amahl.

"Nathan!"

"All right, darlin'. I love you and will call you Sunday night."

Weeping.

"Lenore?"

"Please hang up, Nathan."

"Okay," whispered misery's lover.

Click.

Nathan's pseudo-stoic lay stark and motionless on his rumpled bed a full minute, before his family man whirled, wailed loudly into his pillow, and beat his fists on the bed. Composing himself, he got into his car and pointed it toward their little church. Shara was late. It was past 10:30 a.m., Saturday, and not a sign of her.

Thus began a frustrating morning for both lovers, through Shara's careless telling a would-be suitor, Manny Masters, that her parents would be gone all day. He came, unexpectedly, at 9:00 a.m., and Shara didn't know how to get him to leave. Finally, at Nathan's impatient telephoned suggestion, she accepted a ride downtown from Manny, where she would enter Belk's, wait five minutes, and then come out to Nathan's car.

At 1:10 p.m., getting into Nathan's car, Shara said, "Here; at least I brought you a half a cheeseburger. I couldn't talk him out of stopping at McDonald's, darlin'–I'm sorry. Do you hate me?"

"You know I don't hate you, baby. I only wanted to be with you–and hated having to wait–and wait–and wait."

"Well, I'm here, now, Nathan. Again, I'm sorry. I met Manny at a college function at church. He showed interest in me and…"

"…You naturally returned his interest and told him you'd be home. I do believe you have taught me a lesson in elasticity, gal.

"Elastic or not, I'm sorry I ruined our morning," she whispered.

"Okay," returned his whisper. "What can I do to help until we get there?"

"Love me, anyway?"

"Done!"

Thus, in Room 169 of the Morningside Motel, they made the most of their afternoon: talking, dancing, reading parts of a sexy book, making a bet that she could pee standing up and not spill (he lost), and finding intriguing ways to use a hot fudge sundae. At five, reluctantly, he hied her homeward ahead of her parents' call and potential ire. She would not be able to see or contact him until tomorrow. They both got needed sleep.

*

Awakened at 6:00 a.m., Sunday, unable to sleep, Nathan showered, shaved, dressed in shorts and T- shirt, and jumped in his car. Turning into Shara's Street, *Should I brave recognition?* Should had little to do with it, as he drove forward. Passing the Starr home, he was horrified to see Big J. Carl's car in the driveway. *Dear God, please don't let them be home!*

Lenore was cordial but not pleased to have been awakened at 8:35 a.m. on a Sunday in which she intended to sleep late. Their conversation was brief; she asked him no questions except when to expect him Monday and wasted no energy gauging his welfare. His children were already in front of the TV, and she did not want to get them all riled up and expectant regarding their daddy.

Too casually, she told him that the Trinity University chaplaincy people called, and that he was to call them Tuesday. They were very interested in him and wanted to discuss the possibilities. A few more clipped and distant sentences, and the strangely loving couple hung up, each left to suck wryly on the bittersweet realities of their love.

Impatiently, he fell on the bed and sniffed the sheets for Shara's scent. As his nose pressed against the faint outlines of one of yesterday's wet spots, his nostrils swelled and his heart beat faster with musky recognition.

Lady Chatterly's gamekeeper looked up, in the middle of soixante neuf, *and that busy little man thought to himself, 'Thar she shits, and thar she pisses' in a combination of amazement and stark reality, and here I am with my nose in our drippings, and all I want to do is widen this circle!*

At last, the phone rang.

"Hi, handsome! Get on over here; we can do it in my parents' bed."

"Sure, Paula Play-like, and write a poem for the wet spot!"

"You ought to be able to do that, Rev. Wordsmith."

"Something like, 'We came here; you did not. Hope you enjoy this cold wet spot!'"

"I like it, I like it!"

*

Arriving at their motel, Shara immediately claimed her hour of power over him, her prize for winning her bet about her peeing standing up without spilling (standing facing out, on the seat). She bade him sing to her, she sang, they both learned each other's childhood ditties, he read verses from "the Song of Solomon," to enjoy its amorous declamations, and they both laughed a lot.

"Okay, you have sung for me, and you have read for me, and I've used up twenty minutes of my hour. Now, I want to try something different."

"I'm all agog. Whom do I have to slay?"

"It's nothing like that, Nathan—I want to ask you some questions, and you have to promise me, now, before God, that you will be brutally honest—that you will tell me the truth, the whole truth, and nothing but the truth."

"So, help me, Murgatroyd?"

"I'm serious, darlin."

"I don't think I have anything to worry about—or you either."

Shara stood, ambled to the window, opened the dimpled curtains about six inches, and gazed out, unseeing. Nathan lay down on a bed, fluffed two pillows behind his head, and waited. Finally, she crossed to a chair, sat down, crossed her legs, with her right foot swinging rapidly...

"Well, first, I guess I want to know if you love me as much as you love Lenore.'"

"Yes."

"More?"

"Differently—and, yes, more—in that I am persuaded by my total response to you, that I hope to be with you, always, one way or another, no matter what!"

"Which way do you most want it to be?"

"Both, of course. I honestly wish I could marry you both and have you both totally accept it. Does that shock you?"

"Not really. I've often thought that if we were in a different time or country, we could do that, if Lenore could accept me, too."

"Could you manage three in the same bed and all that such implies?"

"Possibly, even probably. I know Lenore has a lovely body, and if you're turned on by her, maybe I could be, too. The idea is there; I don't know how real it might be. I would worry she might resent me, though, or be turned off by my, uh, body."

"That's more than interesting, Shara. You're more open minded than I thought. I would love to have you both and keep both my kids and my calling. Probably impossible..."

"But if you have to choose between us, which way?"

"As of this moment, I would choose you, though it would be extremely difficult."

"I'm sorry to press you, honey, but 'as of this moment' leaves too much room for other moments. I want you to answer in the long run–forever, even."

Pause.

"Nathan?"

"Shara, you must know by now that no matter what, I have to be with you."

"Is that some kind of commitment, Nathan?"

"Not 'some kind;' I make it freely, from my heart, darling."

"And if I leave home, which I'm determined to do, what will you do?"

"I'll do my best to see that you are in a safe place and as productive and happy as you can be–accessible to me, of course. Where you can either work or go to school, and where you can grow and learn a little more, while I work things out with Lenore."

"What do you mean, 'grow and learn a little more'?"

"Just that–you are all of eighteen years and two months, and you need more time and experiences to sort out what you really want. You ought to go to college, for sure, and you should decide in that context what you wish to do with yourself, vocationally, and with me, personally."

"Nathan, one of the reasons I'm playing this silly game is to get past that kind of response. I know I'm young–and that you're eleven years older–but I also know my love for you, and you just told me you love me enough to sacrifice your marriage, if it would result in our being together, always. Then you turn right around and sound iffy about it. Will the real Nathan Scott please stand up?"

"He already did, Shara, and does so every time he sees you, hears you, smells you, tastes you, feels you, remembers you, or thinks about you. He loves you peremptorily! He wants and needs you to be his wife! He will do whatever he has to do to achieve that, trying his best not to hurt anyone. Finally, he—I—love you so damned much, I'm willing to sacrifice my need for you, if I believe that it would be best for you and, most importantly, if you loved someone else more than me."

"None of those things will ever happen, Nathan. I'm more than positive."

"Shara, I pray that you won't ever ask me to make such a sacrifice, and that you will be happy, fulfilled, and content with me the rest of your life. But I sometimes feel obligated to allow—no, to foster—continued growth and maturation in you, no matter what that might mean. Does that answer it?"

"I think so. I know, in my mind, that your attitude is the correct one. But I also want you to claim me! I want you to dare anybody to touch me, or to educate me in ways that should be reserved for you. Sure, you're certain of your love for me, but it sometimes sounds like you're not so sure about my love for you, and, frankly, Nathan, that bugs me!"

"I could do that—want to do that—absolutely claim you for myself, right now. I feel like doing that every time I miss you or realize that you might be alone with another guy. But I won't and I can't; it wouldn't be right. Not yet. Not now. Do you understand?"

"I do. But I want you to have faith in me, just as you want me to trust you. My mother was all of eighteen when she married my father, and then he went away to war for several years, leaving her pregnant with Jimmy. I don't think he told her it was all right for her to fool around, while he was gone, to help her grow and learn, as you say. Do you understand me here?"

"Yes. May I ask you something, Shara, and expect a totally honest answer, too?"

"Of course."

"Why don't you just turn down all offers, dates, and male liaisons—especially those that might involve a little lickey-face and smacky-mouth—and more?"

"I will in a heartbeat, if you ask me to."

"You know I won't do that; any more than Lenore will demand that I stop seeing you. So why don't you offer it, instead?"

"Wait! Did you and Lenore discuss that very thing? When? What was said?"

"Right before I left for Durham, she asked if I was going to fuck you, and..."

"She actually said, 'fuck?'"

"Yes."

"I thought she'd be, you know, more lady-like."

"She's about the most lady-like lady I know, but she not only says it, from time to time, she does it pretty well, too."

"I'm not about to get into a fucking contest with your wife; I just want to know what was said," surprise and wonder widening her gaze.

"She wanted to know if I planned to fuck you this time. It then developed into the question of whether I was going to love you, too. She even told me that it might be okay were I to seek out another woman, casually, or a prostitute, if it would not involve my loving her..."

"Shriek! What were your answers to both of those questions?"

"Yes, yes, no, no..."

"Nathan, please. As your Mistress Queen, I command you to tell me!"

"Of course, I said yes to both queries. I wasn't going to lie to her. I also told her exactly what I just told you: I want you both; I love you both; I need you both; and I don't have any idea what to do about it, right now, but wait it out, try to work it out, and see what happens..."

379

"Well, let's get back to your earlier question. Why don't I refuse to date all males, but you? Probably, because I trust you, your maturity, and your understanding of me and other kids—er—people my age, and what we need to grow into purposeful, independent, and productive adults. I believe you know what I need more than I do, in some ways, and you have never hurt or failed me. Were you to tell me I'm ready, either way, I'd probably believe it, and do it—but that very fact means I'm probably not ready, huh?"

"That's a great insight, Shara! At the rate you've been growing, I don't think we're very far from the time when we can just can all this other stuff and get married!"

"Do you really think so, Nathan? That would make me so happy. You don't know how much I want to do that—to have you, to have us together, happy and fulfilled, forever! When I leave home, though, it will be because I need to get away, to be on my own, to escape the rule of my parents, especially my father, and to be my own person. If it helps you to solve the burning questions of money, job, and family, great! But I'm going to do it right after summer school, no matter what."

"Lenore thinks that would be a good idea, too, even though she suspects it might be related to our relationship."

"It really isn't, Nathan. I need to do this for me, and for nobody else, not even for you. When I do it, I'll need your interest and moral support, and surely visits, but I need to do it for me, not for us."

Changing focus, she leapt from her chair, looking at him with eyes aflame. "Okay, I've got exactly sixteen and a half minutes left of my power over you. Take off your clothes…"

*

Awakening, nibbling his nose and mouth, she sighed her breath into his nostrils, depositing her intimate *ruach* (רוּחַ), her God-breathed spirit, her proximity, and her life. Kissing him, she traced one trembling finger across his brow, over their uni-nose and united mouth, parting their lips, and entering, touching, and discovering their kissing, moving, tasting tongues, bathing it in their mingled pith.

"Shara, darling, what were your finger doing, just now, in our mouths?"

"It was–I was trying to–crawl inside–of us, to touch and handle–our kiss, so I could–remember it–in every way–possible," she murmured, her lilting words punctuated by kisses cascading over and down his gratefully receptive visage.

"Are you happy, now–right this minute?" she asked.

"I am light and color; I am *allegro vivace* and *glorioso*, lush, gladsome harmony; I am form and comeliness; I am joy and happiness, incarnate; I am bliss!"

"Why are you hap—?"

"Because we have permanently fused more than our bodies; because we have grown into the promise of one, God-breathed spirit, as well as one flesh. Agape and Eros combined, we are no longer potential and devoutly to be desired. We are, here, alive, in this place and in this time, gliding into our future. Because if and when have finally become now and forever. Because I am no longer afraid to love you completely, as your husband, and am only puzzled about how to show it forth, till it come. I am happy in you, on you, about you, with you, for you, over you, under you, beside you, and because of you. You are my life, my wife, and my best investment in eternity! God help me; I can do no other!"

Hot tears of joy seared their faces and sealed their simple vows of happiness. Kissing tears from her face, their mouths met, and gentle Priapus stirred, moving his maned and manic head upwards, toward the romp and prowl of Eros graced by Agape, at last freed to plunge deeply where lay his Key and her Keeper, safe within her delectable folds of Joy.

And it was so, until his thrusts and her buck and spread evoked greater gladness of heart, spilling over, between, and within them, giving song to their voices, and soaring flight to their spirits. The time: 5:35 p.m. Sunday, July 4, 1965; the hour and day of the anniversary of their first coition, now marking, in its zenith, their avowed expurgation of the dreadful dragons of doubt.

CHAPTER 38
THE AFTERMARK

Now no joy but lacks salt
That is not dashed with pain
And weariness and fault;
I crave the stain
Of tears, the aftermark
Of almost too much love,
The sweet of bitter bark
And burning clove.

Love at the lips was touch
As sweet as I could bear;
And once that seemed too much;
I lived on air.

Robert Frost

Though Monday dawned in rain and gloom, serenading their hearts with parting dirge, the lovers tried to enjoy their last several hours together–and to recapture yesterday's bliss. QI nagged him, instead:

Our long weekend has released in me a baneful willingness (not yet a readiness!) to lose my family, in order to secure Shara. Yet, I do not abhor the wistful thought of going home; au contraire, *I miss the wit, warmth, and wisdom of my Lenore, and my lilting little ones who will gather about my knees, pummeling and quickening my heart with their touching hands and winning ways. God, how can I seriously contemplate living without...?*

Though his prayer was aimed at God, he realized that he was talking to himself, as well: *Lord, how can I seriously contemplate walking away from Lenore and my dear children—and the best part of my own heart? Not only would it be godawful for them, but it would also fly in the face of everything I have ever felt and believed. Yet, this is essentially what I promised my Shara. God help me, somehow, to both assimilate and accommodate to what feels like blasphemy at best and treachery at worst. Yet, if I would have–keep–Shara, it seems I must lose–and hurt– everyone else. Not only do I hate that prospect, I excoriate the self who vows it. Am I really that lost? My God, please help me!*

At noon, the spent, naked couple unwrapped their limbs, dressed, gathered their belongings, loaded his car, and returned to the room to sit quietly for a few minutes. Seeing her lust-tousled hair and makeup-smudged face in the mirror, Shara rushed for her pocketbook, ferreted out the necessary manipulanda, and assumed one of womankind's most natural and endearing stances–that of her reflected self in studied reverse. An enthralled student of most all feminine assiduity, Nathan found intrigue in these rituals, and sought to differentiate mystery from necessity; he could not.

Shara seemed to gesticulate hypnotically at a series of serious faces in the mirror, wave her hands like wands before them and above her head, make strange, self-directing noises, and, lo, she was transformed and restored before his very eyes!

An hour later, having decided to forego a restaurant meal, they were parked in their familiar, unfinished subdivision, finishing burgers. The continuing deluge had long since halted any subdivision work, and his car was well hidden behind fifty yards of thickly planted loblolly pines–and sailing, ghostly sheets of a thick, driving rain. Nathan's mood was one of deep, unfocused contemplation and worry.

"Nathan?"

"Yes?"

"Do you think you can–will–should tell Lenore about our bliss and mutual commitment?"

"Yes, yes, no, no, and maybe."

"I appreciate the truth in each of those answers, Nathan. I know you love her, too. Telling her would hurt her, and you want to avoid that."

"Thanks for loving me enough to understand that darling. It's one of the reasons I love you!"

Silence.

"Nathan?"

"Yes?"

"I was just saying your name...."

Silence.

Heavy rain on the roof.

Nathan rolled down his window, in the lee of the wind, and stuck his arm out, soaking it instantly. Cupping his hands, he pushed them into the storm, waiting no more than a few, silent seconds before he brought them back in, brimming. Immediately, he splashed the rainwater into his face and eyes, rubbing it all over his head. Turning to Shara, who was watching him ruefully, his imp grinned.

Perhaps it was the tension of one more protracted, unsatisfactory parting, or the inconsistency of communication; perhaps it was the lack of sleep, or too many orgasms in so short a period; perhaps it was their mountain of bliss, so difficult to re-climb; perhaps it was the Beethoven weather, or it might have been Nathan's own titan, wrestling with the gods of encroaching, hurtful family disaster. No matter: in a burst of spontaneous irrationality, his grin translated from impish to mischievous to devilish to beatific–all in the space of an irresistible moment of decision–or surrender. No matter: it happened, *and to hell with QI!*

Before she could stop him, Nathan had his shirt off, then his undershirt. Kicking off his shoes and socks, he dropped his trousers on the seat, opened the door, and danced out into the storm, wearing nothing but his whitey-tighties.

"Come on in, Shara," he enticed, waving his arms, rubbing rain all over his face and torso, taking a shower, "the water's fine!"

"You're crazy, Nathan!" she shouted, pulling his door closed and watching him happily cavorting in the pouring rain.

"It's wonderful, Shara!" he yelled, water pouring off him. "Take off your clothes and join me! *'Freude, schöener Götterfunken: Tochter aus Elysium, Wir betreten feuertrunken, Himmlische, dein Heiligtum!'*" he sang, *fortissimo*, lifting his arms to Joy, Schiller, his beloved Beethoven, and to the covering, velvet curtains of falling water almost obliterating him from her sight, less than fifteen feet away.

At first, she hesitated, then she smiled resignedly to herself, took off her blouse, bra, and skirt, stripping to her panties. She removed her glasses, held her naked arm out his window to test the water, hesitated a moment more, sighed mightily, held her breath, and threw herself under the steering wheel and out the door. In seconds she was soaked and might as well have been naked. Her rain-soaked panties stuck to her body, revealing her intense signal of dark pubic hair and her delectable backside split.

Roaring his pleasure, Nathan gallumphed to her, gave her a slippery bear hug, cradled her in his arms, and twirled her round and round, as he danced an improvised jig. Grinning widely at her, he put her feet down and crushed their dripping chests together, as she found her footing in the wet grass. Looking down, Nathan licked the water cascading between her breasts, dripping off their erect nipples, streaming down her trim, flat belly, into her translucent panties. Her wet, matted hair hung on her comely, upturned face, as she looked up at him through eyes squinted against the force of the rain. In that crystal, Nature-washed moment, he saw her as God created her to be–young, unpreened, and beautiful, curvaceous, fecund, and alive–oh, so sparkling wet and alive!

Afloat in that moment of clarity and creation, Nathan poured his hands down the curves of his sodden Eve, God's great afterthought, and declared her good–better, he thought, than the male whom God created to ward off His loneliness. Then, laughing his approbation upon this particular creation, he shouted into her ear, over the rush of the wind and the rain:

"I love you, child of the rain, sister of the winds, mother of the earth!"

He kissed her; a kiss for the ages; Adam's first kiss of Eve, naked and unashamed in the Garden, before God allowed his wily serpent to hiss its poisoned enticements; before what was good, acceptable, and perfect, even to God, somehow, absurdly, became bad. And in their kiss was a cleansing–a purging–of all the evil which God foolishly ordained should inhabit and torture humankind, because of the so-called "sin" of wanting–*to know!*

"This is right!" he shouted, cupping her breasts, floating them in his hands, and baptizing them in the blessings of the rain. "This is good!" he cried, slipping her panties down and off her goose–fleshed legs. "This is righteous!" he whooped, as his jockies fell to the earth beneath them. "And this is why we were created!" he bellowed, as he lowered her slippery, pliant form to the grass, alive with droplets and pools and rivulets, spreading her, naked, asoak, and utterly willing, upon the fertile earth that bore them. "And this, and This, and THIS–is the power, Shara–and the glory, Shara!" he yelled, entering, and thrusting repeatedly. "Forever–and ever, Shara! World–without end, Shara! Ahhh–men!" as, together, they became one flesh; one with the earth, air, water, and their own fire–and at One with Life's hallowed Quintessence–Love, Pure Agape, Itself!

And above the swirling, squalling wind, and rain; above the clarifying lightning illuminating their corpus, God roared, through the ensuing thunder: "That's good!"

CHAPTER 39
THOUGH I UNWORTHY BE

Whoso loves, believes the impossible.

Elizabeth Barret Browning

The dry twig lives but in a dream;
The thinness of unruffled nature shall conceive,
And opulent in pregnancy,
Shall bear the world its balm.

Nathan Rhea Scott
July 29, 1965

Most everyone from kids to kings has discovered the utter importance of little things—little things that can control not only our immediate future, but our destinies, as well. So it was with the Reverend Nathan Rhea Scott and Ms. Shara Day Starr, erstwhile lovers, during the hot, fertile month of July 1965.

Who gave what to whom? Lenore would reap it, from time to time, and pass it on to Nathan, who usually sloughed it off. Shara never had it, until her unsuspecting donor was far away in West Virginia, co-directing a senior high conference. Melanie, of course, was too long out of the loop to be either the sower or the reaper of the present crop: *Candida albicans* its name; unwonted shame its game.

The last half of July was exceptionally busy for Nathan, with Dr. Morrison in Scotland, two, large youth conferences and a small group, rustic camp to direct, preaching twice every Sunday, overseeing both junior and senior high fellowships, and the regular duties of the senior pastor thrown in for good measure.

QI realized *I am winding myself up too tightly; but I cannot seem to help it! Tomorrow will be my trysting day! Why, every fifteen minutes throughout the day, do I feel as though I am about to fly apart— or explode? Perhaps it is because I have grown defensively giddy, with Mother dying, far too much to do on the job, guilt about my decision to leave, but more so regarding those loving poles of my heart: Shara and Lenore. To both, I have made lifelong promises. Clearly, something has to give…*

*

As July wound down, the romantic life of Nathan and Shara wound up—to fever pitch. Not only did Shara receive her first pelvic exam, in the process of seeking to stem her yeast infection, but her doctor evidently palpated an ovary hard enough to pop an ovum or two. Unsuspecting, this led to a certain vulnerability, as they continued to meet several times between Nathan's conferences, camp, preaching, and other duties, always using condoms to protect against Shara's infection. With varying degrees of bliss, according to their proximity to each other, the lovers continued to strive…

August, that robust, pre-harvest month, named for the census Caesar, with imputations of his grandeur, was as hot as Hades' ladies. Nathan's ladies were no less hot, but in entirely different ways. Shara, and her Nathan-stoked fires, could not get enough Agape and Eros. Melanie, and her Nathan-enforced virtue, pined, prayed—and plotted. Lenore, and her Nathan-induced, aching heart, could not get enough Nathan. Nathan, and his chattering mind, libidinous body, and aching spirit, could not get enough God. God, according to the bulk of Christian theology, was in His heaven, and all was right with the world…

Wanna bet?

Despite the doctrine of your sovereignty, oh God, the Seven continue to ride, with Lust leading their charge, at least in me. As for pride, avarice, envy, wrath, gluttony, and sloth/acedia (literally, the absence of caring), all constantly look for niches in me, to inhabit me, as is the way with all sins, deadly or not. With the clear exception of charity (Agape: Love), of which I may possess too much, the corresponding virtues of chastity, temperance, diligence, patience, kindness, and humility are perfectly present only in my aspirations. Perhaps that's why these seven, holy virtues are also referred to as "contrary."

Maybe our dilemma, Lord, can be distilled into a simple conundrum: loving to love, loving to fuck, or fucking to love? Perhaps with Lenore it's the former, with Shara the latter, and maybe, as usual, I'm stuck in the middle. Pretty trite, Scott, and how would one know—and what difference would it make? Plenty, depending on the regularity of her menses—which now Shara reports are nearing two weeks late!

OH, MY VERY OWN GOD!

These were the haunts and taunts infecting Nathan and his convoluted life, as his worlds were spinning much too fast and in constant self-collision. *Pining, loving, confounding letters, cards, and telephone calls, when experienced as positive trends, are upbeat, happy, determined and fulfilling—or negative, sad, hopeless, and empty, depending on their proximity to our actual trysts. Like two contrasting, musical motifs, they harmonize around physical and spiritual contact between us, supplemented by two sets of very different, almost competing, daily events. Such are the ways with absent, pining lovers. But Abelard and Heloise we are most definitely not, even if Shara might be enceinte! When Heloise's illicit pregnancy was discovered, Abelard's own students castrated him! Alas!*

August's experiential eddies whipped up a heated whirlwind, within a tempest, spawned by the hurricane weathers of their separate lives. Shara was regularly dating

Manny Masters, who was more than adequate at replacing *Pauvre Pierre*, who had broken up with her 12 days earlier, citing their "incompatibility." Manny was more experienced in the petting department but seemed to be satisfied with less of it than Peter.

On August 11, Nathan transported his family to two, week-long national senior high conferences in West Virginia, where he most successfully taught his invited course on Sex and Christianity to a horde of lusty teens. Jealous Shara later commented:

> The heart of what I would tell your teens is that I know our love is the real thing; we just can't (See? I can spell it right.) help it! As far as their probable charge that you took advantage of me at the tender age of seventeen, pardon my French, but that's a bunch of shit! You fought me off for months before I finally got you to act on what I was positive was our love, not lust alone (but Nathan, I'm still discovering how much I trust our lust—it is incredible!).

Doubting pregnancy, Shara was 98% sure about leaving home and began to flesh out her plan. The main question, of course, was where she might live. Lenore, in on these deliberations, reminded Nathan of Melanie's willingness to board her in Prospect Park, Pennsylvania. Thus, Shara guilelessly wrote Melanie requesting such an arrangement. Equally as guileless, Melanie invited her to live with her while Shara looked for work and figured out what to do next. The next step involved the logistics of leaving.

*

Shara wrote a lovely paean to their relationship, still doubting pregnancy:

What I feel is greater than gentleness, contentment, hope and faith. There is a purity, as if God had touched me and made me new. I feel a quietness of love, a more beautiful surging of warmth, of peace and trust. It is as if the moon is reflecting all that I feel–so majestic as it shines through the trees and provides its soft light–light that seems as soft as a newborn baby, or as fine as a child's hair. It is real; a love so real as to make me cry tears of joy, instead of pain; cries of faith, instead of fear; and hopes of togetherness, instead of anxieties and separation...

Writing Shara after directing his second senior high conference, to no letter, yet, from Shara, he was disappointed but full of present and future realities that, hopefully, did not include a baby:

8/15/65–10:10 p.m., I really do need you, tonight, Shara, and you won't even know about it until Tuesday. Nothing big, so don't worry. I called the Associate Pastor at Miami, and he told me that Dr. Flowers (boss) evidently had some doubts about me, due to my uncertainty about Trinity U. He won't be free to meet me until the last of August, which means I won't be sure about things until then. I wrote a long letter to Dr. Flowers, telling him exactly what is going on with me and Wilmington. It upsets me, though. Things are all so complicated and void of joy, except for my rare times with you. I told Lenore I just wanted to run, sometimes. Of course, I can't, and that is just one more frustration.

In a fanatical, senseless way, of course, I hope you're pregnant as hell, though what that would solve beats me. I told Lenore about my wanting to go down at least once a week, until you or we leave. She reacted unfavorably, favorably, meaning she pouted, pointing her thumb down, but smiled, anyway, not really objecting. She knows I must do it– so, I'll be up this Thursday morning, waiting for you at 9:30 a.m. in the park. My sadness and need are not fatal, of course– probably fatuous. Forgive me and love me anyway, as you always do, thank God!

*

"Hi, Melanie. How's my favorite redhead?"

"Favorite how, Nathan? You don't come knocking any more, or hadn't you noticed?"

"And have you forgotten the reason why, dear heart?"

"Yes; you'll have to enlighten me, again."

"It's pretty simple, Mel; I can love two women at the same time, but I cannot possibly manage three. I had to choose, and you won, of course. Now, you're virtually free of me."

"I thought you managed pretty well for quite a while, though–and I didn't win, dammit, Shara did–and I'm praying Lenore will, too, somehow. That is why I'm willing, even happily ready for Shara to stay with me, until she can get on her feet. I assume that is why you are calling."

"Yes, it is. Melanie. When Lenore suggested that you might be willing to do this, it struck me–still strikes me–as passing strange. Though I don't dare doubt your sincerity, I do wonder at your motives. Why are you so willing to do this, Mel? For whom are you doing it, is probably a better way to ask?"

"Nathan, I don't appreciate your doubting me, though I guess it's a fair question, considering. As you probably guessed, I am doing it partly for Lenore, who needs a respite from Shara, too, even though Shara will be freer to come and go."

"What do you mean by 'needs a respite, too?'"

"I'm sorry, Nathan, I guess I projected that need on to you, given the anxiety that pervades this—your—entire affair. I had no right to do that. Please forgive me."

"Done. Why else, then?"

"I have to admit that I want to know who Shara is. If you love her so much, there must be something to her that I have not been close enough to perceive. But the main reason is because she asked to stay with me, and I saw no reason not to do so. She needs my help, she asked for it very sweetly, and I decided I would give it. It's the Christian thing to do."

"You mean by relieving Shara of some of her anxiety, you might also relieve both mine and Lenore's too, don't you?"

"Yes, of course. Is there anything wrong with that?"

"*Au contraire*, Melanie, everything is right about that, and I deeply appreciate it."

After a little more banter, Nathan thanked her, again, and they hung up. He was satisfied that her offer was sincere, and that it would be a good thing.

Thursday, August 19 came, and so did Nathan and Shara—several times. Shara was over two weeks late, so she suggested that they not even bother with condoms. Nathan used them anyway.

On Tuesday, the 24th, Nathan met Dr. Flowers in a Howard Johnson's just off I-95, to determine whether Miami would work out. They mutually decided it would, and that cemented that! He would begin work at the Miami church on October 1, 1965! The next day the Trinity University people called to invite Nathan to serve as chaplain to students, just as they had a day after he accepted his call from Christ Church, a year earlier. Aghast at such fickle fate, he tried, unsuccessfully, to laugh it off...

After leading a party for over thirty ninth graders, Nathan wrote Shara expressing his growing angst and fear that her probable pregnancy might entrap them both. Still, he pledged his all to his lady in waiting, and foreswore all doubts, no matter what...

Nathan preached twice on the August 29th, then hurried to the post office. *Just maybe...* After reading Shara's familiar, heart-breaking prayers for peace and resolution, still not quite accepting that she might be pregnant, Nathan sat to the task of writing his resignation letters to Dr. Morrison and to the leadership of the church. *Apart from guilt that I am deserting, my greatest feeling is one of enormous relief!*

Nathan's thirtieth birthday passed almost without his noticing, other than to contemplate his existential plight.

I don't see how things could be more harrowing, yet I'm increasingly aware of the miasma a-mixing, just over the horizon. God help us all!

After a bout of morning sickness, Shara wrote that she hoped Nathan would come and visit her in Pennsylvania while Melanie was visiting her parents the third weekend in September. She confirmed her plan to leave home Wednesday, September 8. Nathan didn't receive this letter, before even more hell broke loose!

Friday morning, September 3, Nathan was diligently attending a large backlog of tasks, prior to his leaving, when the receptionist knocked on his door. With wide eyes, she told him his father called and that Nathan was to call home, immediately.

"Is my mother dead?" he cried.

"No," said the receptionist, "It's your sister!"

"Patty has killed herself?" he blurted, mindlessly.

"No, Nathan; there has been an accident!"

A hurried call to a weeping father informed him that Patty had been killed by a military truck that ran into her car in Egypt. Mother was Daddy's greatest concern, however, as she was inconsolable.

"May I please speak to her," lamented the miserable son.

"Oh, Nathan! I wish it had been me! I wish it had been me! I'm going to die, anyway, soon, and it just isn't right that Patty should be killed. Are you coming home? Will you bring your babies? Oh, Nathan; I'm so heartbroken..."

"I know; Mama, I know. It breaks my heart, too. I love you, Mama. I'm coming home right away; and I'll bring your babies, Mama; I'm bringing your precious babies—and Lenore and myself. We all love you, Mama; we..."

The preacher was at a loss for other words, manifest tears filling the aching void, instead. Daddy told him not to come home, yet. The government approved a military flight for (Colonel) Tommy, in Germany, and Patty's body to be flown to NYC, hence to MacDill Air Force Base in Tampa and by hearse from there. Nathan was to stay put, until some idea of family arrival times and lodgings could be worked out.

"But, Daddy," he worried, "what about Mother? Shouldn't we get there as soon as possible?"

"Nathan, you're to do as you're told. We haven't been able to think clearly, I'm monitoring your mother's medications, and there is no room for you and your family, just yet, until we figure more things out."

That was that. Devastated, he called Lenore, who wept with him, both sensing a necessary re-cementing, during his grieving family's reluctant construction of the manifest architecture of death.

"Honey, I'll start packing; you tell whomever you have to tell what's happening, and we'll get through this, together, as usual."

"I know, 'Nore; I know. It is just that I'm not sure we'll get there before Mother dies. I'm afraid Patty's death will simply suck the remaining life right out of her."

"We'll get there soon enough, darling. Let's pray so."

Nathan turned to the other half of his heart–daring to ring Shara's home about 7:00 p.m., Sunday, September 5. Shocked to tears, too, she begged him to visit the next day. She needed him, and she was positive he needed her! And that, too, was so, though, to avoid even more pain for her, he didn't tell Lenore, she thinking that he would be at a new curriculum meeting in Charlotte. *I'll never get used to the sneaking; I hate it! I don't know how to be true to them both, at the same time!*

Further emboldened by his adoring presence–and their ardent lovemaking on Monday, September 6–neither quite convinced of her pregnancy–Shara put her plans for leaving into motion. Tuesday night, she snuck two suitcases out of her bedroom window to a frightened, but very game, Kathy, who took them to Manny, who hid them in the trunk of his car–the ready get-away vehicle.

Meanwhile, Nathan was on the phone, seeking further information. Daddy arranged train tickets for Nathan and family, leaving the seventh, the next day. Mother was sinking fast.

*

Before dawn, Wednesday, September 8, 1965, Shara snuck out of her bedroom window and ran two blocks to Manny's waiting car, where also sat Kathy, not allowing her best friend to leave without an escort and a fond farewell. They drove her north to Bledsoe, about twenty miles away, where Shara caught a bus to Prospect Park, PA. Long faced, but game, the confederates offered all manner of advice and counsel, telling her to keep them posted on her emergent life. Everybody hugged and cried, but she was determined and happy to be taking positive steps, finally, into her own future.

The twelve-hour bus trip, with one change in DC, went by inexorably, while she rehearsed the past two months in her mind, worrying about her poor mother and her beloved little siblings. Only one man tried to impose himself into her space, but she told him she was recovering from TB, which quickly moved him on.

Melanie was waiting for her at the bus station with a small bouquet of daisies–amid baby's breath. She hugged Shara with genuine admiration and appreciation (and perhaps a bit of jealousy), bidding her welcome. In her apartment, consisting of a large bedroom, a bathroom, a small kitchenette, and a spacious living room, Melanie provided an entire chest of drawers, a closet, and two-bathroom drawers. She would stay in her own bed; Shara could sleep on a foldout couch in the front living room, unless she wanted a foldaway cot, instead.

Knowing Shara must be tired and famished, Melanie prepared a hearty vegetable soup, with homemade pound cake, ice cream and strawberries for their simple repast, taken in her kitchenette.

"Melanie, I cannot thank you enough for allowing me this opportunity to step out mostly on my own, until I can become more settled–with a job and all."

"You're entirely welcome, Shara. I know something about being a single woman living alone, and not only will it help you, you'll provide me with company while you're here."

"Speaking of which, Melanie, do you have any expectations as to how long I might be able to stay?"

"None, whatsoever, Shara. We'll just take it a day at a time, regardless of how many days it takes. So please don't worry about a timeline or anything of the sort. Do you have everything you need?"

"I think so. I left so fast; I may have forgotten something. I left my mother a note, but I know she'll be terribly upset. My father will just be furious."

"Just let me know if you need anything I can supply. Have you enough money?"

"For the near term. I want to start looking for a job right away, though."

And so, it went. Shara ate with gusto. Melanie's efforts at small talk challenged them both, neither knowing what the other knew. Shara did not mention a possible baby, and Melanie did not mention Nathan, other than to express her sorrow about Patty–and Nathan's mother. They both shared hopes of meaningful work, so Shara could be about her new life. Melanie assured her she was welcome, then she went to bed, having an early shift.

Shara sat up watching Melanie's small black and white tv in the living room, until right before the eleven o'clock sharing hour with Nathan. To the couch-bed–very suddenly very alone. Comforting herself with her orgasm, which was exceptionally strong and vital, she wept herself to sleep, thinking about Nathan's and her bereaved families, but especially about her mother and siblings, whom she could almost hear crying...

*

Tears and bombastic recriminations were abundantly expressed in the Starr household. Upon going to awaken a sleepy-headed Shara, Donna discovered her note. Shara wrote simply that she loved everybody, was safe, but was leaving because she wanted to live her own life and not an extension of theirs. She added that she would contact them when she knew exactly what she would be doing. Meanwhile, they did not need to know where she was staying.

Big J. Carl was furious, storming about the house, threatening mayhem and disinheritance. Donna didn't tell her little ones, until Jennie read the note that her mother had left in the bathroom. Then, everybody but Carl was crying, whom he called "a bunch of babies."

There followed non-stop Keystone Kops scenes in and around the Starr home. Phone calls, Kathy's visit, denials, Manny calling about his date that night with Shara, Big J. Carl threatening ruination to anyone holding out on him. Kathy's parents querying Kathy; she maintaining absolute loyalty to her best friend, all ending with Big J Carl canvassing the neighborhood, seeking information. None was forthcoming...

Shara was free!

CHAPTER 40
THE VASTY HALL OF DEATH

Her cabined, ample Spirit,
it fluttered and failed for breath.
Tonight, it doth inherit
the vasty hall of Death.

Matthew Arnold

Nathan's little family detrained in Sutherland shortly after 6:00 p.m., July 10, 1965. Sister Jess met them at the station, issuing orders and warnings; who was to sleep in whose house; keep the kids quiet, as Mother is dying; don't bug Daddy, who is not speaking to anyone, waiting for Tommy to arrive with Betty's body and guarding Mother's morphine down to the last second.

Lenore shuttled the kids into a neighbor's home, while Nathan ran the short block to their old home. Charging through the side door, he heard the phone ring and stopped to answer it before he saw a soul or heard the screen door's familiar slam. It was Tommy; he and Patty's body had arrived in New York City and would be home tomorrow.

Nathan entered the kitchen where Daddy was perched, immobile, on a stool, staring at a ham sandwich. He looked up to see Allison and William hugging his second son, shook his hand with tears in his eyes, heard that Tommy and

Patty's body were on the way, offered him something to eat, then shuffled off upstairs to attend Mother.

As Nathan was about to bite down on his sandwich, a soft, insistent summons came from upstairs. Mrs. DePaul, the kind, old nurse who brought Nathan into the world, called down for all to come up. Nathan could hear Daddy sobbing.

Solemnly, the Scott family, minus the two oldest children, plus three sets of uncles and aunts, drooped up the stairs to Mother's bedroom. Nathan was shocked at the person he found lying at an angle, the wrong way, in her long-coveted, cherry wood, four-poster bed: an emaciated, pallid, deeply wrinkled, nearly bald, wild-eyed, non-focusing crone, barely recognizable as Mother, hands weakly flailing, totally uncomprehending of anything, except her pain.

Mrs. DePaul, Mother's midwife of old, smiled grimly and whispered to Nathan: "It's time!"

One by one, in order of age, Mother's and Daddy's brothers and sisters-in-law, and each of their present children knelt before her and whispered something into her unhearing ears. Everyone wept softly. When it was Nathan's turn. Smoothing what little hair she had near her forehead, matted and strangely cool and damp with the sweat of death, he whispered as he kissed her sunken cheek, "Mama, I'm so sorry; please forgive me! I love you! Your babies are here for you, too. I love you! Goodbye—and, and—God keep you."

Last of all, 12-year-old Mildred, with Down's Syndrome, the smallest Scott child, put her arms around Mother's neck, as she did every night, not seeming to notice her appearance or distance, and sang-song to her beloved Mother her bedtime prayer: "God bless Mother, God bless Daddy, God bless Tommy, Patty, Jessie, Nathan, Michael, Stephen, Allison, William, Herman, Mildred, Pinky Cat, and Old Blue Doggie. Make Mildred a good girl; and keep us all safe, we baig for Chrissake, Amen."

"Amen," caromed around the small room grown enormous as its own "vasty hall of death," its walls absorbing helpless gasps.

The Scotts were notably Scots and honored their roots. Not speaking it, they needed a wake to honor the dead, while spitting in the eye of Death. Everyone but Daddy and Mrs. DePaul milled around on the old house's wrap-around porch a moment or two, and then joined Nathan, Michael, and Jess walking the two blocks to the waterfront and out on to the Marina's docks. Whereupon this terribly grieving family began to tell jokes and family stories, laughing and carrying on as though they were at a wedding party. Gone were the tears, except for sudden gulps and bated sobs at certain recollections, hailed and regaled. For a solid hour, this motley, multi-generational family taunted death with humor and good will, none wanting to dwell too long on what was happening back at the Scott homestead.

Thinking it was time, the Scotts trooped back up their street, *en masse*, greeting long time neighbors who came to their front yards offering condolences. Upon entering the spacious Scott yard, their brave jollity bred a sudden sobriety, for there was a hearse parked next to the huge, old oak, long adored by all, but most of all by Mother—and two men carrying a stretcher, holding her still, small frame, covered with a revealing, nondescript, white cloth, as though she were as fragile and weightless as a butterfly.

The awkward, little congregation, standing around on Scott's little acre, on one foot and then the other, watched as the two men finished their grim task, packing her in. Finally, doors closed decorously, the old hearse, spouting clouds of gray exhaust, drove Mother out of the broken cement driveway, between the beloved camphor tree and the cattley guava hedge—and into the pregnant bliss of oblivion.

So, Mother, too, joined "...the innumerable caravan which moves, to that mysterious realm where each shall take His chamber in the silent halls of death...."

Other Scotts, more relatives, and friends began to arrive, along with more food, felicitations, and genuine grief than Nathan thought possible in his small hometown, even for his vaunted Mother. All were heartened by the ancient tradition of feeding death, defying mortality with every bite of donated meats, vegetables, casseroles, salads, breads, fruits, juices, desserts, and trimmings.

Nathan welcomed dear and dark Miss Ada, their Black washer woman and Mother's confederate in surreptitious good deeds in the "quarters," approaching the side steps with a steaming platter. They hugged, she crying softly, praising God that Mother Jewel was no longer in pain, and that Patty was surely with her in heaven. Nathan thanked her, profusely, invited her in, and offered to drive her back, when she demurred. She wanted to walk the five blocks, she said, saying a prayer for the Scotts with each step.

As the mourning family grew by cousins and in-laws, no one went hungry for days, courtesy of a neighborhood and a town deeply appreciative of all that Mother and Patricia had meant to them. The Scotts were deeply moved—and very well fed.

Col. Tommy, escorting Patty's body, arrived at MacDill Field on Saturday, September 11, where a limousine and a hearse drove him home—Patty to the undertaker. Nathan was improvising on their old, well-worn, upright piano, when Tommy walked up the steps to the wrap-around porch, entered the house, allowing the screen door to slam, as all had done most of their childhoods. Nathan could almost hear Mother's eternal admonition, "Don't slam the door; you'll tear it off its hinges!" The brothers shook hands, and Nathan followed Tommy into the kitchen to death-darkened Daddy.

"Tom-my!" bawled the stricken, older man, having waited for this moment to let go. He reached out to his first born in utter misery, coughing and sputtering his grief in his son's trembling embrace. Everything stopped, while father and son held–and held on–signifying and commiserating this family's god-awful, double loss.

On Sunday, September 12, all sat together for the Morning Worship service in the church where Daddy was a deacon, Mother a favorite adult Sunday School teacher, and from whence two Scott men heard their calls to the ministry. They filled three, long rows, while listening to the new minister, the Rev. Maynard, preach on the resolute and overpowering Love of God. Nathan and Lenore, sitting together, held hands. Shara floated to his consciousness but was gently shaded by ambient holiness–and relentless remorse.

Sunday afternoon, Nattie and Beth charmed everyone with their antics. Knowing that Mother would have loved them to distraction, everyone felt her absence a little keener in their presence. Nathan took time to walk behind the house to the clothesline where his cathartic confrontation with Patty had so recently occurred. There, remembering their poignant extremities, he wept his private farewells to his much beloved, older sister.

*

Immediately, he wanted to tell Shara everything! Thus, he risked a solitary sojourn to the waterfront to use its pay phone. Shara was almost beside herself with excitement as Melanie handed her the phone.

"Hi, darling, how are you?"

"Oh, Nathan, I had no idea it could be you. Melanie and I were just about to go to a movie when the phone rang. Wait a minute, let me close the door–never mind, Melanie went outside. How are you? I love you! I'm so sorry to hear about your sister, and now your mother! It must be so very hard for you. Tell me that you love me–and tell me–tell me everything, Na—"

"Whoa, Shara! Take a breath. I assume you must be feeling okay, from your energy. That makes me happier than I've been since I got down here. I'm all right; thanks for asking. Of course, I love you, and I need nothing more than I need your love, right now. Yes, it has been hard, but not as terrible as I thought it might be. I have to tell you that Lenore has been a real trooper, helping me, the kids and everyone in sight."

"I knew she would be, darn it, but I'm glad. I wish I could be there, for I would help and take care of things, too."

"I'm sure you would do just that, Shara."

"I'm sorry, Nathan; I don't mean to be jealous, but I need you so terribly much, now. Nothing is happening in Glocca except pent up desire, and I'm now about 99% sure I'm pregnant–and I must tell you that I'm extremely happy about that–about having your baby! But I babble; tell me everything."

Must I see both sides of that welcome/disastrous news? One is the gladness Shara is expressing because she believes we'll be married by time our baby arrives. The other side, of course, is how this disastrous news may affect everything else, pushing us to act precipitously, or even worse, not to act at all. I must allow her happiness–and see the future through her trusting, hopeful eyes, even though I am scared shitless–for us, both!

She hadn't landed a job, yet, but had some leads, and Melanie was being very nice to her–but her focus was on him. Conversely, Nathan felt the vacuum in his heart fill to overflowing with her, describing only the basics of his interactions, experiences, and plans. Lenore and their children will remain with Allison, the twins, Mildred, and Daddy a while after the funeral, and he will drive Stephen back to seminary. If all goes well, he might be in her arms the following weekend. Shara was ecstatic; Melanie was planning to visit her parents, then, and had been worrying about leaving Shara. They hung up while desperately hanging on...

*

Wanting—needing—to see Patty one last time, Daddy insisted on a viewing of both bodies at the funeral home Sunday evening. It was ghastly! Patty was made up by people who never knew her, and she looked a ghoulish, wax shadow of the vibrant redhead she was in life. Mother's body appeared to be a wilted, desiccated corpse—little more.

When Tommy and Nathan brought Daddy into the viewing room, Daddy ran to Patty's casket, crying her name, trying to hug her. The two brothers gently guided him toward composure, so he could greet the long line of consoling visitors, then instructed that the caskets be closed.

Though old Dr. King had retired, and Rev. Maynard was now installed, both ministers co-officiated at both services. Dr. King, who knew and deeply loved both women, said he would certainly try to serve, but worried about breaking down. At the appointed hour, on Monday, September 13, the church was packed and overflowing, all come to praise God for the lives of Mary Jewel Best Scott and Patricia Best Scott—and to mourn their passing. The Scott family again exhausted three full rows.

"Fear not, little flock . . .," intoned Rev. Maynard, and the funeral service began. Dr. King did more than get through the service without breaking down; he was almost beatific, weeping his love of God and the two, departed souls, striking exactly the right tones between deep respect and admiration and the loneliness of grief—his and others.' His emphasis was on the Love of, and for, God.

Nathan was very pleased to see a dozen Black faces in the church and, later, at the graveside, dear Miss Ada and her brood among them. He remembered Mother's inroads into the "quarters," with her special brand of low-key good will—and wily social and political manipulations—all without Daddy knowing. It was her subtle doing that opened the town's library and small beach to members of that stalwart race, long before any civil rights legislation.

Additionally, Mother was a focal point for special projects succoring dire, personal needs of some of the Sutherland Blacks, who were, nonetheless, kept pent in their place, in his small, wretchedly segregated, Southern town.

Nathan recalled, as a teen, how pleased and proud of Mother he was when he saw some of his own clothes on the backs of young Black children, and not a few new pairs of shoes, some folding money, and other needed items hidden in the basket of clothes he toted to Miss Ada for washing, each Saturday. It was Miss Ada who took proper care of both the clothes and the contraband obtained for the neediest of her race. They called her "Mother Jewel," and Daddy was never the wiser. Nathan never forgot the lessons in overcoming prejudice with love and active concern that Mother Jewel lived so quietly.

The last hymn sung, and the benediction offered, the Scott family was ferried to the old Sutherland Cemetery. As appropriate, the graveside service was short and to the point. God and His love were invoked; Mother and Patty were remembered, again, and praised for their good works; mourners were comforted by scripture; all were admonished to awareness of their own mortality; and the two blessed women's bodies were committed back to the earth, side by side—and to God—in the vasty halls of death. Nathan deflected Rev. Maynard's offer for him to pronounce the benediction, so Mother's favorite blessing, learned at her beloved Papa's knee, was sung, instead.

Bless be the tie that binds our hearts in Christian love; the fellowship of kindred minds is like to that above.

Thus, did the Wheel turn, waiting for no one to catch up; not mourner, not friend nor family, and especially not lovers—or their pregnant expectations.

Is it no small thing
To have enjoyed the sun
To have lived light in the spring,
To have loved, to have thought, to have done;
To have advanced true friends, and beat down baffling foes?
Matthew Arnold

Forgive, O Lord, my little jokes on Thee,
And I'll forgive Thy great big one on me.

Robert Frost

CHAPTER 41
TRAINED AND TRAINING

Desire is always desire for another person, mediated through their body–not merely a body that is the necessary instrument of gratification, but a body that reveals the person, most significantly of course in the face, the voice and smile… Localized pleasure and sexual release are not the aim and object of desire.

All love, not just erotic love, is embodied…. The incarnational, sacramental nature of erotic love… harmonizes well, if not with many traditional expressions of Christianity, then certainly, with the essential incarnational, sacramental logic of the faith.

Paul Avis on Roger Scrutin's "Sexual Desire: A Moral Philosophy of the Erotic"

Thursday, September 16, 1965, found two brothers in their black suits, sitting in the club car of an ACLRR passenger train, speeding north. Talking softly, they enjoyed the familiar, hypnotic rhythm of clickity-clacking wheels rolling over the slight gaps between rail sections. In reverie, they watched the undulating telephone wires diving and sounding, like a school of dolphins frolicking beside the onrushing train.

Before boarding, there were teary goodbyes, childish kisses, and Lenore's fervent embrace pressed on and into Nathan's body. He and Stephen grinned their way through archival family picture taking and both made their tender obeisances to their myriad kin–and to their beloved, boyhood home: "Scott's Little Acre," now bereft of its quintessential heart. They were on their way to pick up Nathan's station wagon in Wilmington, thence to drive Stephen to his seminary in Virginia. Nathan would venture farther north, to reclaim his courageous, recently uprooted, pining, likely pregnant Shara.

"Nathan, you look all but spent–pretty much as I feel. You and Lenore all right? I thought I noticed a little this and that…"

"Behold, the wise, junior seminarian belly-buttons his preacher brother, diagnosing angst and asking for secrets to be unfurled and hoisted aloft…."

"What secrets, Scott-head? I already know everything there is to know! You told Mother that I am the 'pick of the litter.'"

"That was a slip of the tongue, Stephen. I meant to say, 'prick of the shitter,' because that's where you hung out– to hang out–most of the time."

"Surely you jest! Nonetheless, if you'd like to tell me anything, I'm all zipped up and ready."

"Stephen, I'm up to my immortality in fear and trembling, and my foundations are shaking me half to death."

"Are you mostly worried about things theological, psychological, or carnal, Nathan?"

"There's a difference? Why don't you tell me what you have divined might be besetting my *existenz*, and I'll tell you if you hit the mark?"

"I suspect that you and Lenore aren't doing all that well, that's all. I don't have a clue why, though."

Against QI's specific admonition, Nathan began a long, long-needed, risky confession: "Sure, you do, if you think about it. You were part of a crucial *entr'acte*, once upon a time, way back there in 1964, when you offered to bring me my .22 caliber rifle, should things go badly between me and an irate father."

"Great Scot, Scott, you mean Shara's dad–and Shara–and you? Is she–herself, is she–could she be...?"

"Living and moving and having her being almost completely complected with mine."

"What? I don't understand. How is Shara that important in your life? I kinda thought, maybe Melanie. She is with you guys so much and often, but Shara?"

"Two cigars, Ladies and Gentlemen, for this young prophet of perfidy. He hast hit two out of a possible three."

"Don't tell me there's another person out there who is 'almost completely complected' with you, too? Who?"

"God, of course. Aren't you up on your Abelard?"

"Slow down, Nathan. I've only got one bat of a brain, and you're pitching things by me so fast, I can't even see them, must less hit them."

So it went, until Nathan tired of playing banter-ball with such serious subjects, threw caution to the hurdling train's passing scenes and simply enumerated forty-one awful and salient truths of his early, recent, and present predicaments, *seriatim*–from boyhood circle jerks and porn, through early abuse at home, Lenore, sex, marriage, children, jobs, Melanie, more sex, Shara, confounding, wonderful love, Tabormont sex, Big J Carl, her absconding, finally believing herself to be pregnant, and staying with Mistress Melanie.

Pained silence, as Stephen searched for his idealized, older brother amongst forty-one shards of fallible clay strewn all around the pedestal of his erstwhile admiration. By the time Nathan finished his long, detailed reprise of the past, and answered a zillion bug-eyed questions, they had arrived at Wilmington. Off the train, they loaded their stuff into Nathan's wagon and began their drive north to Stephen's seminary.

"Forty-plus, incredibly complicated events and situations that may lead you to either disaster or fulfillment, huh, Scott-head? Dammit, man, what on earth are you going to do?"

"Improvise; let whatever happens, maybe? What I am going to do, after I drop you off, however, is high-tail it to Prospect Park, to have and to hold Miss Shara Day Starr, while mistress-no-longer-Melanie is gone for several days. Actually, I'm contemplating telling Shara about Melanie very soon; maybe tomorrow–at least before I return to Wilmington."

"Wow! That would be Number 42? What do you think she'll say–and feel?"

"She'll be a little hurt–maybe a lot hurt, but, if I know her, and I do, she'll be forgiving, understanding and accepting, when she realizes that I gave Mellie up out of fealty to her! Also, after I come clean, I expect she'll be a helluva lot more intrigued about Melanie."

"Nathan, don't you care about all the pain and harm you're fostering?"

"Of course, I do, Stephen. I hate the strife and pain, the lies, and the sneaking, and I certainly love my wife and children, but I love Shara so much that, somehow (and there's the rub), somehow, I believe that if I stick with her, it'll all work out."

"It's not up to me to tell you what a pipe dream that is, Nathan. You're too smart to actually believe there may be a way to hang on to Shara, a baby, and Lenore and the kids, too."

"Greater faith have you not seen in all of Israel?"

"Something like that. I love you, Nathan, and if I could, I'd try to disabuse you of fantasy. Any chance Christian morality–or critical thinking–can kick in?"

"Would you understand me better were I to say, simply, 'I can't help it!?'"

"Maybe, but could I ask you what you will you do if Shara really is pregnant?"

"Go ahead, ask."

"Ho-ho. How can you treat such a likelihood with laughter?"

"To keep from crying," in unison.

"That's really the poser, Stephen, and, honest to God, I don't really know, right this minute, though I have thought of some alternatives–each one with its own potential pitfalls and cave-ins."

"Such as?"

"Damn! You would make me face up to this, wouldn't you? Maybe that's the reason I'm telling you."

"And?"

"For starters, maybe Lenore, whom I still love, will enlarge her great heart even more and allow Shara to join us–an extended family, sorta. That would be ideal, because I could stay in the church, keep my family."

"You're dreaming Nathan. That ain't gonna happen."

"It's my nightmare, and I can spice it up if I want to."

"What other, more likely scenarios have you dreamt up?"

"Well, there's always the possibility that I will just dump everything else, hold on to Shara and our child, and start a new life, somehow, somewhen, somewhere . . ."

". . . over the rainbow," warbled his smiling, little brother.

"See? Isn't humor better?"

"What else?"

"Tough it out, I reckon, Stephen–improvise–keep on keeping on–with Shara, with Lenore and the kids, with my new job in Miami and the church at large, with the rest of the family, and see what happens. I honestly do not know. Maybe Shara will decide on her own to make the biggest sacrifice, either to keep the baby or put it up for adoption and do something other than being screwed by Nathan Scott–literally and figuratively. She mentions that sacrifice as a possibility, when she's feeling her love for me the most—and her over-riding fear of hurting Lenore, the kids, and others."

"That's the first, half-way rational scenario you've mentioned, Nathan, but wouldn't it be incredibly difficult for both of you?"

"'Impossible,' is a better word. She's hoping for a way we can keep the baby and be together, somehow. I couldn't let her sacrifice alone. I love her—and I need her—too much. 'What selfish gods we be, to seek someone seeking me.'"

"I've heard you quote that, before, Nathan. Is it yours?"

"Just one of my existential realizations, Stephen; something of a universal truth, maybe?"

"Could be. I certainly recognize it as part of my own equation."

Existential pause.

"Sooo, you don't really have a plan, do you?"

"Nope; but I've come this far without—without…"

"…Getting caught?"

"Sorta. Ever since Daddy beat the shit out of me when I was fourteen—for nothing—I've become pretty good at plotting and avoiding things that might cause me trouble. It's a learned skill that most of our earliest ancestors evolved, or we wouldn't be here. Good ol' avoidance behaviors. Still, avoidance is one notch better than escape, any day."

"Yeah, I know, Nathan, I don't much like it as a way of life, either. I, too, learned that skill, if it is a skill, very early on. I was in the kitchen when all of that happened with you and Daddy, and it scared the shit out of me, too. I had already learned to avoid Daddy, by then, but that little tragedy taught me to practice serious avoidance, as if it were another badge on my Eagle Scout sash."

"Survival of the wiliest?"

"That, and of those with the most courage, too, I guess—that would be Shara, wouldn't it, Nathan—and you and Lenore, too?"

"'Coward, take my coward's hand'—we're about to step off of the precipice without a parachute, literally praying that God—and improvising—will provide."

"Hey, I remember that movie: "Home of the Brave," wasn't it, with Frank Lovejoy? 'Coward, take my coward's hand' is a misnomer, though, don't you think? What they were really talking about is courage—courage to trust, courage to try; courage to believe in something bigger than oneself? Weren't those the points you kept emphasizing when you showed it at camp?"

"See? I was right; you are the prick of the shitter."

"Flattery will get you . . . if you don't watch out."

"I'll try to avoid it..."

"So, you have no plan for anyone, except for love—in its various forms—assiduous avoidance, prayer, courage, and hope?"

"Pretty much. Any ideas you'd like to offer?"

"Unless you do leave Lenore—and everything else—maybe adoption, first, and then see what happens—taking things a step at a time."

"That's what I meant by improvising—keeping on keeping on, Scott-head, and toughing it out, although I think Shara would be doing most of the toughing. Which brings me to this: all this talk is theoretical. Even to think about giving up our baby, or asking Shara to do so, or my stepping aside, or any of it threatens me in ways you cannot imagine. Frankly, I think I would pretty much die... I love her so damned much!"

Long pause, while Stephen hugged his brother.

"I hear you, Scott. I almost wish I could go with you, tonight. I'd like to show Shara I respect her, feel for and with her, and that I love her, too."

"Another time, Stephen. Though I truly appreciate your empathy, as well as your efforts at understanding and accepting our plight. I'm not sure whether I'll tell her that I have confided in you. I think I will, though. I don't like keeping anything from her, just as I wouldn't want her keeping things from me."

"Scott-head, can there ever really be that much love between two people, to allow your vaunted 'elasticity,' without risking–everything?"

"Good question, Stephen. Perhaps I'll let you know, betimes.

"Don't expect me to understand or agree with everything you've told me, Nathan, but you may count on me to accept you and love you as my brother, just the same–and to keep my mouth shut."

"Thanks, Stephen; I needed that. I suspect the mechanics of Eros and my dubious activities with three lovely ladies are not the only thoughts carousing in your excellent brain, just now, right?"

"Yes, of course; I admit to a certain excitement trying to imagine... But I'm confused about a lot of things–mostly, how you can do–be–all of this and still serve the church–love God–be a Christian, much less a preacher? Don't you feel hypocritical?"

"Yes, yes, no, no, and maybe."

"Huh?"

"That's a useful mind/word motif that Shara and I use, when faced with questions that have complicated variables and answers. Looking at it from such perspectives helps us to understand and answer more completely, less facilely–and more honestly than yes or no, black or white."

"Explain, please."

"You asked about my feeling hypocritical: First *Yes*, of course, I know my behavior and my deepest thoughts are in contradiction to some tenets of the church—and to at least some of my marriage and ordination vows—even though the ones I feel are the most important and productive of Love, I try, very hard, to keep. That's a sad and regrettable given, but it's not the complete answer. I hasten to add that the hypocrisy you may discern stems primarily from outmoded, formalistic standards and the lockstep judgment by those who insist that we keep them—especially those with no idea of the truth and benefits of elsewise thinking. I feel the weight of that implied judgment, even though I feel no sin in our actions, at all."

"Go on."

"Second *Yes*, I feel very deeply the conflicts that may harm my Lenore and my babies. That I haven't figured out, yet, other than to just have Shara move in with us and be part of the family—a second wife, so to speak, as I said, earlier. And, yes, I know that may seem sexist and—and probably ain't gonna happen, dammit. Absent those consequences, I know Lenore to be wonderfully accommodating, accepting, and forgiving. What an incredible woman she is, Stephen. You know that don't you?"

"Of course, I do, Nathan. And what about the two 'nos?'"

"First *No*, I'm not entirely hypocritical, because our loves, both Agape and Eros, for Shara, and hers for me, have created a universe of good: made me a much better communicator, listener, leader, teacher, preacher, musician, youth worker, organizer and person, in just about every way possible—our Eros, made possible only through pairing it with our Agape, has produced incarnational, near sacramental, righteous results. For what it's worth—their incarnation in us has made me much better in almost all personal areas."

"Including baby-making!"

"Ouch! But you ignored all my other benefits from this God-allowed—likely willed—affair. Besides, did I mention that the great, existential disquietude I have almost always had about my life, my calling, and my sense of self has been transformed utterly, for the good? I'm calmer, abler, much more fulfilled and positively directed and challenged, in spite of present and impending chaos.

"My love for Shara is peremptory—a love that drives almost all competition out, due to its strength, character and depth. It manifests in caring, primarily, for the other person. You've heard the phrase, 'the expulsive power of a new-found affection?' Triple—no, quintuple that, and you're approaching what I mean by 'peremptory love.' Get it?"

"Got it!"

"Good! Now, for the last no. *No*, I don't feel so hypocritical because both Lenore and Shara know everything, except about Melanie. They know everything else, and they love me, anyway. God, of course, is in on everything."

Awakened, QI thought: *Hold it there, preacher, Lenore knows nothing about Melanie, specifically, or about Shara being pregnant, or your promise to marry her. Even if you haven't told Lenore these things, for fear of hurting her, I'd say that is hypocritical.*

"And, somehow, I try to believe that I can work my way through all of this, even by improvising, without doing serious or permanent damage to anybody. That's the challenge I'm facing, and that's also the *maybe*, as in maybe I'll feel hypocritical unless I do everything I possibly can to forestall harm to Lenora, Melanie, Shara, my babies, the church, and now you. If I can do that, any hypocrisy won't matter very much. See?"

"I hear what you are saying, Nathan, but I'm a long way from being convinced that you're not already doing permanent damage. Nothing is quite so permanent as a baby."

"Nor as wonderful, potential, beautiful, fulfilling, loved, and loving, either."

The conversation quieted as they arrived at Stephen's dorm. The two brothers sat in the silence of their intimacy, not wanting to break the fraternal, incarnate bond between them. They had discussed and discovered more about each other and their convergent, if not perfectly aligned, views. Mentally exhausted, but closer than ever, they off-loaded Stephen's suitcase and stood in the darkness looking at each other, then hugged.

Aware that he risked, big time, by telling his younger brother everything, he had desperately needed to tell someone whom it would not destroy. Still, he worried, while sailing up the road toward Prospect Park, that he might have overburdened him. *Another guilt to weigh and pack onto my Sisyphus burthen!*

CHAPTER 42
NESTING

Hither and thither spins
The Windborne, mirroring soul;
A thousand glimpses wins
And never sees a whole.

Matthew Arnold

Life shrinks or expands in proportion to one's courage.

Anais Nin

About 11:00 p.m., Nathan entered an all-night drug store near Melanie's, hoping to find some breath mints, freshen up a bit, and buy a small gift for Shara. He had not seen her since Monday, September 6–ten days–and then for only a few, fast-paced hours, two days before she absconded.

My God, our entire universe has flip-flopped since then!

His first two tasks accomplished, he roved through the store, stopping at a charm display. Shara loved the charms he had given her, including the silver mailbox, with its wee *billet-doux*, so why not? He considered two charms: a silver hope chest and a pair of discretely nude lovers kneeling and kissing, spinning in a small, thin hoop. The nudie charm won, of course. He had it gift wrapped, bought a blank greeting card, and sat down to pen his accustomed doggerel.

Thursday, September 16, 1965, two blocks from your
arms!

> Ringed in love, this couple kneels
> and presses, flesh to flesh.
> How like us, my Darling Core,
> this couple seems to be,
> For they will hold forevermore,
> and we will love, eternally!

> I love you as joy loves laughter!
> Nathan

At Melanie's, entering the small foyer, he stood before her door, hat on head, bag on floor, heart in throat, and bowels in uproar. Knocking, he waited–and waited–and waited, some more.

"Who is it?" came a sleepy, heart-rending voice, unsure and cautious, at 11:30 at night.

"The Fuller Brush Man. Want to sample my wares?"

A shriek of realization, prolonged fumbling with double locks and door chain, and a crying, laughing, kissing, hugging, jumping, holding, patting, babbling, overwhelming Shara inhabited him–doubling his heartbeat and easing forty-plus, disquieting challenges to his *existenz*.

I am home!

Nathan swept his darling purpose into his arms, carrying her like a waif–this kissing, hugging, crying sweetness–through the front door, making straight for Melanie's bed. There, he laid her down, as gently as color on blossoms. She would not, could not, let him go, hugging where she touched, kissing where she looked, and looking where she felt, as she swept his smiling, sacramental corpus with ravishing eyes.

Softly blubbering her love and relief, with jeweled tears of joy, she drew him down to her body eagerly splayed just for him, in all the world, and felt the familiar, confirming counsels of connection crowning her joy, adding the luster of lust to her precious realization.

"You are here; you are truly, totally here! Oh, God, thank you; thank you; thank you!"

QI had little time to consider, as their delirious hearts exiled logic and sense, transformed seconds into months and minutes into years of joy and restoration. Her nightgown around her neck, two young breasts pointed the way to the cessation of waiting. He caroused in her delicious softs and curves, inhaling her musks, cradling, crying her name. Releasing his imprisoned self, he willingly followed her instinctive, coaxing contours, until he joined her, in her, as surely, no man had ever been so conjoined!

Such were the heats of their desire, fanned into corporeal conflagration, purging their fears and anxieties, welding them, together, with the atoning coals of fire from God's most perfect altar, again and again, until the very sounds of their sentient tendering, amid the soaring voices of their manifold, mutual love, prayed, "Here am I! Spend me!"

And it was so!

Puddling in the aftermath of the exquisite, the happy couple lay util, amidst their reverie of release and restoration, Nathan suddenly remembered his suitcase, still outside her apartment door—he hoped. Flopping nude, he opened her door, peered left and right, grabbed his suitcase and Shara's little gift, and fell backward into the living room, smack into the equally naked Shara, bowling them both over, into a clunking clatter that would surely wake sleeping neighbors, if not the dead.

"Shhh," they hissed, in abrupt, jocose caution. Nathan helped her up, fearing that he may have hurt her—or disturbed that which he was almost certain grew within her, and quickly closed the door.

"Are you all right?"

"Yes, Silly, but I'm glad I landed on my butt, instead of my head. I'm afraid our upstairs neighbor will think I've fallen—which I did.

Back abed, Nathan attended Shara's delicious prattle about her sneaking out of her home, her friendly send off, her bus ride, her first days with Melanie, her beginning search for a job, her monumental desire, and sundry other aspects of her new life. Half-attended, was QI's unwelcome prate about *when and how I should tell her about my long, deliciously aggravating—and utterly complicating—affair with Mistress Melanie—who, even now, is hauntingly present, as we occupy her bedroom—and her bed—where, not so incidentally, I most recently fucked my dear wife!*

Fearing a tempest, he was reluctant to roil the gentle waters of their reunion, just yet. We should just sleep, and I should wait until after the breakfast Shara is telling me she will prepare, come daylight. We'll let sweet love, sweet sex, and sweet sleep occupy us.

Spending their first, full night, ever, in the same bed, they slept the softest of sleeps, as though forever...

Came the dawn, opening their unbelieving eyes to the delicious reality of the other. Hearkening to the silken luxuries of love's naked flesh, the happy couple finally roused themselves to break their fast.

"Shara, if you're pregnant, you certainly don't look it. Your belly is as flat and lean as ever. I love the way your breasts have developed, but that could be a function of normal growth. I've read that women peak, physically, around eighteen, and that would be you, Miss Body Beautiful of 1965."

"Thank you, Sir," came the happy response, half lost to him in the sound of beating eggs. "I don't notice any changes, at all, except for my boobs, other than a bit of morning sickness, now and then, worrying Melanie."

"So, you and Melanie have discussed this? What was her reaction to the probability?"

"Well, at first, she sorta fussed at me for not telling her when I wrote her. It bothered her that I might have withheld such important information. I reassured her a dozen times, so she believes that we didn't know. We still have no confirmation except a missed period and morning sickness."

"Gad! I haven't even told Lenore, yet, but I'll wager she'll know as soon as she talks with Melanie. I'll tell her right away, though I suspect she suspects, anyway. Regardless, now that Melanie knows, perhaps she could help you get an appointment with a good ob/gyn, soon—maybe even hers? We need to make sure everything is okay, as well as to get all the information, prescriptions, and anything else needed, including a schedule of checkups, assuming you'll still be in the area."

"I think she'll be glad to do that, honey."

Pause

"Nathan?"

"Shara?"

"Am I a baby for being a little frightened?"

"Most natural thing in the world, but I suspect there are other things in that facile brain of yours worrying you, too."

Silence.

"I don't want to talk about it, now, Nathan. I just want to fix us the breakfast I've been planning since I got on the bus and have us eat it together in our own kitchen—well, sorta—and be a normal couple, for a change."

Cooking noises couldn't disguise the sudden heaviness in the room—the weight of huge present and future challenges, yet to be discussed. It was soon replaced, however, by the lightness of disarming aromas of good bacon, freshly baked biscuits, and scrambled cheese eggs. Nathan quietly set the table, squeezed oranges for juice, and put half a banana on each plate. Then he sat at table and watched his prim and proper paramour cooking breakfast—wearing nothing but her new, nudie charm around her neck.

"I lie awake thinking about what we'll say to each other, when it really comes down to it." Shara broke the silence. "Melanie has asked a few probing questions; it can't be all that comfortable, having an 18-year-old, probably pregnant novice in just about everything but sex, crowding her in her own place. Let's discuss that. Why do you think she's being so, so...?"

"...Magnanimous?"

"Yes, that's the word. Oh, you'd be proud of me; I try to do the crossword in the Inquirer ever–ever*!*–day, and my vocabulary is improving. I want to be able to write and speak as well as you, and I will, someday. Have you noticed any difference?"

"Definitely! I have noticed you leaping ahead of the curve in every way. In fact, I need to tell you a few things, too. I had a long talk with Stephen on the train and later, in the car. I hope it won't shock you to learn that I told him everything."

With eyes almost as big as the food-laden plates she put on the table, she said, "You didn't!"

"'Fraid so, Miss Nekked—be careful you don't dangle your charm—or your nipples—in your eggs."

"Tell me! What did he say? Does he hate me? You told him everything, including our sex and maybe the baby?"

"'Maybe the baby.' There's a phrase that merits a whole other conversation, darling. We've got to slow down and take things a step at a time. So far, this morning (mmm, these eggs are perfect!), so far, we've walked up to four or five, important conversations, and somehow backed off each one.

Where to begin? Would you please pass the blackberry jam—your biscuits are light as feathers, honey."

"Thanks, they're one of the things I really know how to bake. Now you see why it's been so hard not being able to really communicate with you, ever since I got here. I haven't even asked you about your mother and Patty. Oh, Nathan, I was so upset when you called to tell me about Patty, then when you called for exactly fifty-two seconds to tell me about your mother, it was even worse. I cried and cried, just thinking about how hard it must be for you, for Lenore, for Stephen and William, and your entire family!"

"That's six! Anyone wanna go for our seventh heaven?"

"I do think of all of it as heaven, Nathan—at least about most of it—about us—I do, or I would simply sink into the ground, the challenges are so big. And—and it is heaven being here, together, eating our breakfast naked, as if we were married—I feel like we are married, Nathan. Do you?"

"You know I do, Shara, and I, too, want that to happen as soon as we can all get on steady tracks—tracks that will eventually lead to the same station: marriage."

Watch it; promise only what you know!

"Yes. I'm aware that we will have to be on separate tracks, at least for a while, but what about the 'maybe baby?' I'll do it if I must, but I don't much want to go through that without you being right there with me, throughout—preferably as my husband! Do you think…?"

Melanie's phone rang, insistently, stopping their disparate, free form ramble through their vicissitudes and opportunities, the most important one still forming in Shara's mouth.

"I better answer it. Melanie hasn't told everybody in her family about me, yet. In fact, one of the reasons she went home this weekend was to tell them. I'm a little scared."

Shara picked up the phone on the fourth ring. It was Melanie's sister, Shelly, giving Shara a chance to meet her via telephone and to take a message.

"My heart was beating so fast I almost couldn't hear her!"

"You did well. Come here."

Taking her naked self to his lap, she pulled his face into her breasts, pressed him hard into her, and trembled. Then, she was gone–into the bathroom, where he heard the clear evidence of morning sickness.

"'Maybe the baby,' my foot!" he exclaimed to her empty chair before he rushed to help.

"What a waste of a good breakfast," Shara wailed, as she emerged, wiping her face with a damp washrag.

"I'm so sorry, Shara," he empathized, walking her to the bed. "You lie down a little, and I'll clean up. Do you want me to save you a bacon and egg biscuit?"

"Ugh! Don't even talk about it, or I'll throw up, again. Just clean up any way you want, and we'll get to, ugh, food later."

Twenty minutes later, dishes washed, leftovers stored, the kitchen immaculate, Nathan joined his Naked Maja in bed.

"Now, sweetheart, how are you feeling?"

"Much better, thank you. Usually, it goes away within fifteen or twenty minutes, and the cold rag on my forehead and wrists helped a lot, thanks. I just got too worked up, trying to cover everything worrying me at once, then the damn phone rang… Anyway, let's talk about Melanie. Why do you think she's doing this–going out of her way to accommodate me–us, for she seems to know most everything?"

"Do you have a theory?"

"I think she has a serious crush on you, Nathan, but how does that fit into what she's doing?"

I'm glad you're feeling better, though, darling–and that you are lying down, for I have–I have a huge confession relevant to that very question."

The bed rustled and rocked with Shara's reaction, virtually spinning in mid-air, to face him where he sat. Her visage was a mask of expectancy, muscles ready to create whatever face might be required.

"Go on–but if it's really bad, say it all at once, so I don't have to dread it very long."

"I hope you won't think it's so bad, Shara–nothing about calling it quits or anything like that."

Her sigh of relief took an eon of two seconds, before she said, "I'm glad–Nathan, promise me that if you ever do make such a decision, you'll not keep me hanging, and that you'll not try to soften the blow. Just tell me, straight out, without frills or window dressing, okay?"

"You are a very courageous woman, honey, but you don't have to worry about that. I love you far too much even to contemplate such an impossible scenario."

"I believe you; I have to believe you, Nathan, and I trust you, totally."

"Then, let's trot that trust out about now, for I must tell you that Melanie and I started fucking the first day I arrived in Durham, in 1961, to start my job at our church."

Nothing but big eyes, so far. Keep going.

"Lenore took little Nathan and flew to visit her parents, and because we had no apartment yet, Melanie offered to let me sleep on cushions on the floor of her living room. One thing led to–well, fucking. We did that for almost four years, perhaps every two weeks or so.

Intense interest, puzzlement, and wonder flickering alive on her face. No words, yet.

"But I also want to tell you that I literally pulled out of her, five months ago–last April–in Wilmington, before I came, even, and gently but emphatically, told her I would never touch her, again—because I wanted to be loyal and faithful to you and Lenore. I hasten to add that I have completely kept my promise, even though she still implores me to come back to her bed. Finally, you should know that one of the reasons I found it so easy to turn to you in the first place—that I needed you so—was because I was disgusted with myself for carrying on with Melanie."

Shara sat quietly, rapt, beautiful eyes lathering him with her unasked questions.

"Because I had undercut my relationship with Lenore, then, I desperately needed—and wanted—a new relationship—a person pure and unaffected whom I could genuinely love, at least partly to mitigate my lust for Melanie. You were that person, and I somehow knew I would love you enough to—well, stop a lot of things—and you did it, without even knowing it. I haven't touched Melanie since April, almost five months, nor shall I ever do so, again, simply because I love you so very much. Now, I'm ready for your reactions—whatever, but I had to tell you!"

She's watching me; her face showing wonder and determination.

Without a word, knee-walking to the edge of the bed, Shara reached for him and gently pulled him into it, helping him onto his back. Once he was stretched out, she straddled him, kissed him passionately and moved her kisses downward, where she took him into her mouth, urging his surprised flesh to fill it. It did. She didn't linger; kneeling over him, she spread her vaginal lips and sank down on him in one determined move.

So connected, she grabbed his shoulders, leaning on her arms, her nudie charm dangling hypnotically before his eyes, looked deeply into them, and as she began her slow, writhing, reclamation, saying, "Nathan, I *love* you. I've always *wondered* about something like that, but it *doesn't* matter a bit, because I *know* you love me, and that you *don't* love Melanie. As you have said, *many* times, you can't use it *up*, so I'm just going to *love* and fuck you, *now*, until you can think of *nothing* but me—my *body*—my *spirit*—my *energy*, but most of all, *my love*. You just *lie* there and *allow* me to *love* you the *way* I have been *dreaming* about for *over* two weeks. *This* is exactly what I *want*. I love *doing* this. I'm sure *I do* it better than *Melanie*, and *I'm sure* I can keep *your mind* off her, from now *onnn*! Oh, God, Nathan, I love you, love to fuck, fuck, fuck, fuck you. I'm going to come on you, and you in me! This—is the truth about us, Nathan, the only truth that matters, or will ever matter. We are one! Dear God, this is sooo good. I'm spasming like mad…!'"

For once, he was overwhelmed by the indomitable fires that burned in his delectable Desiderata. He simply lay there, captured and captivated, loving her emphatic burrowing into him, as he was buried in her, reclaiming him forever, washing his chest, shoulders, and face with her salty tears, and crooning her deepest love for him, while she reclaimed him.

CHAPTER 43
RAISING MISTRESS MELANIE

So loath to suffer mute;
What we ought not, we do;
And lean upon the thought
That chance will bring us through.

Matthew Arnold

Settling on the sofa that opened to Shara's bed, Nathan lazed his head in her lap, looking up into her contentment.

"Do you want to know anything more about my relationship with Melanie, Shara?"

"Yes, yes, no, no, and maybe," she grinned.

"All at once, or one at a time?"

"The woman in me wants to know some physical and personal stuff, like was she a virgin and did she come easily, use her fingers, or what? Also, was she verbal when she came? Did she cry out that she loved you, like I do? Could she squeeze you back to life? But those things aren't all that important to me. I have seen her in panties and bra, and I know that she wears clothing that usually de-emphasize her gorgeous figure–better than mine, I think. I know her pubic hair is red, like yours."

"Yes."

"Nathan, what's hard to understand is how you ever got her to fu–make love, she's so very prim and proper about everything."

"You might turn that around, Shara; it was very mutual. I'm certain we both fantasized it for seven years, one way or another. It seemed all too easy because we both knew exactly what was happening and why. She wanted me–and I wanted sex–the free, different, and unfettered, mutual sex that I had been fantasizing since puberty. I never believed Lenore to be that open to such, so it was easy to dive right in."

"Well, you can tell me about the sexy parts later, maybe while we're doing it. In a way, it sorta turns me on–but what I'd really like to know is who you were with her; how you acted; what kinds of things you talked about; how she expressed her love, if that is what it was–is; and whether you brought her little gifts, wrote her notes, or anything like what lovers–like we do."

"There was never anything like that, honey. We weren't lovers; we were erotic partners. We never had much time for anything but sex, really: late at night at her place; I'm embarrassed to say after Lenore was asleep at our place; on the road, hurriedly; so, our conversation was usually about that, especially beforehand, when we were both hot."

"I'm so glad you stopped–and that you did it for me. I haven't thanked you for that, darlin,' so thank you."

"I had to stop, because I love you–also I wasn't being fair to Lenore, even though we both thought it was harmless."

"Nathan, can I ask you something else?"

"Certainly."

"When and how did Melanie learn about us?"

"About the time Lenore wrote you, I think; but Lenore could have told her long before that."

"Do you miss her?"

"I don't miss her, romantically, at all. Not even as a friend, for she still visits, regularly."

"So, that brings us back to the original question: why is Melanie doing this for me?"

"I asked her. She gave all the reasons you might think: lingering curiosity about you, and what I may see in you; to help Lenore by providing you with some distraction; and simply to aid you out of Christian charity, which I know is sincere."

"I could just ask her, couldn't I?"

"Think you can do that, honey? It's obvious that you'll have to discuss your probable pregnancy with her, too, if she's to help you find a good doctor—at least for a pregnancy test."

"Okay, but I'd sure like to have you around. You could talk to her—call her—let her know that we really need to find out for sure, so she'll help me with a doctor."

"Good idea. I'll call her as soon as she returns. Shara, I'm very proud of the way you're coping with all of this. You are wise and mature well beyond your years, that's for sure."

"You treat me as an equal; it makes me one."

CHAPTER 44
TOO MUCH?

Fate gave, what Chance shall not control,
His sad lucidity of soul.
This iron time
Of doubt, disputes, distractions, fears.

Matthew Arnold

Till their own dreams at length deceive 'em
And oft repeating, they believe 'em.

Matthew Prior

L enore called, as they lay in the limpid aftermath of
morning. Thinking it might be Melanie, Shara answered
the phone, and Lenore asked if Nathan was there, as she
needed to speak to him on a matter of some urgency. Shaken,
Shara mouthed the word, "Lenore," handed the phone to
Nathan and sat down hard.

"Hello, 'Nore. I guess you figured I'd be here?"

"Yes," icily, "after several calls to our home, several
more to your office, and finally one to Stephen, who, after
some hemming and hawing, suggested that I might try you—
where you are! Couldn't you wait until your mother's and
sister's bodies were cold, before you decided to warm hers—
yours?"

"You have a right to be upset, honey. I should have told you my plans. I'm truly sorry to have failed you, once again. I don't really have an excuse, other than anxiety; can you forgive me?"

Somewhat disarmed, his distant mate moderated her tone a bit, and proceeded.

"Well, Dr. Flowers has been trying to reach you, and I was terribly embarrassed when the home and office numbers I gave him didn't bear fruit. You need to call him right away—he didn't say why, other than that he wants to discuss something about your arrival time and a program he wants you to do."

"I can do that, 'Nore. Again, I'm sorry I put you through that. When did he last call?"

"He called three times, the last time about forty-five minutes ago. I just got off the phone with Stephen—whom I assume you burdened with our—our—your..."

"...Plight? Yes, I told him pretty much everything."

"Nathan, why? He's just starting seminary, you've always been almost a god to him, and now you've probably shocked and dismayed him terribly."

"Honey, Stephen is my brother. You have always known that I love him, and he me, and that we have a very special relationship—one in which we can tell—indeed, have told—pretty much anything."

"In addition to the shock of the death of his mother and his big sister? How could you, Nathan? What happened to your vaunted sensitivity and empathy?"

"Honey, I won't try to explain it any more than to say that our having lost the same people, share the same griefs, and are committed to serving the same God, give us legitimate, mutual entry to each other's most secret hearts—it always has. He is most empathetic, not just for me, but for you, the kids,

Mel–Shara, and everyone. He even prayed with me, seeking guidance for us all."

"But how can I look him in the eye, now? He'll see me as the weak, all too tolerant woman I am. It's embarrassing, Nathan. Would you like it if I suddenly told Allison or Jess?"

"I understand those feelings, and your fear of embarrassment, Lenore, but didn't you tell Melanie...?

"I–I–Yes. You know I did, and I guess I don't have any right to be upset that you found someone with whom to share your..."

"...Perfidy?"

"...Burden, Nathan. I don't think of you as perfidious–only in deep trouble with yourself–and with the God you say you and Stephen love. I'm sorry I spit at you, just now, but it's frustrating not to know where you are, especially when your new boss is trying to find you. You'd better call him right away."

"Nore? Just how much have you told Melanie, anyway?"

"Everything–everything that I know, that is. God–and Shara–only know what I don't. Perhaps you'll tell me, someday."

"If you remember, I told you that her doctor palpated her ovaries during a pelvic last July. I'm very sorry to tell you, now, that due to her very recent symptoms, including a missed period and several bouts of morning sickness, we are about to conclude that she may be pregnant, but we haven't confirmed that with a doctor, yet. I apologize for waiting to tell you, and on the phone, at that, but we only recently accepted it, ourselves."

"I'm not stupid, Nathan, and neither is Melanie. We have discussed that very likelihood. Why else would Shara leave home so suddenly?"

"First, it happened well after Shara decided on her own, to leave home. When she did leave, pregnancy was only a vague possibility, to be quite honest. But, to your point, Shara and I were just discussing asking Melanie to help her see a good gyn/ob, perhaps Mellie's, for a pregnancy test. We are still not absolutely sure, though."

Silence.

"Dear God, Nathan. What are you going to do, now?"

"That's the major, unanswered question, I guess, 'Nore. I also guess part of the answer is up to you."

"No, you don't. Don't put that onus on me. It's not my problem, apart from what it might mean for me, our children, and our future."

Silence.

"Well, Nathan, I'm not going to blow all of my available whistles, suddenly act out and leave you or something, if that's what you're thinking. I'm opting for the long run–and for our family, your job, and our financial future, as well."

"That's good to hear, honey. That's what I meant, anyway."

"Okay, I got it. Anyway, that's one of the reasons Melanie is helping Shara–and why you are where you are, right now, instead of being in Wilmington where you belong. Oh, Nathan, sometimes you make it very hard…"

"It's never been hard to love you, Lenore."

Pause for weeping…

"Let's hang up now, Nathan. I don't like to spend your Daddy's money on long distant blubbering. Call Dr. Flowers and tell him something believable, please."

"Okay, honey. Are you all right?"

"Of course, not, Silly. I just found out my husband is taking advantage of my best friend's good will and accommodation to your–your–to Shara, who is probably pregnant with your child, by staying in her apartment without her permission, I'm sure. I'll bet you're even sleeping in her bed! She doesn't know, does she?

"No, but I'll call her and tell her, myself."

"Yes, please do. I'm too embarrassed."

"You were right a second ago, Honey, let's hang up. I never could argue well over the phone, when I can't see your face."

"Please tell Shara that I hope I didn't shock her into a miscarriage—no, don't you dare say that. Just tell her I'm sorry I startled her."

"I'll tell her, Lenore. I'll also call Melanie when she gets back Monday. I'm leaving here Sunday, to be back in time for both youth fellowships, although I don't have to be back until Monday."

"You didn't tell me that, either. You let me believe that it was urgent that you leave Florida yesterday."

Pause.

"I guess it was pretty urgent, at that," giggled Lenore, incongruously. "I should have known..."

"I'll make it up to you, somehow, honey. Please forgive me and continue to love me. I'm dancing as fast as I can, trying to make sense out of everything, and trying to find a way to do the least harm to the least number of people."

"Has it come to that, Nathan—doing the least harm? Whatever happened to doing the most good?"

"Nothing happened to it. I shouldn't have phrased it that way. It's just one side of the ontological coin I keep flipping into the cosmos, hoping I can get it to land on its edge and stay there."

"Nathan, honestly! You have more metaphors... However, I do understand that one, and it doesn't make me feel any better."

"I'm sorry. It isn't exactly comfort food for me, either."

"See? From coins flipped into the cosmos to comfort food? What's next, peanut butter?"

"Shouldn't we call a halt to this, as it's becoming competitive and..."

"...Heartbreaking? Okay, I'll go now and tell your children that you love them and that you are thinking about them—you are, aren't you? Maybe you could call us when you get out of—when you get back home."

"That's a promise."

"Not another one, please!"

"Goodbye, honey."

"Goodbye, Nathan. I–I–you know I love you, dammit!"

"Yes, thank God!"

Click.

Turning from one distraught woman to another, Nathan found Shara lying on Melanie's bed, weeping.

How much more can any of us take, even rationally? Why does my joy have to bring others misery?

"Lenore's upset, mostly, that I didn't tell her where I was going when I left Sutherland—and that I confided in Stephen."

"I know; I tried not to listen, but I heard your end of the conversation and figured out her responses."

"I'm sorry, Shara. I keep screwing things up, when a little more forethought and consideration would—or could—avoid that. I should have told her. Now she's caught me, and it doesn't feel good—for any of us, does it?"

"No, it doesn't, if you want to know. I hate to feel this way—that I'm the cause of everybody's pain and woe. I should have stopped our relationship before it even got started. Now, here I am probably pregnant with our baby, and I cain–can't–even feel totally right about enjoying you being here."

"Shara, stick with–and by–me, love me the most, now. I can't have both you and Lenore mad me at the same time. That would qualify as my definition of hell."

"Aren't we in some sort of hell, Nathan? One we made all by ourselves. We can't even blame it on the devil if there is such a creature."

I come pretty close, though...

CHAPTER 45
TRANSITIONS

Change finesses the fact that walking or running always result from a series of standing still.

Nathan Rhea Scott
September 30, 1965

Sitting on a bench in Stony Creek Park, munching snacks, Shara looked puzzled.

"Nathan, may I ask you something?"

"Of course, darling."

"If–when–you move to Florida, how are we going to keep us going in any way that satisfies either of us?"

"I know. I don't like to think of that, either. It seems that no matter which way we jump, these days, we land in another dilemma. The Miami decision was the best I could do–and thank you very much Trinity University! At least Bayview is paying me much better, so, I'll have more money for traveling to see you."

Silence for stewing.

"At least, you're with me, now, and all I want to think about is us. I love you so very much. You know that don't you, Nathan?"

"Yes, misty eyes, and I love you more than anything. Don't cry–on second thought, do it for me, too."

Shara leaned her head on his shoulder, leaving a small deposit of salty tears, as she absently stroked his face.

"There is no way I am just going to go farting off to Miami, leaving you pregnant and alone–well, not alone, but as far as our love is concerned, alone. I'll have to figure something out that won't hurt either you or Lenore, of course. The money, both for travel and your medical bills, will be something of an issue, but, if I play my cards right... It's the time about which I'm unsure, for I can't believe my job will be any less demanding than Durham or Wilmington–in fact, I know it won't. That's the problem."

"I gotta tell you that I'm not too happy about that. Have some more tears."

Wiping her eyes on his shirt, she sat up, turned from him, her tell-tale, jiggling foot signaling her emotions.

Silence.

"Okay, I give. What can I say or do, that will bring you back onto this bench with me?"

"I'm crying over here, if you want to know, and I don't want to bother you with my emotions, while you're trying to figure out what to do with me. Thanks for the hanky."

"You're welcome, sweetheart."

Shara took a deep breath, looked at her man, knew she loved him, and decided to heed her own advice. She would just take life a day–a step at a time, hour by hour, if she had to, counting on him to deliver on his promises. Thus, she steeled herself, heroically, unaccountably, given her age and stage, bending herself to the realities, while surely courting her needs–and hopes.

Scooting over, she put her head back on his shoulder and inhaled the essence of the man, tasting the past and concocting menus of him for the future.

"Shara?"

"Yes," she whispered into his right ear.

"May I ask you something?"

"Only if it will make you happy."

"It might."

"Then ask…"

"Will you marry me?"

Gasping, "You know—you have to know—that—that—I would do anything, go anywhere, be anybody, if only—only that can be true, Nathan! Yes, yes, yes! A thousand times, yes! I want to be your wife, to have your children, and to be with and love you always! That's all I've ever wanted, since—since you held me that incredible night in May, when my stunted, little world suddenly blossomed into a vast, sparkling universe. Thank you so much for asking just the right, wonderful question!"

With that, the Man With Love Painting His Visage handed her a small, blue, velvet-covered box, while Shara's eyes glowed cautious delight.

"Should I open it? I'm scared. I hope you didn't…"

Her eyes filled with tears, again, when she saw the shining, silver wedding band in the box. Looking up at him, back at the ring, and back at him, she was literally speechless, tears coursing down her grinning happiness.

"Wha—how—Nath—oh, honey, it's beautiful, but I can't wear it, can I?"

"Why not?"

"Well, you know—but it's so beautiful. Shall I try it on?"

"Here, let me."

Gently removing the box from Shara's shaking hands, Nathan extracted the ring, explained the ∞ engraved inside, reached for her left hand, and slid the ring on her fourth finger, saying, "With this ring, I thee wed—someday soon." It fit perfectly.

QI couldn't stay quiet: *How would Lenore react to this little romantic scene, Scott? How on earth am I going to keep faith with both incredible women? What should I tell Lenore about this, if anything, without hurting her, terribly? I want her to know everything...*

"Oh, Nathan, thank you so much! I do feel married to you, even though we must work through a world of difficulties. I can wear this to work, and no one will think anything about my being pregnant."

Their kiss was long, deep, and breathless. Shara clung to him, burying her lips in his neck, kissing it over and over.

"I love you, my husband. I love you, my husband. I love you, my very own man!"

*

Later, as he re-entered Melanie's apartment with groceries, he met Shara wearing nothing but her smile, lounging on the settee, where he had last fucked Melanie, legs spread, her hands busy at her crotch.

"I want you to do it to me like you did it to Melanie, Nathan. I want to know, and God, I want you! I've been wanting you since we got back from our picnic this afternoon. Get your clothes off and do it to like you did Melanie, right here..."

He did.

"Wow!" Shara managed to pant, holding him to and in her, legs around him, while he pressed her against the front door. "It's strange, I was—am—me, of course, but I put myself in her—her body—and I felt—feel—her pleasure, too."

"Shara, I don't really want to make love to Melanie, I want only you."

"I know," she said, squeezing him back to tumescence, "but you got into it."

"What I am into is you, Shara," thrusting deeply into her, against the door.

"How can that be, Nathan? We're built the same, only I expect she has more experience than I do. Ummph, I

446

can feel you growing inside me, and it feels wonderful. Ohh, I could come again in two minutes."

She did.

Coming down, they moved their heat to Melanie's bed. Relishing their cuddling, her head on his left shoulder, his arm around her, her right hand on her crotch, and her newly wedded left hand on his "paw patch" of a right collar bone, they snuggled toward sleep.

"How does it feel to be sleeping with Mrs. Nathan Rhea Scott...?" she mumbled into his left ear.

CHAPTER 46
KEEPING ON KEEPING ON

Sometimes even to live is an act of courage.

Lucius Annaeus Seneca

"Nathan, what have you enjoyed most about our 'homely honeymoon,' as you put it, here in Melanie's apartment?"

"Let's see here, now—there was you, then you, you, you, and Shara Starr Scott. How does that sound?"

"You didn't really answer, but I like the 'Scott' bit. Were Melanie to discover my legal pad, she'd find my practicing signing that. Speaking of Melanie, tell me again what you said when you called her, while I was in the shower."

"First, I liked shopping with you. That activity sealed our relationship, domestically. Not to take away from our picnic, watching tv; cooking; eating your homemade meals—especially your brownies; reading with you; taking pictures of and with you; especially our long walk by Stony Creek; watching your naked butt bounce as you fled into the bathroom when the doorbell rang; watching you comb your hair, fix your face and shave your legs; cleaning up and Nathan-proofing Melanie's apartment, today; and all twenty-six times we made love.

"Me, too, all of those! I also cherished sleeping with you, cuddling, and waking up in your arms. And your call to Melanie?"

"It was most interesting, as I fore-skinned. She was flustered; I apologized for invading her space, asked if she would mind if I visited several times while you share her digs. I complimented her profusely for the obvious sacrifices she is making in your–our–behalf."

"And she really said it would be all right for you to visit?"

"Indeed. She followed that up by saying that, if we would let her know in advance, she would stay with friends, to give us privacy. She also asked how long I thought you might be here, adding that you are welcome for as long as it takes. That introduced the subject of pregnancy, so I asked if she minded assisting you in getting an appointment with a good ob/gyn. She readily accepted."

"Did she mention Lenore?"

"She admitted having talked with her. I didn't press her on why she was doing this, as it seems obvious. She wants to please me, by accommodating you, and she wants to please Lenore, by assisting you to become independent, preferably far away from me. Plus, a considerable part of her feels empathy for you. Simple–and as complicated–as that."

"Good gosh, Nathan, do you really think she's identifying with me?"

"Yes, I do–our relationship, your pregnancy, the whole thing. That is the Melanie I know–caring, empathetic, loyal, consistent, and determined. She really does have a good and innocent heart."

"Well, that makes me appreciate her more. I think I may be able to relate to her woman to woman, now, if what you say is true."

"She'll retain her natural reticence with you, probably, but she'll be warmer and more forthcoming, I think."

"I'm glad you called her."

"We talked about one more thing: what to do if your parents come calling."

"Oh my God, Nathan, I forgot about that! I want to call Mom, to let her know I'm okay. I could do it from a pay phone, so they couldn't trace the call."

"The question is how long will it take for them to find out where you are? Soon enough, probably. Maybe tell them what city, but not your address. You might even ask if it would be all right for you to visit–before you start showing much."

"What did Melanie say about all of that?"

"As you know, her father is a district attorney, and she says she is perfectly ready to involve him, if the Starrs start something. In fact, the more I think about it, the more I think you should call them tomorrow, after your interview, tell them you're all right, that you're staying with an older, Christian woman who is helping you with job interviews, that you don't hate them, and you just want to live your own life. Ask Melanie, first, whether you should tell them her name, if knowing who she is might ameliorate their fears."

"I wouldn't mind talking with Mom and the kids, but I do not want to talk with my father. Let me see what Melanie has to say and how my interview goes Wednesday afternoon, and then I'll decide. I do worry about Mother–my leaving didn't help her, any."

"Sounds like a plan."

"I'd better leave, now, honey" he whispered, "if I want to get past DC before the rush. Come here, you most beautiful, wonderful girl in the world."

Their kiss lasted a full minute; their tears for hours...

*

The Scotts left for Miami right after their Wilmington church sendoff, Sunday, arriving there on Tuesday, September 28. The truck was already off-loaded, and their meager furnishings unpacked and set up by the Women of the

Bayview Church, making everything ready for them when they walked in the door. Nathan would report to work, virtually across the road, promptly, at 8:00 a.m., Friday, October 1, 1965.

Shara called him at his new office on Saturday evening bubbling with news. She had dared to call home, gratefully and tearfully welcomed by Donna Starr and her siblings. Her father was on the road, and Jimmy was out. With Melanie's courageous blessing, she told her mother she was staying with Melanie in Prospect Park, reminding Donna that she had met Melanie several times at church.

Though Donna knew not to plead and beg, she asked 'why,' more than once, and tried to convince Shara that she would be welcome, with everything forgiven, should she decide to return. Shara cried with her, but remained steadfast, telling her mother that she loved everyone, even her father, but that this was something she had to do. She purposefully withheld her address and phone number, even though such would be easy to discover.

Awe in her voice, Shara whispered, "Nathan, we're going to have a ba-by! Melanie called her doctor Thursday, and he saw me right away. I had the test that very day, and they called around 4:30 today. The immunoassay, or whatever it's called, was positive, and the doctor said the test is about 70% accurate. His examination of my uterus convinced him that I am truly pregnant, about 60 days in, and that the baby will be here about mid-April if all goes as expected. I'm thrilled, of course, but a little scared. How are you? I miss you so much."

"Shara, I'm happy and apprehensive, too. It seems so impossible, yet you have the proof, now, as you expected. I love you, and I already love our little one."

"You don't sound all that excited, Honey. Don't you get it? We're going to have a baby, get married, somehow, and live happily ever, after! I even have the ring, to prove it!"

"I definitely get it, little mother, but–no, not 'but,' and I so want your–our–description to come true. We'll work on it as hard as we can, that I promise, and God will have to help us through the next seven months, even as we help each other."

"I know, and I'm praying as hard as I have ever prayed that everything will work out. Oh, Melanie wept with me, when I told her, tonight. She even hugged me, and she's been treating me like I'm fragile, since. She saw my ring and didn't know what to say. I told her we got it mostly for work, so people wouldn't wonder and gossip. She said that was a good idea, and guess what? I have a job! Shriek! Oh, Nathan, everything seems to be falling into place. I'm so happy, right now, that I could scream."

"Me, too, honey. Tell me about the job, first."

"My job is with this big company in Prospect Park, not two miles from our apartment– 'American Standard' or 'Standard America,' maybe; I have forgotten which. I'm to be a part time girl Friday, doing mostly filing, answering phones, some typing, standing in for other girls, occasionally. I'm to earn a whopping, minimum wage of $1.25 an hour, plus 15% after three months. I only work half days, Monday through Friday, to start, with the probability of working more, as I progress in my office skills. Whether morning or afternoon shifts will depend on others' schedules. I'm so excited. Oh, guess what else? I saw not one, but two, pregnant women in the office area, so I don't think I have to worry about that."

"Good grief, Shara, you're batting a thousand, aren't you? I'm thrilled for you–for us. We're on our way, babes."

Thou art but man; thou art but man...!

CHAPTER 47
LOOK OUT!

In adversity remember to keep an even mind.

Horace (Quintus Horatius Flaccus)

A tired Shara unlocked the door, tossed her pocketbook on her bed, kicked off her shoes, went to the bathroom, and was getting undressed, when a knock on the door stopped her in her tracks. Melanie was at work until 8:00 p.m., so Shara crept up to the peep hole, just as the knock sounded more insistently.

"This is the police! Please open the door!"

They had been expecting something, but not the police–or what happened, next. Several days earlier, Melanie received a phone call from Big J. Carl, insisting to speak with Shara, who shook her head vigorously when Melanie mouthed the words, "Your fa-ther!"

"I'm sorry, Mr. Starr, she's not here, now. Perhaps I can take a message."

"Well, I happen to know that she is there, Miss Charles, and I demand to speak to her."

"Sir, with respect, you can demand all you want, but you shan't bully me, nor shall I allow you to bully her, unless she wants to be bullied, which she doesn't."

"You both better watch out, my girl. All I have to do is get a lawyer, and I can have you arrested, and Shara institutionalized."

"With waning respect, Sir, I am certainly not your girl. You can get your lawyer, and I'll get my father, who is a district attorney, and we'll see who's institutionalized."

"Now, Miss Charles, no need to get huffy. My wife and I are the wounded parties, here. I'm not sure why you're doing this, but by keeping Shara away from us, you are severely hurting Shara's mother."

"Sir, with respect for her mother, Shara has spoken to her, as you know, and they are working on things that may alleviate some of that pain. Shara is safe, she has a job, she is my friend, and as long as she wishes she may stay here in my apartment, under my protection, if need be. I hope that won't be necessary, but I have already checked with my father, and an injunction against harassment, even by relatives, is easy to obtain in Pennsylvania. She is eighteen and can claim legal independence from you, as you should know."

"Well, Miss Pris, you'll have lots to answer for, one day. I, too, have means that you might not like."

"If that is a threat, you should know that threatening or abusive language such as that can be considered assault and/or harassment in a Pennsylvania court—a serious misdemeanor, for your information."

"I'm not threatening you, now; I'm just trying to appeal to you—and to your conscience. Shara's mother needs her, and from what I can discover, you're standing in the way of her return."

"Mr. Starr, you have discovered nothing, if you believe I am the cause of her living here. You might look to yourself for that! I did not pack her things or have the slightest thing to do with her leaving your domicile, nor did I force her to ask me if she could stay with me. So, I'm not standing in her way, at all. She's free to leave any time she wishes, to come and go as she pleases."

"Well, we'll just see about that! You'll be hearing from me, you, you…"

"Bang!" went the receiver in Melanie's reddening ear. Grinning, she asked, "How'd I do?"

"Wonderful, Melanie! I've never heard anybody talk to my father like that. I don't know exactly what he said, but I was cheering my head off, when I heard your responses."

"Thank you, Shara. However, I think you should be careful in your travels, and not be alone–stay in a crowd, as much as possible. He may have been bluffing, but he said he knew you were here. That suggests detective work. You know your father, so you have a better idea of what he's capable of doing. Just the same, be mindful of your environment at all times."

"Good advice, and I'll take it. I wouldn't put it past him to spy. I can't thank you enough for helping me, Melanie."

Melanie colored as they hugged.

Now, four days later, Shara was peering through the peephole at a tall, uniformed policeman who knocks, again.

"What do you want, officer? I'm alone here, and I'm not dressed, so if you don't mind, please speak your business through the door."

"I'm officer Petree, badge number 90, of the Prospect Park Police Department, and I'm looking for a Miss Shara Starr. Are you her?"

"What do you want with her, Officer?"

"We've had a complaint that she may be staying here against her will, and I've been charged with the duty of ascertaining her situation. Now, if you are Miss Starr, please open the door. Keep the chain locked, if you wish, but I have to see you."

"I am Shara Starr, and am here of my own free will, unharmed, happy, with a job, living with a friend who is at work, now."

"Miss Starr, I have to see you and identify you, so I can report back that you are safe and sound, on your own, and not under any sort of duress. Please, at least crack the door, so I can identify you."

Shara complied, uneasily, opening the door as far as the chain lock would allow. The officer was in his thirties, with a friendly manner, as he showed Shara his badge and his credentials. In turn, she held out her NC Driver's License, confirming her identity.

Satisfied, he asked, formally, "Are you Shara Day Starr, formerly of 1484 Northampton Street, Durham, North Carolina?"

"Yes, I am."

"Are you living here, at this apartment, freely, without coercion or pressure of any kind, of your own free will?"

"I am."

"Now that we've established who you are, and you have said you're here on your own, would you please allow me to look around inside, to ensure that no one else in there may be threatening you?"

"Well, I don't know."

"I could come back with a warrant, I guess, but wouldn't it be simpler just to cooperate, so you can get back to your business, and I can get back to mine?"

"All right, but I am going to leave the door open."

Shara unlocked the chain and stepped back, so the policeman could enter. He took a very cursory look around the apartment, smiled at her and told her the second reason he was there.

"Now that I have established that you are here of your own free will, that you are of age, and that you are under no present coercion, I need to inform you that your parents are at the station and would very much like to see you. You are under no obligation to come, of course, but personally, your mother seems to be in pretty bad shape, and I don't see what harm it would do just to talk with them."

"Why on earth are they at the police station. No one has broken any laws, have they?"

"Not that I know of. Your father made an official complaint, asserting that you were being held against your will in this apartment. He was informed that if his complaint didn't turn out to be true, there is nothing we can do to make you come to see them, or to go home with them. Their intent in coming was to see what they could do, legally, to get you to return home."

"If I go see them, can they make me go with them?"

"No Ma'am, they cannot. You are free to come and go as you please in this Commonwealth, as long as you don't break any laws."

"I don't have transportation, right now, and I don't even know where the police station is."

"It's not exactly kosher, but I can offer you a ride. I'm not driving a cruiser, so you would be riding in my personal car, which is my business."

"Then, call ahead, while I listen, and tell them I'll come with you in a few minutes."

Officer Petree used his walkie-talkie to call in, and Shara heard his dispatcher confirm the details. She would meet with her parents in the presence of Officer Petree.

*

Shara added anger to her angst when she spotted her father's big car parked right in front of the station.

"Do I really have to do this?" she complained.

"No. But, if you do it now, it might make things smoother, later."

"Okay, let's go. Where are they?"

"Right this way, Miss Starr."

The officer ushered Shara into a nondescript room, where sat her nervous parents. Donna rushed to her, crying, hugging her fiercely, stepping back, looking her up and down, hugging her, again, and repeating the process several times.

"I'm, sorry, Mama, but it's something I have to do."

"I know; I know. You told me that on the phone, but I just had to see you, to know that you are all right, and not in any kind of trouble—you're not, are you?"

"No, Mama," she said, tearing up, too, and I'm glad to see you. I have missed you and the kids."

"Well, I'm here, too, dammit, Shara Day, and I think you're being a spoiled brat, behaving this way and causing us all this trouble. We have lost friends because of your and Jimmy's cavalier behavior, and I don't appreciate it one bit. You ought to be ashamed of yourself—staying with that—that, what is she, anyway, a lesbian?"

Before Shara could respond, Officer Petree said, "Now, Mr. Starr, let's all calm down a little and try to avoid harsh words and accusations. Miss Starr doesn't have to be here. She came because you asked her to, so let's make this meeting as civilized as possible, okay?"

"Carl, I asked you to please not do or say anything to make it worse. Let's just ask Shara what we came to ask, and then let her decide what she wants to do."

Big J. Carl grunted his reluctant assent. Officer Petree smiled, and Shara sat down, foot swinging and jiggling her tumbling emotions.

Trembling, Shara spoke, "May I say something?"

Officer Petree nodded, J. Carl grimaced, and Donna smiled. "Daddy, with respect, the main reason I left home is to live my own life, just as you are living yours. Of course, I appreciate all that you and Mom have done for me, preparing me for just this step. Another reason is due to responses like you just made. You don't seem able to see me as anything but a helpless girl, good for nothing but to do as she's told. You put Jimmy and me down for wanting to live our own lives. I simply couldn't live with that any longer. I hope you understand."

Clearly agitated, Carl almost rose from his chair as he responded, "Well, it's little bratty speeches like that that show you are in no way mature enough to know what you're doing. I fought in two wars, and I know how hard it is out there. We have fed you, clothed you, kept you safe, and the thanks we get is this spit in the eye. I hope you understand that!"

"You make my case, Daddy. For some reason, you cannot see beyond your own opinion. You've both taught me to take advantage of opportunities, just as have you. That is exactly what I'm doing, even though you disagree."

"Of course, I disagree! You're being spiteful, childish—and stupid."

Before Officer Petree could intervene, Shara looked at both the policeman and her mother and said, "See what I mean?"

The remaining conversation was brief, uncomfortable for all, and resolved only one thing: Shara would consider visiting for Thanksgiving, even though her father simply growled at the suggestion. No, she would not come home, now. Yes, she was working and liked her job. Yes, she had enough money. Yes, Melanie was helping her to acclimate—and is not a lesbian!

Big J. Carl couldn't stop himself, and told her he could make her come home, if he wanted, and then she would be sorry. Officer Petree said the interview would end immediately, if Carl got out of line again. Donna pleaded with her husband to allow someone else's will to prevail, just once. He turned away, frowning his angry frustration.

Shara heard greetings from her siblings; that Kathy was at UNC, dating and doing well; that Manny had called several times, to inquire about her; and that people at church had asked about her, too. A few more mild pleasantries and Officer Petree announced that Shara was free to leave any time.

"Mama, I don't like hurting you," she whispered to her mother, out in the hall, "but you see what Daddy can be like. I just can't live under the same roof with a man who treats everyone like slaves. I'll try my best to come home Thanksgiving, but if he starts at me, or at you, or at anyone, I'll leave, immediately."

Crying, again, Donna hugged her daughter and said she understood. She thanked her for coming to the station and asked her to forgive both her and her father for any hurts they might have caused her in the past. "I love yous" were exchanged between the two, a goodbye pointed at her father, and Shara was out the door.

As Officer Petree let her out at her apartment, he said, "I don't like to pry, Miss Starr, but I thought you handled yourself very well, back there. I have a daughter almost your age, and I can see that your father can be—well, overbearing. Your mother will—does—deeply appreciate your coming down, as do I. I believe you have quite a head on your shoulders and appear to know exactly what you're doing. You have my admiration and respect. If you ever need anything I can provide, please don't hesitate to call on me. We're here to serve, as well as to protect. Please be careful; you're a lovely young lady, and there are plenty of bad guys who might want to get—to know you, if you know what I mean. Take it slowly, do your job, and think about your mother, from time to time; maybe call her. Goodbye, and God bless."

Still shaking from the confrontation, Shara thanked the officer, ran inside, where she collapsed on Melanie's bed, and cried herself to much needed sleep, wishing she could talk to Nathan—who was already up to his eyeballs in his Miami job. That's how Melanie found her.

Finally, she was truly free...

*

With Nathan, however, things were more heat than light. Being the new associate pastor in charge of Christian Education at a church of over 3,000 members was at least three times as demanding as his past, two appointments. He was responsible for a private school, from preschool (in which little Nathan was enrolled) through the 9th grade; a Sunday School of well over 1,000 participants of all ages in upwards of 50 classrooms around the huge church complex; a Youth Club for 175+ juniors (4th through 6th grades) that met Tuesday afternoons for supper, songs, and lessons; Sunday evening junior high and senior high youth fellowships of 125+ and 100+ participants, respectively; an active, 50+ member collegiate group; and a young adult Koinonia Fellowship of at least 80 that met each Thursday evening.

Nathan's job involved fine tuning and overseeing everything educational; curricula; recruiting, training, and supervising teachers and youth leaders; supplying classrooms and teachers; visiting; planning and leading retreats for youth and adult groups; recreational activities across the board; vocational counseling for senior highs; youth and adult personal counseling by appointment; occasional teaching in every department, especially youth, young adults, and adult classes; preaching at least once a month (for one of three morning worship services and an evening worship service in a newly erected, stand-alone chapel); regularly meeting with three church committees: Christian Education, Outreach, and Missions; supervising two secretaries and a full-time educational administrator for younger children, a school principal, plus a host of additional staff and volunteers; attending weekly prayer meetings with both men's and women's groups; and meeting with the senior minister and the other associate minister (of Visitation and Outreach) at least bi-weekly. Add to this areal and regional committees, invitations and assignments, occasional trips to Sutherland, to check on Allison, Jessie and Daddy, regular workouts at the Y, and normal sacerdotal duties such as visiting, assisting in Morning Worship, marrying, baptizing, burying, and serving on community committees, as needed.

Though the pay and benefits were excellent, Nathan was immediately swamped. Making it a point of professionalism to hit the ground running, he evaluated and revamped much of the entire program; led popular, recreational parties for juniors, junior and senior highs, collegians, and the young adult group; began the process of knowing each young person, personally and well; met with each teacher and youth leader privately; and introduced the new, graded national curriculum, both locally and regionally.

In a word, he met himself coming and going, rushing, and studying, preparing, and delivering, observing, planning and administering, counseling, trying to honor and strengthen his own primary family ties, and attempting to love and do right by a lonely, pregnant 18 year-old a thousand miles away, whose needs and expectations only grew in his absence.

Shara's needs, inevitably clashed with his job, his family, his ethics, and his sense of balance, given their differing, substantive demands. As much as he loved and needed her, too, he had great difficulty finding time and energy to communicate effectively with her, much less resolve the major issues and problems caused by the steady approach of an unavoidable reckoning day, now fewer than seven months away.

After their wonderful time in Melanie's apartment, Shara grew more anxious, without specific and permanent plans. She tried not to despair at her lover's constant refrain, however gently stated, "Yes, but how?"

Realizing Nathan's dilemma, Lenore wisely saw opportunity to stake her legitimate claim and rose to the occasion, offering availability and comfort to his spirit–and especially to his body. Understanding his enormous sex drive, she tried her best to meet it, head, and tail on, offering adventurous experiences, when he had time for sex. Lenore had always been comfortable and good in bed; now she sought expertise . . ..

CHAPTER 48
CONVINCING OR CONVICTING?

He who has a "why" to live can bear almost any "how."

Friedrich Nietzsche

Shara's October began successfully enough, coming off her long weekend with Nathan in Prospect Park, a growing friendship with Melanie; a part time job; transportation; an ob/gyn doctor she liked; a transformative meeting with her parents; and promises, promises, promises from her distant lover–now too often otherwise engaged. Shara was not one to hide her innermost feelings. Where Nathan was concerned, though, she was ever gentle, loving and understanding. Her first letter to his newly rented post office box expressed her emphatic hopes–and her growing, existential tensions.

> 8:30 p.m., October 8, 1965 (Abridged)
> Dear Nathan, at last, I can write this much belated letter! I feel so very close to you, now, that my heart sings of joy and yet cries because of the desperate loneliness I feel. I have your picture beside me, and Beethoven's 9th symphony is playing. As I look at your picture and hear the music soaring through me, I want so to stretch my hand out and feel the warmth of your hand in mine, or feel your arm around me–holding, holding the way I remember the last time. I want to feel your lips meeting mine, stirring

my being to gentle passion and the desire to be loved as well as loving! I want to know you, again!! I want to experience each moment repeatedly—yet I cannot lapse into the past, for the future is more important! These tears that stream down my face now announce the hope I have. They say more than my words can express now, yet even tears are insufficient if you cannot see them fall and kiss them away. If only I were gifted, like you, with the wonderful use of words—words that would depict the gut feelings I possess.

Right now, I want to express my sexual needs. I also want to laugh, to cry, to run, to dance, to shout, to scream, to be able to play the piano and create songs of the emotions of life the way I feel them. I want the baby to be here—to see the life in its small body and know it is depending on us for everything!

I want to tell people—someone—of my pure love. To say I enjoy you, our sex, our very being together! I want to live so much, to be the person I am inside, instead of the half product my parents taught me to be. I need to prove myself— to create something with my hands, with my mind, with my very soul. I need to know I'm contributing something to somebody. I need to be important; important because I can do something worthwhile!! I'm tired of sitting on my butt and watching people die or waste in this maddening society of ours, because of some stupid laws. No one can be himself! You've got to be the person people expect you to be.

I can't have a baby without a marriage certificate, even though I love. Our love must be legalized so we can hold our "place" in society. You can't be like the rain, the wind, and stars—they just are.

Two people molded us after themselves and their fears and guilt. And our child shall also be molded–but God, I hope I/we will not fail the way I feel my parents failed me. I try to understand but there's only hurt and confusion! I want to love them, but I don't know how. I want to say, "thank you" but for what? Why can't I know the love they have? Do they even have any love?

Oh Nathan, I want to know so many things–things that only God knows. I don't want to limit myself–I need to know I am doing something valuable. I wish I knew if anyone has been really affected by my actions, my life. You're in a position where you really help people and see the fruits of your labor. Like church!!! When I go to church, I want it to mean something. Last Sunday at Communion I sat there and felt so apart from all the many people around. I wondered how many people knew what was happening–why in the hell they were there, and did it mean anything? I wanted to pray but felt I would "stick out." I needed to be alone in church and cry. I needed to be alone with God and just tell Him how I felt. I needed to speak aloud just as if He were right beside me, listening just like you. I needed Him to see my tears and what they mean.

I want to know what to do with this unborn child of ours because I'm scared!! Scared because it's all new to me and because of the responsibility. I'm going to be responsible for this baby's life, and I want it to be a happy, honest life!!! I don't want to hurt the baby because of my uncertainly now. More than anything in the world, I want to keep and love my child, but the question is should I and can I, properly!!!! It's going to be alive soon and I so want it to be alive. I want you to be the father but occasionally, the terrible pain of doubt cuts my heart. Doubt not about our or your love but in our union. Like you keep saying, "Yes, but how? Yes, but how?"

I feel almost drained now for some tears have fallen, yet there are so many unshed!! I feel I must get to your letter now (I received it today. Rejoice!!!) It's sorta hard to come down to a more practical level after the above emotional reaction.

First, let me say how wonderful it was to hear from you. I was looking for that letter and I'm glad you didn't wait any longer. I'm glad things seem to be going so well, and I hope they continue to do so. I'm very anxious for you to tell me all about the church, its people (young and old), and how you really like it. It really is important to know all this, for it is so much a part of you—one which I would love to share!

As far as I know I'll be going to Durham Thanksgiving, depending on my job. If I can't get off, I'm going down one weekend before Thanksgiving or before I'm well rounded.

I've been feeling quite well (physically) so far. I did lose my breakfast again Friday morning, but I was rushing around too much. My real problem is my sleep! When I got home last night, I fell asleep while I was writing you—I just couldn't keep awake! This is the one thing I ask you to understand. It's not that I didn't want to finish, it's just that I couldn't. Understand? Good!!

I miss you very, very much. Often when I think about you, big ole tears gather in my eyes and it's all I can do to keep from crying. At times I don't want to believe you're in Florida, so I close my eyes and think of you only 3 hrs. away. But you are in

Florida. and I must accept it even though I don't like it. I'm just waiting, hoping, and trusting that we'll have our life soon!!!!

There is so much more to say, but if I don't stop, you'll not get this Mon. (I'm taking it to the airport when I get Melanie!) I shall write more tomorrow, as I do have more to say! Nathan if this letter says nothing more than I love you, I'll be satisfied! As hard as it is to love at a distance, I do love so intensely and deeply. Our moon is reflecting all that love now in its beauty–if only we could share those moments. I see it and I remember all the moments we've shared and are yet to share. There is always hope and love–they will never die, no, never die as long as there is life in me. I love you as I love life, for you make it real and valuable and always will. Be content for there is a way–we shall find it!!!!!

My love forever, Shara

Nathan interpolated between swelling pride and deepest pain at the vehemence and clarity of Shara's loving and suffering expressions. He worried, anew, how they were to survive the next months. *Clearly, she needs closure on our continuing relationship, despite my vague, hopeful promises, and she needs me to be close enough to touch!* Fighting the urge for drastic, ruinous action, he knuckled down and tried to write Shara a weekly letter, at least. As October sailed ahead of him, rapidly approaching November, Shara wrote following an exchange of hot letters:

2:10 a.m., October 26, 1965 (Abridged)

Hello, My Love, oh how my hot cunt burns for you this moment! I have just finished having two orgasms straight in a row and my vagina is throbbing like mad now. Both orgasms were achieved in less than 15 minutes. I had been reading some sexy material and just couldn't stand it anymore...

I'm sure I could go another round but I'm too tired. I would rather go with you. I don't understand this terribly strong desire these past couple of days, but oh man, how I would love to have you inside me–hard as a rock! I'm terribly sleepy now– especially after 2 orgasms, so I better push off to bed– wish to God you were in it! Good night darling, I love you!!!

That letter stimulated a renewed determination to find a better way to communicate. Nathan bought two sets of simple, identical, portable, battery/ac powered, three-inch, reel-to-reel audio-tape recorders, complete with on/off, two speed microphones, and a supply of boxed and mailable, thirty-or sixty-minute tapes to fit, and sent one set to Shara. By using them they would be free to say and hear what was on their minds and feel closer, at least. It worked. Both made full use of their tape recorders. Nathan learned the schedule for the Philly area mail sacks at the Miami airport: a stamped tape dropped in the Philly sack before 1:20 a.m. was usually delivered to Shara that same day.

With Melanie, Shara shared her frustration with the "how?" question and Nathan's inability, thus far, to answer it. After watching a moving program on adoption with Melanie, Shara said, "I'm still hoping that Nathan can find some way to fulfill his promise to me about getting married and raising our baby together, as parents should, if at all possible."

"I certainly agree that such would be ideal for you, Shara, and I can't help hoping, even praying, that such an eventuality might develop. At the same time, since I am an advocate for all concerned, let me gently remind you that, not only does Nathan still love Lenore and his children, but that they need and want him, too."

Tears of repressed realization filled Shara's eyes, as she thought how to respond. She heard herself saying, "I know, Melanie, and it kills me. That's why I have also been thinking very seriously about stepping aside, or at least giving up our baby to adoption."

Melanie immediately opened her arms to her young friend, and Shara cradled there, contemplating the damned and damning prospects for something other than marriage...

In her next tape, she shared her conversation with Melanie and imagined hearing him gasping with the heavy horror of that somewhat likely prospect. Still, despite impatience, guilt, and confusion, she couldn't quite give up, especially considering their baby—and her great love for Nathan. Thanking him for his tape, she promised to do a sexercise tape for them both, soon. At three months, she was relieved that there were no physical problems, at all, other than desire. Her doctor was pleased with her progress, and so was she.

"Give your penis a squeeze for me, and know that I love you, love you, love you! I want, so much, to be your wife. I know you want that, too, and knowing that keeps me determined, so don't mind my tears. I must hold on to that hope, Nathan, despite the almost overwhelming evidence that I should let it go. I'll tape, again, soon, and it'll be a hot one. Send me a couple of sexy novels, so I can at least enjoy reading how others do it. I tried to insert a banana, but it was too squishy—or I'm too tight. Maybe a hot dog would feel a little more like you. Man, I'd hate for Melanie to walk in and see that! The tape's about to run out, so, know my love and that I..."

Accordingly, Nathan, in agony, prayed for a miracle, hardly believing such were even possible in the twentieth century...

My God, my God, why have I forsaken thee?

CHAPTER 49
"... FOR THE VERY WORKS' SAKE."

Believe Me that I am in the Father, and the Father in Me; or else believe Me for the very work's sake.

John 14:11

Love is everything they said it would be. Love made sweet and sad the same.

Jane Siberry

Nathan's work continued more demanding than anything he had ever imagined. Yet, despite his angst and focus on his dilemma, he thrived and flourished, professionally, as never before. Since childhood, he fed on the energy of others, however challenging, in playing, cooperating, learning, or fighting. Thus, his candle burned brightly in the sun and insouciance of south Florida climes and times—at both ends.

Though Nathan's church work produced elements of satisfaction, he was agonizingly aware of his inability to keep his many promises to Shara, without destroying everything else. Fearing he was becoming a liar as well as a reneger, such realizations were overwhelming in their concomitant guilt and sadness. His fervent prayers, when he could muster them, were for relief—that would leave neither Shara nor Lenore hurt or abandoned.

When not taping Shara, some midnights found him in the dark, stand-alone chapel, trying to play through his existential fears and guilts on its concert grand. As Nathan played, he prayed:

God, we both know how upside down everything is now, especially with those I love. It has never been my intention to love one and hurt the other, but that appears to be what I'm doing. Please help us—all of us—to find a way to let our love prevail, without harm...

But how do I pray for something I can't even visualize, Lord, apart from the impossible: finding a way to live and love together? My only certainties are my great love for everyone and my colossal failure to make that real and obvious in anything like satisfactory, harmless, and successful ways. I can ask for forgiveness; not for loving, but for acting upon that love incompletely, inadequately, and even morphing it into what looks and feels like treachery, even to me. I don't lie, but I dissemble; I promise without fulfillment, and still, I cannot abandon my loves—except, God, it feels as though I do so on an almost daily basis, when I don't live up to my or their needs and expectations.

I need help, Lord, and I don't know how or what to ask of you. A miracle, other than the God-given miracle of too much love? Forgiveness? For loving? I cannot; I do not repent of my love for Shara, of my over-arching love for my family, or even of my job and the people I've sworn to serve. I do confess and repent of my weakness, that which doesn't allow me to see all of this as the perfidy it probably actually is, such that I can know of what to repent. God help me; I can do no other! I love them all...!

*

Despite the squeeze of mounting professional responsibilities, November revealed many ways for Nathan to make a difference in the life of his huge, dynamic, and flourishing church. Dr. Flowers was as energetic and galvanizing as Nathan, and they both learned that they would either work beautifully together, or clash. Happily, they were in harmony in most things, so Dr. Flowers gave Nathan his head and bade him do as he would and could, as long as he brought him and the board along with him. Such a blank check provided just the incentive the young minister needed, and he forged ahead, fully, in every area–except Shara...

As he expected, many of his young people were manifestly hungry–almost desperate–for a trusted adult who would actually listen, not to mention having something worthwhile to say. His afternoon counseling requests tripled almost overnight, forcing him to implement his own counseling triage, taking those who seemed most needy before those with lesser needs (e.g., the fifteen years old girls who asked if a girl was still a virgin, if she had been "fingered").

At home, the Scotts were often interrupted by trusting persons in need. On several occasions calls came in the wee sma' of the night. Lenore groaned, as he quickly dressed and drove to the problem site: church, jail, accident, hospital, home, or bar...

Many midnights, from November on, found him parked in a grassy, airport field, away from buildings, watching planes land and take off, while taping his lonely lady. Airport cops checked on him several times, until they got used to seeing his car and left him alone. When finished taping, he applied the necessary postage and drove to the back of the airport mail center where men were still filling sacks bound for major postal hubs. Handing in the little tape boxes, he took a ribbing from the loaders, but didn't mind. The service was very dependable.

*

Though Nathan constantly prayed for solutions to their manifold plight, he could not articulate a specific petition that would not hurt someone, inevitably. However, he prayed constantly for any solutions, miraculous or not, that would hurt the fewest people. What occurred changed the course of all their lives, forever–quite miraculously...

At a meeting of the Primary teachers in the church's private school, Nathan led a Bible study on John 14, on November 15, 1965. One of those teachers, Merilane Martin McLean, about Nathan's age, asked to speak to him privately, afterward. In hushed terms, she confided that she and her biology professor husband, Dr. Andrew McLean, were frustrated in trying to become pregnant. She was so taken with his Bible study, she said, that she wanted to ask Nathan to pray for conception—or for an appropriate adoption opportunity.

Adoption? Yes, adoption! Oh, my very own God!

Nathan struggled to stifle the rush of adrenaline exercising his body, while QI was doing back flips in his brain! *Good God! Yes, God is Good! Is it really a miracle? Not too fast now. No eagerness. Honest concern, empathy, as real as gravity. Careful, now. Ease into it. She is precious, too!*

"Merilane, of course, I'll pray for you and Andrew to have a baby, one way or another. May I know how long you have been trying?"

"Well, it's a little embarrassing, but I feel you will understand."

Merilane began a rush of words, compressed by urgency and reality. Listening and intently watching her face, the young minister saw goodness, love, and steadfastness dressed in the stress of hopes forestalled. He could hardly believe the importance and timeliness of the miraculous opportunity she presented, completely unawares. Yet even that thought produced concomitant guilt for not considering Shara enough, the while.

"I was certain you'd understand. We've been trying virtually since we got married, six years ago, have gone to doctors, tried all sorts of things, including different, er, positions, exercises, and diets but nothing has worked. I'm thirty and Andy's thirty-three, and we don't want to wait forever. We both love children and have always wanted a family–never using con–never taking any steps to–to forestall pregnancy. Two years ago, we determined to try everything safe and recommended, and if nothing happened by now, to adopt."

"I see."

"So, the two years are up. My doctor told me last week that, given promising research in fertility, other methods would likely be forthcoming in future years, but if we are absolutely determined to have a family, soon, it might be time to consider adopting. We are, so he recommended a service group, Bighton Homes, which house and care for–you know–unwed mothers, then handling their babies' adoptions–and we're seriously considering applying. We will need some character references, and I immediately thought of you. Will you help, as well as pray for us?"

Close to relishing a religious experience, QI sang, *There really is a God, and, and She's an adoption agent!*

A great calm o'ertook Nathan, as he grasped the potential miracle before him. "Believe me for the very works' sake" had been the center piece of his Bible study, not fifteen minutes earlier, and here was a totally unexpected, Godly work, as miraculous to him as the blind seeing, the deaf hearing–and possibly a kind and loving partial solution to his and Shara's dilemma!

"I shall pray, of course, and certainly write a recommendation, Merilane. I have admired your teaching and have enjoyed interacting with Andy–as fine a deacon as we have. You two are certainly worthy of the miracle of a baby, and I'll be glad to help any way I can."

"Thank you, Nathan. I was sure we could count on you. Do you have any information or feelings about Bighton Homes?"

Please, God, don't let me screw up!

"They do wonderful work in very difficult situations, even though the adoption process is quite involved—as it should be. It involves the birth mother being assigned a *nom de naissance*, living in, and she is never allowed to see her baby, or to know very much about who adopts it. Though there is great effort put into matching babies with potential, adopting parents, confidentiality rules, which is usually a good thing. I take it you have contacted them."

"Not yet. It's such a huge step, we've been praying about it, and I needed—we both needed advice. Because of their understandably lengthy processes, we have always hoped for something more personal and private."

Smelling the smoke from the altar, like unto Isaiah of old, Nathan inwardly heard the voice of the Lord, crying, crying, "Whom shall I send and who will go for me?" With this coal of atoning fire touching his lips, and torrents of love and atonement drowning his soul, his heart leapt up with his fervent prayer, *Here am I. Send me!*

Now!

"You might—you might find this difficult to believe, Merilane, but I'm currently counseling a wonderful, young woman who is considering entering such a home, or otherwise putting her coming child up for adoption."

Watching her face blossom with possibilities, he saw her heart's ascent into hope, almost beatifying Merilane's visage. Her eyes widened, she gasped audibly, reached out her hand to touch this news, to fondle it, and to make it real. Then, she began to burble...

"Really, Nathan? Oh, Dear God, has she committed to that, yet? When is she due? Can you tell me something about her—about her background, understanding that confidentially is a given? Oh, please forgive me for jumping in like this, but Nathan...!"

Steady, Nathan. Not too eager. Just stick to the facts; don't blither or try to convince her of anything. She is wonderful and should not be manipulated. And, yes, Dear God, don't let her see my tears—at least not yet.

QI was right, and Nathan followed his own, considered advice. Briefly, he nursed Merilane's clear and certain eagerness with the salient facts about Shara. Young, of age, healthy, and attractive; of sound mind and body; good student, college-bound, after the baby; from a white-collar, middle-class family; her father a college graduate and an officer in two wars; one older and three younger siblings; currently working and estranged from her parents in another state; all church going Christians. Very sadly, but realistically, she and the father may be about to conclude that there is little hope of keeping the baby.

Father, a young professional with advanced degrees; from an excellent family; genuinely loving and moral; a committed churchman; totally unavailable, unfortunately, for marriage any time soon. Both very much in love, but also very much up against it, seeking some way to get through their predicament without harming anyone. Their parents must never know; she's living with an older, wise, confidential, Christian, female friend, who has promised to see her through whatever happens. She is working part time, and she and the father have been seeking God's will for several months, now. Though they want to keep the baby, she is realistic, thinking she—they—are not ready, in almost any way, for such a responsibility. She is healthy, under an obstetrician's care, just past her first trimester with no problems, and is expected to deliver mid-April.

Merilane listened, wide-eyed, and Nathan could almost feel the thrill dribbling down her back—very much like his own. Her wonder at this fortuitous coincidence and the possible fulfillment of their prayers clearly charged them—both.

Nathan waited, while tears began to gather in both of their faces. Looking at him with unconfined joy, she whispered, "Nathan, can it be true? Are you in a position to—to maybe tell this woman about us? Of course, I need to speak with Andy, and I'm sure he'll want to hear as many facts as you are able to provide. But, but Nathan, it seems almost miraculous… Something–Someone–prompted me to speak to you, today–it had to be the hand of God!"

Just say, "Amen."

"Amen," choked the convicted, nearly convinced preacher, to QI, to Merilane, and to very God, Himself, whom he had been trying to "believe…for the very works' sake," all his adult life. At the same time, he felt a vast, cold void vacuuming his heart, thinking of his beloved Shara, her desperate longing for him and for a family of her own. His Prometheus may well be about to be unbound, but nowhere was there the necessary fire for him to bring to his beloved, that she might be warmed and healed of her misery to come

*

"I take it you know this couple, personally, Nathan?" spake Dr. Andy McLean, ever the scientist in search of reliable and valid data. It was a day later, and Nathan had not approached Shara with the prospects.

I'm waiting for a convincing interest–nay–a solidly committed affect and determination in these worthy, eager, and prospective, adopting parents–of our child.

"Yes, Andy; I know them very well, and they are both very near and dear to me."

"I take it that you haven't, yet, said anything to them."

"Correct. Nor do I think you should just jump into this, until you are sure, until all, or at least most, of your questions and doubts are behind you. What else would you like to know?"

"Well, it's touchy, Nathan. Naturally, I would like to think that neither the father nor the mother is promiscuous, but quite obviously, they aren't exactly following the rules."

"Obviously, as you say. But is it too flippant of me to say that the baby is?"

"Good point. I know enough about genetics, though, to know that they count for a lot, and that this baby won't arrive *tabula rasa*. What else can you tell me, without giving away confidentiality?"

"In addition to what Merilane has already shared with you, this couple is very much in love and has been so, for two years. I won't go into their specific circumstances, but, clearly, they would much prefer to get married and keep the baby. However, it is also clear to them, both, that marriage is out anytime soon. We–they–have been waiting and praying for God to help them–that something would happen to make clearer and better their options–and His will. Bighton, or similar, was one option; abortion, of course, was never once considered."

"Nathan, I also know a little something about adoption statistics, including that a certain percentage fail, probably due to genetics. However, I also know that the younger a baby is adopted, the greater chance nurture has to affect its future. No one wants a pig in a poke, to be crass. That's why I'm pressing you a little about these people. Let me just ask what I'm thinking. You seem to know a great deal about them, vouching for them at every turn. Are you related to either of them?"

"Yes."

"I suspected–no, no suspicions here–I rather thought so. That almost cinches it for me, because you are at the top of the heap, spiritually, educationally, morally, and as far as I can tell, genetically."

"I must agree with Merilane—the very fact that we are discussing this, and the way it developed into a possibility, seems miraculous, especially in light of the Biblical passage we were studying, that stimulated her conversation with me, afterward."

I mean it, don't I? My God! No, our God! Maybe He does stick His finger in the temporal pie, after all—and yet we can still decide to ignore His offer, if we want.

QI's fabled objectivity waned in the face of the will of God's.

"I'll talk once more with Merilane; we'll pray about it, maybe discuss it with her doctor, who is ready to connect us with Bighton, and then we'll get back to you, one way or the other. It's clear that the situation you have shared with us is apt to be more ready and available, without a wait list or endless processing, and with maximum information about the couple, which, by the way, you have done a super job in describing, without giving away too much. We both deeply appreciate it, and, uh—Nathan, I, I—please forgive my emotions—I don't cry very easily, but this seems so God-blessed and ordained, it almost overwhelms me."

Invited by none other than God, Nathan embraced the man, sharing his conviction, a likely baby, and the joy of answered prayers. Reiterating, they shook hands, and Nathan walked home to tell his wife what might happen—one step liltingly light, the next weighted down by the unwieldy chains of despair, burdened by the leaden limp of losing love. Lenore, though, was alive with hope, immediately, tearing up, both with and for Nathan—and so typically of that incredible woman, for Shara.

The phone rang at 10:45 p.m., and Nathan ran to get it, pausing a good five seconds, taking a deep breath, before answering it.

"Nathan, glory be to God! Merilane, who is on the other line with me, and I humbly ask you to contact the couple we have been discussing, and to broach the subject of our officially and legally adopting their baby, as soon as possible after it is born. Please tell them, for us, that we are totally committed to loving this sure gift of God as our own, and that we will do whatever we have to do for the mother, including paying for her medical services, either where she is now, or, preferably, here in Miami, where you and Lenore can be a special part of this miracle with us. We would like you, Nathan, to be the go-between if you will. We'll get our lawyer to do all the preliminaries, including satisfying the legal dictates of the state, if you'll handle the contacts and arrangements with the mother–and father, too, of course."

"Yes, Nathan," laughed a crying Merilane, "God has looked into our hearts–all of our hearts–and He has seen fit to say, 'Yes.' I cannot tell you how excited and humbled I am–we are–to be the potential recipients of this clear miracle. Our baby, please God!"

"Yes, congratulations to you both! I'll contact the couple, lay it all out, as we have discussed, and get back to you as soon as possible, he sniffed, unable to transcend their joy."

"When do you think that might be, Nathan?" they spoke, almost in unison.

"I'm not sure. I should see them face to face, to counsel with them that this may be the very hand of God, and that it could be the best for everybody concerned. Still, it is their decision, and they must make it unmanipulated by me. Only God, Himself, has that authority, but I'm so filled with faith, right now, that I can almost–almost assure you that His, your, and their purposes will be mutually fulfilled in this matter."

"So be it, Nathan. So be it, Dear God!"

Hanging up, looking at Lenore's tear-stained face, Nathan almost broke. Gasping, he accepted her outstretched, loving, understanding arms, allowing himself to be enfolded, like the Prodigal she must think him, come home...

Not so fast! Yes, this may well be the answer, but at whose expense? I love Shara to distraction, and I will not allow her to be used or abused by manipulation or any trick or deceit. I must approach her with honesty yet love her the while. It is mostly her decision! How to do that, Preacher? How to do that? I do love her, so!

The next morning, Lenore weighed in on just that question.

"Nathan, I know you're trying your best to do no harm, especially to Shara, whose decision this really must be. May I suggest that you, in your own, loving, and inimitable way, simply describe exactly what has happened, in sequence, and allow her to ask questions. You might tell her, for me, that this decision can be only hers, and that I am praying that she will make the one with which she can live, without guilt, despite anything and anybody. As much as you might want to, I do not think it would be fair of you to try to influence her, at all, except to answer, as honestly as you can, all her concerns. Then, let her decide."

Angels, if there be angels, sang at her simple kindness and concern. No matter, Nathan's heart immediately harmonized with his mate's, and incredible love passed between them, in their simple moment of eternity.

"Thanks, 'Nore. I was thinking along the same lines. You have helped confirm that."

"What has she been expecting, up to now, Nathan. Can you be honest and tell me?"

"Sure I can. She's been hoping and expecting that, somehow, we can have the baby, be together, get married, and live happily ever after. It's the 'somehow' that gives her–and me–pause."

"Have either of you ever articulated what the potential costs of that crushing scenario might be?"

"Of course, honey, constantly! I know you don't mean to insult her–or me, but she–we–constantly bemoan what such would do to you, to the kids, to my job and career, to finances, to everything. She has said many times that she should, 'somehow,' step aside, has even mentioned adoption, after seeing a special on it on TV, but that 'somehow' is no more easily contemplated, much less executed, than the more hopeful, other one."

"I can understand that; I really can. I know what is like to be in love with you; to have your children, and now, there she is, up there... Oh, Nathan; I'm so sorry for you both! It must be God-awful just to live, day to day, with the pressure of your morals, your family, your baby, your everything threatened, no matter which way you turn."

"It's awful wanting, needing, especially loving–you both, 'Nore. In another life, perhaps it would be possible to invite her to join us, have the baby and live happily ever after– but evidently not in this one, though I can make a philosophically logical, even ethical case for it."

"I don't think I want to hear that, though–at least not now."

"See? Not in this lifetime. Maybe in a hundred years, if society learns not to be so, so damned rule-bound with the one thing that should never be regulated or stifled–love. There will never be too much of it–we just haven't been able to figure out how to adjust to that reality."

"Maybe, honey, but I don't think you should be telling her that. How–and when–will you tell her?"

"I won't tell her anything, except the facts.

"Please be gentle. Like you, I'm suddenly very fearful of damaging Shara further. I haven't begun to sort out what all this might mean for us…"

"Damaging her 'further,' huh? Have you considered that she may be the least damaged of us all, and that the growth she has experienced due to this–this…"

"…Affair, Nathan?"

"If that's what you prefer to call it. I think of it as a genuine love relationship, impossibly complicated by my love for you and our children."

"You put your relationship with her on a par with your relationship to us, then."

"Yes, to be very honest, I do. But maybe you could be a little more understanding, for before we moved here, I was beginning to swim in an ocean of other possibilities. This job, and yes, the wonder of you, have sorta leveled the playing field, again."

"I already knew that, Nathan. How could I not know, with your many trips, most of which were billed as 'the last' or 'nearly the last.' However, I take no joy in hearing that you now see your wife, family, job, and other responsibilities external to Shara Starr on a par with a pregnant eighteen-year-old, who ran away from home because of you, and who is living with a friend of ours, who is doing us a big favor."

"'Nore. I didn't cause her to run away. She made that decision entirely on her own, without my input, not knowing that she might be pregnant, at the time. As for the rest, it is what it is; I hate even the thought of hurting you, but, in all honestly, I can no more help loving you both than I can help breathing. And as for our friend Melanie, well…"

"What does that mean, 'well,' about Melanie? She's bending over backward to help us all in this situation, and I don't appreciate your–your suggesting that there's anything wrong with her or her sacrificial actions."

QI rang every alarm bell in Nathan's head, reminding him of the many promises to his erstwhile, red-haired mistress that neither would ever tell Lenore about their long affair. Nathan simply turned them off, for God was in his head, now, too.

"Lenore, while we're discussing monumental decisions and ways to handle them, I think it's time I came clean about something else that has haunted me, and you, if you only knew, for years."

Now, alarms sounded in Lenore's head, hearing his voice grow calm, low–and a bit harder–a rarity.

"Is it related to you and Shara? I don't need more surprises, Nathan."

"Yes, most definitely, it is related to Shara and to you, and most especially to Melanie. I probably shouldn't tell you, for I know it will both surprise and shock you."

As Lenore's face turned almost white with exactly that shock and disbelief, Nathan related the whole, sordid story of his long affair with Melanie. He also recalled to his stunned wife his early, erotic drawings that he now confessed were done in a futile effort to disentangle himself from her best friend, and how he had finally pulled out of her and her body, literally, before he came, successfully ending their nearly 4-year, illicit relationship last April. All out of a newfound fealty to both Shara and to Lenore, he emphasized.

"You mean you did it in our house, while I was there?"

"Many times, yes, just after you and I had made wonderful love, even. In both her old and new apartments, my car, even once in the church, when she stayed after Koinonia, and no one was around–in the Bridal Room, yet. Yes, yes, yes, dammit, there, and wherever we could find a few minutes of privacy, and I'm not the least proud of it. It almost ruined me, you, my job, and by extension, even Shara. It was because of my discontent about Melanie that I turned to Shara in the first place, looking for something, someone who could give me what I was losing with you, with the church, with my job, even with God, then. I haven't touched Melanie since April; however, she begs me to do so almost every time I see or talk with her."

"You know, honey," spake Nathan's shocked paragon of love and understanding, weeping softly, as she reached for him, "I never told you that those drawings of fucking you showed me turned me on, then. I was, and am, amazed at your sex drive, and how pleased I was–still am–when I can get you to focus it on me. Evidently, I failed to accomplish that enough, which turns out to be loss for all of us."

Lenore, the loving woman so empathic and quick to understand that she wrung the neck of a kitten ensnared by a fishing lure, rather than to see it suffer a second longer, was not one for hysterics. Rather, she loved the ones she loved, no matter what–an utter paragon of Agape. This amazing and enabling capacity arose now, for though she was aghast at Nathan's confession, she simply came to him, put her arms around him, nuzzling him and weeping–silently, relentlessly, until he couldn't help but hold her close and appreciate her rising heats.

For reasons known best to Lovely Lenore, her Agape had no trouble, at all, inviting her Eros to join her in her simple, loving act of reclamation. As she wept, she moved her thighs against him, and began kissing him, caressing his genitals through his pants, unzipping him, and inviting him so utterly believably, that Nathan's all too dependable penis soon arose to reward her smoothings. In minutes, she had him on the couch, both naked, kissing him, rubbing her beautiful, lithe body all over him, taking him into her mouth, then sinking her body down upon him, nailing herself to him, sighing and murmuring her ardent claims, once more, wiping and rinsing Melanie from him, forever, as they both reclimbed their own, familiar mountain.

Coming down, Nathan still in stark amazement and appreciation at Lenore's calm, accepting reaction, heard her whisper, "I have always known that she loves you, Nathan. Poor Melanie. How she must be suffering, now!"

CHAPTER 50
REPRIEVE?

Necessity is the mother of taking chances.

Mark Twain

With Lenore deeply asleep on the couch, an overwhelmed Nathan dressed and walked back to his office, to make the fateful call.

"Hello." It was Melanie.

"Hey, Melanie; Nathan, here. I need to speak with Shara if you don't mind."

"Why should I mind? But first, how are things at home and at your work, stranger?"

"Busy; back-breaking, actually, but I'm getting the hang of it. You?"

"The usual. I'm enjoying getting to know Shara better. She's a very real help around here, cleaning, cooking, picking me up, and so on."

"I'm glad, Mel. I'll tell her you said so."

"No need; she heard me. Here she is."

"Hi, Nathan, I was just thinking about you–then, I do that all the time."

"Hello, darling. I need to speak with you privately if possible."

"Is everything all right? I'll turn the tv up. I don't think she can hear much if anything."

"Okay, sweetheart; I'll get right to it. Three days ago, a wonderful, young couple in the church came to me, wanting my help regarding their desire to adopt a baby, because they don't seem able to have one. The wife asked me to give them a reference to a Bighton Home, as adoption seems to be their best next step.

"I was almost overcome at the prospects, as I'm sure you can understand, but equally as wary, even though I heard the flutter of angel wings whispering a miracle. Of course, I agreed to help, if possible, and told them that I am counseling a young, pregnant couple worried about what to do, because marriage seems impossible, soon. They were immediately interested and hopeful–overwhelmed–actually, with the prospects. I realize, darling, that this is sudden and unexpected, but I felt I should share the idea with you, immediately–to see if you might think this is something we should consider– allowing them to adopt our baby?"

Very pregnant pause . . ..

"Honey?"

"Oh, Nathan, I'm crying a little. I was just thinking about how–that's all I ever think about, and certainly adoption was one of the things I thought about, but I never thought something like this would–could–happen. Is it what you want?"

"Honestly, honey, no, no, yes, yes, and maybe."

"I know. I could–run through all, uh, of those answers, myself. Tell me about these people and what has been said, so far, and don't mind me if, if I sniffle and cry (God, Melanie's bringing–me a–a box of tissues) the whole time I'm talking to you."

Hurting, not simply because Shara was hurting, but because he felt the same anxiety and grief that so much was at stake for so many, Nathan briefly filled in more details of the offer, including their willingness to pay for everything, their wanting to fly her to Miami, paying for an apartment, using their own doctor, and asking him to coordinate everything.

Weeping still, Shara asked if he could possibly come up, so that they could discuss it face to face. Yes, but the earliest would be after Thanksgiving. Confirming her plans to go home on the 24th, returning on the 26th, she asked if he could possibly fly up the evening of Sunday, the 28th, for a day or two. Yes, he would make that happen.

"Do you have a reaction, Darling? Anything I can tell them, at this point?"

"I have your exact reactions: no, no, yes, yes, and maybe, and you may tell them that."

"Oh, Shara, please just forget the whole thing if it doesn't seem right to you. You shouldn't make any decision you'll regret, later."

"Darling, I'll regret any decision I make, now, with so much at stake. I just have to think about it; discuss it with you, while I'm in your arms, and not on the phone. Please understand."

Nathan listened to her weeping, unable to hold back his own choking emotions.

"Baby, I'm sorry. I should have waited to tell you until I could be there–to love and hold you, and to try to work out what is best with you!"

"I'll be all right, Nathan," she gasped. "It's just hard to realize that now, we really do have to decide. The 'somehow' we have always talked about is here, and it's hard to face! My every instinct is to shout, 'Noo!' but my good sense tells me that it might be the best thing to happen out of this whole–whole…"

"…Mess?"

"I wasn't going to express it that way. I need you so much, right now. Hurry to me as soon as you can."

"I will, darling, unless something intervenes."

"Yeah, like maybe we'd be in Mexico or somewhere, getting married..."

*

Nathan left his office around midnight, returning home to an animated and interested wife. He told her about his conversation with Shara, that she was upset at the thought, but admitted to having considered it, herself, recently.

"She is going to think about it quite seriously, 'Nore, but she doesn't want to make a final decision until she is with me, face to face."

"What do you want to happen, Nathan?"

"Do I know? Everything. Nothing. Something in between. I do want the pain to go away—hers, yours, and mine. That will take something as radical as adoption, so, yes, it feels much like a Godsend to me. I am hoping that Shara will agree to it, and that it won't kill her. I've admitted that I don't want to give up either one of you, so that figures into the developing equation, too. How about if we move Shara in with us, and we, all three, raise the baby? Don't answer that... "

"Nathan?"

"Yes."

"How in the world did you two manage to get pregnant? You're much too smart to take real chances—and I imagine Shara knows her body. So, what happened?"

"I honestly do not know. I hope talking about this doesn't upset you, but we always either used protection or figured to be within four or five days of her period, either way, which, as you know from our own, premarital precautions, all the books say are safe. When we all had that yeast infection in July, her doctor gave her a full, pelvic exam, including palpating her ovaries. I suspect he popped an ovum or two, and we saw each other five days later, the 25th day of her cycle—which was always as regular as clockwork. We used protection, anyway, so I'm at a loss. She said her ovaries hurt for several days after her pelvic, but that the pain was gone before I saw her. I figure she conceived on July 28; Melanie's doctor told her she would probably deliver around the middle of April, which works out just about right, if you count the normal forty weeks to term, from the first day of her last period."

"God moves in mysterious ways, doesn't He, Nathan?"

"So do you, Honey," he grinned, gently kneading a naked breast.

After making love, Lenore wanted to do it, again. When Nathan rolled his eyes in wonder and anticipation at her evident, sexual surge, she offered that she was reading a pre-publication copy of Masters' and Johnson's, *Human Sexual Response*. There was no surge, just a greater willingness to get what she needed from him—and maybe the knowledge to succeed.

"Anything for science, 'Nore," he whispered, as he slid into her willing readiness.

For Lenore one orgasm was usually enough; a habit from very early childhood, when she accidently learned to come by humping her pillow, with no idea what she was doing, besides receiving great pleasure—inducing almost immediate sleep. Lenore eventually found that she could come again, within ten to fifteen minutes of any orgasm, but she sometimes had to work at it, herself, too, which wasn't her style or even her proclivity. After her third orgasm (and Nathan's second), she wanted to talk about Melanie, while he stroked her and petted her most sensitive areas.

"You say that it started your first night in Durham, while I took Nattie to visit my parents. How?"

"Do you really want me to go into all of that? Isn't it sufficient for you to know that it was totally unplanned and opportunistic? We sorta gentled into it, then I felt like hell, guilty and ashamed, and promised God and myself, repeatedly, in writing, that I would never do it again!"

"It's the 'repeatedly' that gets me, I think, Nathan. I can see, maybe, once, or twice, but repeatedly over three years and eight months—almost four years? That's a long time to act and to feel guilty, afterward."

"Lenore, again, I don't think you want to do this."

"Of course, I do, Nathan—it involves the two people I have always trusted the most, I would like to understand why—how—that trust was misplaced."

"Okay, honey, but if it gets to be too much, stop me. Clearly, I was not satisfied with something. I was so disquiet about things, most things, and I was operating on energy, alone. I know that I always loved you. That never changed, and it never will, regardless of what happens. So, why did I keep fucking Melanie over forty-four months? It's not an easy question, and I certainly have no easy answer. I could wax sociological and blame it on a too early, too young marriage; on an off the charts sex drive; on your tendency to have one orgasm, roll over and go to sleep; on my need to be much more creative in sex; on my perception that you judged my mammoth sex drive negatively, as in our honeymoon photography and those posters I drew; the sense that I didn't—don't—deserve you; on a psychological quirk; on genuine sin; even on her delicious body, one which I eyed for four years before we married and for seven years, thereafter, before I sampled it; or on the fact that I knew she wanted me, and that it was just too easy, costless, and rewarding, sexually, to stop."

"Which, Nathan?"

"Maybe any or all the above, or for some reason that doesn't come to mind. I don't really know. Maybe because I was clearly invited, and because I could. Also, theoretically, philosophically, even ethically, I have always had a problem with Biblical strictures of celibacy before marriage and fidelity after marriage. You can't use it up, and, very often, it just seemed to me to be a big issue over a little tissue, not significantly different from a kiss, a dance, or even a handshake, outside a mature love relationship. Just because the touching is genital shouldn't set it totally apart from other friendly or shared touching.

"Finally, I never once, in all those 44 months, loved Melanie, or stopped loving you, even for an instant, so I concluded, early on, that there was little harm to anyone in getting our rocks off. It never once threatened our marriage, directly; it didn't even take a lot of time, and hour, now and then. You once told me that you wouldn't mind very much were I to screw a prostitute or someone I didn't love. *Voila!* Melanie!"

"I guess somewhere in all of that there might be some truth, Nathan, but what about your religion? Didn't you feel hypocritical?"

"Stephen asked me the same thing when I told him about Melanie. At first, I prayed about it almost constantly, but even that faded into my growing belief that what we were doing was inconsequential to all but ourselves. Bottom line: Even after my relationship with Shara evolved into sex, neither Melanie nor I believed we were hurting anyone, or we couldn't have continued. It became a rewarding, virtually costless habit– minor addiction, if you will. You know that she loves you, loves the kids, and would be mortified were she to know I told you. Perhaps she just wanted to get her piece of the sexual pie; you'll have to ask her, when the inevitable facing up occurs."

"You expect me to bring this up to Melanie? I don't know about that."

"Nore, it's inevitable. I'll have to confess to her that I told you, ultimately, and that will open the door for all sorts of talking, confessing, forgiving and restoration, don't you think?

You don't love her one bit less, knowing this, and I believe she knows that. I would love to be a mouse in the corner, however, when that conversation comes around."

"Don't you dare tell her, Nathan—at least not until Shara is out of—until she finds her own place. Promise me. No, don't. Promises seem to sit rather loosely in your ontology—or is it in your teleology or cosmology?"

"Most likely in my penis, where my brains are, Lenore."

"I shan't follow that lead, Mister. You were explaining the absence of hypocrisy from a religious perspective when you got side-tracked. Please continue."

"From a religious perspective, I had—have—come to believe that Pauline Christianity is terribly hung up on the sins of the flesh, when Jesus, himself, didn't appear to get all excited about it. He forgave the woman at the well and the woman taken in adultery, but he didn't tell them they couldn't fuck, did he? You've heard me rail at Paul—that self-appointed, elite misogynist, with TLE—temporal lobe epilepsy—likely, whose emphases and caveats continued a prudish and paternalistic approach to 'evil' flesh, especially female flesh—and to the useless, material earth, itself, caught between God above and Satan below. Balderdash!"

"Yes, I recall your having those sentiments; many of them have made some sense to me, too, as you should have realized by my willingness—eagerness, really—to engage with you in sex long before we were married. You're right, now that I think about it. I don't feel threatened in the least by poor Melanie's love for you—however expressed."

"Repeatedly, I told her that what we were doing was purely sexual and friendly, and that there could never be anything else to it.

"And potential pregnancies?"

"She's on the pill, as you doubtless know."

"I understand your voracious appetite, and I know I don't have the same need for frequency—or variety. But I can't help but recall with some bitterness that there were dry spells for me, Nathan, especially back in Durham. I now know you were doing it with both Melanie and Shara, then, so maybe I'm pissed that my needs were ignored. I fault both of you—all three of you for—for that selfishness and insensitivity."

"Guilty, as charged, Lenore. I am deeply sorry."

Pause.

Lenore's hands reached for his crotch, her lips kissing his neck.

"You want to do it again? At your service, always. We could try some things differently if you're willing."

"I'm willing, as long as it doesn't hurt. One thing more, before I turn sluttish, however; aren't I as good in bed as either Melanie or Shara?"

"I wondered when you'd get around to asking that, 'Nore. Of course, you are! I don't want you to be sluttish—unless it comes from within, then it would be great. However, I relish innovation and make believe, not pretense; mutually pleasing acting is okay, though. I also relish honest attempts at spoken fantasy, maybe involving others, variety, and experimentation, as long as no one gets hurt . . . .."

CHAPTER 51
INCUBATIONS

The mind is a very useful tool along the path, but the heart is the path.

John Clark

"**O**h, Shara, I've missed you so! Come to me!"
She did.

She had Melanie's car; Melanie was gone for three nights. They had her apartment and her blessing. Three nights to rest and nest and consider what to do about their baby. Three nights they needed to incubate their future, and three nights from which they hoped would rise a new day for everybody concerned, one way or another.

Neither was ready to jump right into things, so Nathan decided to tell Shara of his conversations with Lenore about Melanie first.

"You told her? Why? How? Oh, Nathan, do you think that will upset her so much that she will . . ."

". . . Kick you out? I don't think so. Lenore had the same reaction. You know what, Shara? Lenore could not have been more understanding, both of my long affair with Melanie, and with my–our need to see each other while deciding."

"How did she react? Cry? Shout? Hit you?"

"She did exactly what you did, Shara; she fucked me, immediately, passionately, and emphatically, as though to wash Melanie from me, forever. Then she commented that she has

498

always known that 'poor' Melanie is in love with me, and is worried about how upset she must be, now."

"Lenore and I are more sisters than I thought, Nathan. I know exactly why she did that. Partly for the reasons you said, but another part of her simply wanted to prove to you that nothing matters as much as having you. I understand that, totally!"

"I hadn't thought of it that way. Humbling, either way."

"Speaking of humbling, it's time to share our thoughts about the baby. I think I have it figured out, but I absolutely want your honest, heart's—and mind's—reactions. Promise?"

"Of course, if I can stand it."

"I know. You'll have to stay there in that chair and just let me talk, even if I cry. I want you to wait until I've said all I want to say, then you can react."

"I'll try, wonderfully mature and sane woman; I'll try."

"First, I want you to know that more than anything in the world, I want to be your wife and the life-long mother of this baby—but with you, not apart, sneaking, scraping, conniving our way through a necessarily less than totally committed relationship. So, if you tell me, now, that there is no way, at all, for us to do that by time the baby gets here, I'll go on to my next thought."

"Sweetheart, it breaks my heart to sit over here, watching you cry, going through this hell I've brought upon you. Can't I hold you?"

"No, Nathan. I'm crying because it hurts, and that's normal. If you start holding me, now, I'll never get through this, and we'll be back where we started."

"I'm hushed."

"Then, please tell me if you are willing and able to make the kind of commitment I need—I must have—if I'm to keep the baby and be its mother: that you will do whatever it takes, by April, for us to be together, formally and forever."

"Willing, of course. Jesus, Shara. I, I, don't know how—I'm not sure if—I don't see... Now, you've got me crying, too. Let me take a deep breath or two, then I'll answer you."

"Take your time, Nathan, only be totally honest. I know you; you don't want to hurt me or anybody, so you may try to grace the question. Not this time. Please tell me your God's only truth."

Pause.

"Okay, I'm thinking how to put it, Shara. But I guess there is no way to sugar coat it, is there? As much as I want—need—what you want, in all honesty, there is no way I can bring that off in time for the baby, or probably even within year or so of its birth. Do you want me to go into detail as to why?"

Crying harder, but retaining her mature demeanor, Shara said, "No, I understand why. I just wanted us both to look at that option square in the face, decide and then go to the next possibility, if necessary."

It's necessary, of course, and I, I—wait a minute. What's happening here?

A certain numbness settled into Nathan's body, as he heard her speaking as though from afar. Worlds were colliding, and he could no longer avoid their collisions. QI was sidelined, confused.

"All right, second. Since I can't have you and the baby at the same time, and I'm not prepared in any way, except by my love, to take care of it by myself, in a proper manner, I propose that we give it up, hoping and working toward the time when we can be married and have our own children. Isn't that the next best thing, Nathan?"

From somewhere behind his eyes, Nathan heard his own voice say, "Regrettably, yes, so it seems..."

"Then, I'm ready to discuss the adoption proposal made by the couple in your church. I think I can handle that—and believe that it is the best, though it breaks my heart into a million pieces."

Nathan heard her voice, saw her sitting there, beautiful in her cogent misery, ready to do the two things any committed woman least wants to do: lose her baby and possibly her man at the same time.

How many more pieces of our hearts have we left? How can I ask this of this woman? I love her, dammit, and I cannot allow her to carry the whole burden, even though I know that is what she is trying to do—to protect unworthy me.

"Wait a minute, Shara. What did you say? You're ready to give…?"

Seeing his utter misery and his attention flooding away with the tears coursing down his face, Shara realized that he was simply unable to make such a decision; nor, could he ask her to do it. Drawing deeply from her heart of love for him, she was aware that, despite his usual strength and caring, no matter his cool head in the face of tragedy, he was incapable of deciding for so much pain and loss—and that she must do it for them both.

Touching him, shaking his shoulder, "Nathan, are you all right?"

"Sorta—give me a minute," his face still contorted by pain. "I just couldn't get my mind around… Trauma can do that to thinking persons—just make them stop thinking; stop knowing; stop being, even, for a moment or two."

"Nathan, you have to know that this is best—for everyone concerned—even me, when I look at things through the eyes of a future that does not include our marriage by mid-April, when our baby…"

Not willing to finish her sentence, feeling her strength puddling with his tears, she realized anew that her love for him was willing to suffer anything, if there was any chance of their being together permanently. Uncharacteristically, he simply looked blankly at her, tears still streaming. Finally, he held out his arms to her and she flew into them, burying their co-misery in their embrace, salting their faces with wretched tears. Then, holding–and somehow holding on–they calmed, weightless, yet more weighted than ever.

Of flat affect, drained, and despairing, Nathan turned her face to his, kissed her as gently as starrlight, sighed and spoke, haltingly: "I agree–that it is probably the best–the most loving–thing we can do in the near term. And, yes, it will give you opportunities you would have to postpone–maybe forever, if you were to–to keep the–our–baby–either with or without me–college, a career, and so on. If that's what–you truly believe is best–I'm with you–both in the decision–and in this God damned misery."

"That's what I'll decide, then–but Nathan, I want you to come up one more time, to make if final. That's my only condition: at least one more visit with you before I–we–make that final decision."

He stood, pulling her up with him, held her at arm's length, looked deeply into the most beloved face in his short life, absorbed in agony, and sobbed, "Shara, I'm so sor—...!"

CHAPTER 52
NEW WINE

Lust invites love to play house.
Love invites lust to live in it.

Nathan Rhea Scott
December 15, 1965

To love for the sake of being loved is human,
But to love for the sake of loving is angelic.

Alphonse Marie Louis de Lamartine

Perhaps it was inexorable. Nathan and Lenore bought a house–three days after his return from Prospect Park. Seven miles north of the city, several blocks off the interstate, it was in a quiet neighborhood crowded with established, typical Florida cinder block, VA homes. All of 1,600 square feet, it sported terrazzo flooring with bedroom carpeting; a large dining/living room/kitchen, opening to a jalousied lanai; plenty of windows; no heat or air conditioning; hall leading to three bedrooms and two full baths; heavy gauged, wire fenced back yard, complete with bearing grapefruit and orange trees; circular drive and car port: $18,500, with an assumable, VA mortgage charging 2.15% over 29 years. Their sparse furniture barely made it livable, but Lenore loved it.

The significance of this purchase? As obvious for Lenore as it was dubious to Nathan, for almost the exact same reasons: an anchor for Lenore; a potential ball and chain for Nathan, both aware of the effect it could have on Shara Day Starr.

Never to be Scott, now?

The opportunity had arisen suddenly. Dr. Flowers called and urged Nathan to snap it up. They moved in on December 11, 1965.

Dr. Andy and Merilane McLean were among the volunteers helping them pack, load, unload, and unpack, all in one day. The McLeans were upbeat, happy, and well satisfied with Nathan's intermediary role, leaving almost all the many, non-legal details to him. No one questioned the need for another visit, understanding the moral, physical, and emotional depths involved.

Lenore was concerned at Nathan's flat affect since his return. He reported that the experience with Shara was very much like cutting out his own heart, except that it was Shara's heart that worried him the most. He was in shock for a few days, which could explain how/why he passively acquiesced to Dr. Flower's urging to snap up the house. Nathan seemed a dead man walking.

Intermittently taping Shara, while making rounds at two hospitals and a detention hall, Nathan worried about telling her. She knew they had to move by January but thought they would find another rental. The implications of buying, instead of renting, were clear enough for Lenore, who insisted that he carry her over the threshold, for a glass of barely tolerated champaign.

"To our new life," she toasted.

And how would Shara react to this sparkling, little scene? Once again, I'm catalyzing joy, at the expense of pain and dismay.

"Wail, Shara," he taped, "you may be surprised to hear that we moved into our new digs Saturday. It all happened incredibly fast–and unexpectedly." His brief, exculpating explanation felt much like treason, even though Shara offered half-hearted congratulations.

"Honey, I will be able to visit you December 18–21, Saturday through Tuesday, until my evening return flight. I am to marry Liz Oberon to Charlie Moore in Raleigh on the 18th, at two. She was on the regional Senior High Council with you and Kathy. Charlie was two years ahead of you at First church. They came to visit me while I was in Wilmington. The wedding will be in the Trinity Church. I'm flying up on Friday, December 17, for the rehearsal. Melanie will arrive here, as I leave for North Carolina

"After the wedding, Saturday, I'll fly to Philly, arriving at 8:15 p.m., hoping you can meet me. We'll have the apartment to ourselves! Dr. Flowers approved the whole thing, agreeing to my seeing 'the natural mother,' as he calls you, to make 'gut-wrenching,' final decisions and arrangements.

"Shara, I'm all right. You asked if I were still having 'moments of denial.' I don't sleep all that well, unless I'm dead tired, so I've been working extra hard, lately, so I can just drop into bed."

*

As Nathan packed for his trip to Raleigh and the wedding, he included several, new articles of clothing for his pregnant paramour. Such were purchased, on the sly, despite the amused salesclerk who giggled throughout his efforts.

"Before you go pick up Melanie at the airport, Nathan, may I ask you a few questions?"

"Sure, 'Nore; have at me."

"Well, I have two concerns. First, I'm wondering if I should tell Melanie that I know about–about your affair with her."

"To what end, honey?"

"That's what I have been asking myself. I don't feel right about knowing and having to act as though I don't. You know how I hate sham and pretense."

"In spades!"

"Yes. Melanie has always been the best friend I have in the whole world, besides you, and I don't feel right about not dealing with this rather large truth. I'd like to tell her that I love her, still, and to forgive her, if she asks for it. It's bound to prey on her. Doubtless, we'll talk about your situation with Shara, and Melanie's incredible sacrifices, but it will ring a little hollow, due to these damned secrets we both have. See what I mean? You're to pick her up in less than an hour, and I want to know who I'm supposed to—no, not supposed to, but who I am and who she is, now. I don't want to fake anything, and I do want to, well, I want her to know that I understand."

"You have an urgent need to forgive her, don't you, honey?"

"Yes. It's very important to me. Moreover, I think I understand how—how you both finally lit the fire that I have always noticed smoldering between you, Nathan."

"Was it that obvious?"

"To me, yes. I've known she was in love with you since college. I've also noticed her blush and color when you pay attention to her. She acts completely different when you're around. I also noticed that she became progressively bolder about dressing—or undressing—around you. For whom else would she wear sexy, black underwear when she came to visit—and it was obvious that she wanted you to see it, wasn't it?"

"I noticed, of course, 'Nore. I just didn't notice your noticing my noticing. Come clean with her, if that is what you want—or maybe she'll take this occasion to tell you. Who knows?"

"All right, honey. Thanks. I'll wait to see what unfolds, while she's here—and you're there. She may decide to tell me the truth, at that, though I tend to doubt it. Maybe there will be a way I can make it easier for her, if telling me is on her heart."

"Speaking of truth and hearts honey, you already know I am constantly seeking ways to continue with Shara that won't hurt anybody, after the baby. But that seems so unlikely, especially soon, that her idea of 'stepping aside' begins to seem reasonable—but devastating—to both of us. I hope that doesn't shock you too much, but I have always dreamed of having you both, in some sort of workable arrangement. That seems more improbable, now. If true, I need—to contemplate freeing her, so she can get on with her life, go to college, and, and…"

Nathan couldn't finish the thought.

Lenore didn't say a word; she just opened her arms to him, both physically and emotionally, as she always did, and he sought refuge there, again, as he had done so very many times.

"It's so hard, 'Nore—so God-damned hard!"

"Yes."

"Thanks for being you. I love you; you know."

"Yes."

*

Melanie arrived at the Miami airport at 10:00 a.m. for her long weekend stay with Lenore, while Nathan visited Shara. She was met by a tense Nathan and wanted a kiss which he deftly dodged; it landed on his ear.

"The better to hear you with, my dear," he laughed as she tried, again. "Come on, let's get your baggage."

"All right, but you could at least kiss me properly and not be such a kill joy."

"I ain't never killed no joy in my life, nohow. I may have wounded one a little, though. Anyway, when are you going to give up on me, Melanie? I ain't worth the powder it'd take to blow me up."

"I don't want to blow you up, Nathan. You know that. But I would like you to treat me with respect, and with a little bit of honor—and maybe affection. It's not as if we don't know each other—inside and out."

QI suppressed *I like inside best.* Instead, "Melanie, you've been a dear friend to me and my family for years, and I can't tell you how much I appreciate what you're doing for Shara—and me. You're a saint!"

"I'd rather be a sinner with you, and you damned well know it, Mister Scott."

Turning into the grounds of his church, Nathan explained that he needed to get something from his office. Melanie simply followed him. Inside his office, she closed the door and came up behind him, as he was retrieving Shara's gift bags from an upper cabinet. He felt her breasts against his back, first, and then her arms around him holding him tightly against her.

"Oops!" he said, as he whirled, removing himself from her clear and pressing offer. "No thank you, Mel. We've got to get home, eat and visit a bit, before everyone takes me back to the airport."

Meekly, she followed him back to his car, where she apologized, wiping her eyes. In the car, where intensely creative and lubricious activities were sometimes enjoyed by its present occupants, Melanie was her demure, poised, well-dressed self—exuding muted sexual desire and availability. Despite himself, his QI, and years of fervent prayers, he felt the inescapable, conditioned response of lust creeping through his body. Glancing at her, he immediately knew exactly what was beneath her smartly designed outfit.

She noticed his noticing, for she turned toward him, brought her left leg up on the seat, cocked her knee toward him, where a flash of a delectable, white thigh invited his look, as well as his hand—he had only to reach out and touch somebody. Wise to the ways of this man, her face flushed deep red with lust, she looked at him looking at her and whispered, "Nathan, I know you want me–and you know I want you. Can't we go somewhere and enjoy each other, one last time, before you cast me away, forever?"

Swallowing his lust in great gulps, holding fast to his avowed intent, he replied, "Of course, I want you, Mel, but I can't have you, and you can't have me; not for old times' sake, nor because we're both hot for each other, nor for any other reason under the sun. I don't mean to be cruel, but it's not fair of you to come on to me, knowing how much I desire you, but also knowing that I–we–are going through one of the most difficult periods of our lives. It is important that I hold myself together throughout this episode, and you are already doing much more than you should, helping. So, with great respect and deep admiration, plus a rampant erection, please put your leg back down where it belongs, shift your skirt to "demure," and let's both shape up. We'll be home in about five minutes, and I don't want to go in flushed."

Melanie sighed a long sigh, ending in more quiet tears, and muttered, "I'm truly sorry, Nathan. I had to try. I'm not seeing anyone, and my drives are huge, especially seeing Shara every day, knowing what, how, when, and now where you have made love to her. I fantasize that, and I fantasize you. Is that so terrible?"

"No apology necessary, Mel. You were just doing what comes naturally, and I wanted to respond in kind, but I just can't. Please understand."

"I do, of course. Again, you can't–or at least you shouldn't–blame me for trying. In a way, I'm proud of you. I don't know what I would have thought, had you given in to my needs, again."

"So, that was a test?"

"Not really, except now it has become one—that you passed with flying ..."

"...Erection?"

"Did I notice?" she smiled grimly, "but that makes your refusal even more telling. Like the night you left me frustrated on the bed, you were able to stop, this time, before you started. That's good for Lenore; it's good for Shara, but I fervently believe that it was—is—a loss to us both."

"Loss of sex, Melanie, not friendship. I still love you, in my own, awkward way, and I shall always remember our—our times together."

"Thank you for that, at least."

They drove the last 2 minutes in silence, Melanie pretending to take in the south Florida flora and climes.

"Here we are—our little home in the woods. Welcome to 'Scott Free,' which is what we've named it, except it'll cost us a bundle, over the years."

QI was amazed. *I passed a test—a huge one, at that.* He was smugly congratulating himself, when Melanie suddenly reached over, in full sight of his house, grabbed him and kissed him on the mouth.

"I love you, Nathan Rhea Scott," she said, breathing heavily, "and probably always will."

She was out of the car before he could say a word. Discombobulated, he sat there a moment, trying to recover, when Lenore opened the front door, rushed up to Melanie and gave her an honest hug. Then, she told him to get Melanie's bag, for heaven's sake, and come on in.

And it was so.

*

Driving Nathan back to the airport for his trip north was hilarious, with Nathan cracking corny jokes, singing kiddie songs, and the kids responding with their own silliness.

Mommy noted that, honestly, she didn't know which of the three was the silliest, but that she was going to vote for Daddy.

"Noo, I'm da silliest," sang Beth.

"No, you're the smelliest," responded the five-year-old.

"Nooo, I da prettiest. Mommy, Nattie say, 'smelly.'"

"No, I'm the ugliest," snorted the driver, trying to head off sibling conflict.

"Nooo, you're the bestest," sang Nattie.

"Who's da Mommiest?" asked precocious two-and-a-half.

"I'm just here to keep peace in the family," sang Mommy.

"What does that leave for me, then," asked Melanie, sitting between the two rapscallions.

"That's easy," said the bright lad, "you're the luckiest because we love you, and Daddy and Mommy love you, too."

"And why does everybody love me?" she asked.

"Because you give everything when you come." Little Nathan hollered, causing immediate agreement from his little sister.

QI almost choked at his son's naive accuracy. At the airport, he gave all big hugs, including Melanie, who made sure it was pubes to pubes, as Lenore watched with her calm, all-knowing gaze.

*

As his plane approached the Philly airport, after a delightful wedding experience, Nathan wondered whether to share his pondering with Shara. *Should I share my recent, utterly depressing, and damning thoughts about our future—Lenore's joy in our new house, the fading promise of marriage—freeing her to find what's best, or at least better for her?*

QI counseled *forthrightness and transparency in all things Shara. Should I remind her that marriage seems an impossibility, especially soon, though I love her and that it might be best that she be free—of me? That I would do all in my power to see that she got every opportunity for meaningful independence, education, or whatever she wants, after the baby is adopted, but that she might be best served to move on from me and my impotent promises…?*

Nathan had always trenched around such an abortive idea, ever seeking twin valleys in which to live his life and his loves. *Must I—we—awaken from that dream, replacing it with separation nightmares for us both? It would seem so, this side of bigamy. Shara probably realizes it, too, or why would she even contemplate "stepping aside?"*

And so it went, until he saw her just outside the gate, grinning and looking *much the same—only a little heavier, or is it only the coat she's wearing? She is well into her 6th month and ought to be showing more than she was at the end of November. Oh, God, she's wearing a maternity smock; she's precious!*

Grabbing her and lifting her off her feet with his enthusiasm, he immediately put her down, careful not to hurt her or the baby. They kissed for at least a minute, each ravenous for the essence of the other.

"Oh, Shara, you're so cute in that smock. God, I'm so glad to see you."

"Do you like it? Melanie gave it to me, just before I took her to the airport this morning."

"I do like it, Little Mama. That was incredibly nice of her to do that."

Inside Melanie's place, it took very little time for the starving couple to try to take their urgent fill of the other, with Nathan insisting that she get on top, lest his weight cause discomfort. Shara's orgasm was so intense she collapsed on him in her delirium, reclaiming him with each thrust and pulse.

Later, as Shara followed him, naked, into the living room, Nathan eyed her growing pregnancy with sudden approval. *What's this? Pride? Yes, I am proud of her. She's more*

512

beautiful than ever, with her growing tummy creating a little, round platform above her wonderful, black forest. If I believed in auras, hers would be golden and shimmering.

Shara squealed with delight when she saw two maternity smocks, two pairs of maternity pants, two pairs of warm socks, and two cotton panties with elastic fronts. She immediately stepped into a pair of dark blue slacks, pulling them up to her dismay, thinking them too large for her.

"The sales lady said they should fit a junior size 7 about 5-7 months preggers, but if they didn't right away, you'd grow into them."

"I hope you didn't spend money we don't have on me, honey, but I'm glad you brought these. Now we don't have to go shopping for them. You are the most thoughtful husband a girl could have."

Show her the dildo.

"What on earth is that? It looks just like a penis–balls and all, except he–it's more circumcised than you."

"That's what it is, Honey, only it's made of pliable rubber–for obvious purposes."

A lust of wonder came into her eyes, as she timidly took the 6-inch, prosthetic penis, turned it this way and that, and finally put it to her nose and sniffed.

"It's made for a different orifice, Shara. You'll need to keep it under wraps, though. It's still illegal in some states; I don't know about Pennsylvania. Many southern states outlaw this and other sexual paraphernalia. I had to order it from New York, and it came in a plain, brown wrapper, as advertised."

Suddenly inspired, she put the balls end against her crotch, holding it up as though she were a man and humped the air. Running to a full-length mirror, she repeated her bumps and grinds, watching the dildo move in and out of an imaginary vagina, giving her goose bumps.

"Wow, Nathan, I almost know what it might be like to be a man, with this thing. What's it called, again?"

"It's called a 'dildo,' now, but it was called an 'olisbos' around 500 BC and was used in fertility rites, orgies, and between women. They were made of ivory, wood, horns, and sometimes jade. They were popular in America until the 1930s, when the prudes outlawed such."

"I didn't even know such things existed. I've heard a guy call another guy a 'dildo,' but I had no idea what it meant."

Amused and amazed, Shara was anxious to try it out. After washing and warming it, she lay on Melanie's bed, spread her knees, and began. Being fully lubricated from their recent efforts, it slid right in, opening her eyes as widely as it did her vagina.

"I can't believe I got it up me just like that. Now what? I feel it, but it isn't the same as feeling you. For one thing, I should've warmed it more, and for another, it doesn't exactly feel like you–but it's much better than a hot dog!"

CHAPTER 53
HOPE DEFERRED

Hope deferred makes the heart sick, but when the desire is fulfilled, it is the tree of life.

Proverbs 13:12

Sex, maternity clothes, cuddling, talking, listening to music, and eating took a goodly portion of their remaining, waking hours. Nathan simply put off what seemed inevitable: to earnestly suggest what he absolutely did not want to suggest. Instead, he asked her about her life in Prospect Park and beyond. She told him about her boring job, modeled her new maternity clothes, and tried some new recipes. The picture of young, female beauty, it made his heart wither, to think that he might–could–should–lose her.

Nathan shared more of Lenore's reactions to his Melanie confessions, fully reported Melanie's persistent advances and his responses, causing Shara's mouth to gape at Melanie's boldness. Then the conversation shifted to other matters.

"Would you have wanted me to get an abortion, if they were legal, Nathan?"

"Absolutely not! That thought never once occurred to me–it's our child–and it's illegal. Besides, that would not have been up to me, just as adoption isn't; it would've been up to you."

"I never thought of it, either. I don't think I could have done it, no matter. As you say, that's our baby in here, and I very much want him to be born: a combination of our bodies and love. Don't you think it would be murder?"

"Yes, yes, no, no, and maybe. I would hate to decide that, as I'm not qualified—no men are. Pregnant women are—hopefully in consort with their men and their doctors. Hard and fast rules and laws often ignore prevailing circumstances—and that will get us into a deep discussion of ethics—what should be the principle, as opposed to the precept or law, to guide such moral decisions?"

"What principle might justify an abortion, then?"

"Relevant circumstances, Shara. Fletcher, an Episcopal priest who developed 'situational ethics,' wrote that there is only one absolute good, and hence, only one absolute law: the law of Love: Agape, the unconditional love for all people in all circumstances. He wrote that justice is love applied, that situations and people matter more than hard and fast rules or laws. His principle asks, simply—and perplexingly—what is the most loving thing to do? This Law of Love is best served if more specific precepts, for example, laws against abortion, are set aside, in favor of the most loving results possible."

"Go on; I'm following you."

"Some hold that women bring pregnancy upon themselves, so let them bear the consequences, ignoring the male partner and the prospects for the coming child, the mother, and siblings. What if she were desperately poor and already had a house full of kids, if she were the only means of support for them, and adoption was simply not available—or what if she had been raped, or forced into sexual slavery? There are lots of 'what ifs,' that may not be treated justly by blindly applying a hard rule, practice, or law. What would be more or most loving in such cases, to abort the fetus, or allow worse things to happen, either to it and/or those connected with it, after birth?"

"Well, I can see what you mean. Just to blindly apply some law, especially a law that doesn't consider other important facts."

"Shara, do you remember Nancy, the Black, former prostitute and junkie, who worked in the whore house with Temple Drake in "Sanctuary," the movie I showed at Camp Promise?"

"Yes, she was the one who smothered Temple's littlest baby, to keep Temple and her two children from running away with that awful killer, Candy Man. Temple was about to do deadly harm to both herself and her children, and Nancy couldn't stand to see that, so she stopped Temple by taking the life of the innocent girl. But that was still murder, wasn't it?"

"You bet, according to Mississippi law—and to Nancy. If you recall, she readily accepted her guilt and punishment. Why?"

"Because, in her heart—her conscience—she did what she thought was right—the most loving, the most saving. Right?"

"Right. You also remember that Temple Drake visited Nancy, whom she loved, the night before Nancy's execution, wanting to help and to understand. Nancy readily accepted her guilt and coming execution, to Temple's horror. When Temple asked her how she could be so calm, not even trying to help herself, Nancy just kept saying, 'Believe, Chile! Just believe!' Believe what, Shara?"

"I'm not sure—believe that Nancy had done a good thing?"

"Certainly, she thought so—a 'better' thing, perhaps. Yet, Temple, the mother of the little girl, might have felt quite

differently about that. What else do you suppose Nancy
wanted Temple to believe?"

"Hmmm. I guess she wanted Temple to believe that
she was already forgiven, and was going to meet God with a
clean conscience?"

"Thou hast said it, Shara! Nancy loved Temple and
her innocent children enough to stop Temple from going back
to the Candy Man and ruining all their lives, but she didn't
want Temple to believe that she, Nancy, was condemned by
God for her act. She wanted Temple to realize and believe the
depths to which love can and does take us, even in adverse
extremity. Nancy believed she was already forgiven. In her
mind, she had done the most loving thing. But more
importantly, she wanted Temple to believe that she, too, could
be forgiven of her hand in Nancy's unlawful, but possibly
ethical action. She wanted Temple to believe both of those
things—in the awesome power of love and forgiveness!"

"Okay I get it. You're comparing Nancy's killing the
child with an equally as 'necessary' abortion. Right?"

"Right! Paul Tillich, the existential theologian, wrote,
'Love (Agape) is the ultimate law.' I try to believe that, because
I also try to believe in Christ's ultimate commands: 'Love God
with everything you have and love your neighbor as yourself.'
However, I readily admit that it gets a bit hairy trying to decide
two related questions: how do we measure Agape, and how
can anyone predict what will happen in the future? Nancy
simply assumed that Temple's leaving with Candy Man would
be ruinous, and that Nancy's deadly action would compel
Temple to stay— but she didn't really know either of those
things. Nancy acted on what she thought would happen."

"A leap of faith, huh?"

"Exactly. Ultimately, we cannot know the answer to
either of those questions, which forces us back on something
other than law or too narrow a precept. For me, though it may

seem entirely too facile, I am content to try to do as both Augustine and Luther admonished: 'Love God and do as you please.' Loving the God of Love should affect my behavior in His direction."

"So, tell me in plain English, do you, Nathan Scott, believe abortion can ever please God?"

"Maybe. It depends on the circumstances, Shara. If there are only two choices and both are evil, such as the choices Nancy thought she had, then the lesser of those two evils is/becomes good, by definition, and that's what Nancy believed. If I, Nathan, love God, I should do as I please, because my love of God will deeply affect what I please. I believe I should be free to act harmoniously with the love of God, because I want to thank and to please God. The arbiter, the judge, in this life, must be my conscience, or the conscience of the persons involved. Not just the Bible, not just the Torah or Talmud or the Koran, and certainly not just anything else, like laws. They all help, of course, but I must leave all that to God. That is what Jesus was getting at, when he clearly said, 'Judge not, that you be not judged.'"

"Man, I'm glad I didn't have to face such a decision."

Now, Scott? Is now the time to be Shara's Nancy?

"But, honey, you do. If you make your final decision today, won't it be because you believe it is the decision most consistent with Love?"

"Well, when you put it that way... Nathan, can I ask you something?"

"Yes, as always."

"Did you love God and do as you please, when you started up with me, fell in love with me, made love to me, and now love me, despite your family, the church, your job, and even God?"

This woman is sharp as a razor. How I love her insights and perspectives, even when they pillory me!

"Shara, I–we–have been answering that question, daily, since that incredible night in May, on the boathouse deck and beyond. To most others, the answer would be, 'no;' that I only pleased myself and you and didn't think about pleasing God. And, to an extent, they would be right. I never thought what we were doing was *displeasing* to God, for I simply assumed that pure love, Agape, admixed later with Agape-drunk Eros, was consistent with everything we humans know about nature, evolution, and the purpose of life, itself–the purpose of God's creation. No, my dilemma has always been the same as yours: how can I–can we–finally fulfill our pure love, without hurting anyone else, especially Lenore and my children, for I have always loved them, too, and always will. So, yes, I believe God's love was part of my motive in seeking you out to love. I was virtually lost, otherwise, and acted accordingly."

"I knew something like that would be your answer, Nathan. My answer to that question is that I trusted–trust–you and not only followed where you led, but did my own leading, when it appeared to be consistent with what I was learning about love–almost entirely from my relationship with you. I believe we have both acted consistently with our Love for each other but that our love for others was almost always secondary, and that's why it has been so difficult to figure out the 'how?' We both still struggle with our love, all our relationships, our baby, and our future, of course. Right?

"So, it seems, alas!"

Do I suggest loving, hard decisions that seem to be hanging in the very air, now, or wait?

"I have accepted my responsibility about those things, Nathan, and, yes, you are quite right about your dilemma, because it is mine, too. I don't want to hurt your family, and the 'somehow' that we have been hoping for these many months just doesn't seem very possible, does it?"

Nathan sighed, "I guess it's time to address that dilemma, isn't it darling? But first, what have you finally decided about an adoption?"

"I've come to a solid decision if that's what you mean. I think I should, and I will, give up our baby to be adopted by your friends in your church. That's final. I will not change my mind—not even with the purest love for me pouring from your shocked face, right now. If I must, Nathan, I'll look away…"

Expecting that decision, it still shocked him into silence, as wispy tears blurred his vision, not only of her beautiful, steady face, not twelve inches away, but of their dream, as well. He—and it—were crushed under the god-awful weight of godly love, regardless of QI's sigh of relief.

"I see. As much as it pains me, as I know it pains you, darling Shara, I must agree with you. It certainly appears to be the best possible—the most loving—solution to our current dilemma. Do you want to say more?"

"Yes. I had to be the one to make this decision, because I'm the one who must go through the next four months and the birth. You can't give up the baby. Only I can do that. However, like Mr. & Mrs. X, down in Florida, I want you to handle the details, be the go-between. That way, I'll have you near me most of the time, won't I?"

"Yes," he whispered, the pain in her face shredding him.

Pause.

"Nathan?"

"Yes?"

"Aren't you going to say anything else?"

Suddenly grabbing her in an embrace so tight, it frightened her, he held on for dear love, knowing the moment of his truest love had arrived.

"Shara! You have to know that I love you!"

"I know that darling. You're not changing your mind, are you?

Laughing and weeping at the same time, Nathan just held on and rocked his precious gift in his clinging arms, trying to imprint her on his heart forevermore.

"No, honey. I'm just having a sadness fit. I absolutely hate it, but I think–don't you? –that it also may be the–the most loving thing for me to–do–is to free you from me, so that you can go about your life without me, and without the ethical weights attached to me. Just as you have spoken about "stepping aside," I've been thrashing about that idea. You have to know that what I really, truly want is to marry you and live with you the rest of our lives, but that just doesn't seem possible any time soon, without egregious harm to innocent people. Shouldn't I free you from that hopeless plan, for all the right reasons?"

There! It's out! The worst–and the most loving–God help us both!

"Lose the baby and you, both!?"

"I hadn't thought... I'm just looking for the decision with the most love in it?"

No matter: the raw meaning of his words, amounting to promise breaking, so blatant that they needed no repetition, floated above them, echoing, and mocking their embrace, their love, their history, and their hopes, as well as his integrity, his word, his strength, wisdom, and his most precious, closely held promises! QI held his breath...

Shara was silent for a moment or two, allowing his question to sink in. Then, she spoke.

"Nathan, I know what you're doing. You're trying to solve our dilemmas by thinking what would be best for me, as you always do, in the short term, right?"

"Yes, you are that important to me!"

"I know that. I, too, have been thinking similar thoughts, but mostly for the near term, after the baby is born. That's why I've mentioned 'stepping aside' several times. Neither of us wants to see everything else that is dear to you harmed or ruined. That's a given. But just as I am the one who has the final responsibility of deciding to give up our baby for adoption, I believe I am the best person to decide what will be best for me in the future, as well—and it isn't giving up on our love, that's for sure!"

"Shara, given the realities we face, then, as honestly as possible, what are your expectations, both for the near and future terms?"

Tears welled in her eyes, as she stroked his face, now within inches of hers.

"Nathan, you have to know that I love you more than anything on earth. I am also aware of the challenges—and dangers—of continuing that love. Lately, I have been remembering a sermon you preached once, in which you addressed hoping, even when circumstances indicated that hope was lost. Do you remember that?"

"Yes. It was based on Proverbs 13:12: 'Hope deferred makes the heart sick, but when the desire is fulfilled, it is the tree of life.'"

"Yes. I think it applies, here, don't you?"

"So, you're thinking that even though things may look hopeless, now, we need to depend on our pure love to perpetuate that hope, even though we will have to defer it until such time as it may be fulfilled with minimal harm, becoming our 'tree of life,'?"

"Exactly! By deferring, but also hoping, it will give us both time to prepare for an eventual life together more based on what you call, "the fullness of time," rather than on the fullness of my womb."

"Of course, you're right, darling! Come here!"

Falling into each other's arms, once more, they both trusted the clear evidence that God had already worked in mysterious ways, and that He should continue to be involved. They were content, as they stroked their love on each other's bodies, and invested it, again, in their deferred hope, still absolutely alive in their hearts!

"We believe; just believe!" she whispered, kissing his eyes.

CHAPTER 54
WINTER'S PORTENT

Hope is a waking dream.

Aristotle

With renewed hope and resolve, and openness to new options, they looked forward to Shara's coming to Florida to have the baby and anticipated only as much of the future as they could foresee. Such were the temper and steel of their love. They were free to mark time, trusting God and each other to find the way to the eventual fruition of their "tree of life," in real time and place–to come.

So mought it be!

*

Lenore was all obreptitious eyes and anxiety, while they bathed the kids and got them into their pajamas. They were doubly excited, full of tales about Melanie and her gifts, and that they were to fly to the Granddaddy's house on Thursday where, they assured him, Santa would surely find them.

"Cause, 'cause Grandaddy dot a chimley," piped Beth, the fixer, always making sure things went right.

"Grandaddy has a biiiigg yard, lots and lots of trees, oranges and tangines and kumsquats and a porch with posts and toys an,' an' a water hose I can squirt," responded her big brother.

"Indeed, he has, chilluns, and you know what else he has?"

"No-oh, what?" they sang.

"He has presents for you from a million aunts and uncles and Ma Trish and Pa Jack—so many that I'll bet you couldn't count them."

"I can count, Daddy. Wanna hear? One, two, fwee, four, fi, sis, seben—uh seben, what comes afta seben, Mommy?"

"See if you can remember, Beth. Try again," said patient, teaching Mommy.

She got all the way to "eleben," this time, to her own and her parents' pleasure.

"Well, I can count to ten hunnerd. Watch: one hunnerd, two hunnerd, three hunnerd...," all the way to ten "hunnerd," sure enough.

Because of the celebrity of the season, all four Scotts piled up in the master bed, for their bedtime rituals. In addition to "Old Texas," and "Animals A-Comin,'" Nathan added "Silent Night" and "I Wonder as I Wander," his dulcet baritone holding the pitch. Prayers were heard, hugs and kisses exchanged, parents watching each other with love and appreciation, as two wee ones laid themselves down to sleep. Mommy and Daddy repaired to the kitchen table to debrief.

"Granddaddy called, honey. He has the tricycle in the attic."

"That's great, 'Nore, and the peddling fire engine?"

"It hasn't arrived, yet, but there's still hope for tomorrow. What will we do if it doesn't arrive in time? Sears promised."

"Put an 'IOU one peddling fire engine, Love, Santa' note in Nattie's stocking, maybe. We'll think of something. I'll bring the other presents when I drive over Friday night, after our three, candlelight Christmas services. If you've already gone to bed, I'll put out the rest of the Santa stuff, if I can tell where each person's loot is placed."

"Well, mister, how did it go with Shara? You know I'm dying to hear."

"It went gladly, then sadly, at first, as you can imagine. She agreed, with perfect, ethical logic, great sadness, as well as a modicum of palpable relief, that she would give up the baby for adoption to 'Mr. & Mrs. X,' as she calls them, and that she is looking forward, as much as possible, to coming down here to have it."

"Well, I'm glad to hear that, finally. I hope she–and you–weren't too upset."

"Not this time; I was more prepared for it. With a few tears, maybe. And, by the way, I signaled success to Merilane and Andy, who were Mary and Joseph, tonight, in the Living Nativity. She almost fainted, and they dropped their roles long enough to give me–and the whole of Christendom–huge smiles."

"I'm glad they're glad, but back to Shara, please."

"We had a long talk about abortion and ethics and related subjects, which led me into my talking about the adoption as a decision with the most love in it. Then I braved suggesting that my letting her go would be another such decision."

Pause.

"And?"

"I immediately realized that my timing was awful, considering… Then Shara said she had been thinking the same way, but primarily for the near term. She realized I was thinking of what might be best for her, again, but as with giving up the baby, she insisted that I let her be the best arbiter of that. We agreed that hope springs eternal, so, rather than total cessation, we agreed to continue to nurse earlier hopes for the future. If not now, maybe someday, after she goes to college, and I figure out what ..."

"...To do with your family?"

"...to do that has the most love and does the least harm. My job, for instance. It's enough for three people, honestly."

"Only because you never, ever say 'no' to anyone—except me."

"Honey, I don't say 'no' to you, do I? I just can't always say 'yes.'"

"Big difference," she pouted, eyes filling and body tensing. "I take your point about your timing, as you say, considering... But what do *you* expect from such vaunted hopes?"

"I told her that I absolutely love her and you both, and that I hope that there may be some way to mix this oil and water, so that it comes out something other than salad dressing."

"Don't make too light of it, Nathan. There are lives at stake, here."

"Of course."

Breathless pause.

"How was your visit with Melanie? I know the kids enjoyed her. Did you feel any differently about her? Anything?"

Breathing.

"As you weren't saying..."

"Oh, Nathan, I don't know what to tell you. This stupid soap opera couldn't get more involved—or banal—but all too real! It's not as though we have lost our love for each other—our intimacy, but when she talks about you, she—she—glows, dammit, knowing something that she doesn't know I know; it's upsetting. Several times I almost told her what I know, but she was so blithe and cheerful being here, being loved by the kids, and by me, and so full of what she is doing for you and Shara–for you, mostly–I just didn't want to pop her bubble, or risk upsetting the arrangement. I do wish she weren't so willing to let you visit there, though, but I squelched that little hurt, too."

"As usual, Lenore hopes all things, bears all things, loves all things..."

"Nathan, please don't patronize me, I..."

"Sorry if it came out that way, 'Nore. I actually meant it as an amazing realization–and my highest compliment."

"Well, it's hard to say, 'thank you' to a compliment that points up my stupid willingness to suffer."

Taking a chance, Nathan said, "Lenore, do you remember the McLeish play in verse, 'J.B.,' the modern re-telling of the Book of Job?"

"Of course–we saw it, together."

"Then, I'm sure you remember the most telling line and the gist of the entire play."

"Yes," she wailed, "spoken by J.B.'s wife! 'You wanted justice, didn't you? There isn't any; there is only love.'"

Real tears, this time, as too much truth caromed about. Nathan knew not to say much more, but he risked tendering his hand across the table and taking hers. She started to jerk away but squeezed back in time with her sobbing: a rhythmic sadness, played on the leaden drums of her overly stretched–and sometimes wretched–loves.

CHAPTER 55
DAY UNTO DAY

Goals are not meant for prediction, but for inspiration.

John Clark

There are no shortcuts to any place worth going.

Beverly Sills

January, that two-faced month, renews the cycle, but guarantees no better results, despite our fatuous resolves. Resigned to focus on home and work, once again, Nathan re-compartmentalized his life, spending most it as a minister, and reserving too little of it for his lonely, five months pregnant inamorata–even through his handy-dandy tape recorder.

In Shara's tapes, she reported missing her desolate man almost desperately, was otherwise lonely, bored by her job, looking and longing for April, when things would come out, one way or another. Decidedly, the hours did not, "…too swiftly fly!"

Melanie discovered Shara's dildo and was aghast, at first, then curious, then matter of fact, saying she understood. Shara suspected that she may have used it a time or two, as well.

Melanie's second shift at the airport allowed too little together time, which was both good and bad for Shara. Her sex drive seemed to be growing which she attributed to increased hormones and decreased contact with Nathan. The baby was especially active when she had orgasms, which became something of a secondary pay off.

Shara sought Nathan's help and advice about college next fall. Having altered the course of her life, to achieve greater independence, she found herself almost entirely dependent on the care and concern of others. She had to fight against feeling helpless. He did his best to reinforce her efforts to plan for herself, helping her with scholarship information and application.

*

Spinning too many, breakable plates on the ends of duty's upright schticks, Nathan bounced from one urgent task to another: taping a loving but impatient and increasingly anxious Shara; individual counseling every afternoon (twice heading off possible suicides); several presentations or sermons a week; training sessions for new teachers and youth volunteers; periodic weekend retreats for each grade, 7-12, seriatum; meetings with his senior high council; regional committees; prodigious correspondence, hospital visitations; classroom observations; staff meetings; etc., with too many oft-postponed, homemaking and parental duties (and privileges!). Nathan felt himself in a professional groove, avoiding a rut, but in danger of excluding his greatest loves...

*

Taping Shara, he told her he had called the dean of students at Tabormont College, and that they are sending her admission applications, scholarship information, the college handbook, and other literature about the college, right away. He had sent other students to Tabormount, and it was just the ticket for Sara. *The ticket to where? I know not, but I must do all that I can to enhance her future.*

Handing the finished tape to one of his new friends at the airport post office, Nathan watched him ceremoniously drop the little box into the Philly sack, heard a crack or two about "how good she must be in bed," and went home to Lenore, who sought to rate the same thing about him. A little later, she whispered in his ear her appreciation for his attention—and his performance before he sank into exhausted oblivion.

CHAPTER 56
GESTATING LOVE

The freethinking of one age is the common sense of the next.

Matthew Arnold

The moving finger writes and having writ–probably needs an editor.

Nathan Rhea Scott
February 9, 1966

B oth Nathan and Shara were extremely frustrated that he could not get away long enough to visit. At seven months pregnant in February 1966, she was showing enough to require maternity clothes all the time, having gained all of nineteen pounds, weighing 132. He sent her a credit card, so she could buy what she needed–but she needed *him*!

Though they had been audiotaping each other almost every other day, the tapes began to grow shorter, and the time between tapes grew longer, as well. Though this alarmed them both, a certain adjustment was taking place that might allow an easier separation, once the baby was born...

Yes, yes, no, no, and maybe...

March 1966 came in like every other day in Miami: warm to hot, billowing, white cumulus clouds sailing, ocean breezes gentling the exotic flora, and plenty of people going about either their businesses or their retirements. Far away, near Philadelphia, an eight months pregnant, almost nineteen-year-old young woman was rather ruefully contemplating her future, with and without the father of her unborn child.

Shara's focus was on two things: first, she said into the recorder's microphone, she wanted to hand her baby into Mrs. X's loving arms, herself; second, she wanted advice on financing college. She was excited about the prospects of going to Tabormont College (TC), which had accepted her for admission in the fall of 1966, thanks to Nathan's advocacy.

TC sent Shara an application for financial aid, along with all sorts of information about the college. She called home with the good news, only to hear her father declare that he would have nothing, whatsoever, to do with such a plan, and that if she wanted anything but courtesy from them, she would get her "sassy little ass" down there, stay at home, and go to DTI. Then, if she behaved herself as a daughter should, they'd see what they could do about a residential college after her sophomore year. Plus, she should concentrate on interior design, about the only area in which "you show the slightest talent."

She turned him down, flat, saying that she was learning to be independent, and only wanted a start. After big J. Carl got off the phone, Donna whispered that she could probably slip her a little money, now and then.

Still speaking into her microphone, while staring out the window at a cold, blustery, wintery Pennsylvania afternoon, she got teary-eyed when reiterating her tentative, but recurring, pressure to cut the intimate strings between them, after the baby was adopted. In a moment of genuine panic, however, she told him that she still had dreams about his scooping her up and taking her away, afterward, to start a life together, in California, maybe, where nobody would care who they were. There was a pause, as she got herself together, then she began to anticipate her flight to Miami, mid-April.

She was considering getting a chic, maternity outfit, to look her best for him.

Anesthesia was another source of concern, as she wondered what kind her Florida doctor would use. She wanted to be awake, if it wasn't too painful. Admitting to fearing the delivery, she began her recording sign-off by expressing a lonely, fervent love for Nathan, for their baby, and for Mr. & Mrs. X. She was almost certain it was a boy, and wanted to name the baby, too, before she gave it up for adoption. Did Nathan have any suggestions...?

*

Nathan's tape to Shara of March 13, 1966, was filled with his need to be with her, despite the ridiculous demands placed upon him, how much he truly missed her, and how happy he would be to see her in one month minus one day (April 12, 1966). The McLeans (X's) gave him their first check to begin to pay for Shara's care, starting with her plane fare and housing while in Miami.

Nathan reserved a nice, efficiency apartment near the hospital, from April 11– May 30, 1966. Promising that he would visit her as often as possible, he confessed to wanting her, even though Lenore was doing a fair job of keeping their few intimate moments more than interesting.

Moving on to other things, Nathan reported the gist of his interactions with his many counselees. He also told her about his last senior high retreat at a Boy Scout camp just north of the Everglades. The retreat theme was, "Man's Need and God's Action." He used the movie, *Cat on a Hot Tin Roof,* to stimulate discussion about "mendacity," and about the need for God in resolving relationships when the tide was out. He taught that when relationships are based on love and concern for what is best for the other person, and not simply on the need for self, God was most active in those relationships.

After the retreat, some deacons questioned his use of such a film with youth but relented when they saw his discussion questions and heard the rave reviews of the adults on the retreat, including those of Dr. Andy McLean (Mr. X). However, they warned him not to stray too far afield from standard Christian fare, whatever that was. Dr. Flowers winked at him and gave him a furtive thumbs up.

Because of Dr. Flowers' leadership at the regional and national levels, he was gone a lot, leaving the preaching of five sermons a week to Nathan and the Rev. Jack Eastman, which duties they shared, equally. Nathan's sermons seemed to strike chords in people, because he preached to himself. He preached what he knew he needed to hear, due to his screwed-up situation and the pride that got him there. It didn't hurt his ego any when he learned that two delegations from pastorless churches came to hear him preach in February and March. Both churches wanted him, but he cheerfully turned them down.

There is no way in the world I would ever take the job of pastoring a church, solo. My job is with children, youth, and their families, one way or another, and if I must leave for any reason, college teaching will be my next endeavor.

*

In late March, just as Nathan was sitting down to a late dinner, Lenore called him to the phone. It was Merilane and Andrew McLean, both, and they had something to tell him. QI began a rapid-fire listing of possible negatives.

"Well, McLeans, you've got me on pins and needles. What's going on?"

"We might as well just come right out and tell you, Nathan. We're pregnant!" laughed Merilane.

With shock ringing in his ears, he plopped down in a chair so hard, he almost broke it. Lenore's eyes were circles of

"What? What? What?" from across the room, and Nathan had to catch his breath before he could utter a word.

That word was, "Damn! That's good news–isn't it?"

"You bet it is, Nathan," replied the proud progenitor. "We've all agreed that 'God works in mysterious ways.' I guess when we gave up trying so hard, agreed to adopting a baby, and just loved each other, He decided to make another miracle!"

"Indeed so, Andy. My–our–heartfelt congratulations. I have spent none of your money, yet, so, if this means you'll be wanting it back..."

"Good Lord, no, Nathan. We're going ahead, full speed, with both babies. It'll be a little like having twins, which run in my family, anyway, so nothing has changed, except that you are talking to two of the happiest, most grateful people in the state."

"Wonderful! When are you expecting, Merilane?"

Lenore sat down hard!

"I'm just over two months, Nathan, so we figure we'll have two in diapers by Hallowe'en. God's own 'trick or treat,' I guess. Andy says there's something a little bit spooky about all of this. What do you think?"

"Maybe we should chalk it all up to the Holy Ghost!"

Later, in bed, after Lenore's willingness to go for two, he lay satiated in her arms, QI mulling over the McLean's surprise–both surprises.

"Nathan, what would you have done had the McLeans backed out of their adoption agreement?"

"Ask you to adopt the baby with me and raise it as our own–which is something I should have asked long ago."

"You're serious, aren't you? Would that mean that Shara would come along, too? Would we adopt her, as well?"

"It would be a solution, wouldn't it? At least she'd be with us, where you could keep an eye on both of us."

"Who wants to see you fu–making love to Shara? I don't, though you might not mind, at all, from what I know of your sexology."

"Of course, I fantasize all three of us in the same bed, Lenore, as equal partners. You might even like the novelty, as well as the pleasure. For that matter, we could even move Melanie in and make it a 'moresome,' couldn't we? Have you decided when you might tell her what you know?"

"I'll get to that in a minute, darling husband, but right now, I really want you to stop putting me off with your wit and tell me what you would have done had the McLeans called off the adoption."

"I told you the truth, 'Nore. At this late stage, there wouldn't be much else that would be decent, fair, and the most loving action, would there?"

"Hmm. I'll have to think about that. However, I have to say that I'm relieved they are going ahead as planned. Have you been sharing your recurring thoughts about–not dropping–but maybe distancing from your intimate relationship with her?"

"We both discuss it, frequently, in fact. I don't think she has any illusions about the likelihood that I'm just going to drop her, now that the baby will be taken care of. As you know, I've helped get her into TC, after they had closed their acceptances for next fall. She's getting excited about it, even though her father refuses to give her any financial support, as I think I told you. We may have to help her find some, even if..."

"...Even if you wind up paying for it?"

"Yes, partially. I think I have that obligation, don't you?"

"Yes, but I don't, nor do our children. You would take away from us, to assuage your conscience about her?"

"If I must. Although I wouldn't be assuaging my conscience; I would be helping someone I dearly love, on purpose. You already knew that, Lenore."

"Nathan, with you, one never knows exactly what has happened, what is happening, much less what might happen in the future. I do love you, you know, even if you are unrepentant. And maybe tonight we'd try for three, if I weren't so sleepy—and satisfied. I hate to admit it, but I guess I can see what your other women see— no, feel—in you—or you in them— or, or, oh, shit!"

"Lenore, I do believe you've done gone went and embarrassed yo'self, Ma'am."

"Good night, darling. I'm going to turn away from you now and go to sleep. Don't go sneaking into the kitchen and calling Shara, either."

"Yes Ma'am, Mister Grandpappy."

CHAPTER 57
THE HOUR COMETH AND NOW IS...

There is no remedy for love but to love more.

Henry David Thoreau

When Nathan saw her coming down the escalator, grinning, he melted. She looked so young–and then he realized with an unexpected pang that she was trying to look sophisticated and refined. *Wearing a light green maternity skirt, with a matching green bolero jacket over her filmy white blouse, topped off with a very large, wide brimmed, matching green hat, worn to the side of her head, over her long, dark hair, she looks like a kid playing dress-up, with a pillow stuffed under her skirt.*

When she stepped off the escalator and began running toward him, he noted that she was wearing green heels that matched her dress, as well. Then, her hat fell off, she batted after it, inadvertently sailing it toward him, its flying saucer shape holding it up. Two men reached for it, but Nathan beat them to it, scooping it and her into his arms, in a single, memorable motion, holding her lightly, tapping anew the overwhelming love he felt flowing through him, as she fit snugly into his arms–despite her protruding tummy.

Shara!

When she looked up, longing to be kissed, they noticed tears in the other's eyes and, unaccountably, both laughed. Then he kissed her; kissed her to ease the months' absence of kisses; kissed her to taste her, again; kissed her to begin to slake the thirst that was stirring in his being; kissed her to express the rapturous love that she evoked in him, no matter her tummy, no matter his marriage, his family, his church, but yes matter his God.

Shara!

Their kiss expressed and foretold, at once, cementing his foundations of hope and promise, again, as he molded her into him, not caring who saw. Not a word was spoken for an eternity, as they kissed the days, weeks, and months away, bringing their love, ineluctably, up to date. As her tongue entered his mouth, he breathed her in, almost consuming her essence, entering her as she entered him, becoming one flesh, once and for all.

Shara!

The clapping around them finally broke through, QI alerting him to the small gaggle of people appreciating this sweet slice of life. Shara grinned her embarrassed grin, as Nathan simply bowed in several directions, put her hat on his head, took his prize by the hand, and marched her toward the baggage area, with clapping and whistles still ringing in their ears.

Shara!

She couldn't stop talking; about her outfit; about Melanie's gift of the shoes; about almost missing her plane and having to stand by on her half-priced, youth fare ticket; about the man who sat next to her who said she looked like his daughter and kept asking her embarrassing questions; about the plane ride, itself, with funny sensations in her womb, making her nervous; about having to use the tiny rest room on the 727 jet; about worrying whether Nathan would really be there; about TC's offer of a combo scholarship and loan, that would mean she could go to college there without too much worry; about how much the baby had moved down, allowing her to breathe more easily; and about how unbelievably glad she was to be there, next to him in the car, again, assuming their favorite position.

Shara!

She curled up on the bench seat, her head in his lap, talking to his belly and his genitals, alternately, while trying to keep from falling into the foot well, due to her oversized tummy.

"Nathan!"

"Yes?"

"I was just saying your name. Nathan; my Nathan. I'm really here with you, and I know everthing will be OK, now. Where are we going to eat? I'm starved."

Shara!

After eating at a Howard Johnson's, with Shara eating part of his meal, they drove to the rented apartment, both to check it out and to relax a bit. After he opened the door, she wanted to be kissed and carried in, appropriate, she said, to the occasion.

He put her hat on his head, again, swooped her up in his arms, turned sideways, and sidled into the room in little baby steps, the broad rim of her hat bobbing up and down, ridiculously. Once inside, she snatched the hat, sailed it across the length of the room, onto the sofa, and began her orientation. Pleased enough, she began to undress, "...to put on something more comfortable."

"May I watch, or does Madam desire privacy?"

"It isn't privacy Madam desires; I've been thinking about that since I woke up this morning. There isn't much room for privacy in here, anyway," she said, already down to her maternity pantyhose and bra. Those came off a little more slowly, so he helped her balance, as she worked her way out of the hose. Staring at her black forest, apparent through her maternity panties, Nathan, slowly ran his hands up, over and around her tummy, feeling her pregnancy with paternal curiosity and amazement at the miracle within.

"Do you think he'll move, so I can feel it?"

"I'll let you know. He was kicking my bladder on the plane. That's why I had to use that silly restroom. The stewardess stood outside the door when I told her I might need some help. She is just a few years older than me and has a kid of her own, so she understood. She treated me like royalty the entire trip, which made me very happy–and special."

"Dare I say the obvious? More than special; you are wonderful, Shara!"

Then did his hands reacquaint themselves with her beautiful, larger breasts, nipples extended more than he remembered, from darker areolas. Feeling their heft, he tentatively put his lips over one nipple, lightly licking and sucking.

"You'd better stop that if you don't want a raving sex maniac on your hands. I'm still so horny that I have to jerk off three or four times a day, and that still doesn't satisfy me."

"I'll cool it, then. I don't think my baby would appreciate my penis as a roommate."

"Oh, but listen, Nathan; on my last visit to my doctor, he was delivering a baby, so I saw a lady doctor, instead. She examined me more thoroughly than he usually does, and pronounced me incredibly healthy, with every expectation of a normal delivery. So, I got up enough courage to ask her about sex during these last weeks, and she laughed and said she saw no reason why not, if we both want it. As long as we follow a few precautions, like using a rubber, because semen has stuff in it that may stimulate contractions and bring on the birth."

As she spoke, Shara looked at him looking at her, and noticed his rather obvious erection. She reached out and stroked it through his pants.

"Should we try it, Nathan?" said Madam Hope.

"I don't know, Shara. I don't want to hurry anything, right now. But I do want to hold you and, well, let's see what happens."

Gingerly, Nathan lay next to his pretty, pregnant lover, spoon fashion, holding her fast against him, recommitting her body to memory. Legions of memories marched through them, as they reconfirmed their sentient contours, and settled back into loving, instead of longing; then they gentled into the inimitable peace of restorative sleep.

Nathan awoke feeling a strange sensation beneath his left hand. Holding Shara's nascence, as they lay together, he felt it again. A movement; a signal; a readiness. His child was preparing his primary entrance by pushing against the walls of his gestating haven, alerting his father of his special life. Spreading his hand over the recurring trusion, he gently pushed back three times in hail and welcome. Pause. Repetition, until the genetrix awoke with a jolt. Disoriented for only a wink, she placed her hand over Nathan's, guiding him in his sensate perusal of her impatient, incubating child.

Shara slowly gentled his hand lower, through the forest and onto lubricious lanes, until he found her readiness, exploring and polishing it into an intimate renascence of realized and realizing ardor—her lover's hand, instead of her own—at last. Thus, the sacramental reincarnation of heart and spirit, through the flesh, once again uniting the happy twins of Agape and Eros, without a word spoken. For this eternal instant, at least, they were at one!

*

During the ensuing days, Shara was content only when Nathan was present, providing the comforts of courage and anticipation to what she must inevitably face, essentially alone. She was well prepared, intellectually, for the event, but the fuzziness of the future did little to calm her.

What are the X's really like? Will the medical powers allow her to see and hold her baby, as planned? Will she be able to give it up, after all? How close will Nathan be allowed to be? What if she identifies him as the father, under the anesthesia? Will she be able to stand the pain? What will it do to her vagina? Will she get her figure back—what about striae? Will she be able to wear her new bikini? Will her parents be able to tell? What is Lenore really thinking? Will she be able to see little Nate and Beth—she loves them, too. How often will Nathan be able to get away and see her, both before and after the birth? Last, but certainly not least, Did you bring any condoms?

Such questions haunted her into many tears—of joy and sadness, equally distributed across the waiting hours. Her joy in their experimental sex was monumental and reclaiming, with Nathan under her, lusting, loving, and looking up at her ecstatic face, as she came, again and again.

She suffered most when Nathan was home or at work. There was a phone in her apartment, but she was wary of using it, hoping Nathan would check on her more often, instead. He did his best to be with her, make love, take her around the area, even walking on the beach.

She loved their beach strolls, recalling them whenever she felt overwhelmed. She was uncomfortable, physically, of course, and impatient as well as frightened—the perfect admixture of competing emotions, causing maximum angst. It took Nathan's steadiness and love to put it into perspective, with his practiced patience, explanations, and assurances— while he, himself, cavorted in quease and quandary.

Nathan was experiencing his own angst, of course, as plans bumped into the reality of frustrating expectations. In vain, she wanted him with her almost all the time. Their sex was wonderful, even though Nathan was afraid of hurting her when she bucked so hard, straddling him, and claiming him with near abandon. Once, she removed his condom, thinking to stimulate the birth by his semen, as well as luxuriating in the sense of keeping part of him inside her, when he had to leave, again.

Lenore was sympathetic but impatient when he was with Shara. She had not yet seen the girl, though she planned to do so after the birth, to provide a sense of mothering to her, as she expressed it. Nate and Beth were hyper, because their parents were hyper, and the circle repeated itself. Work–and the piano–allowed Nathan his only gravid relief.

Andy McLean wrote Nathan another check to cover hospitalization and other expenses; Merilane chose her own doctor for Shara's successful office visit and the delivery. They were paying him separately, so Nathan didn't have to worry about that. Andy's lawyer drew up the legal papers required for the adoption and sent them to Nathan for official implementation.

Nathan's responsibilities were to alert the hospital *factota* of what was expected of them, including the resident social worker, who was to determine that Shara knew what she was doing, and to notarize the adoption. He also contacted the obstetric charge nurse, to ensure that the nursing staff knew Shara was to see and hold her baby, which was against general hospital procedure in "XXX" cases.

Nathan was designated the official mediator and one of two, required witnesses. He would be the person handing the papers to Shara when the time came, interacting with medical and hospital staff, throughout, to ensure that the whole affair went as planned and as smoothly as possible.

The McLeans were anxious, too. Merilane experienced some morning sickness, and her hormones kicked in some depression. This worried Nathan, but Andy took it in stride, insisting that nothing short of tragedy would forestall the adoption. They wanted the baby as soon as possible after it was born, and Nathan and Lenore agreed that they would bring it to them, as the baby could be discharged only to him.

The McLeans spent many happy hours preparing for the advent, with her parents visiting, bringing arm loads of baby paraphernalia and anticipation–their first grandchild, after all. It got back to Nathan that everyone hoped the baby would have red hair. Andy and Merilane recalled that one of the natural parents was a kinsman of Nathan, so that expectation seemed normal enough, but a little worrisome to QI.

Heavy, heavy hangs over was a constant QI refrain, keeping Nathan focused, alert, and ready. Though he couldn't spend as much time with Shara as he wanted, he was there every lunch and after dinner up until her bedtime, 10 -10:30 p.m. He called her every morning at least twice and visited each morning a couple of times, during the interminable, five days of waiting.

Despite a few moods and crying times, she is Shara the Courageous–probably the most courageous–and sacrificial–person I know. His admiration soared to challenge his love for ascendency, in his heart and mind. QI marveled at her, as did Lenore, when she allowed herself to ponder.

Everyone involved had nothing but the highest regard for this young mother, who was obviously doing what she believed was the best–the right, most loving–thing to do. Only Shara doubted her own courage; she was plain scared. Nathan's reminder that courage is possible only when fear and/or danger are involved, helped a little–maybe.

Nathan's office phone rang at 9:30 p.m., on Sunday, April 17, 1966. Shara was leaking amniotic fluid and experiencing the first twinges of labor. He called Lenore and was at Shara's side in 10 minutes. She showed him the pre-birth, mucous plug that was expelled when her cervix began to dilate, so he called the hospital.

A nurse told him to bring her in when the contractions were three to five minutes apart, lasting for about sixty seconds, each, for at least an hour or more. The seriousness of the contractions should render it difficult for Shara to talk much between them. Though she didn't match all these criteria by midnight, they decided to go in, anyway.

Shara was admitted to the Northside General Hospital at 12:30 a.m. on April 18, 1966. The examining nurse didn't want to call the obstetrician until they were sure, suspecting a false alarm, but they alerted the resident anesthesiologist, who took blood samples and started an IV with a mild sedative. Shara was asleep in no time, so they sent Nathan home.

Shara had dilated a little at 8:00 a.m. but the contractions were not consistent. Her doctor checked her out, finding both she and the baby doing well. The charge nurse assured Nathan that he would be called when things looked imminent. Now, Lenore was nervous, too, asking a barrage of questions. Nathan went to the office to escape her intensity, having enough of his own.

No call by noon. Nathan couldn't concentrate, sending him to a nearby classroom and a decent piano—but not so far away as to muffle the sound of the phone. He played wild, abstract tempi, many, rapid runs, and sudden *pianissimos*. During such a *pianissimo*, he heard the phone's insistent *fortissimo*, and he almost broke his neck answering it. Things were definitely happening; the anesthesiologist was doing his stuff; Shara was out, surprising him, as he was expecting an epidural anesthetic; and the obstetrician was with her, considering how much help she might need.

Calling the McLeans, he heard Andy's "Whoopee!" in the background, as Merilane told him that things were imminent. When Nathan called to alert Melanie, she wept, obviously worried, saying she had done all she thought she could have done to make Shara's stay with her comfortable and welcome. Nathan thanked her profusely, of course, and promised to apprise her of progress. Lenore was quiet and tense, quite worried for Shara and the baby.

At the hospital by 2:15 p.m., he was told Shara was fine, well-attended and that the birth could be any minute. He joined two other fathers in the waiting room, all three nervous and frustrated with waiting. Nathan didn't deny their assumption that he was a father-in-waiting.

About 3:15, a nurse pulled him aside and told him that Shara had delivered a fine, red-headed lad at precisely 3:02 in the afternoon (*exactly two years, to the day and perhaps to the very minute, from our portentous, Vesper Dell hug!*), coming in at six pounds, three ounces.

Shara was groggy, and they were waiting for the placenta. He could see her after she was returned to her room, probably in about forty-five minutes. Meanwhile, he could view the boy through the nursery window, after the pediatrician had thoroughly checked him out, cleaned him up, and circumcised him.

There were seven babies in the nursery, all swaddled, some crying, and improving their lung power. Nathan knew immediately which one was his, by the wisps of red hair on his otherwise baldish head. Numb, Nathan's expected elation was countered by his coming distress, and his worry about Shara's ability to handle it.

He wanted to feel the joy of fatherhood he had known twice, but it would not come. He felt doomed, no matter what he did. QI could not get him past the irrefutable knowledge that *I don't even have the honor of sacrifice, because that is Shara's courageous role.* QI accused himself of self-pity, so he shaped up enough to go check on Shara's availability, again, for the fourth time since 3:15. It was now after 5:00 p.m., and he had calls to make.

At 5:15, he was ushered into Shara's private room, where the nurse shut the door as she left. Shara's face was pale, her hair only minimally brushed, and she seemed to be asleep.

Nathan wanted to grab her and run away with her, but he tip-toed to her bedside, reaching for her. She opened her eyes at his touch, focused, and smiled a wan, relieved smile, while a tear gathered and overflowed.

"I did it, honey!"

"Yes, you did, and he's a fine-looking little fella, red-hair and all. Did they tell you that?"

"No, they—they don't tell me anything. They just smile and say the doctor will tell me what I need to know—other than that he's a boy and all right. I was sure he'd be a boy. I don't remember much of anything, though, after they started the anesthetic, until just a few minutes ago. What time is it, anyway?"

Nathan told her what he knew, but she dozed, off and on. Finally, the charge nurse came in with the social worker, who wanted to speak to him. Outside her room, the social worker told him she had been in consultation with the hospital administrator, and they decided that Shara was not to see or hold her baby, for fear of losing the adoption. The hospital didn't want to be responsible for that possibility. Nathan held back his frustration, asking only if he might speak to the administrator. He was rather curtly informed that he had gone for the day.

Upset, Nathan slipped back into Shara's room, finding her semi-awake. He explained to her that there was a mix up, but that he would take care of it no later than tomorrow morning. Meanwhile, both he and her doctor wanted her to do nothing but rest and get her strength back. It had been an ordeal.

Back at his office, he made the happy calls to Lenore, Melanie and the McLeans, all of whom were relieved and joyous–especially the Mcleans, wanting to know when they might receive their baby. He advised them to wait until he got clearance from the bureaucrats at the hospital, that there had been a mix up about the mother being able to see and hold the child, as previously agreed, but that he would take care of it in the morning.

Eight a.m. came, along with Shara's urgent phone call, as he was dressing.

"They won't let me see my baby," she wailed, repeatedly, clearly beside herself.

"I'll take care of it, Shara. Try to relax, honey, and rest. I'm working on it."

His call to the administrator of the hospital got nowhere, for he was elsewhere. So, he called Shara's doctor. After Nathan explained, the doctor put in a call. It worked. When he got to the hospital Shara was holding her baby, with two LPNs hovering. Donning a gown and a mask, he held the baby, too.

Shara was totally relaxed and her old, feisty self by that afternoon. The hospital administrator and social worker were there, asking her to sign a release form, holding them harmless, should she decide to keep the baby. She refused to sign anything, until she talked to her pastor. Enter Nathan, who asked them to step out into the hall.

"I realize that you guys are just trying to protect the hospital and your own rear ends, but please stop harassing this girl, if you want to avoid a lawsuit. She will sign nothing of the sort; the adoption is on; she is ready for it tomorrow morning, so just go away and leave her alone."

They just turned on their heels and walked away. The social worker looked back and spouted petulantly, "Tomorrow, in her room, at 9 o'clock sharp. Bring the consent forms." Only QI stopped him from giving her the finger.

CHAPTER 58
WHAT THOU DOEST, DO QUICKLY!

Courage is fear that has said its prayers.

Dorothy Bernard

We must be willing to get rid of the life we've planned, to have the life that is waiting for us.

Joseph Campbell

The greatest courage lies more in contemplation than in action, and nowhere was that truer than in Room LR-X of the Northside General Hospital of Miami, Florida, on April 19, 1966. There gathered before one Shara Day Starr, courageous child of God, and by His grace, unmarried, and mother to "Baby XXX Starr," about whose future they were met: the Rev. Mr. Nathan Rhea Scott, witness, and official adoption mediator; Janet Heller, MSW, hospital social worker and Notary Public; Rosa Jane Spake, RN, obstetrics charge nurse; and Caroline Childress, LPN, Shara's primary, a.m. care, shift worker, who was holding "Baby XXX Starr." As soon as Shara saw Ms. Childress come in with baby, she sat up and reached for him.

"Not yet," said Ms. Heller. "Not until she has signed the consent. Then she may hold the baby this last time."

Nathan's stare into her officious eyes was almost intense enough to turn the aptly named social worker into a "pillow" of salt, for her apparent desire to make the procedure as painful as possible. She stared back—then lowered her eyes.

"I'm sorry, Ms. Heller, but there are no contingencies here. Until this consent form is signed, Shara is his mother. And, by specific agreement, she may hold him, periodically, until she is discharged, thank you. Ms. Childress, please give the baby to Shara."

Nurse Spake simply nodded her assent, so Ms. Childress carefully put the baby in Shara's outstretched, aching arms. She immediately drank him in with wide, teary eyes and abundant love. Nathan looked at his beloved holding their red-haired child, cleared the pain and denial from his throat, and spoke, again.

"Shara, honey, it's time for you to sign this consent form that I am obliged to read to you before you do so. Are you—are you—ready for me to read it?"

Shara, with tears still streaming, but a smile on her face that became a virtual halo to all in the room, except for Ms. Heller, nodded, yes. As Nathan read, she held "Baby XXX Starr" close to her face, drinking in his quiet, ruddy, sleeping features.

"CONSENT FOR ADOPTION. KNOW ALL MEN BY THESE PRESENTS: that I, the undersigned mother of the un-named infant, born at Miami, Florida, on the 18th of April, 1966, out of wedlock, relinquish all rights to and convey custody of said child to the parties named in the PETITION FOR ADOPTION, to which this CONSENT is attached, to be adopted as their legal child and heir-at-law, and to release any and all rights I may have to the custody or control of said child, and waive all notice of such adoption and consent to the same. IN WITNESS WHEREOF, I have hereunto set my hand and seal this 19th day of April 1966, at Miami, Florida."

Nathan, standing by the bed, his hand trembling on her shoulder, showed her the consent form, when Ms. Heller broke in and said, "You must indicate, for me and these nurses that you understand..."

"Ms. Heller, I must ask you to keep your peace. I will propound the necessary questions. With waning respect, you have but one job, here, our lawyer tells me, and that is to sign as a witness to this difficult event, and to notarize Shara's signature. Now, if you don't mind, I'll continue. Thank you."

"Shara, you'll have to forgive Ms. Heller. She has been most anxious to see that you understand what I have read to you. Do you?"

"Yes, Nathan. When I sign the paper you are holding, and it is witnessed, I'll no longer be the mother of my baby—except—in my heart. I understand that he will be adopted by two people who will love him and care for him as their own son, and that I will have no rights to him, at all. Is that it?"

Ms. Heller looked down in what, for her, slightly resembled shame. Both nurses were weeping as Shara handed the baby to Nathan, who handed him to Nurse Spake. Shara took the consent forms and pen from Nathan's shaking hands, re-read the form, sighed, and with tears blotting her signature, signed both copies over her name, already typed in.

"Now give me back my baby, please."

Ms. Heller started to object, but Nurse Spake smiled through her tears and gently laid "Baby XXX Starr" back in Shara's longing arms. Nathan quickly signed both copies as witness and handed them to Ms. Heller, saying, "What thou doest, do quickly." She did, officiously signing with a flourish, and notarized them with a second signature and her compressing seal. Then, she took the papers, turned at the door to look at the leeching joy haloing Shara's bed, sighed a wearisome sigh, and left.

It was done.

Shara gazed long and lovingly at her son, soon to be another couples,' kissed his cheeks, held his tiny hands, looked at his kicking feet, smoothed his tuft of red hair, kissed his forehead, put him against her swollen breasts. On her own whispered suggestion, she handed him back to Nurse Spake.

Nathan felt like a falling stone but did his best to keep it together. Nurse Spake spake soothingly to the little one, as she and Ms. Childress prepared to leave the room with the baby. Looking back at them, she said, "You'll have to forgive Ms. Heller. She is not a happy woman and seems to enjoy stirring others' feelings. I apologize for her. Shara, you are a very courageous woman, and I greatly admire you. God bless you in whatever you do, for as long as you live. You make sure she's well taken care of, Rev. Scott."

Amen to that!

Alone together, an emotional vacuum sucking all the joy and hope from their earlier dreams, Shara held out her arms to Nathan, as he reached for her, trying not to fall on her in the high hospital bed. They clung desperately.

"Nathan," she wept, "can I ask you something?"

"Anything, darling. Anything!"

"How do you feel, right now?"

His reply was a gasping sob... Now, she was comforting him, realizing that he felt their loss almost as deeply as did she. They continued to weep and to hold each other, until a knock at the door separated them. Wiping his eyes and straightening up, Nathan managed a "Come in!" It was Ms. Childress, holding a heat lamp, come, she said, to give Shara a wash and rub down, check her stitches, and show her how to use the heat lamp to soothe the pain. Nathan took his cue, told Shara he would be back later, and walked out into the most cheerless of all possible worlds.

Not twenty feet away, a mockingbird was singing its heart out, as he got in his car, but he heard it as a dirge. In his office, it seemed to QI that he wept forever, until the phone rang, forcing re-orientation to time and place. It was Lenore, of course, wanting–yes, wanting–as she always did, to be of some help to her husband, whom she knew to be in abject misery. He was able to share some of his burden, but he reserved the bulk of his onus for God, the only entity he knew strong enough to carry it, besides courageous Shara–whose burden was far, far heavier than his.

Nathan visited both Shara and the baby, repeatedly, on Wednesday, knowing that on Thursday Shara would be discharged, and that he and Lenore would take the baby to the McLeans. Nurse Spake left orders for all three shifts to allow Shara at least 15 minutes with her baby, every four hours: little enough, but a giant boon to Shara, who ruefully memorized the features of the child she gave away.

*

Came the dawn of the McLean's long-awaited happiness and Shara's discharge from the hospital. Nathan and Lenore came to fetch her and her load of pads, vitamins, pills, ointments, and instructions on how to heal her stitches, exercise her tummy, and lessen her surprisingly few stretch marks.

After shyly giving Shara a hug, Lenore offered to take her hospital stuff, along with her flowers from everyone to her apartment, while Shara got dressed. Nathan sneaked a last, agonizing look at their baby in the nursery. Then, Nurse Spake and Ms. Childress both rolled Shara to the front door in a wheelchair, where they all waited for Lenore to return with the car.

When Lenore drove up the circle drive, the nurses rolled Shara to the car, hugged her, and saw her safely into the back seat, with Lenore hovering. Shara was genuinely moved, as were both Scotts, at their simple human kindness. Nathan drove off the hospital grounds and started to turn toward Shara's apartment, when Lenore, who had been quiet and pensive, spoke.

"Don't turn here, Nathan. We are not going to that apartment. We're taking Shara home with us. I will not have her staying in that—that place, all by herself, after what she has been through. She is coming home with us, and that's the end of it!"

Both Shara and Nathan were stunned. Shara began to cry, trying to thank Lenore for the goodness that she had obviously spilled all over them, covering them with her grace. Nathan looked at Lenore with such gratitude and appreciation he almost shouted his love for the woman. It was then that Nathan noticed that Lenore had packed up all of Shara's clothes and toiletries and placed them in the way back of the station wagon—where, most likely, their baby had been conceived.

"You're a saint, Lenore," was all he could get out.

They drove in a stunned silence, laced with enormous gratitude to Lenore. In ten minutes, they were home. Once inside, with all of Shara's paraphernalia and flowers, Lenore put her in their bed, in the master bedroom, with its full bath, closet, and the privacy she would need to take care of herself.

The kids, who came in with their sitter, were fair beside themselves with this welcome homecoming, hugging everyone, repeatedly and dancing about Shara, their favorite babysitter of yore, who hugged them with both light and tears in her eyes. Sure she was all right and knew where she could find everything she might need, Lenore hugged her, again, told her they would be back soon, and they left. What they didn't tell her was that their next mission was to take the baby to the McLeans, who were anxiously waiting, with Merilane's parents.

As they drove back to the hospital, Nathan kept looking over at his calm, assured wife, knowing not what to say. He already knew she was loving, caring and generous to a fault, but this was almost unbelievable–another Godly miracle!

"Don't look at me as though I were some kind of saint, Nathan. I just did what I very well knew I would want done for me, in similar circumstances."

"But, how, when, what made you decide this at such a late date? Not that I think it was too late, or anything, but what happened to–to…"

"…To make me behave as a woman, a mother, and a Christian. I opened that apartment door, saw how Spartan it was, saw Shara's clothes and things strewn around, saw that little couch bed, and the one, little flower that you must have given her, all dried up in a water glass, and I knew in an instant that I could not leave her there. It would have been too cruel to do so, and we should have known that all along."

"But we discussed it, honey, and you thought that it would be best for her to stay in a place of her own."

"Yes, I did, but I had no idea how–how empty–how stark it would be, especially after the sacrifice she just made. I just couldn't do it–leave her in there, crying herself to sleep each night, all alone. It's done. She's to stay in our home, for better or worse, but I want you to do your best not to shower her with your wonderful sympathy and presence, or she'll never get over you. We must help her heal, help her plan a future for herself, one that does not involve you very much, including college, and then send her on her way as soon as she's comfortable enough to move. I have no deadlines; in case you were going to ask. We'll know, and so will she."

Awed silence.

"My God, Lenore, you really are a saint. Thank you. Thank you for Shara, thank you for me and thank you for being you. I love you."

"I'm not a saint, Nathan. As I said, I'm just a woman, a mother, and a Christian; simple as that."

"And as complicated."

Arriving at the hospital, Nathan checked in with the discharge officials, signed the appropriate forms, paid the remaining bill, and here came Nurse Spake with the baby, who was sleeping peacefully. Nathan took him from her, looked at him long and ardently, and then handed him to his wife, who immediately warmed to him, woman, mother, and Christian that she was. Nathan thanked Nurse Spake again, especially for her ultra-kindness to Shara, got in, and began the most arduous journey of his life, so far.

Nearing the Mclean's house, Lenore asked him if he wanted to present the baby to Merilane to which he nodded, yes.

"Nathan, you're as white as a ghost. Do you want to stop before we get there, so you can get it together enough to get through this without falling apart? Somehow, you've got to convince them that you are truly happy to be delivering to them their most precious gift–even though you are really giving them one of yours. I know it must be killing you–and, and, oh, Nathan, how in the world did all of this happen? I'm holding your flesh and blood in my arms, loving him, because he looks like you, has your red hair, and you're going to give him away. I know it hurts you because it hurts me, too. This child is the half-brother of my children, and they will never know him as that."

Lenore wept.

Nathan parked in the shade of a huge live oak tree, while Lenore cried. Now, his role was comforter, which he tried to fulfill by placing the baby between them on the bench seat and leaning over him to kiss Lenore's tears away. *My God, will this thing ever end? Emotions, emotions, and more emotions, drowning us, and, still, we haven't completed our journey.*

Steeling himself, Nathan straightened up, gave Lenore some tissues, combed his hair and wiped his eyes, straightened his tie, kissed his wife once more, handed her the baby, and drove straight to the McLean's. As they turned into the driveway, all four adults hurried out to the car, smiling so broadly their teeth glistened white in the bright, Florida sun.

Nathan parked, calmly got out, opened the door on Lenore's side, took the baby from her, turned, looked at Merilane's radiant, expectant face and said, "Merilane, here is your gift from God. I know you will love him, always."

Speechless, all smiles and tears, the McLeans hovered over the boy, now in Merilane's unbelieving arms, she clucking and laughing with instant delight. Suddenly remembering their minister and his wife, they invited them in for refreshments, gladly accepted. Once inside, the new Grandmother proudly showed them the baby's room, fully equipped with just about every baby gadget imaginable, including a lovely blanket that she had made, herself, awaiting her new grandson.

"All I have to do is sew his name on it," she gushed, reminding herself that there had been no final word on that. "Let's go back and see if these newborn parents have decided what to name that little angel."

Nathan choked up when he re-entered the living room and saw Merilane sitting in a rocker, holding the baby closely, rocking and softly singing to him. *Madonna and child if ever there were—so mought it be. I must not cry; I must not cry!*

"Andy, are you going to tell us what you two are going to name this little chile?" Nathan asked, in tremolo, but smiling his brightest.

"We should make you wait until you baptize him, Nathan, when my parents get down here next month. You will do the honors, won't you?"

If QI had teeth, they would have dropped out, for this caught Nathan's vaunted objectivity off guard. *I hadn't even thought of, even less expected, that I would have that—that what? Honor? Duty? Agony? All three?*

Lenore looked at him with knowing love, as he nodded his affirmative, not quite being able to speak.

"Good. So, now we'll tell you. This baby's name is henceforth and forevermore: 'Moses Schmedley McLean,' because we got him from the bull rushes."

"Andy, stop that. You'll scare him to death—and Nathan and Lenore, too. Tell them what we're naming him and stop your silliness, professor."

"Yes, Dr. McLean, do tell," smiled Lenore.

Taking the baby from his clinging wife, holding him securely over his head in his up-lifted arms, Andy intoned," I hereby dub thee, 'Marshall,' for my father, 'Nathan,' for obvious reasons, and 'McLean,' because, well, because that's the best Scottish name I could come up with—and—and so be it, please God!"

Nathan, who thought he'd had all the stunning moments possible on this signal day, was stunned all over again. As others clapped, startling little Marshall, he merely grinned, bowed his silly bow and looked at a knowing Lenore. Then, they drank their iced tea, ate their cookies, hugged all around, held the baby—young Marshall Nathan McLean—and left.

"You drive, please, Lenore. I can't think, much less drive."

"You'll be all right, honey. Just think; we've got a sad, lovely, lonely, girl—woman, now—at our house, plus two delightful children—waiting for you—for us—to take care of them. Your day has hardly begun, Nathan. Yes, I'd better drive, while you screw up your own courage, so we can end this day fittingly—at the right hand of God, with the sheep, instead of the goats."

Say amen!

"Amen!"

And it was so.

EPILOGUE: OF SO DIVINE A GUEST:
A SAINT'S FOLLY

I know of only one duty, and that is to love.

Albert Camus

Love may be or it may not, but where it is, it ought to reveal itself in its immensity.

Honoré de Balzac

Let no good deed go unpunished

John P. Grier
Andrew W. Mellon
Clare Booth Luce

The next few days were agreeable and calm, in that all in the house focused their love and concern on Shara–who beamed it right back at them, but especially at Nattie and little Beth–in the day times. Her most intense, nighttime beams–for Nathan–she held back, deferring to the sister–mother, almost–who Lenore came to be to her.

Lenore could not do enough for her, back rubs, intimate instructions, and empathic conversations. She shared what she knew of postpartum issues, stitches, striae, tummy and vaginal exercises and cramping–all while touting the fabulous future that surely lay in store for Shara, during and after upcoming college. What they tacitly acknowledged and shared, but didn't discuss, was their intense love for and from the father of their children.

To her credit, Lenore found herself caring a great deal for Shara, now bereft of her child, due to her magnanimous sacrifice for the common good. Shara returned the compliment.

Meanwhile, more conflicted than ever, now that he gut-watches and experiences the magnanimity of both women, Nathan found himself almost giddy with the pleasure of having them both under one roof–not quite together in one bed, yet, as they were in his heart.

Slowly, perhaps inevitably, considering the love and concern filling this house, I find myself tipping my own concerns and affection to– or is it back to–Shara? What am I going to do with my love for both–for all? Will it be ever thus–this see-sawing of love in relentless quandary? What if she were to stay? Dare I hope for that, at all? It would be bliss!

Life in the Scott house, now enlivened by another, needy female, began to adjust slowly to its new realities. The first two weeks centered around ensuring that Shara was comfortable, on the mend, physically, and supported emotionally by all. She was utterly appreciative and thankful, rising early from her confinement, helping as much as she could with both children and housekeeping, freeing Lenore to do other things. Seeming happy with her self-imposed situation, Lenore's attention to Shara never wavered, morning, noon, nor night.

"Lenore, you have to know how very grateful I am that you are allowing me to stay with you–and Nathan–and your children, until either I am ready to leave, or you believe I should go… I realize that, under the circumstances, having me here is not only a sacrifice, but several kinds of burdens, as well. I do not want to overstay my welcome."

"Thank you for sharing that, Shara. The circumstances to which you refer are clear enough, but so is your need. I welcome the opportunity to try to meet at least part of that need. I have no timeline for your stay, of course. As you say, when you—or we, together—understand that you will be okay to leave on your own, well, that will be the time, don't you think?"

"Yes," whispered Shara, tearing up.

Lenore hugged her.

Nathan appreciated Lenore's sacrifices but began to suspect that some of her sincere attention to Shara might also be to guard against my propensity for same. For his part, though sorely tempted, he held in his burgeoning love for Shara, while practicing his sincere gratitude and loving admiration of his dear wife. Thus, something of a balance was achieved in their home—but decreasingly so in him, missing the fullest expression of his love for Shara...

Ensuing days saw Nathan offering, and Shara happily accepting, unpaid, secretarial work in his church office—with the door open. His staff knew only that the Scotts were taking care of this young woman for a while, with Dr. Flower's knowing approval.

I'm pretty sure they speculate, but that's just the way it must be. The trick is to withstand my temptations due to our closeness in the car and in the office, while providing Shara with meaningful work and a less romantic relationship with me. How to do that with sincerity, when my heart fair leaps with both want and need for her. So far, I'm holding my own, instead of holding her, heeding Lenore's daily caution, "close, yes, but not too close…"

Even though Shara was cocooned in the love of the entire Scott family, she was sorely aggrieved at the loss of their baby and at Nathan's practiced caution—and distance. Despite the miraculous emergence of ready, loving, adoptive parents, more than delighted to receive him as their precious own, the enormity—and finality—of her sacrifice, seemingly of both baby and probably Nathan, haunted her into private weeping and lonely, longing despair—in dark of night.

Three weeks after Shara's sojourn in their home began, Lenore didn't stir when Nathan sat straight up, alert, in their sofa-bed in their living room. *There it is again—like a kitten's muffled mewing. Shara! Dear God, she's crying, softly, trying not to let anyone hear. What to do? Lenore specifically asked me to be wary of being trapped by her grief and needs. No way can I ignore them! I must see what's wrong—as though I don't know.*

Slipping out of bed, Nathan tiptoed up the hall, to the slightly open door of the master bedroom. Her quiet sobbing racked him. Torn between rushing in and grabbing her and not doing anything that would upset the delicate balance that now permeated their home, Nathan peered through the door into the moon-lit bedroom.

Shara, lying on her tummy, wearing only a short night gown, was crying, panting, and gently humping the bed—her right hand under her, busy at her crotch. She was whispering something into her pillow. The only words he understood were, "Oh, Nathan…!"

Oh, my dear Jesus, she's crying, masturbating, and fantasizing—me!

Pulling back, so as not to intrude on this, her ultra-private extremity, Nathan listened at the door, amazed, ashamed, and abashed at having wrought such angst, especially on one so beloved. Fearing to intrude on her passion, Nathan was stunned—and utterly moved.

She still wants me! I have done this to her, and she still needs me. Why am I surprised? I still want her in every way, too! What should I do? Do I go in, hold her, comfort, and reassure her, or go back to bed as though I'm unaware of her pain—much less of her passion? It would be cruel to ignore her. Maybe she wanted me to hear her. Her door is ajar, maybe not an accident?

What about my Lenore? She's a heavy sleeper, but what if she wakes up? It's so damned obvious that I still love Shara, no matter our unexpressed resolve—and Lenore's expressed expectation—to let our relationship dwindle, allowing her to grow—and go—on her own, now that she's had the—our—baby.

With Hell's bells ringing in his ears, Nathan ceased being his own interlocutor, stole back to his and Lenore's sofa bed, dressed, to reduce temptation, and tiptoed back to Shara's door, listening for further sounds. He heard soft weeping, as Shara came down from her lonely, anguished need. QI's unhelpful caveat: *Even though past is prologue, the fatuous wheel does not need another push, just now, Scott.*

No matter; for future's runes were cast for all, as was he cast by his abiding, undeniable, strident love, into her room, where, holding and soothing her, kissing her hot tears, and caressing her welcoming face, he reassured her that things were going to be all right—that he would not—could not—ever let her go—that he would be with her—love her—somehow, even while she is in college—and beyond. His own tears washed her face, as he held, caressed, and loved her with his earthy, ethereal, eternal passion—loved this lorn and lovely, young woman—his Shara—back to her essential, trusting self—as he had always done.

Surely, she must know me, by now!

Shara melted into him, as rain elides into the sea, reciprocating entirely, passionately, relentlessly trusting—again. Nothing solved, planned, or resolved; back to the hopes, determination, and dilemmas of the past, and to the unrolling of a parlous future, facing up, yet again, to their one, sure Reality: their eternal, uncompromising, crucially pure Love—no matter what!

And it was—and will be—so!

But that's another story…

The End

Made in the USA
Middletown, DE
30 January 2023

23319370R00338